ALONE WITH HIM

Josie slowed her horse and directed him into the shade where the golden peaches were swelling with every new day of sunshine. Josie inhaled the scent of grass and rich black dirt. The sensual earth breathed in rhythm with Josie's own breast, heightened her senses, smell and sight, and most of all, touch.

Bertrand dropped his reins to let his horse browse among the trees. Before he helped Josie from her saddle, he took hold of her booted ankle and gazed into her face. "Such a proper young lady, one might think, until one sees you on a horse." He tilted his head to consider her. "Are you brave enough to walk with me in the orchard, no chaperone, no spying eyes to keep you safe?"

Josie's breath caught, and she held the pommmel to keep her hands from trembling. "I will walk with you anywhere, Bertrand. You know that."

BOOK YOUR PLACE ON OUR WEBSITE AND MAKE THE READING CONNECTION!

We've created a customized website just for our very special readers, where you can get the inside scoop on everything that's going on with Zebra, Pinnacle and Kensington books.

When you come online, you'll have the exciting opportunity to:

- View covers of upcoming books

- Read sample chapters

- Learn about our future publishing schedule (listed by publication month *and author*)

- Find out when your favorite authors will be visiting a city near you

- Search for and order backlist books from our online catalog

- Check out author bios and background information

- Send e-mail to your favorite authors

- Meet the Kensington staff online

- Join us in weekly chats with authors, readers and other guests

- Get writing guidelines

- AND MUCH MORE!

**Visit our website at
http://www.kensingtonbooks.com**

Always And Forever

GRETCHEN CRAIG

ZEBRA BOOKS
KENSINGTON PUBLISHING CORP.
www.kensingtonbooks.com

ZEBRA BOOKS are published by

Kensington Publishing Corp.
850 Third Avenue
New York, NY 10022

All Kensington titles, imprints, and distributed lines are available at special quantity discounts for bulk purchases for sales promotion, premiums, fund-raising, educational, or institutional use.

Special book excerpts or customized printings can also be created to fit specific needs. For details, write or phone the office of the Kensington Special Sales Manager: Attn. Special Sales Department. Kensington Publishing Corp., 850 Third Avenue, New York, NY 10022. Phone: 1-800-221-2647.

Zebra and the Z logo Reg. U.S. Pat. & TM Off.

ISBN 0-8217-8019-0

First Printing: April 2006
10 9 8 7 6 5 4 3 2 1

Printed in the United States of America

For my mother,
Louise Anna Laird,
who taught me to love books.

Acknowledgments

Always and Forever entered the world with help from my friends Julie Williams and Hurshel Farrow, who read every word at least twice and showed me where I'd gone wrong. Thank you both. Berniece Rabe and The Lone Star Night Writers encouraged me throughout the last year, and Nancy Bray critiqued an early draft. My daughter, Amelia Rose Griggs, is a fine critic and helped me find my way several times. My editor at Kensington, Hilary Sares, showed me how to make it better. And thanks always to my husband, Steve Craig, who makes all things possible.

Part I

Chapter 1

Toulouse Plantation, August 1823

Elbow John stepped into the pirogue with one leg and shoved off with the other. Josie, who dreaded the loops of black snake that sometimes dropped into the boat, breathed easier when Elbow John poled out from under the cypresses into the full sun.

"You put dat bonnet back on yo head, mam'zelle," Elbow John said.

Josie, five years old, shook out the bonnet strings. "Cleo doesn't have to wear a hat."

"Cleo don' get no freckles." He handed Josie a gourd. "See can you get dis boat bailed."

Josie set to bailing, but Cleo, four, reached for the gourd. "Lemme do it."

Josie held on and Cleo tugged at it.

"Y'all don' start, now. Mam'zelle, you set down. I needs yo eyes to find de fust trap."

Josie let go of the gourd and Cleo tumbled backward. "You all right?" Josie stayed low in the boat as she'd been taught and helped Cleo sit up. Then she squeezed out the back of Cleo's skirt and handed her the gourd. "You can bail."

Cleo set to work with the gourd and Josie scanned the water, searching for a cane pole sticking out of the surface. "I see it! Over there."

Josie and Cleo together hauled on the rope, but they couldn't break the suck of the mud holding the trap. Elbow John took the line and with his good arm raised a tangled mess into the boat. Water and mud streamed out of the busted trap.

"What happened to it?" Josie said.

"Ol' blind gator likely chomped it. He got more teeth than sense, don't he?" Elbow John tossed the trap back overboard and picked up his pole. "You gals keep a sharp eye out. Next trap coming up 'round dis bend."

With better luck, the three fished the traps till they'd emptied every one into a burlap sack. "Dis one fine day," Elbow John said. "God in His heaven, and crawfish in de bag."

Cleo pointed to the mud on Josie's white dress. "Look at dat."

Josie smeared it, trying to rub it away with her grimy hands. Maman would be so angry with her.

"Don't worry none, mam'zelle," Elbow John said. "Bibi wash it for you, and Madame Celine won't know nothin' 'bout it."

The girls lay back on an old smelly pillow and watched blue dragonflies hover above the water. A snowy egret took flight, showing them the way down the bayou. Elbow John poled them back to the landing, hauled the pirogue up on the bank, and tossed the bag of crawfish over his shoulder. "Les us get out o' dis sun."

Hand in hand, Josie and Cleo led the way to the big house, Josie in her soiled white dress, Cleo in her too-small hand-me-down. Muck clung to Josie's leather shoes, mud oozed between Cleo's bare brown toes.

As they approached the grounds of the big house, voices came to them through the trees. The murmur grew into a clamor, and Josie turned to Elbow John with a question on her face.

John listened. "Lawd, I hope dat ain't what I tink it is." He dropped the bag of crawfish and sprinted toward the courtyard behind the big house, Josie and Cleo struggling to catch up.

The girls drew up at sight of the confusion in the courtyard behind the house. Three dusty men, strangers, were forcing men and women from the dark little houses in the quarters into an oversized wagon. The people resisted, crying and arguing and pulling back.

Elbow John steered the girls around a corner of the big house. "Neither one of y'all needs to see dis."

Josie and Cleo held on to each other. "What's happening?" Cleo said.

"Nothin' make no difference to y'all. Madame Emmeline done sell off some hands, dat's all."

Josie believed Elbow John's body, not his words. His voice shook, and his hands trembled. Cleo gripped Josie tighter. She was scared too.

A single wail cut through the din, and a woman screamed, "Let go o' me!" The girls stared at each other.

"Bibi?" Josie whispered. She and Cleo broke free of Elbow John and ran to the courtyard. They pushed through the crowd to the big wagon.

"Bibi!" Josie shouted, but Bibi didn't hear.

Bibi clambered to get out of the wagon. The redheaded slaver grabbed at her to shove her back. She twisted away from him and threw her leg over the side. He grabbed her again and she scratched at his eyes. Finally, the man threw his fist into Bibi's jaw, and she collapsed.

"Maman!" Cleo cried. She tried to climb the wagon wheel to get to her mother.

"This the one?" the redheaded man said and pointed to Cleo.

"Gotta be. She's going right to her."

While Bibi lay stunned in the bottom of the wagon, the man manacled Bibi's ankles to a bolt on the floor. Then he helped Cleo climb aboard and sat her down on top of her mother. Bibi quit struggling against the chains and hugged Cleo to her.

Josie started to climb the wheel too, to get Bibi out of the wagon and take her back into the house where she belonged. But Mr. Gale, the overseer, caught her and pulled her down. "Mam'zelle Josephine, you best go up to your mother."

She stretched her arms toward the wagon. "Bibi! Cleo!"

Mr. Gale carried Josie, kicking and struggling, over to the back gallery steps before he set her down. "Go on up to your mother, there's a good girl," he said.

"Maman!" Josie ran up the tall staircase to the back gallery overlooking the courtyard. Her mother stood erect, motionless, her gaze fixed on the scene below. "Maman, they put Bibi in that wagon." Josie grabbed her mother's skirts and tugged. "Maman, Cleo's in the wagon!"

Maman, her back stiff and straight, neither comforted nor explained. Her lips were curved, but her eyes were hard, unreadable. Josie shrank from her.

A slaver's whip cracked, and Josie gripped the railing, her panic rising. She sobbed and pushed her hands through the bars as if she could reach them—Bibi, who woke her with a kiss every morning, who sang her to sleep at night, who dried all her tears, and Cleo, who shared all her whittled toys from Grammy Tulia's cabin.

Grand-mère Emmeline, square shouldered and clad all in black, appeared on the gallery. The voices below swelled in supplication.

A muscled young man called to her, "You don' sell me, Madame Emmeline. I won't run off no more. I promise."

Another hollered, "You know I cut twice de cane dese others."

And from grizzled old Henri, "Where M'sieu Emile? He not do dis!"

Josie flung herself against her grandmother's skirts. "Grand-mère!"

Grand-mère patted Josie's back, then crossed her arms. Josie sobbed, her fingers pulling at her hair. She saw Cleo clinging to Bibi's neck, both in the big wagon.

Without warning, Papa's black stallion charged into the courtyard, scattering the slavers.

"M'sieu!" the slaves cried out. "M'sieu!"

Papa pulled hard on the reins and the big horse reared.

"M'sieu, don' let dem sell us off!"

"M'sieu, you got to hep us!"

Josie leaned over the gallery rail to see him. "Papa," she breathed.

Papa slid from the saddle and ran up the stairs. He leaned close into his mother's face. "This is obscene. You have no need to sell these people."

Grand-mère shrugged. "You have gambled a great deal these last months, Emile. And lost."

Papa turned away from his mother in disgust.

"Emile!" came a desperate voice from the courtyard. Papa's eyes found Bibi and Cleo in the wagon below. He paled and wheeled on Grand-mère. Grand-mère cocked her head toward Maman.

Papa locked eyes with Maman in silent duel, and Josie quailed at the fire passing between them. Papa's face dark now, he tore back down the stairs to the wagon and reached up to pull Bibi out, but the chains held her fast. He turned on Mr. Gale. "Unlock these manacles," he demanded.

The overseer glanced up at Grand-mère, then held his palms up. "The sale's been made, M'sieu Emile."

"Let's move out," a slaver called, and the wagons began to roll.

"Stop," Papa called and lunged toward the lead mule. The slaver spurred his horse between Papa and the mules, knocking Papa off his feet.

The wagon driver snapped his whip, and the mules picked up speed. Papa scrambled to his feet, too late. He grabbed at his hair with both hands as the wagon rumbled down the lane.

From the gallery Josie gripped the railing and watched the wagon roll away. Bibi held Cleo tight, her eyes fastened on Papa as if her whole being reached for him. Couldn't Papa stop them?

Papa ran up the stairs, pushed past Maman, and banged open the door into the house. Maman followed him with quick steps, and Josie ran after her.

In Maman's room, Papa was rummaging through drawers and tossing them to the floor.

"Your jewelry box. Where is it?" he said to Maman.

"Emile, you can't mean to—"

"I haven't the cash in the house. I need the pearls."

"Emile, I will not have you take my pearls for that girl. I will not have it."

Papa grabbed Maman's wrist. Josie struggled for breath from behind her mother's skirt.

"Let go," Maman said. "I won't give you my pearls."

Papa shoved her onto the bed with Josie still clinging to her dress. Ignoring Maman's sobs, he ransacked the wardrobe until he found the pretty painted jewelry box. When it wouldn't open, he smashed it against the hard floor, and Maman's bright rings and necklaces spilled across the boards.

Papa snatched up the dark blue velvet bag that held

Maman's precious pearls, the ones he'd bought her in Paris on their wedding trip. "Emile," Maman pleaded.

Papa's boots thundered across the floorboards as he left the house. Josie heard his spurs jangle down the gallery stairs, and then his stallion's hooves clattering across the courtyard.

Maman pulled herself off the bed and stood perfectly still, her eyes on the door Papa had gone through. Josie gathered the jewels from the floor to offer them to her mother, but Maman began to sway, her face seeming to dissolve like the wax doll Josie had left too near the fire. Josie shuddered, and Maman cried a single high note that ended only as she buckled to the floor. She knelt there, her face in her hands.

Grand-mère Emmeline glided into the room and regarded her daughter-in-law. "Well, Celine," she said, "your plan has failed."

Josie pulled a pillow to her as a shield against her grandmother's deep dark eyes, but Grand-mère's attention fixed on Maman. "Our Emile has more gumption than we anticipated," she said. "That, at least, is a pleasant surprise."

At the end of that long day of whispers and stillness, Josie leaned out her window and strained to hear Papa's big horse over the singing of the cicadas. When he came, it was deep twilight.

The stallion carried him directly under Josie's window. Cleo sat in front of him and Bibi rode behind, her arms around his waist. He'd brought them home.

Josie ran to the back gallery to follow Papa to the stables. She wanted to hold on to Bibi, to laugh with Cleo that Papa had let her ride the big horse.

"Josephine." Grand-mère sat in the oak rocker, watching the dark slide through the trees and over the barn. "You may not leave the house."

"But Bibi is home." Josie could hear the whine under her words. Grand-mère hated that.

"You'll see her tomorrow. Go to bed."

Josie had never gone to sleep without Bibi tucking her in, kissing her, and telling her sweet dreams. She stood a moment in the empty bedroom, then turned around and padded on bare feet to Papa's big black chair in the study, the one he sat in while he smoked and looked dreamily out the window. She was almost asleep when Papa found her there. He lit a candle, then kissed her as he lifted her from his chair and placed her snugly on his lap.

"Bibi and Cleo are home again," Papa said.

Josie nodded, looking deeply into Papa's soft gray eyes. This was the Papa she knew, not the wild-eyed man who took Maman's pearls.

"They're with Grammy Tulia in the quarters, but after this, Bibi will sleep in your room again, as always." He stroked Josie's light brown curls. "And now Cleo too. You won't mind having Cleo sleep in your room, will you?"

"No, Papa. I won't mind."

"Good. You're big girls now. You should be friends." He shifted her so he could look at her directly. "Now, Josephine, listen carefully."

"I'm listening, Papa."

"Josephine, I'm giving Cleo to you. I'll have the papers drawn up that make her your very own. Do you understand?"

Josie nodded. Papa had brought her a porcelain doll from New Orleans for her birthday, but this was even better. Cleo was a real girl who could walk and talk and play with her.

"And, Josie," Papa said, "you must always look after Cleo. You'll do that, won't you?"

"I will, Papa."

Chapter 2

Josie kept her promise. When winter came and Cleo's feet were cold, Josie gave her a pretty pair of shoes from her own wardrobe. When Maman handed out the rough cotton sacking for the slaves' new clothes at Christmastime, Josie gave Cleo a blue linen dress and another green one from among her frocks.

It was easy to love Cleo. She was pretty as a brown doll. She could play games and knew all kinds of rhymes she learned from Grammy Tulia in the quarters.

Josie knew she pleased Bibi when she took good care of Cleo. Bibi would see Josie share her drawing pencils or help Cleo button her shoes; later, she'd pull Josie into her lap and hum to her while she brushed the long brown hair. Papa too smiled on her when she played with Cleo.

Maman, however, did not reward Josie's kindness to her slave. When Maman entered the nursery from her adjoining room the day after Christmas, she found Cleo wearing the embroidered blue linen dress. "Where did she get that?"

Josie's throat grew tight. "I gave it to her, Maman," she said, her voice very small.

"Well, she can't have it. She'll wear the sacking like everyone else on the place."

Cleo sat with a cornhusk doll in her lap, her dark eyes trained on Maman's pale face. Maman marched across the room, grabbed Cleo by the arm, and jerked her up. "Don't you look at me like that." She tore at the buttons in the back and yanked Cleo's arm out of the sleeve.

Cleo might have been a rag doll for all her reaction, but Josie began to cry. Maman's face was so mean, her lips just a white line and her blue eyes hard and little.

"What's all the ruckus?" Papa stood in the doorway. His voice sounded mild, but Josie could see his face looked tight and angry, almost as angry as Maman's.

Maman released Cleo's arm and whirled on Papa. "Look what she's wearing."

Josie stopped crying, watching. Since the summer, when Papa had taken Maman's pearls, Josie had become attuned to the undercurrent of tension in the house. Maman was angry all the time now. Josie knew she didn't like Bibi or Cleo, and now she didn't seem to like Papa anymore either.

"It's intolerable," Maman said.

Papa walked over and bent down to Cleo, pulling the dress back onto her shoulder. "It's just a dress, Celine."

Maman whirled out of the room, slamming the bedroom door behind her. Josie heard her throw herself across the bed.

Papa buttoned Cleo's dress. "You look very nice, Cleo."

He straightened up and held his hand out for Josie to come to him. When she stood before him, he took her face in his hands and looked into her eyes. "You are never wrong to do a kindness, Josephine. Remember that."

He kissed her on the forehead. "Run along, both of you,

and find Bibi. Tell her you're to have a slice of cake and a glass of milk."

By the time Cleo's little brother was born, the girls, seven and six, were inseparable. They had become adept at finding ways around Maman's strict rules and frequent admonishments, and the current goal in their sneakiness was to see the new baby.

Maman forbade the baby's presence in her house, so Bibi had to run from the big house to the quarters all through the day and night to nurse Thibault. Maman had also forbidden Josie to go to the quarters, but she found ways to slip off to Grammy Tulia's cabin nearly every day.

"Ain't a prettier face in heaven," Grammy said. "Not even you two gals was any prettier dan dis baby."

Cleo put a finger on Thibault's rosebud mouth. "Look at that—he trying to suck on my finger!"

"Les put a little honey on yo thumb and see how he like dat."

Cleo put her sweetened finger back in Thibault's mouth. He delighted the girls when he smacked his lips and sucked.

Josie leaned over the hand-hewn crib. "Can I try it?"

"Sho. Dip yo finger in de jar."

The next time Josie and Cleo visited Thibault, Josie smelled her Papa's tobacco in the cabin. The time after that, she saw he'd left his pipe on the mantelpiece. *My papa loves babies,* she thought.

Months later, Thibault was just as pretty. He was a contented baby, sweet natured and smiling. But he was oddly quiet. At nearly a year old, he still didn't show much interest in the toys Josie and Cleo brought from the nursery.

On a bright summer morning, while Maman was still sleeping, Bibi washed Josie and Cleo's faces and told them to wait till she came back, and then she'd give them their breakfasts. But the house was quiet, Grand-mère already in her office and Papa out with his hounds; no one would miss them. The girls carefully closed the door behind them and climbed down the back stairs, then ran down the lane to Grammy Tulia's house.

When Josie and Cleo shoved the gray wooden door aside to go in, they found Bibi in the rocking chair, Thibault clutched tight to her shoulder. There were tears on her face.

Josie stood on one side of the chair and Cleo on the other. Cleo put a hand on Thibault's head. "He'll be all right, Maman," she said. "Thibault's a good baby."

Tears flowed from under Bibi's closed eyes. She shook her head and rocked.

"What's wrong?" Josie whispered. Sometimes Cleo got to come to the cabin when Josie had to sit with Maman. Cleo knew things she didn't, and Josie often felt left out. "Why's Bibi crying?"

"Thibault is simple."

Josie looked at her without understanding.

"It mean he can't never be a smart man. He gon' be simple, like Smilin' Nick. You know which one he is? He cuts cane with the others."

Josie nodded. Everybody knew who Smilin' Nick was. Even the overseer, Mr. Gale, treated him extra good because he smiled all the day long.

Bibi opened her eyes and looked at Josie for a long moment. "I know you just a little thing yo'self." She took hold of Josie's wrist. "But you got to know, Josie. You got to take care of dis one and Cleo too. You hear what I'm saying?"

Josie nodded. "I'm almost eight."

"You hear me?" Bibi tightened her hand around Josie's arm. "Dis here baby is yours, yours and Cleo's. If something happen to me, or to yo papa, you de one dat see he taken care of."

Josie nodded. They all belonged to her: Grammy Tulia, Bibi, Cleo, Papa, and Thibault. Every one of them belonged to her. And she loved them all.

Childhood days rolled on, hardly a day less happy than the one before it. Josie and Cleo played hide-and-seek with the overseer's children and even with Cleo's darker cousins from the quarters. Sometimes, when he was old enough, they took Thibault with them to catch tadpoles in the creek or to search for quail eggs. Thibault smiled whether they crowned him with honeysuckle or filled his pockets with caterpillars.

Elbow John, his right arm permanently cocked from a logging accident, watched over them during the day. He'd follow along absentmindedly while the girls explored the swamp at the edge of the plantation or climbed on the cypress knees where the cottonmouths hid in the black water. If the girls grew drowsy with the afternoon heat, he'd sit with them under the live oak tree behind the house and tell them stories from Africa he'd learned from his grand-père.

Now and then, Josie and Cleo would quarrel.

"I'm the princess," Josie asserted.

"You always the princess. It my turn today. I'm the princess, and you the knight."

Soon they were shouting and crying, and Bibi sent them to opposite ends of the house. Hours later, when she allowed them to be together again, they hugged as if they'd been lost from one another for long, long years.

When Josie turned eight, Maman sent Elbow John back to the stables. Josie was to have lessons, she was to keep her petticoats and her hands clean, she was to become a young lady. Tuesdays and Thursdays, Madame Estelle drilled Josie in English grammar. On Mondays and Wednesdays, Mademoiselle Fatima enthused over French literature. Fridays, Monsieur Pierre insisted Josie sit straight in front of the piano as she practiced scales. Afterward he held her in his wooden arms to teach her to dance.

Josie would so much rather be outside climbing a tree or helping Louella haul water. But Maman had hired tutors to counter just that sort of behavior. Other daughters of good families did not spend their hours like little hoydens.

So the tutors came, and Josie had to curtail her jumping and running and swinging. Cleo keeping her company, she sat with Mademoiselle Fatima who, with her mustache and moles, leaned in too close when she read from Perrault's fairy tales, the spittle flying from her mouth. Monsieur Pierre was not above rapping Josie's wrists if she let them drop at the keyboard. Worst of all was Madame Estelle, who demanded absolute perfection.

"Put, put, put," Josie recited. "Run, ran, run. Sit, sat, sat." She could discover no pattern to the English verbs, and she suffered from the disgusted sneer on Madame's face when she made a mistake. Sometimes she appealed silently to Cleo, sitting on the floor in the corner, and Cleo would mouth "swam" at her, or else shrug her shoulders, equally ignorant.

Only Papa looked in during study time. Usually he simply leaned against the doorjamb for a few minutes and listened to Josie conjugate an English verb or read a few lines of *Montaigne,* which for all she understood of it might as well have been in English.

One particular morning, as Josie labored under Madame Estelle's tutelage and Cleo sat on the floor copying letters on a scrap of paper, Madame took Papa aside.

"Monsieur Tassin. Perhaps you are not aware the little slave attends Josephine in her school hours. I am most uncomfortable with this flouting of the law." Madame referred of course to book learning as a forbidden activity for a slave; indeed, teaching a slave to read had been labeled a crime by the wise men of Louisiana.

Papa looked at Josie and Cleo, both of them blatantly listening, watching for his reaction. Amusement played across his mouth. "I wasn't aware, madame, that you were endeavoring to tutor both girls."

"Of course I am not. But you see how it is. The slave girl listens to everything; she is even so bold as to practice drawing the alphabet. She will soon be learning to read if we are not careful."

"Josephine, you are not teaching Cleo to read, are you?"

"No, Papa. Indeed I am not." She sent a guilty glance toward Cleo, but Cleo wore a blank expression, the one she put on when Maman scolded her.

"Nor am I. So you see, Madame Estelle, the only one from whom Cleo might learn to read is you, and I am sure you are guilty of no such crime."

Madame Estelle pursed her lips and stiffened her back. "I understand perfectly," she said. "I'll not trouble you about it again."

Josie studied dutifully if without enthusiasm. Cleo's progress nearly matched her own, and the conspiracy continued.

It was because of the piano that Josie consciously became Cleo's ally and her mother's adversary. Before that day, whenever Maman was hateful to Cleo, Josie had felt helpless. She often would cry when Maman scolded or shook Cleo. Then she'd wait for Maman to leave the room before she crept to a dry-eyed Cleo to give and receive comfort.

The day Josie asserted herself, she was practicing the pieces Monsieur Pierre had left for her while Maman lay down for her afternoon rest. Occasionally Maman would call to her to count the beats or check how many sharps she was supposed to play, but mostly Maman slept through the hour. When Josie tired of playing, she'd quietly relinquish the bench to Cleo.

Cleo had never benefited from Monsieur Pierre's direct instruction, but she was blessed with an ear and that ineffable something, talent. She could play whatever she'd heard, and Maman never noticed the difference behind her closed bedroom door.

But Cleo forgot herself this afternoon. She began to pick out the tune of a melody she'd learned in the quarters, an old song the men and women sang when they chopped cane or picked cotton. Josie sat on the sofa looking through the stereopticon Papa had brought from New Orleans. She didn't at first hear Maman come into the room.

Cleo saw her immediately. She froze, her hands still on the keyboard. Josie looked up to see Maman and Cleo staring at each other. Maman moved first. She covered the distance from the doorway to the piano in three quick strides, grabbed hold of Cleo's headscarf and hair in one bunch, and yanked Cleo's head back.

"You little bastard." Maman slapped Cleo, hard. Cleo gasped, but she'd long ago ceased to cry when Madame punished her.

Josie, however, couldn't bear it. She ran across the room and caught Maman's raised arm. "No, Maman!"

Maman's face was in that white fury Josie dreaded. "I'll deal with you later, young lady." She pulled her arm out of Josie's grip and raised it to strike Cleo again.

"Maman!" Josie grabbed her arm again and dragged her away from the piano.

Maman pointed toward Cleo. "You put her in her place, this instant, or I will have her whipped."

Josie shook her head. "She belongs to me. Papa gave her to me."

In a swish of skirts, Maman spun back to Cleo. She seized a handful of black hair and hauled Cleo from the bench. Cleo's head hit the edge of the bench as she fell and a gash opened over her right eye. Maman didn't stop at the sight of the blood. She pulled Cleo farther from the piano, both hands tugging at the loose hair.

Josie threw herself against Maman. "Let her go!"

Maman fell back and across Cleo. Josie went down with her, struggling to force Maman to let go of Cleo's hair. She cried and pulled at Maman's fingers.

Maman scooted back across the floor, her face twisted. She put the back of her hand against her mouth and stared at Josie. "You take their part. You're just like him." Maman sobbed, both hands covering her face.

"She belongs to me," Josie whispered.

Cleo lay stunned, wordless, the blood flowing across her face and onto her dress. Josie stared at the blood, then at Maman's trembling hands.

"Maman?" Her mother rocked back and forth, deep gulping sobs shaking her. "Maman?" Maman turned her face away.

Josie crawled over to Cleo. She helped her stand up and, arm in arm, the two of them left the parlor in search of Bibi.

It was days before Maman left her room. When finally she appeared at table, it was as if nothing had happened. Ashen faced, but decorous, Maman made small talk with Grand-mère and Papa and enquired about Josie's English lessons. Josie felt she could breathe again for the first time since the incident at the piano.

Maman resumed teaching Josie the womanly art of needlework. On Saturday morning, with no tutors in attendance, Maman said, "Bring your basket and sit with me in the parlor."

Josie hesitated. She had been about to follow Cleo outside to find Elbow John. They were going to ask him to take them to the bayou. After winning the battle to protect Cleo, though, Josie did her best to please her mother. She sat down near the window and threaded a needle.

She didn't complain, but she did keep an eye on the clock. She took a few stitches in the doll's dress Maman had cut out for her, and then she checked to see how many minutes had passed. If the old repeater hadn't been ticking, Josie would have been sure it had stopped.

After an hour, Josie's eyes hurt. "Stop squinting," Maman said. "If you don't keep your face quite still, you'll have wrinkles before your time."

Grand-mère had wrinkles. Grammy Tulia had wrinkles. They looked fine. They looked like themselves. But, Josie had to admit, Maman was much prettier than either of them. Maman's parents were both German, and her hair was buttery yellow, her eyes the color of morning glories. That's why Josie herself was not dark like Papa and all his nephews and cousins and aunts and uncles.

The sweat on Josie's hands made the needle hard to hold on to, but her mind was not on sewing anyway. Cleo was probably fishing in the bayou with Elbow John. Or she might be in the quarters playing with Thibault. Whatever she was doing, Josie was sure it was more fun than sewing.

When the clock finally chimed ten times, Maman said, "Let me see what you've done." She shook her head. "Josie, your stitches are quite irregular. I'm sure other nine-year-olds sew better than this. You simply don't try."

"I do try, Maman," Josie said softly.

"You've given me a headache," Maman said. "Leave me now."

Josie carefully tucked her needlework back into her basket, curtsied to her mother, and sedately crossed the room. Once out of sight, she ran through the house, heedless of the clatter her shoes made on the cypress floors.

Josie ran to Grammy Tulia's. If Cleo wasn't there, she would play with Thibault. He liked it when she drew pictures in the dirt for him. But no one was home. Her shoulders slumped. Where was everybody?

The blueberries were coming in. Josie picked up a syrup bucket from Grammy's porch and hurried through the quarters to the blueberry patch. That's where she found Cleo and

Elbow John, Grammy and Thibault, picking berries in the heat of the day.

"Look here how many we already picked," Cleo said. "Louella said we could make a pie, you and me."

"Let's get on out a dis sun," Elbow John said. "Yo maman have my hide, I let you get freckled again, mam'zelle."

"But I haven't picked hardly any. I just got here."

Cleo plucked the straw hat off her head and plopped it on Josie's. She turned to Elbow John. "Now can we stay?"

"Well, I guess a few minutes won't hurt none."

Thibault, toddling with his tiny pail, attached himself to Josie, and she showed him the berries low on the bushes.

With full pails, the party headed back. Josie and Cleo went on to the cookhouse for long drinks of cool water from the cistern. Louella had her oven hot and ready. "I done got the crust rolled out. You two gals pick through dem berries, put some sugar and cinnamon on 'em, and we make us a pie for M'sieu Emile."

"Maman likes blueberry pie too," Josie offered.

"Mm-hmm," Louella said. "Go easy on that cinnamon, Cleo. It don' take much."

Hours spent in the cookhouse with Louella were more fun than anything else, even fishing with Elbow John. Josie measured out the sugar and stirred in Cleo's spoonful of cinnamon. "Does it need a dab of butter?" Josie said.

"Dat it do. You know where de butter is."

Cleo laid the bottom crust in the pie pan, Josie poured the berries in, and they both crimped the edges of the top crust.

They left Louella to watch their pie in the brick oven, and all through the afternoon, as she and Cleo followed Elbow John down to the bayou for him to check his traps, Josie imagined how proud Papa would be of her for making him a pie. And Grand-mère too. Grand-mère believed Creole women should be capable, useful members of the plantation. Maman did not agree. She told Josie to be a lady, to keep her hands clean and her hair tidy. Josie labored every day to please both Grand-mère and Maman.

It was much easier to please Papa. He smiled at her whether she was messy or clean, idle or busy. He'd love the blueberry pie.

Chapter 3

Spring, 1836

"Hold still," Cleo insisted, muttering around a mouthful of hairpins.

Josie met Cleo's amber eyes in the mirror. Cleo had a way of making her feel like a child sometimes, but Josie let it go. She didn't want to quarrel today.

Cleo labored to fasten three pale pink rosebuds in Josie's upswept hair, but their weight inevitably pulled them loose. She had tried pins and ribbons and was resorting to the thin green wire they used for corsages.

"I don't want green wire in my hair!" Josie said.

"Do you want these flowers or not?"

Josie eyed Cleo's black curls. When she'd taken a turn at hairdresser, she'd had no trouble fastening roses in Cleo's thick hair. She suppressed a sigh. Her own hair was not nearly so luxurious, nor as glossy. But it wasn't an ordinary brown either. More like dark honey, she decided.

Josie sat up taller and inspected herself in the mirror.

Nice looking. Not bad at all, really. But she'd be more careful about freckles this summer.

Papa stuck his head in the door. "Is there some grand ball tonight I don't know about?"

Josie, as always, brightened in her father's presence. "We're practicing, Papa. For all the balls in New Orleans next winter."

Papa's eyes drifted to Cleo, and Josie felt the old ache. Always her father's attention shifted to Cleo, but he was *her* papa.

Papa leaned against the doorjamb. "*Tu es très belle,* Cleo," he said. "Did Josie fix your hair like that?"

"*Oui,* monsieur." Cleo smiled and turned her head to show him the elaborate hairdo.

Josie felt invisible. She sat very still until her father remembered to look at her again.

"I like your hair like that, Josie."

Josie tilted her head and put a hand to her curls. "Do you, Papa?"

Papa checked his breast pocket for a cigar. "You're more beautiful than the queen of France," he told her.

Josie laughed, but she suspected it might be so. Her papa had actually seen the queen when he was in Paris, and he'd said she was small and dark. Josie was already taller than her mother, and no one would ever call her dark.

He bit the end off and stuck the cigar in his mouth. "The two of you will turn every head at the ball," Papa said and left them.

Papa had done it again. He seemed to forget, now and then, that there would be no balls for Cleo. Josie glanced at her in the mirror, but Cleo's face was closed. A curtain covered her eyes whenever she was reminded of her place. How could Papa be so thoughtless?

Maman often scolded Josie about treating Cleo better than she deserved. "Cleo is your servant, not your friend," she harped. But Cleo was so much more than a servant. Josie hated it when Cleo was put "in her place." Yet Maman was right. Cleo's lot in life was God-given, and she, and Cleo, would have to accept that.

As for Papa . . . How could he pay as much attention to Cleo as he did to his own daughter? Josie knew the answer. Papa loved her. Josie didn't understand it, but she knew it was true. And it wasn't fair. Papa belonged to her, not to Cleo.

Josie's mouth grew tight and she avoided Cleo's eyes in the mirror. When Cleo tried to twine the roses in the honey-colored hair again, Josie said, "Never mind. I'll do it myself."

Cleo's arms dropped to her sides.

"You must have chores to do," Josie told her, pretending interest in the brushes on the dresser.

Cleo left the room with that wordless resistance Josie hated. When Cleo closed her face and retreated into the slave's protective silence, Josie felt she herself had been put in her place.

Josie picked up the roses. "Drat," she said under her breath. She could not get the flowers to stay in her hair, and she regretted having been so cold when she sent Cleo away. She gave up on the flowers.

I shouldn't be so jealous. It's a failing. If I don't watch out, I'll end up as mean and suspicious as Maman.

Poor Cleo, Josie reminded herself. For Cleo, there would be no silk gowns, no twirling around the room on a hand-some gentleman's arm. *Maman won't like it if I say I'm sorry. But I can ask Cleo to go to the cookhouse with me. I'll show her how to make divinity.*

As Josie rose to find Cleo, she heard the first notes of a minuet. Ah, this was Cleo's revenge. Cleo knew Josie wanted more than anything to play beautifully, but somehow the feeling in her heart could not reach her fingers. Now Cleo

breathed life into the minuet Josie had been plodding through
for weeks. Josie had the lessons, Josie read the notes, Josie
practiced—but Cleo somehow made the music shimmer and
sing.

Josie sat down again and fingered the lovely pink rosebuds. Papa's footsteps crossed the parlor floor. His booming
baritone burst into accompaniment as Cleo began a piece
she'd heard Josie practicing.

Josie's shoulders sagged. She pressed the roses in her
hand until the thorns pierced her palm. The swelling ooze
dripped onto her white lawn dress.

In a few days, Josie and Cleo's hard feelings forgotten,
springtime eased toward summer like the seamless flow of
the Mississippi. Bees buzzed among the wisteria, blue jays
splashed in the birdbath, and squirrels scampered in the
moss-draped trees.

As the morning sun warmed the roses, their scent spread
to the gazebo where Josie sat with her mother. Josie dropped
the embroidery to her lap and watched the shadows of the
oaks play on her mother's face. Maman seemed to be listening to some inner whisper as she gazed at the rose garden.

"Does your back hurt you, Maman?"

She smiled. "A backache is a small price to pay for a
baby."

"Bibi, would you bring the footstool, please?" Josie said.

The peace Maman and Bibi had achieved over the years
was easily strained by personal contact, so when Bibi returned, Josie lifted her mother's swollen ankles and slid the
red velvet stool under her feet.

"You may dismiss her," Maman said. Josie glanced at
Bibi, who picked up her darning basket and left them to their
coffee.

Maman held her hand out. "Let me see your sampler, Josephine."

Josie sighed and yielded the linen square to her mother. Here she was nearly eighteen, and still her embroidery was at best mediocre, even on the days she made an effort to be precise. Maman demanded such tiny stitches, and anything that tiny was a blur to Josie.

Reading was difficult too. Some of the books Mademoiselle Fatima left with her were printed in such dense type they gave Josie a headache. Bibi suggested she ask her Papa for reading glasses like the ones he wore on the end of his nose, but Josie balked. Ladies did not wear glasses, not if they wanted to be beautiful. Instead, she secretly handed the books to Cleo to read to her.

Maman shook her head. "Josephine, you don't apply yourself, my dear. You must pick out these stitches in the blue-bird's tail and do them over."

No use to complain. Whether she stitched or restitched, Josie would have to spend the morning embroidering. When she saw Cleo striding from the house, free from the tyranny of the needle, Josie envied her.

Cleo curtsied to Celine. "Madame sends me for Mam'zelle Josephine," she said.

Josie suppressed a groan. From one chore to another. Grand-mère no doubt wanted to go over the account books with her again. It was expected that, as the only heir, Josie would become president of the family business someday, that she would manage Toulouse all by herself as her grandmother did. Her papa had long ago proven himself unfit or unwilling, it hardly mattered which, to handle the plantation. Even if the new baby were to be a male, it would be years before he could take over. When Grand-mère grew too old, Josie would be responsible for the plantation until he was of age. But the accounts bored Josie more than embroidery did, and anyway, someday she'd have a husband who'd take care of business.

Cleo's playful look over Maman's head gave Josie hope that it wasn't the account books this time. She folded her embroidery into the sewing case and excused herself. As soon as they were out of Maman's hearing, Josie said, "What does she want?"

"You know the old Cajun, Monsieur DeBlieux?"

"The one who brings gator tails."

"Only today it isn't gator tails. It's hearts of palm. But listen, M'sieu sent his son instead. Your grand-mère is busy, and she says it's time you learned to buy and sell."

Josie, far enough away from Maman to escape censure for unladylike behavior, snorted in disgust. Josie aspired to be a fine lady, to dress well, to host grand parties and be beloved and pampered by a man like Papa. Buying and selling were not part of that vision.

When the girls entered the cool underhouse where much of the Toulouse plantation's business was conducted, the Acadian boy was leaning against a brick pillar with his hat pulled low on his face. He seemed so relaxed, Josie wondered if a person could actually sleep standing up. She took in his faded work pants and bare feet, but his shirt was clean enough, and neatly mended at the elbow.

"Monsieur?" she said.

The boy breathed deeply and raised the brim of his hat. He had been asleep. Abruptly, he pushed himself from the pillar and swept the hat from his head. "Mademoiselle," he said.

Josie stared at the brown eyes fringed with thick black lashes until the curve of his lips told her she was making a fool of herself.

"You have something to sell, Monsieur?"

"*Oui*. I have the heart of the palms. A basket of them."

"How much do you want for them?"

"*Mon père*, he say . . . twenty picayunes for all."

Josie realized she had no money. She roused enough presence of mind to turn to Cleo. She would send her for the household purse. But Cleo, without taking her eyes from the tall, lean figure of M'sieu DeBlieux's son, pulled the purse from her apron pocket and held it out.

"Twenty picayunes?" Josie said. She had no idea how much hearts of palm were worth, but Grand-mère had lectured her often enough about never paying the asking price for anything. She looked the boy in the eye and nearly lost her sense of purpose when he held her gaze.

"I think," she began. She cleared her throat. "I think fifteen would be a fairer price." She glanced at Cleo, but Cleo's mind was obviously not on the transaction.

The boy smiled. "Fifteen it is, then, mademoiselle."

She'd been right. He'd asked too much, and she was shrewd enough to catch him. Grand-mère would be pleased. Josie loosened the string and peered at the small collection of odd coins. It was bewildering, this assortment of an English shilling, a Russian kopeck, and various coins of Spanish mint. She sifted through the reales, half-dimes and eleven-penney bits to sort out the picayunes.

She counted out the coins into the boy's palm. It was calloused, but the fingers were long and slender. As he accepted the picayunes, Phanor somehow stroked his thumb against Josie's hand, and she felt a jolt.

"*Merci, mam'zelle*," he said. He tipped his hat, looking Josie right in the eye, and then ran his glance over Cleo as he swaggered to his wagon.

The young Cajun was hardly out of sight around the house when the two girls leaned into each other, hands over their mouths, giggling. Josie put a hand to her breast. "I thought I wouldn't be able to breathe. Did you see his eyes?"

Cleo grinned and fanned her face with a handkerchief in mock heat. "He must be the devil's child, to be that good looking."

"Oh. I should have asked his name," Josie said.

Grand-mère appeared from the shadows of the underhouse. Josie and Cleo both dropped their hands and stood soberly. "It's Phanor. Phanor DeBlieux. And he is an Acadian."

Josie glanced at Cleo. They'd heard Grand-mère's discourse on the Cajuns before: still living in the swamps after four or even five generations in Louisiana, more interested in Saturday night dances and fishing than hard work. They'd never amount to anything.

"A good Acadian family," Grand-mère said, "but Acadian. You would do well to remember that while you are admiring Monsieur DeBlieux's son. What have you bought from him?"

Josie picked up the basket and pulled the cloth aside. "Hearts of palm, Grand-mère. The whole basket, only fifteen picayunes."

Josie withered under her grand-mère's stare. "How much did Phanor ask?"

"Twenty picayunes, so you see I drove a hard bargain, Grand-mère."

"And how many of these will you eat at supper?"

"Just a piece of one, but—"

"And how many of us sit at table?"

"Well, Maman, Papa, you, and—"

"After dinner, you will help Louella in the kitchen. She'll have to pickle these to keep them from going to waste. Until then, I think we might review the account books to see what we have paid Monsieur DeBlieux for hearts of palm in the past."

Josie followed her grandmother into the house, already counting the minutes until she'd be free. The actual ciphering involved in bookkeeping came easily to Josie. She could even multiply double digits in her head, which meant she didn't have to strain her eyes to see Grand-mère's tiny figures. "Expenses vary with the seasons," Grand-mère was saying, "and you'll need to account for that in your yearly forecasting."

No, Josie's distaste was for the actual application of the arithmetic. She could do that too, if she had to, but like Papa, she'd much rather gaze at the river rolling along toward New Orleans. Or be in the cookhouse. If she'd been born to another life, she often thought, she'd want to be a cook. She wondered if the hearts of palm would be good seared in the pan with a little butter and rosemary.

The heady scent of summer roses drifted in through the office window. From her seat next to Grand-mère, Josie could see the climbing roses wrapping the gazebo in a blanket of deepest red.

"Josephine!"

Josie jumped.

"You *must* attend, Josephine." Grand-mère's exasperation made her snippy. "Unlike your father, you will not have the luxury of depending on someone else to run Toulouse."

"I'm sorry, Grand-mère."

At noon, Grand-mère released Josie to help Maman dress for dinner. Always before Maman had suffered from nausea, and the smells of bacon or pickles repelled her. With this pregnancy, though, Maman was spared those symptoms. A good sign; maybe she would finally carry this one to term. Yet she had no appetite. Her belly grew and her legs swelled so that she walked with difficulty; at the same time, her face was becoming thin and drawn.

The others had not yet arrived in the dining room. Bibi was filling the water glasses when Josie stood behind Maman, ready to push her chair in. With an odd groan, Maman swayed and grabbed the table for support.

"Maman . . ." Josie pushed the chair aside and took hold of her mother's arm, but Maman's weight pushed her off balance. Bibi rushed to help, and for once, Maman did not shove her away. Together Josie and Bibi sat her in the chair. Bibi dipped a napkin in a water glass and began to bathe her face.

Josie fetched the stool in the corner. She took her mother's ankle to lift her foot, but the warm wetness startled her. She pulled her hand back—it was blood. She moved Maman's skirts away. Streams of blood flowed down both legs.

Josie looked to Bibi. Her wide eyes were signal enough, and Bibi fixed on the growing red pool under the chair. "Get your father," Bibi told her.

Papa rushed into the room, swept Maman into his arms, and carried her to the bedroom. "Bibi, get the old woman," he said over his shoulder.

Josie followed him, but Papa said, "Josie, you're not to see this. Tell your grand-mère to send for Dr. Benet." He began piling pillows under Maman to raise her hips. "Hurry," he told her.

While Josie ran to the stable to fetch Elbow John, Grand-mère wrote the pass for him to be off the plantation. She met Josie and John at the back steps.

"Once you've found Dr. Benet, John, go on to Vacherie for Father Philippe." She handed him three folded notes. "This one with the bent arm on it is your pass. This one is for the priest; see the cross on the paper?"

The priest too? Maman must be in mortal danger. Josie crossed herself and found the rosary in her pocket.

Grand-mère handed Elbow John the third note. "This one for Dr. Benet has a medicine bottle drawn in the corner."

"Yes'm. I sees it. Me and dis ol' mule go fast as we can."

Josie followed Grand-mère into the house, taking care to touch the *benitier* of holy water on the doorjamb. As Josie crossed the threshold of her mother's room, Grand-mère put a hand out.

"Please—" Josie said, but Grand-mère shook her head and closed the door.

Josie put her ear to the door panel. "You're only in the way, son," Grand-mère said. "Leave us."

When Papa opened the door, Josie saw the old midwife from the quarters hovering over Maman. For the last thirty years, Ursaline had delivered most of the children on Toulouse Plantation. Surely she could stop the bleeding until the doctor arrived.

Papa's face was very pale and his hands shook as he took Josie's. "I fear she will lose the child again," he told her.

"I'm sorry, Papa. I know you want a son."

He took her in his arms and held her tight a moment. "Come with me to the gallery. We'll watch for Dr. Benet."

Papa paced. Josie ran her rosary through her fingers over and over for comfort, but her mind was not on prayer. "Can you sit down, Papa," Josie finally said. "It'll be a while yet."

He shook his head. "Go speak to your grandmother again."

"She won't let me in."

"Just ask her if the bleeding has stopped."

Josie reported Ursaline had stanched the bleeding. Still, Papa watched the river road for the dust cloud Dr. Benet's carriage would raise. If the doctor had been out on another call, it might be hours more before Elbow John even found him.

The day dragged on, Papa becoming more and more morose, alternately pacing and sitting with his hands steepled under his chin.

"You need to eat, Papa," Josie said. He nodded absently, and Josie walked through the strangely quiet house and down the back steps to the cookhouse. She'd fix a plate of cold meat and bread, and maybe some preserves to tempt him.

Josie stepped into the shadowy kitchen. "Louella?"

"Come in, *enfant*," Louella called to her. "It hot in here wit all dese kettles cooking. Madame Emmeline want hot water and mo' hot water ready fo when *le médicin* get here."

Louella's brown face glistened with sweat, and the bandana on her hair was wet. When Josie felt the full force of the fire, she tugged at the embroidered scarf around her neck.

"I've come for a plate for monsieur, Louella." She flushed when she saw the big earthenware jar on the table. Louella had somehow found time to trim and slice the hearts of palm for pickling without any help from her. All that remained to do was to pack them in the jar with vinegar and oil.

"I'll come back and finish the hearts," she said. "After I take Papa something to eat."

"*Non, chérie.* Don' worry yo'sef bout de hearts. Boiling water no work at all. You sit wit your papa." She sliced bread and meat. "You need to eat, too, *enfant*."

Bibi came in with an empty basin and Josie jumped up. "How is she?" When Josie saw the stains on Bibi's sleeves, she sat down again heavily.

"It not fresh blood, *ma chérie*," Bibi said. "Ursuline stop de bleeding."

Josie caught the glance Bibi exchanged with Louella. "What is it?"

Bibi shook her head. "Wait fo de doctor, Josie."

Josie insisted. "I'm not a child, Bibi."

"*C'est vrai*," Louella cut in. "Mam'zelle Josie grown, Bibi."

Bibi looked into Josie's eyes. "Well, den. Ursuline say dere no baby in your maman."

That didn't make sense. Mama's belly had grown larger every month. Josie shook her head. "It's just Ursuline. She's too old. Her eyes are all milky, and she can't see anymore."

"It not her eyes dat tell her dis, *chérie*. Ursuline use her hands. De belly, it have no movement, and the shape, it not a baby. 'Ave you not seen how ill your maman been dese weeks?"

"Lots of women feel ill when they're expecting. Tante Marguerite threw up every day, and Jean Baptiste is a fine baby."

Josie watched Bibi's face close down, the slave's first defense. When Cleo or Bibi or Elbow John did that, Josie felt blocked out and lonely and apart.

She picked up the tray Louella had prepared. "You'll see," she said. "When Dr. Benet comes, you'll see."

The priest arrived first. Father Philippe was a tall, thin man who radiated the odor of bad teeth. Dust covered his boots, and white circles under the arms of his black tunic revealed the extent of old sweat. He kissed Josie's hand and then asked to see Madame Tassin immediately. Grand-mère admitted him to Maman's bedroom and again shut Josie out.

It was approaching dusk when Dr. Benet drove up the alley of oaks to the front of the house. Josie watched from the front riverside gallery as Papa helped him down from the carriage. The doctor's only concession to his aged, gaunt frame was to accept a hand getting in and out of the high-wheeled carriage he needed for traveling down muddy roads. His voice rang with the vigor of a much younger man.

"I'm sorry to have taken so long, Emile," the doctor said as the men climbed the gallery stairs. "I was on the other side of the parish. How is she?"

Papa told his old friend what he knew and escorted him to the bedroom, where Father Philippe still prayed with Maman. Then Papa returned to the gallery to take up his pacing as Josie sat motionless in the rocker. Half an hour later, Dr. Benet and Grand-mère emerged from the house.

"How is she? Is the baby all right?"

"Sit down, Emile. It's complicated."

Josie yielded her seat to Grand-mère.

"She's lost a lot of blood, as you know," Dr. Benet began.

"But the baby?" Papa said.

"I'm coming to that, Emile. You've noticed, of course, Celine's growth. She did indeed appear to be carrying a child."

Emile's head dropped. "It's lost, then."

"I haven't made myself clear, my friend. The growth is not a child. Her abdomen is swollen with tumors."

"I don't understand. She's—"

"Don't be simple, Emile," his mother snapped. "There is no baby. There was no baby. Celine has a belly full of tumors."

Josie's hands found her rosary.

"Tell him the rest," Grand-mère said.

"The tumors have ripened, Emile. The pressure of their own growth is bursting them. Do you see?"

Papa made no response. Josie held on to the gallery post, suddenly weak.

Grand-mère shifted her feet impatiently. "Get on with it, François."

"Celine has lost a lot of blood," Dr. Benet went on. "Your Ursuline did well to pack the bleeding. That gave us some time. But the bleeding will come again. Maybe tomorrow, maybe tonight. And that will be fatal."

Papa stared at the shadows under the eaves. "Does Celine know?"

"She knows," Grand-mère said.

Josie slipped away to her mother's room. *Dr. Benet can't know the future. Maman will lie very still, and she'll heal inside. She's too young for God to take her yet.*

In the yellow light of the candles, Maman's face was sallow. Father Philippe sat close by Maman, his head bowed. Josie couldn't tell whether the poor man prayed or slept. She sat down on the other side of the bed and took her mother's hand. "Maman, how do you feel?"

"Only very tired, Josephine. The pain is gone."

Father Philippe rose from his chair. "Mademoiselle, now you are here, I will excuse myself for a moment." He patted Maman's hand. "I will return soon, my dear."

"Josephine," Maman said, "hand me my rosary."

As Maman counted the ivory beads and recited the prayers, Josie knelt. She reached for her mother's lace sleeve so as not to disturb the prayers of her hands and closed her eyes to say her own prayers.

When Papa found her in the candle's glow, her knees ached. "Josie," he said and took her elbow. Maman was sleeping, the rosary wrapped around her fingers.

"I want to talk to your maman now, Josie. You have said good night to her?" She nodded.

Josie sat in the adjoining parlor, Cleo keeping her company. They watched the hands of the clock creep around the face. An hour passed. A bar of light shone under Maman's bedroom, and the murmur of Father Philippe's voice stopped.

"Do you think Maman is awake?" Josie said.

Cleo left her chair and put her ear to the door. "I don't hear anything," she whispered.

"I'm going in." Josie tapped twice and then turned the crystal knob. The candle's glow spread over the bed, and Maman was a vision lying on the cream pillows. Her hair fanned out over the linen and her eyes shone in the pallor of her face.

Josie smiled and breathed out in relief. "Maman, you look like an angel."

Maman raised a hand for Josie to come to her.

Father Philippe was folding his vestment, the vial of holy water on the table nearby. Papa stood in the shadows, gazing out the window into the darkness. He turned, and his wet face glistened in the candlelight.

Papa moved a chair for her. His voice husky, he said, "Sit

with your mother, Josie." He patted his breast pocket for his cigars. "I'll be on the gallery. Cleo, I believe Father would appreciate a glass of wine."

The others left the room, and Josie took her mother's hand. "Maman, you're cold." She tucked Maman's other hand in and pulled the covers up higher.

"Thank you, Josephine."

"How are you, Maman?"

Maman gestured to the cobalt bottle on the table. Her speech was slow and sleepy, and the lines of pain in her face were gone. "Dr. Benet allows me as much medicine as I need."

The laudanum bottle stood next to a bowl of gardenias, Maman's favorites. Bibi must have brought them in. How kind, Josie thought.

Maman squeezed Josie's hand. "It will all be over soon." Maman's eyes closed.

Josie began to rise. "You need to rest."

"*Non*, don't leave me, Josephine."

Josie sat down again. "I'll watch you sleep, Maman."

Maman's eyelids fluttered and then closed. Her breathing was shallow but steady, and Josie thought again how beautiful she was.

Maman's eyes opened wide, and she stared into the shadows. "Josephine. It's coming." She pulled her arm from the covers, clung to Josie with both hands. "I told him I forgave him, Josephine. But it isn't true. I can't forgive him." Fear whitened her face and thinned her voice into a whisper. "And now I have to meet God."

Maman's hands were so cold. "Papa?" Josie called over her shoulder. "Lie back, Maman. You need to rest."

Maman's hands let go of hers, and Josie shouted, "Papa!"

Papa rushed into the room. Maman lay collapsed on the pillow, eyes staring, her arms outstretched.

"It's Maman," Josie said. "She's . . ."

With one sweep, Papa threw the covers back.

Josie recoiled. Her maman's gown, the bedding—drenched in blood.

"François!" Emile called, and then louder. "François!"

The doctor hurried through the gallery doors. He picked up the limp wrist and felt for her pulse. He dropped her hand and pressed his fingers to her neck. The doctor shook his head. "She's gone, Emile." He placed his hand over her eyes and gently closed them. "She's gone."

Josie stood in the shadows behind Papa. She whimpered, and Papa grabbed her to keep her from falling. Bibi hurried into the room, Cleo close behind. They slid a chair under Josie, and Papa sat her down so she couldn't see her maman on the bed.

Josie bent over her knees and trembled. Cleo wrapped a shawl around Josie's shoulders and sat on the edge of the chair with her.

Grand-mère Emmeline entered, her gray hair loose but her robe neatly tied. She placed her hand on Josie's shoulder for a moment, then nodded to Cleo to help her.

Together Grand-mère and Cleo pulled the covers up and straightened them so that the pool under Maman's body was hidden. They arranged the white hands, chose a gardenia from the bowl and placed it on her breast, then smoothed Maman's lovely hair.

"Josephine," Grand-mère said, "come kiss your mother good-bye."

Josie collected herself and faced the candlelit bed. A moment ago, Maman had lived. Now, the stillness of the body total and complete, there was no mistaking that death had taken her.

The only sound was the sibilance of the burning candle. Josie put a hand to her mouth against the mingled scent of gardenia and blood and leaned over to kiss her maman's forehead. Josie then gathered her rosary and knelt at the bedside.

Abruptly, Grand-mère's harsh voice broke the stillness, and Josie turned in alarm.

"Emile! You forget yourself," Grand-mère said.

Papa was in the big velvet chair with Bibi standing before him. She stroked his hair. His arms encircled her waist, and his head rested on her breast.

Chapter 4

Papa sent Josie to bed in the hour before dawn. The mockingbirds were already singing outside the window when she entered her bedroom. How strange, she thought—as if nothing had happened.

Cleo pulled the mosquito net aside for her and folded the coverlet down. She began to close the shutters, but Josie stopped her.

"Leave them open, please."

Josie lay in the bed and waited for the early light to erase the shadows in the room. She relived every moment of the last hour—how lovely Maman had looked in the candlelight, then the panic in her eyes, the coldness of her hands, the strange words.

Josie puzzled over the outrage in Grand-mère's voice when she spoke to Papa. Bibi was like one of the family. Had it been so awful for her to comfort Papa? At last Josie's eyes closed on childhood memories of Bibi's soothing, loving hands.

Late in the morning, Bibi opened the netting and placed a

cool hand on Josie's forehead. Josie reached her arms up to her as she had all the mornings of her childhood, and Bibi sat on the bed and held her tight.

"There was so much blood," Josie said.

"Shh. You don' need to tink about dat."

Bibi rolled the mosquito curtain over the canopy. "I bring you a cup of Cleo's good coffee, wit two sugars de way you like it. M'sieu Emile wit Dr. Benet. I gon' fix your hair, and when *le médicin* leave, you try to get your papa to rest."

When Josie entered the dining room, Dr. Benet rose and held out a chair for her. "My dear, let me help you to some coffee," he said.

"I've had mine, Doctor, thank you." She looked at her papa, and Bibi was right. The skin under his eyes sagged. He hadn't shaved, he hadn't slept. He needed to rest.

"I'll be back tomorrow for the funeral, Emile." Dr. Benet picked up his hat. "I'm sorry, my friend. I'm sorry I couldn't save her."

Papa stood to shake his hand. "You did what you could, François. Thank you."

Dr. Benet followed Bibi to the front entrance. Papa remained standing, staring vacantly at the dining table.

"Papa," Josie said. She left her chair and took his arm. "Papa, come to bed."

Josie took him to his own room. He sat on the side of the bed while she took his boots off, and then she helped him swing his legs onto the coverlet. She loosened his collar, pulled the mosquito netting down, and closed the shutters.

Grand-mère waited for her in the parlor. "He's asleep?"

Josie nodded.

"You've made a good beginning, Josephine." Grand-mère had already dressed in her black linen gown. Her hair was neatly coiffed, and her face showed none of the fatigue and loss her son's betrayed.

"You are now the mistress of your father's house, Josephine. You will have new responsibilities in the Tassin family's social obligations. And now that there will be no male heir, you will continue learning to run Toulouse.

"More immediately, though—sit down, Josephine—we must plan your mother's funeral. There will be perhaps fifty people here, and they all have to be fed; some of them will stay the night, and we will have to find beds for them. It won't be just the family. Many of them you won't have met, and some are not even Creole."

Grand-mère Emmeline delegated Josie to ready the beds for all the overnight guests. Grand-mère herself draped the mirrors and oversaw the cooking, the china, the extra servants they'd need in the house.

While Josie mended mosquito nets, Cleo and Bibi spread the linens to air. Elbow John put up the spare cots with help from his nephew, and Josie learned how to fold the corners of the sheets and tuck them under the mattress.

Josie worked on the gallery and in every bedroom, except her mother's. She avoided Ursaline, the midwife, and her apprentice Marie when they carried baskets and basins out of the room. Only Grand-mère looked in on them as they changed the bed and washed the body.

At noon Bibi brought a pitcher of cool lemonade and a plate of ham and cake. "Sit down, mam'zelle. You wear yourself down you don' eat."

"Where's Cleo?"

"She in de laundry. You sit here on de gallery, you catch de breeze. I send Cleo come sit wid you. She need to eat too."

"What's Papa doing?"

"Elbow John fixing his bath. You can see yo papa after."

By midafternoon, Josie had the house filled with makeshift

beds reassembled from the frames stored in the barn. Some of them were made up with worn linen, but each had a plump pillow and mosquito netting.

Josie found her grandmother in the cookhouse. Grand-mère's sleeves were rolled up and she wore an apron over her black dress. Grand-mère knew how to roll a pie crust as well as Louella, and the next day, they would need more food than any one cook could provide. The sweat beaded on her forehead and upper lip, but not one curl escaped the cotton cap on Grand-mère's head.

Louella's two scullery maids were bustling around the cooks, and Josie sought a corner at the table where she'd be out of the way.

"Mémère, the beds are ready."

Grand-mère handed Josie a basket of pecans. "These need shelling and picking."

Louella tied an apron around Josie's waist and passed her a nutcracker. Grand-mère filled a pie with sausage and potatoes, then rolled out the next crust.

"Tomorrow, Josephine, you will be hostess to a great many people. The family, of course, including the Chamards from Cane River. But some of the newcomers, *les américains*, will come to pay their respects."

"My English is not so very good, Mémère."

"You should know by now, Josephine, that people find a woman charming if she listens, not if she talks." Grand-mère gestured for Josie to pass her the sugar bowl.

"I want you to pay special attention to the Johnstons," Grand-mère said. "They've built a big house on the old Rénard place. Louella, where's the cinnamon?"

"I'll get it," Josie said.

"Mr. Johnston is going to need cane shoots to plant the new fields next spring," Grand-mère said. "I want him to buy them from us. Your father has lost heavily at the track again this past winter, and we need the cash. So you will see to it that the Johnston family is welcomed and made comfortable."

Josie squeezed so hard the nut shattered instead of cracked. Grand-mère's mind was always on business; she even expected Josie to conduct business on the very day of Maman's funeral. *I'll never be so heartless, never.*

Cleo came in and curtsied to Grand-mère Emmeline. "Monsieur DeBlieux is here, Madame. The son, that is."

"Good. I sent word I'd need provisions. Josie, go see what he has. We'll need it, whatever it is." As Josie wiped her hands, Grand-mère added, "Mind your purse."

She would not embarrass herself this time, Josie resolved. He was just a Cajun, no matter how good looking he was. She held her hand out to Cleo. "I'll carry the money."

Josie and Cleo found the young man standing in the shade of the underhouse, not slouching against a pillar. Phanor removed his straw hat when he saw Josie.

She studied his sober face. No hint of the mocking amusement she'd seen in his eyes last time.

"Mademoiselle. *S'il vous plaît*, may I offer you my condolences?"

Josie dipped her head.

"My maman passed on in the new year," he said. "I am sorry for your loss."

"*Merci*, monsieur. And I am sorry for yours also."

After an awkward moment, Josie said, "What have you brought, monsieur?"

"In the wagon, under the trees. Let me show you."

He uncovered the baskets and itemized the hens, the fish, the black-eyed peas, the eggs, the dried apples.

"The fish, they are no charge," Phanor told her. "*Mon père*, he say I ask too much for the heart of the palms." He did not look at either Cleo or Josie. "If you please, the fish are to balance our account with Madame Emmeline."

His embarrassment erased how foolish she'd felt the last

time they met, but Josie decided she would still be careful what she paid out of the little leather purse. She had mostly forgotten all the tedious figures in the account books, but she did recall a notation of five cents for a basket of crawfish, and she took it from there. She ignored Cleo's nudge when she bargained for the hens, and then she counted out the coins into Phanor's hand.

"There is one more thing, mam'zelle," he said as he climbed into the wagon. "My sister, she make you a cake. For all the people who come tomorrow." Phanor handed out a large round cake wrapped in a flour sack.

"Your sister is very kind. *Merci,* Monsieur DeBlieux."

He settled the hat on his head and smiled at her. "Phanor."

"*Merci,* Phanor."

While Cleo and Elbow John took care of the provisions, Josie wandered down the alley of oaks to the levee. She sat on the dock and watched the Mississippi roll by. Muddy and brown, littered with logs and trash floating downstream, it wasn't as pretty as the Cane River. Josie had twice visited her Chamard cousins on the Cane. The upcountry side of the family would be here tomorrow.

For the first time since before dawn, Josie had time to think about Maman. Her eyes—it was as if a candle in Maman's eyes had blown out. Her golden hair had gleamed in the light as it always had, though.

Josie hugged her knees and pictured the previous morning, only a day ago, when she'd sat with Maman in the gazebo. Maman's feet were on the red stool, and a little brother stirred inside her. Or so they had believed. Josie wished she could ask Maman what she'd meant at the end. Was it Papa she couldn't forgive? And for what?

An hour passed, and the sun ate the shade where Josie sat. Maman had told her and told her to stay out of the sun; her freckles would multiply overnight. *I should have listened more, and I should have been more careful with my embroidery.*

When a bloated dog floated against the dock, Josie pulled herself up with a hand over her nose. There were things to do yet today, anyway, and she headed back.

Papa appeared on the gallery and motioned for Josie to join him. Freshly barbered and smelling of wildroot, he kissed Josie and looked at her carefully.

"Your eyes are red, Josie."

She began to cry again, and Papa pulled her to him. As he stroked her hair, Josie remembered how Bibi had caressed Papa the night before, and how Papa had wrapped his arms around her. She had never seen Papa embrace Maman like that. But it confused her, and she couldn't think about it now.

Josie sat on the gallery with Papa and listened to the carpenters bumping into the house with the casket. They pretended not to hear the rattle from the room where Maman lay as the men poured a layer of charcoal on the bottom of the casket. Then it was quiet, and Josie tried not to think about her mother's body being lifted into the long box.

After a late supper, Papa, Grand-mère Emmeline, and Josie each carried a lighted candle into the parlor where the casket had been placed. Ursaline and Grand-mère had padded the charcoal with a length of cream silk and had dressed Maman in her favorite blue gown. All around her body they had arranged roses and gardenias, which would be replaced with fresh blossoms before the funeral.

And so began the wake. Dr. Benet and Father Philippe kept vigil with them, and their nearest neighbors, Monsieur Cherleu and the Cummings family, would join them soon.

"Her rosary, Josephine." Grand-mère meant for her to place the beads in Maman's hands, stiff now and colder than they were last night. Josie held back.

"I'll do it," Papa said.

Grand-mère frowned and flicked her black handkerchief.
"I can do it, Papa."

Father Philippe said a prayer, and they crossed themselves. Then Grand-mère Emmeline raised her candle and,
in her long-legged way, marched from the room. Papa knelt
at the side of the casket and leaned his forehead against his
clasped hands.

Josie stared at Maman, so pale in the candlelight. The
lines around her mouth were smoothed away, and she looked
young and at peace. She'd never be impatient with Josie
again when she ruined her sewing. She'd never be angry
with Papa again, or hateful to Cleo and Bibi.

Josie put a hand to her eyes. *That's not what I want to remember about Maman. Maman was beautiful, and she was a
lady.* She thought of Grand-mère's shrewd, hard face when
she was about the plantation's business, and that was not the
woman Josie wanted to become. She would be like Maman.

And yet, she thought, Maman had not been happy, and
she hadn't been kind. *Maman's heart was not so big as
Papa's. Surely I can be a lady and be like Papa too.*

Chapter 5

Josie didn't have a black dress. The last time there'd been a death in the family was when Oncle Augustine, Papa's elder brother, had drowned in the river. Josie was five inches taller now. Grand-mère pulled Maman's black silk from the wardrobe and held it up to Josie.

"Try it on."

Bibi helped Josie out of her dress and into the black one. The buttons up the back didn't meet across Josie's shoulder blades, and the hem hardly came to her ankles. Grand-mère let out a disgusted snort.

"Well, then. Wait here."

Grand-mère came back with a dress from her own wardrobe. The silk taffeta was so old that the black dye had a purple cast to it. Josie wrinkled her nose against the reek of cedar chips and pulled the dress over her head.

The bodice hung limp on Josie's frame, and the skirt dragged the floor. Tears filled Josie's eyes, but she didn't dare let Grand-mère see them.

"After breakfast, sit down with your needle, Josephine.

You can hem that skirt in half an hour, and take a tuck or two in the bosom."

Grand-mère bustled on to other duties, and Josie let loose. She cried as though the dress itself had broken her heart.

"Josie, Josie," Bibi said. "I help you wid de dress."

"It stinks, Bibi! How can I see people when it stinks like cedar chips?"

"Wash your face. Go to breakfast. I take de dress outside and let de wind blow through it. And I ask Louella if she know what else we can do."

Before Josie had to greet the first arrivals, Bibi had aired the dress, Josie had taken it in, and Cleo had ironed it with a cloth dampened in lavender water. Cleo fixed Josie's hair and helped her into the purply black gown. The two of them stood in front of the long mirror and stared at the dress.

The dark gown washed out Josie's complexion and robbed her hazel eyes of their green tones. The freckles on her nose shone through the powder, and Cleo had accidentally singed one of Josie's curls. Josie was sure she'd never looked so awful. She thought, just for a moment, of Grammy Tulia's cabin, of a safe haven while the strangers were here for Maman's funeral.

"One more thing," Cleo said. She left the room only a moment and came back with Maman's perfume bottle. She dabbed Josie's neck and inner elbows, and after a slight hesitation, she dabbed the dress itself. "That'll help," she said.

Josie joined Grand-mère in the alley of oaks in front of the house. The servants had set up tables from the front gate to the road. The two rows of trees funneled the river breeze, and the canopy shaded the lane. Thibault was peering under the table drapes while Elbow John, cleaned and combed, oversaw the women setting the china and glassware.

"Thibault," Josie said, "what are you doing?"

Thibault hung his head.

"You're not in trouble, Thibault. It's all right. Do you remember me?" Josie hadn't been down to the quarters in such a long time.

He lifted his head and beamed at her. "You Josie."

Josie glanced at Grand-mère, but she hadn't heard. "You must say 'Mam'zelle Josie,' Thibault. What are you doing under the tables?"

"It my job. I the snake hunter." He showed her the forked stick in his hand. "I find a snake, I call Elbow John. He kill it fo me."

"You be careful, Thibault."

Josie's head turned when the steamboat whistle blew. In another ten minutes, it would dock and their first guests would arrive. From the garden, Grand-mère crooked a finger at Josie to come to her. As she passed the statue of the Virgin, Josie genuflected, then joined Grand-mère in the rose-covered gazebo.

Grand-mère looked Josie over. "You'll do," she said. "I want you to sit here until luncheon is served. People will want to pay their respects, and you will receive them here." Grand-mère was scheming, as always, Josie thought with distaste. The scent of the roses would help to mask the smell of cedar chips emanating from her.

A small local steamboat churned upriver and crossed the flow to the dock. Several people disembarked quickly, the eldest man's voice carrying as he shouted last-minute instructions about being picked up again later in the day.

"These are *les américains* I told you about," Grand-mère said. "That's Monsieur Johnston, and that's his wife in the silly hat. The children are Albany, see the young man, the plump one with the sandy hair? And Abigail. It will do no harm if you become friendly with the daughter, even if she is Anglo."

In due course, the visitors came to Josie in the gazebo.

After their introduction, Abigail Johnston kept Josie company as friends and business associates of the family stopped by her bench to offer their sympathy. Josie nodded, said thank you, and counted the minutes until the formalities were over. Her head ached, and she wished Abigail would leave her.

L'américaine had immediately put Josie off her footing. Abigail wore a stylish gown of gray silk trimmed in white. Her blond hair was swept up and topped by a gray lace cap. Josie felt her own shabbiness keenly.

Maman's sister Marguerite, elegant in black lace but red eyed and blotchy, entered the rose arbor. "My dear Josephine," she managed before grief overcame her. She sat next to Josie and held her hand while she struggled to control herself. She wiped her eyes and blew her nose. "You must rely on me, Josephine," she said hoarsely. "I will try to be a mother to you, whenever you need me." She kissed Josie's cheek and, with her handkerchief at her nose, joined her husband among the rose beds.

Tante Marguerite's genuine sorrow brought Josie's own grief to the surface, and she was having a difficult time. Yet Abigail didn't seem to notice.

"All of us Americans," Abigail drawled, "paint our houses white, generally. But here your little home is green, yellow, red. And the Oulette house across the river from us. I believe there are four colors in their paintwork. It's all very quaint. Almost foreign."

Doesn't she realize she's the foreigner here? It's true, then, what they say about les américains. When Cleo came to call her to dinner, Josie thought she'd been rescued, but Grand-mère had business ever on her mind. She maneuvered the Johnstons so that Josie was surrounded by them.

The black dress was heavy, and the sweat ran down Josie's sides in rivulets. The shade and the breeze under the oaks revived her somewhat, but she couldn't eat. Bibi kept filling her glass, and she drank, but the fried chicken on her plate nauseated her.

"Mercy," Abigail said as the gentleman across the table passed her a plate of pickles.

Mercy? Josie thought. *That's an English word. Oh, she means "merci." Good heavens, her French is worse than my English.*

Abigail's brother Albany said a few words to Josie, she hardly noticed what. The buzzing of the flies looking for an escape from the sugar-water trap filled her head so that his voice seemed far away.

At the ringing of Father Philippe's bell, everyone gathered in the courtyard where the priest had set up his altar. Josie, Papa, Grand-mère, and the many aunts sat on the front benches.

"*Dominus vobiscum,*" Father Philippe intoned. "*Et cum spiritu tuo,*" the mourners answered.

After mass, Father Philippe led everyone to the family graveyard on the knoll south of the house. The little cemetery smelled of fresh earth and heat. The sun pounded Josie's aching head, but Father Philippe had claimed the only shade, and Grand-mère stood next to him.

As the priest's voice buzzed on, Josie's attention was on Papa. Poor Papa, who stood erect and silent, but whose face was wet with tears.

Tante Marguerite too wept for Maman, but, strangely, Josie could not cry. Her eyes felt hot and swollen, but there were no tears. The noisiest mourner was Abigail Johnston. Josie watched Albany pull his sobbing sister out of the crowd and lead her away. Then Papa's hand tightened on hers, and Josie felt his arm tremble. Papa would need her from now on.

The house began to settle down. The children slept on pallets while the women gossiped in the parlor and in the *garçonnière*. The young mothers leaned against the headboards of the beds and let their elders fill the chairs. On the riverside gallery, the men gathered in the twilight to smoke their cigars.

Josie climbed the ancient knoll to receive the slaves' condolences at her mother's tomb. Elbow John stood just behind her, but Josie wished Cleo or Bibi were with her. They were needed to wait on the company, though, and Papa and Grand-mère were occupied with the Chamard kin from the Cane River.

Josie's head ached fiercely. This would be her last task of the day, and then she could retreat to her bed.

Still wearing the sweat-stained black dress, the purple cast lost in the dim light, Josie stood at the head of the newly whitewashed crypt. The river breeze brought the scent of magnolias and the promise of rain.

In ones and twos the men, women, and children from the quarters came to the little cemetery. They placed bundles of wildflowers on the crypt, a necklace of shells, a handful of glass beads. Ursaline, who everyone knew practiced *vodou* at the same time she wore a wooden cross around her neck, dug a quick small hole at the base of the tomb and as quickly covered the offering. Maria laid two red feathers on the crypt, and more flowers covered the first gifts.

Josie acknowledged everyone who passed by her. The ones whose names she didn't know, she thanked with a nod and a *"Que Dieu te bénisse."*

Having paid their respects, the slaves lingered around the graveyard. The lament began softly, gently, as Old Sam's humming reverberated through the crowd. Some began to moan and others cried out. Josie swayed with the rhythm until she feared she'd be overcome. She reached for Elbow John, who led her away from the increasing intensity of the keening.

The wailing and the singing rode on the breeze toward the big house as Josie followed Elbow John through the night. Thunder growled from the west. John held the candle high, but it only made the darkness that much blacker outside its circle.

There was still a light in the cookhouse. As Josie neared the corner of the log building, she heard Louella's voice.

"You gone put a bundle of stickers on her grave?"

"*Non*, I don' do dat, Louella. I don' be so mean." That was Bibi's voice.

"After what she do to you and yo poor boy?"

Josie stopped and looked in the window at the two women grinding corn by lamplight. Louella and Bibi, they had mothered her all her life, cared for her and loved her. But were they talking about Maman?

"Dat a long time ago, Louella, and only de good God know if Thibault be simple 'cause she beat me." Bibi lifted her chin. "And M'sieu Emile, I 'ad the best of 'im, I know dat."

Elbow John took Josie's arm to pull her along, but she resisted.

"Madame Celine don' hate me mo' dan she could help," Bibi went on. "I put no stickers on her grave. And Cleo neither."

John whistled then, and the women glanced at each other and hushed.

Josie wrenched her arm from Elbow John and ran on to the gallery, guided by the glowing ends of cigars. She made a hasty good night to the gentlemen and found her room at last. She closed the door, and was glad there was no candle lit on her table. Glad, too, to be alone.

Not caring if she tore the buttonholes, Josie struggled out of the ancient dress and kicked the hateful thing under the bed. Tante Marguerite had brought her an extra black dress from her own wardrobe, and it would be fresh and sweet-smelling.

Prickly with heat, Josie washed from the basin. Over and

over, she squeezed the wet cloth, letting the water run over her to drench the towel on the floor. A lightning flash lit the room, and merciful cooling rain began to splash on the bricks outside.

The drapes billowed and the rain spattered in. Josie lowered the window and watched the drops bead on the glass and run in little streams to the sash. Thunder boomed on the river, and Josie remembered another storm when the rain had pattered hard against the windows. She'd been very young then.

She and Cleo had been playing with dolls in front of the fireplace. The wind had rattled the windows and rain pelted the glass, but she'd felt cozy and safe with Papa nearby reading the papers and Maman tatting a lace collar.

Josie was struggling to dress the new porcelain doll Papa had brought from Paris for her sixth birthday. Cleo, in her flour-sacking dress, played alongside, pulling tiny pantalets onto one of the old dolls.

"Maman, her arms are too big for the sleeves," Josie said.

"You see I'm busy, Josephine," Maman told her.

"Let's have a look," Papa said. He put aside the newspaper and pulled Josie into the space between his legs. Gently he worked the velvet sleeves over the doll's arms. "There," he said. "Once you get her hands in, the sleeves fit well enough." He kissed the top of Josie's head and picked up his paper.

Mama studied Cleo sitting before the firescreen. "Did you see that Cleo's hands were clean before she handled your doll?"

Cleo kept her head down as if she hadn't heard.

"Yes, Maman," Josie said. "Cleo's hands are clean." They weren't, but Josie hadn't wanted Cleo sent away. It was dull playing alone.

Bibi came in carrying the tea things, moving slowly with

her belly grown so big. Josie already knew that this woman who sang to her as she dressed her in the mornings, who kissed her scrapes and bruises, who slept at the foot of her bed each night—she already knew that woman was invisible in Maman's presence. Cleo smiled at Bibi, though, and Josie worried that Maman would see.

"The tea is ready, madame," Bibi said.

Maman motioned with her tatting needle. "On the table. You may pour for Monsieur Emile first."

Papa set the newspaper aside to accept his tea. Josie watched him, and she watched Bibi. She didn't know what she was looking for, but she felt the change in the air whenever Bibi and Papa and Maman were in the room together.

Maman's eyes were on Papa, but Papa's eyes were on his teacup when he said, *"Merci*, Bibi."

Bibi poured tea into another of the delicate cups and turned to serve Maman. But Maman just at that moment was rising from her chair and knocked the cup with her elbow. The tea spattered Maman's silk gown. The blue china shattered on the hardwood floor.

"You clumsy cow!" Quick as a snake, Maman slapped Bibi's face. The kerchief on Bibi's head flew off, and Josie was embarrassed for her that her wooly hair was uncovered in front of Maman and Papa.

"Now, Celine," Papa said. "It was just an accident."

Maman's lips were tight and almost white as she looked full in Papa's face.

"Don't you take her part. Don't you dare take her part."

"I'm just saying, Celine . . ."

Papa glanced at Bibi as she held her belly and bent down to retrieve the kerchief.

Papa said again, "It was an accident."

Maman turned her shoulder to Papa. She grabbed a handful of Bibi's hair and yanked her up.

Josie began to cry. Cleo trembled, her eyes on her mother's

face as Maman slapped Bibi again and again, the white hand bright against the brown cheek.

Papa rushed to gather Cleo in his arms. Cleo first, Josie remembered. Then he grabbed Josie's hand and took the girls to his own room, away from the sound of Maman's slaps, of Maman's chanted "slut, slut, slut" in time to the blows.

In the bedroom, he pulled Josie and Cleo into his lap and rocked them, humming to cover the sounds from the parlor. Josie breathed in the smell of his cologne, of tobacco and pomade, and held Papa's big hand in both her own.

She heard Bibi leave the parlor, her steps heavy and uncertain. Then Maman's sobs began.

"Maman's crying," Josie said.

Papa shook his head and hummed louder.

Josie looked at Cleo on Papa's other knee. Cleo leaned against his chest, her thumb in her mouth. Papa had put red pepper salve on Josie's thumb all last summer, but Cleo, just as big as Josie, could still suck hers. Josie reached over and tugged Cleo's hand down.

Cleo's eyes flashed, and she put her thumb back in her mouth, snuggling deeper into Papa's lap.

"He's my father," Josie said, and pulled at Cleo to unseat her from Papa's knee.

"Josie," Papa said.

Josie shoved Cleo and reached for the kerchief that covered her black curls.

"Josie! I won't have this. You're not going to be like that, not you." Papa stood up and pushed Josie onto her bottom. "Sit there," he said.

He sat in the rocker and pulled Cleo back into his lap.

Cleo's thumb went into her mouth and she leaned her head against Papa's chest. On the cold floor, Josie curled into her own lap and sobbed. The rain blew against the window, and Papa lit his pipe.

* * *

The night of Maman's funeral, then, as lightning cracked through the clouds, Josie understood. Maman hated Bibi and Cleo because Papa loved them. And the baby Bibi carried . . . that was Thibault, Papa's baby.

Josie covered her face. Shame weakened her knees, and she collapsed to the floor, as she had done at Papa's feet so many years before.

Chapter 6

Far into the night, lightning struck the old live oak in the courtyard. Josie felt the blast before she heard it. She fumbled with the netting and rushed to the window. Cleo, from her pallet on the other side of the room, was right behind her.

"Move over," Cleo said. She opened the sash and pushed the shutters aside, heedless of the rain spattering her.

The tree, only forty feet from the window, blazed like a giant torch even in the downpour.

Papa rushed into the room with a candle held high. Josie didn't know the two men who followed him. They were fully dressed, and the scent of tobacco and liquor told her the men had probably been playing cards in Papa's room.

Papa put the candle on the table. He picked up Josie's shawl from the chair and wrapped it around her shoulders. "You'll catch a chill. Cleo, child, close the window."

Josie held herself stiffly as Papa put his arm around her. Her feelings for him were raw, and she felt she didn't know him, not now that she understood about him and Bibi.

He turned her to face the gentlemen, and she recalled her bare feet and state of undress.

"My daughter. Monsieurs Chamard and Medout."

"Mademoiselle Josephine," Monsieur Medout murmured and nodded formally.

Josie shifted her gaze to the other gentleman, whose cigar tip glowed red in the dim candlelight.

"Bertrand, perhaps you remember your cousin from the days before you went to Paris?"

"Mademoiselle." Bertrand Chamard removed the cigar from his mouth and bowed his head slightly.

Josie felt his eyes penetrate the thin fabric of her nightgown. Awareness of her own body, of her breasts, her belly, her most private place flooded her senses. She dropped her eyes for a moment, but she couldn't turn away from his gaze.

"I believe I do remember a girl with straw in her hair, missing her front teeth." His smile gleamed in the candlelight.

Papa seemed suddenly aware of his daughter's unreadiness to receive his friends. "Well, excuse us, Josie. I wasn't sure how close the lightning had hit. Go back to bed, my dears. I'll see Mr. Gale watches the fire."

Josie's face burned as Bertrand Chamard's eyes lingered on her. And had his eyes not probed the shadows where Cleo stood in her nightdress?

The gentlemen withdrew and Josie moved back to the window to watch the fire defy the rain. This Chamard, how rude he was. And disturbing. The candle flame had reflected in his eye, his dark hair fell over his forehead. The loosening of his cravat had revealed the skin at the base of his throat. Though they had not touched, Josie felt the heat of this man, felt the power of his sex.

Cleo slipped an arm through Josie's. "How many times did we sit under that old tree?"

At the touch of Cleo's warm brown skin, Josie had a sudden vision of Papa touching Bibi. He had touched her nanny the way Josie wanted this man Chamard to touch her.

She'd had the best of him, Bibi said. Cleo was the embodiment of her father's sin, and Josie felt unclean at her touch. She pulled away and retreated to her bed.

In the following days, people recalled the last full moon had been blue, and others said no, the moon hadn't been blue, but the river had had a strange green tinge to it the week before the rains began. Whatever the cause, the rains swelled the creeks, the bayous, and the river.

Frogs hopped in the courtyard, and one morning Bibi yelled so loud that Emile came running. She'd stepped on a garden snake on the gallery stairs and nearly dropped her basket of laundry. Emile kicked the snake off the step and called to Elbow John to get rid of it.

Josie leaned out her bedroom window to see what the commotion was. Papa stood close to Bibi, one hand on her arm, his face alight with pleasure. "It wouldn't have bit you, you know. It's just a racer."

Bibi leaned into him, her smile forgiving him the mocking tone.

Josie didn't want to see them together, especially not when they thought they were alone. She pulled back into the room and glanced at Cleo, who was mending a pair of stockings.

"What was it?" Cleo asked.

"A snake on the stairs," Josie reported. "Bibi stepped on it, but Papa kicked it off."

Cleo smiled. "Maman doesn't like snakes, does she?" Her attention was on her sewing.

Josie gazed at Cleo's lowered head. Her hair curled loosely

while Bibi's was kinked. Cleo's skin was lighter than Bibi's, too, and Bibi's was lighter than Grammy Tulia's. Who had been Bibi's father?

She should have noticed sooner, Josie thought. So many things made sense now. Papa's protection of Bibi and Cleo, Maman's resentment.

That's why Papa gave Cleo to me. My sister, my slave. So I would protect her from Maman.

Josie burned. That Papa could do this to Maman. And to her. That Josie, his true daughter, had to share her own father with his slave child.

Cleo glanced up to find Josie staring at her. "What's the matter?"

Josie turned her pinched face back toward the window. "Nothing," she said. Cleo hadn't seen Papa and Bibi just now. Cleo didn't know what she knew. Or did she? People in the quarters would talk. Maybe Cleo had always known. Maybe Josie was the only one who hadn't understood. She stared at the gray sky where more clouds gathered.

Everyone along the river began to watch the sky. While Grand-mère and Mr. Gale worried about the crops, and Papa fretted that his hunting was spoiled, Josie grieved for Maman and tried to understand what her father had done. She watched him sometimes as he smoked his pipe on the gallery or poured himself another brandy in the evening. Who was he after all? She could not excuse him, and she felt the papa she'd adored was a stranger.

The rain let up for a while late in the morning, and Josie wandered up the knoll to the little family cemetery. Only the sound of the big river came to Josie through the trees. How lonely for Maman, she thought.

The storms had left their mark on the cemetery. One huge

puddle made an island of the crypt. Mud spattered the white-washed stones. Fallen twigs and leaves littered the mucky ground.

It simply wouldn't do to have Maman's final resting place so bedraggled. Josie couldn't find Elbow John, and most of the slaves were digging runoff ditches in the fields. Cleo, she didn't know where Cleo was, but Maman would not want Cleo at her crypt anyway. Josie would clean it up herself.

Back in the house, Josie unrolled her stockings and rummaged for her oldest shoes in the back of the wardrobe. She carried a bundle of rags with her, found a trowel among the gardening tools in the carriage house, and trudged back up the hill to the cemetery.

Josie sat for a moment on the little stone bench and tried to feel her mother's presence. She wanted to tell Maman how sorry she was she had never understood what she suffered. Maman, humiliated all those years, Bibi right under her own roof. How awful. No wonder Maman had sometimes been cruel. Josie closed her eyes. She tried to remember her mother smiling and happy, but she could not. The strongest image in her mind was of Maman staring at death, afraid to meet God with bitterness in her heart.

Josie wiped her eyes. She crossed herself and prayed to the Blessed Mother that Maman would find peace.

She stood up and eyed the little sea surrounding the crypt, and then plunged in. The water poured into her old shoes, chilling her in spite of the steamy heat. She began with the rags, wiping the mud off the stone. That done, she began trying to move the standing water with her trowel just as she would bail a boat.

The bailing didn't work. Water flowed into the slight depression where the stones had settled as fast as she could slop the water out. *Forgive me, Maman, for what I'm about to do to my dress,* she thought. Then she dropped to her knees and began to shove mud into the upper runoff channels.

Worms wiggled in the upturned earth, struggling to escape from their flooded world. Josie didn't mind the worms. She and Cleo used to poke a stick in the ground and then rub another stick against it to bring them to the surface. When they had a pail full, Elbow John would take them fishing in the bayou. How Maman would have fussed if she'd known, but Bibi had hidden the soiled dresses from her. *So many things I did with Cleo and Elbow John, and Maman didn't know. Poor Maman.* She had kept to her room so much. Josie was sure her maman had never seen the early mist hovering over the bayou, or the flight of a crane startled from its feeding.

"Mam'zelle."

Josie started. Phanor DeBlieux stood not ten feet away. He carried his rifle and a full bag over his shoulder.

"*Excusez-moi,*" he said. "I didn't mean to frighten you."

"No, only startled," she said. She raised herself from the mud and hoped she hadn't smeared dirt on her face when she'd pushed her hair back. Somehow, muddy pants legs and all, Phanor de Blieux looked good enough to . . . Josie pulled herself back from that thought. "You've been hunting?"

"*Oui.* I have a possum." He set his rifle against the pine tree. "The rain has been hard on the tombs. My maman's too."

"I'm trying to block this channel," Josie said. "I don't know what else to do."

"You will let me help you? I'll show you how I repaired Maman's crypt."

He picked up the trowel and deftly dug a trench all around the tomb. Josie sat on the little stone bench and watched his long fingers at work. At higher ground, he led the runoff channels into his trench and at the lower end, he fanned the trench into smaller crevasses.

"If the rain doesn't let up, you may need to have someone haul fill dirt up here," he said.

Josie pulled her skirt aside and made room for Phanor on the bench. As he wiped his hands on one of her rags, Josie said, "Your mother died in the winter?"

"*Oui.*" He shoved his hat back. Josie saw him swallow hard. Would she still have trouble talking about Maman in half a year?

"She had bad lungs, for a long time," Phanor said.

"I'm sorry."

Phanor breathed deeply. "She was a good woman, my maman."

"And now it's only you and your father."

"*Mais, non.* We are five. Papa and me, my sister Eulalie, her husband, and the baby, Nicholas."

"It's nice you have a sister."

Josie caught sight of Grand-mère Emmeline crossing the courtyard. If she should look up the hill and see her sitting with Phanor, unchaperoned . . . Grand-mère stepped into the cookhouse without looking their way, and Josie said a quick silent prayer of thanks. "I must go," she said.

Phanor nodded, a sad smile on his face. "A dangerous moment, eh?" He tossed the possum sack over his shoulder and picked up his rifle. "*Au revoir,* mademoiselle. I will maybe see you again."

Josie watched him disappear down the hillside opposite from the house. She didn't want him to leave her. Heedless of decorum, and safe from Grand-mère's eyes, Josie slipped down the muddy slope after him. "Monsieur," she called.

She slid into the grassy patch where he waited for her. When he held a steadying hand out to her, she took it and her breath caught. His grip was warm and firm.

"I didn't say thank you," she said. "Phanor." She felt very bold using his first name, but he had once invited her to. Even so, she knew her face reddened when she said it.

"You are welcome—Josephine."

She should probably not allow him to use her familiar name, she thought. But she'd just used his, and it seemed a silly formality when the two of them were muddy from the knees down.

"But," he added, "Cleo, she calls you Josie. Shall I call you Josie?" The gentle tease on his lips said he knew it was improper as well as she did. She was about to insist on Josephine, but Phanor reached down and plucked a wiggly purple worm from her skirt.

Josie had to laugh. It was absurd to be formal with an earthworm on her dress. "Josie, then. But," she warned him, "if Grand-mère is near, Phanor, you must say 'Mademoiselle Josephine.'"

"This I know. Even my papa is careful with Madame Emmeline. And they knew each other as children."

"They did?"

"Oh, yes. Their fathers used to hunt gators in the bayou together. Papa says in the old days, my grandfather and your grandfather had big cookouts at the lake, and the two families would picnic on the shore."

"Cajuns and Creoles? I mean, my grand-mère . . . "

Phanor nodded. "I understand. I will not forget you are Mademoiselle Josephine."

Josie ended an awkward moment. "Do you like possum meat?"

"Mmwa," Phanor said and kissed his fingers. "My sister, she roast it with sweet potatoes and apples. I will bring you a possum some day, and your cook, she will know how to fix it."

Josie lost herself for a moment in his brown eyes. Such beautiful eyes. Phanor held her gaze and moved toward her. Her breathing quickened. They were very much alone. Was he going to kiss her?

She tilted her face up in readiness for his lips, his lovely full lips. She took a step forward, but her smooth leather-soled shoes held no traction. Before she could catch herself, her bottom thudded onto the muddy ground.

A burst of laughter escaped Phanor's lips, the same lips she'd wanted to kiss only seconds before, and she thought she would kill him. She glared at the hand he offered her.

He grinned, set his rifle and bag down, then hauled her up by her arms. She brushed against his body when he heaved her up, but she stepped away quickly. Could he feel her breasts through his shirt?

She tried to straighten her skirt with all the dignity she could muster. She wouldn't look at him. He must think she was a fool, and a wanton at that. She'd been about to kiss him!

"Please, Josie. I'm sorry I laughed, but it happened so quickly. I couldn't help it."

She turned a frown on him, but he only smiled back, his black eyes merry. "I do apologize, truly I do."

She crossed her arms over her chest and cocked her head at him. "Truly?"

"*Oui*, truly." He put his hand over his heart and wiped the smile from his face.

"Well, perhaps I will forgive you, then—someday."

His moment of contrition was over, and a hint of amusement played around his lips again. "I will live for that moment." He picked up his rifle and bag once more. "Would you like me to help you back to the house?"

"Oh. Oh no. That would look very odd indeed." She looked back in the direction of the house where Papa and Grand-mère were going about their day, confident Josephine was behaving as a young lady ought to. And here she was alone in the woods with a young man. In a dress covered in mud. Thinking impure thoughts.

The weight of propriety descended on her once again. "Thank you, no. I will not require assistance."

He tilted his hat to her and turned to leave. She'd been too abrupt. She hadn't meant to be harsh.

"Phanor?" He stopped and looked back at her. "Thank you," she said.

He smiled and headed into the trees.

Josie slogged through the mud toward the house and pondered whether it was quite proper to be friends with Phanor. After all, he was Cajun, and poor, and—could he even read? She didn't know. Imagine not knowing how to read. *Oh, but he was so very kind to help me with Maman's crypt. And it's not just that he's handsome. He's smart. And strong. I like him, and I won't be a snob like Grand-mère.*

On the way back to the house, Josie stopped in the carriage barn to return the trowel. It was dim in there, and Josie squinted to find the hook where it belonged. A rustling in the far buggy caught her ear, and she thought she'd better tell Grand-mère the squirrels were nesting in the carriage house again. But the rustling became a giggle.

Who would be in the carriage house? Maybe some of Elbow John's younger grandchildren had sneaked in to play. *I bet it's Laurie and some of her cousins. We all spoil her silly, cute as she is.*

Josie moved to the high-backed carriage to see what Laurie was up to. *I bet they're giving their dolls a ride.*

But it wasn't Laurie at all. It was Cleo—with a slave boy! Josie was sure she smelled Maman's perfume too. Grand-mère would have Cleo beaten for that if she found out. Josie had never had to protect Cleo from Grand-mère before; it might be more difficult than with Maman.

Cleo's laugh was forced. "You caught us," she said.

Josie examined the boy sitting so close to Cleo. A handsome boy, high cheekbones and a slender neck. Bold too. He didn't let go of Cleo when Josie eyed their clasped hands.

"Who's this?" Josie said.

"Dis Remy. He Elbow John's grandson."

Josie looked at Cleo a long time. Her sister. And Papa's favorite. What would Papa think about Cleo sitting out here with a field hand with sun-scorched hair? Cleo didn't have permission to court, and she had no chaperone.

Not unlike Josie herself a few minutes earlier. Was Cleo as lonely as she was, then?

"Why are you talking like that?"

"Like what, mam'zelle?"

"Like the . . . slaves . . ." Josie's voice trailed off.

Cleo's eyes flashed. She climbed out of the carriage, pushed past Josie, and ran out.

Remy and Josie stared at each other. Now she remembered him. He had played with them at Grammy Tulia's sometimes, when they were little. Nobody could catch him when they'd played tag, and he'd once helped her pull the burrs off her stockings. Now he had the broad shoulders and long legs of a man.

"I know you," she said.

Remy sat as if frozen on the carriage seat. Josie had meant to reassure him, but she saw fear flicker in his eyes. She had no doubt he was imagining the whip across his back.

Josie had never witnessed a whipping, never heard a slave cry out in agony, but she'd seen the scars on the backs of slaves who'd been whipped. She would never be the cause of such suffering. When she was mistress of Toulouse, there would be no whippings.

"It's all right," she said. She reached her hand out and touched him gently. Then she left him in the shadows.

Chapter 7

Cleo ran over the sodden ground back to the courtyard, her jaw clamped to keep from crying. *Just because Josie doesn't have a sweetheart,* she thought, *doesn't mean I can't. If Josie is jealous of Remy and me, well, she'll just have to be jealous.*

But, she thought, *I shouldn't have left Remy in the barn with Josie. Maybe I should go back. And say what—Remy's too sweet for you to be mean to, Mademoiselle Josephine?*

In truth, Josie was never mean to anyone. But Josie had not been herself lately. That sour mother of hers was still her maman, Cleo thought, and Josie missed her.

Bibi appeared on the back gallery above her. "Cleo, where you been, child? Don' you know it time to set the table?" Bibi eyed the pavement she had just swept. "Look at dose footprints you making!"

Cleo had tracked mud all across the courtyard bricks. "Damnation," she muttered.

"Never mind 'bout dat now. Get on up here."

Cleo pulled her shoes off and stuck them behind the wine

racks in the underhouse. Madame Emmeline didn't care whether Cleo was barefoot or not, but she wouldn't abide her being slack with her chores.

Cleo hurried up the stairs to get the dining room ready for dinner. Through the open doors, Monsieur Emile's cigar smoke wafted through the house from the front gallery. She'd watched him the last few weeks, since Madame Celine died. The first few days, he was more grieved than she'd expected, but he seemed himself again now.

She never called him Papa, not even to herself, though she had always known he was her father. When she was a child, he had gently touched the top of her head whenever he passed by her. He had smiled at her as often as he had at Josie. And he had held Maman on his lap those mornings when Celine and Josie were in the rose garden.

Josie was so dumb sometimes, Cleo thought as she set the plates on the table. Josie never seemed to know anything Madame Celine hadn't wanted her to know. And now that Josie had found out about Remy, Cleo guessed there'd be trouble.

"None of her damn business, anyway," she said under her breath. She folded the last napkin and poured water into each glass. She'd done her part until Louella sent the dinner over and everyone gathered. She popped a fig from the preserves dish into her mouth and licked her fingers.

Emile clomped in from the gallery, and she plucked another fig as he entered the dining room from the parlor.

"I'll have a glass of wine, Cleo," he said.

Cleo poured him a claret, knowing Madame Emmeline would harp at him for drinking so early in the day. It was the rain, Cleo thought. He was bored and restless.

"Will you go hunting this afternoon, monsieur?" Cleo asked.

"*Non*. It's nothing but mud out there. The game have gone looking for a little high ground."

Cleo heard Madame stomping her feet on the back gallery. "Cleo," she called, "bring me a mat to wipe this mud on."

"*Oui*, madame." Cleo wondered where Josie was. She'd certainly had time enough to change from that muddy dress by now. Josie had been so odd lately, cold one minute and then loving again the next. *Probably planning to stick her nose in my business,* Cleo thought. *Like I didn't see her with that Cajun boy up there on the hill. And I'll have to clean her damn shoes.*

By the time Emile had seated Madame Emmeline at her end of the table, Josie entered in a fresh linen frock. "*Bonjour*, Mémère, Papa."

Cleo served the soup and stood back while dinner progressed. Madame talked business, as always. Monsieur Johnston had agreed to buy his start-up cane from her, and they had negotiated a price. If only this incessant rain didn't ruin the shoots.

Madame picked up her spoon again. "Josie," she said. Cleo saw Josie start. She'd been woolgathering instead of listening. She was in for it now.

"Josephine." Madame spoke sharply. "The business of this plantation concerns you more than anyone. Pay attention."

"I'm sorry, Mémère. You were talking about the rain?"

"Is there something more important than the cane on your mind, young lady?"

If Josie planned to make trouble over Remy, Cleo thought, now's the time.

"On my mind?" Josie said. Cleo caught her glance, and Josie held her eyes. "*Non*, of course not, Mémère." So she wasn't going to tell.

"Well, then," Madame Emmeline continued, "you'll do well to listen to your—" She stopped midsentence and gaped at Cleo. Cleo had taken Madame's soup plate away even though it was half full.

"What are you doing? You stupid girl, put that back."

Cleo shared a fleeting smile with Josie and repositioned Madame's soup in front of her. Cleo habitually distracted Madame Emmeline whenever she fussed at Josie. It made Madame angry and gave her someone else to rail at. Cleo was well aware Josie had protected her from Madame Celine; she could do the same for Josie with Madame Emmeline.

Madame reclaimed her dinner, and then she affected a casual tone. "Josephine, I've had a letter from Monsieur Johnston. About the cane, of course, but he mentions his daughter—you remember Abigail? She invites you to visit them next week. Only for a few days, just to get better acquainted."

"Oh, it's too soon, Grand-mère. I really don't want to—"

"Of course you do, Josephine. It'll be good for you to make a new friend. And now the dressmaker has finished your mourning clothes, you have no excuse for sitting about moping. You should be with other young people more."

Cleo knew Josie would appeal to Emile next, but that wouldn't do her any good.

"Papa needs me here," Josie said.

Emile admired the color of his claret. "I believe your Grand-mère is entrusting you with a business assignment, Josephine." He put his glass down. "In order to ensure the Johnstons' considerable wealth finds an outlet in our pockets, she wants you to befriend the girl, charm the family, and, tell me if I'm wrong, Maman, to win the son as well. Not such a lot to ask. Have I understood you right, Maman?"

"Emile, you are impossible. You know how these things are done, yet you will not stir yourself to make friends with either Monsieur Johnston or his son. They are looking for connections with us Creoles, and you waste this opportunity."

"I'll go, Papa."

Cleo knew she'd say that. Anything to keep the old lady

from carping at Emile. Besides, the old lady was right. That's how business was done. It's just that Emile had no taste for it. He had his books and his hunting.

Cleo had long ago observed that Emile spent much of his time doing nothing. He sat on the gallery in the rocker, smoking his cigar, watching the Mississippi roll by. As long as he could hunt early in the morning, he was content the rest of the day. After supper he read, unless he was playing cards with his friends.

Josie sat and stared out the window a lot too. She and Emile were alike in that. And in their disinterest in the plantation. As hard as Madame was, Cleo thought, she was the one who kept Toulouse running.

"I'll go, Grand-mère," Josie said.

"Of course you will. And you will have a lovely time. How nice that you have a new wardrobe for the occasion," Emmeline said.

An all-black wardrobe, Cleo thought. *Josie looks awful in black.*

Cleo served the vegetables and slyly omitted the stewed okra from Josie's plate. Madame wouldn't tolerate finicky eaters, so Josie had to clean her plate every meal, and she hated slimy stewed okra.

Emile raised his glass to Josie. "You are an angel, Josephine, and I do agree that you need to get out of this dreary wet house. Go, my dear, and enjoy yourself." He finished his wine in a gulp and excused himself.

Madame Emmeline eyed his untouched food, no doubt calculating the number of half cents wasted on his plate, Cleo thought. No matter. Cleo loved stewed okra. She would eat it herself after Madame left the room.

And so Josie was to go to the Johnstons. That meant Cleo would have to see to it that all Josie's smallclothes were washed and ironed, her stockings mended and laundered, and all the new mourning clothes carefully folded into the trunk. Abigail had written that she had plenty of maids in the big house, and Josie need not bring her own. That was fine with Cleo. She could meet Remy every day while Josie was gone.

In Josie's bedroom that night, the girls lay in the dark talking. A year ago they might have discussed Posey Purr's latest litter and who should be given the kittens. There'd been few times these last weeks, though, when Josie set aside the distance she'd put between them. Tonight, Josie said, "That Abigail called our house little. Like it was a cottage or something."

"This big house? How big must her house be, then?"

"Papa said the new *américains* all build huge houses."

"Are they all rich? Richer than Creoles?" Cleo said.

"Did you see that gown she wore to the funeral? I bet it came from New York, or even Paris."

"Well," Cleo said, "she talks through her nose."

"And her French is terrible."

They were quiet a moment, and then Josie said, "My English isn't very good. I'll feel like a fool every minute I'm there."

"Maybe you should pretend you don't know any English at all. Then they'd have to speak French."

Josie snickered at that, but her anxiety radiated through the room. "My clothes are all black," Josie said. "Mostly cotton, and all black."

"I think you need to wear some rouge."

They settled into silence. Cleo reflected on the close call she'd had. If Josie had told on her, she could have been switched for slipping off with a field slave when she was supposed to be in the house. Remy would have been flogged.

Cleo had seen a man flogged—her cousin Jean. It hadn't happened on Toulouse in a long time, but Mr. Gale knew how to wield his six-foot whip with the four knotted ends. Jean had lain in the cabin for a week, hardly able to move after Mr. Gale had flayed him for running away. That was a long time ago, and it was the last flogging on Toulouse. Still, Cleo knew the whip still hung on Mr. Gale's porch.

But there would be no beatings, thanks to Josie's discretion. Cleo didn't see how she could have endured a flogging. A beating with the whip left scars, scars that forever marked you as a slave.

Chapter 8

Every day it rained some more. The wind and the heavy downpours tore the rosebuds apart, and the dahlias dragged their heads in the mud.

Josie stood in the rain on the Toulouse dock while the men loaded her trunk onto the riverboat. The wind whipped at her skirts and Elbow John struggled to hold a big umbrella over her. She stared at the current swirling in the middle of the river. Anything dropped overboard would be sucked under, like Oncle Augustine was, and he'd known how to swim.

"Ever see such a rain? Look to me like the whole world gonna drown," the boat captain said.

Emile laughed. "I put my faith in the Bible, Mr. Hurley. 'Neither shall there any more be a flood to destroy the earth.'"

"Could fool me, Mister Tassin. These clouds go clear up past Vicksburg, they say."

Emile kissed Josie on the forehead. "I want you to have a good time, *chérie*. Abigail seems a nice girl, and you need to know someone besides your cousins. The Anglos are here to stay, I think."

Josie's stomach roiled at her father's touch. She did not return his kiss.

"*Au revoir*," he said. "I'll see you at the end of the week."

Josie climbed the ramp onto the boat and stood under the overhanging gallery of the second deck. Papa stood in the rain and threw her a kiss. Josie looked toward the gallery where Cleo waved to her, but she did not respond to either of them. Her heart was heavy as lead.

The river pulled the boat away fast. The water was full of logs and branches, an empty skiff, even a dead cow. Josie chose to watch the riverbank instead. She waved back at the little boys Mr. Gale had positioned every fifty yards to watch out for inroads in the levee, then she retreated to the salon and from there watched the rain pelting the brown water. She hoped Elbow John had found a dry place on the boat for the trip downriver.

Half an hour downstream, the boat rounded a curve and Josie caught first sight of the Johnstons' mansion. It stood three stories tall, gleaming white in a momentary sunburst through the clouds. No wonder Abigail had said the Tassin house was little.

At the dock, Elbow John handed Josie over to the Johnstons' butler Charles. Josie looked again at the imposing house and wished she were home. She gave Elbow John a quick hug and then followed Charles up the long stone path to the house. Huge round pillars supported the gallery roof, and the front windows gleamed with new glass. Josie straightened her bonnet and shook her skirt, hoping it wouldn't cling to her legs. Then she nodded to Charles and he opened the big double doors for her.

Josie had never seen such an entryway. Toulouse was a typical Creole home, the front doors leading directly into the parlor, and on the opposite wall, another set of double doors invited guests into the dining room. The Johnstons' front door, however, led into a large hallway whose ceiling reached the third floor. Midway down this hallway, small palm trees in porcelain planters flanked two red velvet settees.

Charles took Josie's wrap and led her into the drawing room, where a cheery fire dispelled the damp.

"Miss Abigail will be down in just a moment, Miss Tassin."

Josie sat on the edge of the black horsehair sofa and hoped her skirts wouldn't drip on the floor. She twisted her handkerchief as she took in the opulence of the room. The rosewood table glowed, and the tall mirror over the fireplace reflected the green silk wall covering. The darker green damask curtains swept from the ceiling to puddle on the floor in an excess of fine fabric.

Josie heard quick steps on the stairs. Abigail would probably eye her wet skirt and windblown complexion, but there was nothing for it. At least she didn't smell of cedar chips.

Abigail rushed into the room, both hands outstretched. "You're here at last! I'm so glad to see you."

There was not a hint of disdain in Abigail's demeanor, and Josie smiled in relief.

"You poor thing, you're drenched," Abigail said. "Sit here closer to the fire. As soon as Suzanne unpacks your things, we'll go up and change. How was the boat ride? Isn't the river frightening when it's like this? Does it rain this much every summer?"

Josie laughed, a little too loudly. "But *non*, this rain is too much," she said in awkward English.

"My father worries the river might flood his fields. He has the darkies out building the levee higher. Did you see them piling the dirt when you were in the boat? Your father must be doing the same at your plantation."

Josie suspected her father would not think of that precaution, but Mr. Gale might suggest it. Anyway, they had the boys on lookout atop the levee.

After their coffee, Josie followed Abigail up the grand staircase to Abigail's rose pink room. They chatted about clothes, the girls they might both know up and down the river, and most especially about the young men Abigail had been introduced to in New Orleans. She was already nineteen and had been to six balls last winter. Besides the older men who asked her to dance because of her father, Abigail counted three men as absolute possible suitors, and she described each of them to Josie in minute detail.

The three hours before supper were happily spent dressing and arranging their hair. This was justified because at the Johnstons', it was the evening meal that carried the weight of the family's social life. Abigail knew the latest hairdos and she directed her maid just how to arrange Josie's hair with a single fat sausage curl over each ear. The rest of her hair was gathered into a curly mass on top of her head. Josie felt very sophisticated as she preened in front of the mirror. She regretted the lack of colored ribbons, but the period of mourning for Maman was only just begun, and she chided herself for being so trivial as to miss a pretty ribbon.

Abigail looked wonderful. She'd adopted the practice of melting fine beeswax and smoothing it over her face. "My cousin Samantha, from Oxford—she showed me how. You want to try it?"

Josie eyed the warm pale wax. "Not today, thanks." What would happen when Abigail smiled with the wax on her skin? Would it crack? Or melt in the heat? She had to admit, though, that the thin layer of beeswax on Abigail's face made her skin as perfect as porcelain. Cornsilk hair curled around her ears, and the blue gown made her blue eyes bluer. Still, Josie thought as she turned to the mirror, her own light brown hair was very good. She hadn't so many freckles as in past summers. And green eyes were considered an asset, though in truth hers were hazel.

The ladies joined the misters Johnston in the parlor. The son, Albany, reached six feet, all of him rather colorless. Though his black boots shone, the buff of his jacket blended with his hair and skin. When he took her hand, bowed, and murmured something about "a pleasure," Josie noticed his pale hair was quite thin on top, in spite of his being only in his mid-twenties. Even so, he exuded a . . . something. Josie decided it was money. Albany Johnston exuded an aura of wealth and refinement.

During supper, Albany turned to Josie now and again, mostly to comment on the unusually rainy weather. Josie found him dull, a little stiff, and a bit too fleshy for her taste, but she appreciated his effort. He seemed shy rather than un-interested, and she smiled at him to be kind.

She couldn't help but compare him to Phanor DeBlieux. How much more confident Phanor was in his straw hat and bare feet than Albany was in tailored jacket and leather boots. Phanor didn't need fine clothes. He was of the rich black land and the bayous, his character firm and sure. His shock of unruly black hair and the flash of his smile filled her mind's eye. But, she reminded herself, Phanor was a poor Cajun, and had no refinement at all. For a Creole girl of good family, regrettably, he simply was not marriageable.

"Miss Josephine," Mr. Johnston broke into her reverie. "I believe we have a kinsman of yours arriving tomorrow. Bertrand Chamard?"

Chamard. The man who came with Papa to her room the night the lightning struck the tree. Josie's face grew warm as she recalled the dark eyes that had peered at her in the candle-light. She had thought of him often, and of how, merely by gazing on her nightgown, he had made her body glow, her breasts swell. And now she would see him again.

"A cousin, my papa said. I hardly know him, though, and I don't know exactly how we are related."

"Really? How odd," Abigail said.

"I can well understand your not being acquainted," Mr. Johnston said. "Bertrand's been in France since his school-days."

Josie's fingers strayed to the curl over her ear. Bertrand Chamard must have found Toulouse as quaint and small as Abigail had. And she herself—he'd find her small and plain next to Abigail Johnston. Or maybe not. Albany certainly seemed to find her attractive.

After noon dinner the next day, the rain recommenced in earnest. The girls lay on Abigail's silk-draped bed and talked until even Abigail's chatter lapsed into dreary silence. All the while Abigail had shown Josie the house, had entertained her with fashion magazines and gossip from Town, Josie had been preoccupied with the night she'd first met Bertrand Chamard, reliving the heat of that moment in her bedroom. Josie wanted to ask Abigail how she knew Bertrand Chamard, what she thought of him, if he had ever looked at her the way he had at Josie. But she didn't dare.

Abigail had run out of ideas to entertain her guest. They were bored. They couldn't just lay about all afternoon, Josie thought. They needed something to do.

"You didn't show me the cookhouse, Abigail. Why don't we make cinnamon cakes for supper?"

Abigail propped herself up on an elbow and looked at Josie. "Make cinnamon cakes?"

"Or a cobbler. You probably still have a barrel of apples from the fall."

"You cook?" Abigail said.

Josie suddenly realized why Abigail hadn't shown her the cookhouse. She had probably never been in it. "I can make a few things." Josie felt her face flush. "My grandmother insisted I learn something useful."

"Useful," Abigail said. "Well. I can't say I know how to do anything so useful as that. I would hardly have time, anyway, between practicing the piano and studying French and writing letters . . ." Abigail held a hand out and examined the smooth skin, the delicate nails. Josie closed her fingers against her palm. She still had one very short nail from when she'd torn it to the quick helping put the extra beds away after Maman's funeral.

What a *faux pas*, she thought. No one expected Abigail to contribute to the running of the household. She and her mother were truly ladies, always dressed beautifully, always available and charming. Josie juxtaposed Mrs. Johnston's smooth, merry countenance against her maman's perpetual scowl of discontent, her grand-mère's habitual frown. Mrs. Johnston never had occasion, she supposed, to count the gains and losses of the plantation or to balance Mr. Johnston's gambling losses against the season's cane profits. Or to every day have to see her husband's lover and bastard in her own house.

Josie shoved that heartache away and eyed the sumptuous rose damask covering the bed, the chairs, even the windows in Abigail's room. There were no age spots in the mirror where the silver lining had yielded to the climate. There were no nicks or stains in the rosewood dresser. Josie yearned for such luxuriance, both the material extravagance and the evident pampering of the ladies of the Johnston family.

But how the afternoon did drag on.

The following morning, the maid pulled the heavy drapes aside to reveal a sunny blue sky at last. Josie put a hand up to shield her eyes and hoped the rain was over.

The sun burned off some of the damp throughout the day, and Albany proposed a ride along the river road. "Do you ride, Miss Josephine?"

"I have my own bay gelding at home—Beau, I call him."

"Then, Abigail, why don't you and Miss Josephine join

me. We'll ride on the high road to avoid the worst of the mud."

Damp earth and honeysuckle scented the air, and the sun steamed a hazy miasma just above the road. The three of them loped along, and Josie relished the freshness of the breeze in her face, the freedom of easy motion. She wanted to gallop. She used the whip to signal her horse to pass Abigail's mare, leaned into the gelding's great neck, and grinned back at Abigail.

Josie puzzled over Abigail's expression, mouth and eyes open wide, and then, in the corner of her eye, Josie caught the blur of a deer darting across the road. The gelding neighed and reared back, and Josie began to slide off the saddle. She squeezed her right knee around the pommel, but the horse struck the ground with his front hooves full force, unseating her, and then it reared again.

Josie slid off the gelding's hindquarters, helpless to stop herself, and landed on her back in the mud. Abigail yelled at her mare to turn round, turn round as Albany galloped past her after the gelding, mud spattering Josie from his horse's feet. Through the ground under her back, Josie felt the vibrations of a fourth horse thundering toward them.

The rider yanked his horse to a full stop, and as Abigail began to raise Josie up, the man leapt from his saddle and commanded, "Wait. She may be hurt more than you know."

Abigail laid her back down in the mud, looking intently into Josie's face. Josie was struggling for breath, and her eyes were wild with the effort.

"The breath was knocked out of you, Josie." Abigail took her hand and squeezed it. "I've had that happen before. It'll come back by itself. It will."

The man felt her ankles, then her lower legs. "Can you move your feet?" he demanded.

Josie gasped as her diaphragm at last began to pump air into her lungs. She glanced at the man. My God, it was

Chamard. He had his eye on her boots. "Move your legs," he said again.

She did, first one and then the other. His hands were on her. To be touched so intimately—and her skirt must be awry, revealing her pantaloons. She blushed in embarrassment, and at the kindling of her blood. She breathed deeply, waiting for him to look into her eyes.

"Does this hurt?" he said. "Or this?"

Satisfied nothing was broken, at last he looked into her face. She'd never seen eyes like his. The color of brandy in candlelight. Deep, and warm.

"You've had a nasty fall, *chérie*."

Albany trotted up with Josie's horse in tow. "How is she, Chamard?"

Chamard glanced at the horse trailing Albany instead of at Albany. There was a hint of censure in his voice. "She will do, now she has decided to breathe again." He winked at Josie. "Her pretty neck is not broken, nor are her long legs. She'll do."

Josie tried to raise herself, but the mud sucked at her back. Chamard took an arm and lifted her to her feet with one hand. She leaned against him, thrilled at the pressure of his arm under hers.

Albany dismounted and stood rather uselessly. Chamard held Josie's arm, and Abigail fussed at her other side. Josie drew away from both of them, remembering her dignity. She could stand by herself.

"Miss Josephine," Albany said, "you have to be more careful on these wooded lanes. You never know when a rabbit or a deer . . . the woods are full of game, and—"

"It could have happened to anyone," Abigail interrupted.

"Yes," he reasoned, "but my point is that Josie looked away from the road for a moment and so was not prepared when her horse reacted."

"I still don't see . . ." Abigail argued.

Josie ignored them. Chamard was examining her hairline. He thumbed a smear of blood away where a rock had caught her. "It's not bad," he said. "I don't believe we will have to send for Dr. Benet."

Chamard tilted her chin up. "I believe you are very lucky," he said. "We have the soft mud to thank for that, and your wits to hold on to the reins as long as possible." He held her chin a moment too long, she thought, and she began to blush again.

Then he surprised her. He bent his head and sweetly kissed her lips.

The world stopped for a moment. Then Josie became aware that the argument between Albany and Abigail had ceased. They were staring at them. In the silence, Chamard seemed suddenly aware, too, and he straightened.

He turned a jovial face to Albany. "My cousin is recovered, and I take that as a blessing, Johnston. Perhaps you will allow her to ride with you on your horse back to the house? I would take it kindly. My stallion is not fit for a gentle rider."

"I'm perfectly capable of riding by myself," Josie protested.

"Please, cousin," Chamard said. "I would be more at ease if you would ride with Johnston."

Those lovely eyes appealed to her, and she relented.

Albany offered his arm and led her to his mount. Once she was in the saddle and he astride behind her, he reached one arm around her to hold the reins and with the other held her around the middle. Josie was aware of Albany's hand pressed against her ribs, but it was not the same sensation as her cousin's hands on her. With Johnston's body behind her, she was simply hot.

When they reached the stable, Albany slid off first. Then he held both arms up to Josie. She allowed him to lift her down, and as he set her on her feet, he said in her ear, "I'm so glad you're all right, Josie."

Josie pulled her head back. He'd dropped the proper Miss Josephine, she observed. "Thank you, monsieur," she said formally. She glanced at Bertrand Chamard. He had the look of a man trying not to smile.

Chapter 9

Toulouse

The morning Josie boarded the riverboat to visit the Johnstons, Cleo wrapped two shawls around herself. The wind and the rain made it a nasty day, and Cleo wanted to wave good-bye to Josie from the dock.

Josie had been distant off and on since the funeral, and Cleo missed their old camaraderie. Surely if Cleo kept herself ready to be friends again, Josie would come around. Grief didn't last forever.

Cleo followed M'sieu Emile and Josie through the front gate. Emile turned around and waved her back. "Go back to the house, Cleo. No need of your getting soaked," he said.

Cleo was about to protest, but Josie didn't even look back, so Cleo nodded to Monsieur Emile and hurried to the shelter of the upstairs gallery. A pang of loneliness grabbed her as she watched Josie board the boat. She raised her hand to wave, and for a moment she thought Josie saw her, but there was no hand raised in return. What would a week among those *américains* do to Josie? She might be even more distant when she came home.

After dinner, the clouds grew thinner, and the wind shoved them farther south and east. Cleo finished her chores and checked that Madame was busy with the accounting books. Monsieur Emile was in his room, probably reading or taking a nap.

Cleo wanted to pick out the minuet Josie was learning, and she wanted to study the notes in Josie's old beginner's book. No one but Madame Celine had ever minded Cleo playing the piano, though lately Josie had seemed a little put-out. *Well,* Cleo thought, *she should practice more if she wants to play better.* M'sieu encouraged both of them, though Cleo was sure he'd rather sing with her than with Josie. Josie got nervous and made mistakes when he sat with her.

Cleo wouldn't miss the tutor's skinny, faintly odorous figure standing stiffly behind her, beating the time with his foot, as he did with Josie. But Cleo had only heard the piece twice. She wished she could read the notes on the page. In the spring, she'd begun to decipher the mysterious symbols in the beginner's book she'd found in the cabinet. Maybe by next summer, she'd be able to read music.

No sooner had Cleo opened the keyboard of the old Chickering than Madame's favorite little pickaninny found her.

"Cleo, you wanted, you," Laurie said. Her hair was twisted into little pigtails all over her head, and her black eyes shone with the importance of delivering a message. "Dat Cajun fella, he here. Madame say you see to it, she busy."

"Is it the young Cajun or the old one, Laurie?"

"I seed Cajun wid a hat on his head. I don' see no young, no old." Laurie held the coin purse out. "This here full of money. You best be keerful, Cleo. Madame done count all dem pieces of money."

"Go on with you, Laurie," Cleo said, and waved a hand at

her in irritation. *It might be Phanor*, she thought, and so she hurried to Josie's mirror to check her headscarf and smooth her dress before she went downstairs.

Phanor leaned against his wagon, his pants rolled up to his knees to save them from the mud. When Cleo stepped from the underhouse, he tossed aside the grass stalk he'd been chewing and watched her walk across the courtyard to him.

Conscious of being admired, Cleo swung her hips a little more than she might have and held her chin just so.

"*Bonjour*, mademoiselle."

He had that teasing look again. Cleo didn't know what he was so stuck-up about. She raised her nose a little more.

"*Bonjour*, Phanor." She drew his name out in as condescending a manner as she knew how. But she didn't get his goat—he laughed and flashed his white teeth.

"How are you this fine day, Cleo? The sun, he has decided to show his face, and maybe he will dry up the mud in the road."

How could you be mad with a boy whose brown eyes were afire with fun? She smiled up at him through her dark lashes. "But you brought your wagon through the muck."

"*Oui*. Old Gus and Toine here," he said, gesturing to the mules, "they'll be tired when we get home."

The gate of the wagon was open, and Cleo hiked herself onto the back end. "An empty wagon this time?"

He hitched his hip onto the wagon next to her. "I've come to buy, not to sell. Our henhouse, she floated off yesterday, the chickens a-clucking and a-squawking till a big ol' gator, he snatched the whole house, pulled it down under the blackest water you ever see."

Cleo's eyes widened. "You're flooded out at your house?"

"*Non*, not the house. Just the chicken coop. We're safe and dry in the house. You ever see a Cajun house back in the swamp?"

Cleo shook her head no. She noticed he wasn't shy about eye contact. He knew how he affected girls, all right. She looked right back at him, a vampish look on her face to match the wolfish gleam in his eye.

"Well, we Cajuns," he said, "we are ready when the water rise. My grand-père, he built our house on tall pilings, higher even than your house here. We keep the skiffs under there when it's wet, and the wagon when it's dry."

Cleo admired the way Phanor's hands interpreted his words, but she couldn't resist a poke at his self-assurance. She waved her own hands in the air, artfully mimicking Phanor's pantomime of snapping gator jaws and flapping chickens.

Phanor made as if to goose Cleo in the ribs, and after they'd laughed and exclaimed, they settled into companionable silence. He was a charmer, this fellow, but Cleo felt at ease with him. Her heart was already spoken for, and flirting with Phanor was only in fun.

She thought about Josie and how much she liked this lighthearted Cajun. Maybe he could have lifted her mood. If she were here. "Did you know *les américains* paint their houses white?" Cleo said.

"I've seen them. Our house, I think it must have been yellow once, like yours. But now it's kind of gray all over." He shrugged. "No one to see it back in the bayou."

Cleo swung her legs comfortably. Then Phanor touched her hand.

"I believe I see you with someone," he said.

Cleo pretended complete innocence. "I don't know what you're talking about."

He raised his black eyebrows at her. "You sure? 'Cause I think I see you with that boy Remy."

"You know Remy?"

"Sure, I know Remy. He and some of the other fellows hunt coons, possums out our way. We hear them in the night calling out to the dogs, and sometimes we go out with them. We have guns for the killing, and they have the dogs. We bag plenty of game that way."

Phanor hesitated. "Where's your mademoiselle?" he said.

Ha, Cleo thought. He knew about Remy, but she'd seen Phanor and Josie together too. She spoke to him in a singsong voice—"So you want to see Mademoiselle Josephine?" She gave him a sideways look, and he smiled, only a little sheepish. "She's visiting *les américains* downriver this week."

He looked up at the house, as if he might see her there anyway. He looked back at Cleo in mock accusation. "So you have idle hands, with your mistress gone? You know what they say about idle hands."

"I still have chores," Cleo defended herself. "But you are right. I have time for other things now, like the piano."

"You play the piano? Maybe you'll play for me? I'll sit here in the wagon and listen. Then another day you come down to the river with me, and I'll fiddle for you."

"I'd love to," Cleo said. She slid down from the wagon. "As soon as I sell you those chickens."

The next morning, the mockingbird wakened Cleo as it celebrated the return of clear skies. She stretched luxuriously and snuggled into the soft bedding. Josie's bedding. Bibi had slept elsewhere, Cleo could guess where, and so she had slipped into Josie's high bed with the soft white sheets and the feather pillow.

Louella's "Here, chick, chick, chick" drifted up from the chicken yard. Cleo pushed the mosquito netting aside. When Louella finished tossing corn to the chickens, she would start on breakfast, and Cleo had coffee beans to grind and water to fetch before Louella lit the cookfire. She splashed some water on her face and pulled the blue hand-me-down dress over her head.

After breakfast, Cleo hurried through the smoothing of the mattresses, the making of the beds, the emptying of the chamber pots. She swept the dining room and cut fresh flowers for the center of the table.

Cleo was to watch for Phanor from the front gallery. No need for Madame to know he was on the plantation again so soon. She took her mending to sit where she could see the riverbank, and soon Phanor appeared on the levee riding bareback on his mule.

Cleo checked that Madame and Mr. Gale were still in conference, then she slipped on a pair of Josie's old pattens to save her shoes from the mud and clomped to the levee where Phanor waited.

He eyed the platforms under Cleo's shoes, then grinned at her. "Walking in those things, you look like you carrying a pig between your knees."

"Oh! You are too mean!" She laughed, though.

They found a felled tree atop the levee down stream a ways, fairly dry from a day and a half of sunshine, and made that their parlor. Phanor tied the mule in the shade to graze and muse on mule mysteries.

While Phanor tuned his fiddle, Cleo took off the pattens and the shoes and made herself comfortable on the log. The day before, after selling the chickens to him, Cleo had played her best pieces for Phanor and then walked to the gallery rail. Phanor had raised his hands in silent applause, and she'd forgiven herself for the sin of pride.

Now Phanor stood with the fiddle under his chin. He stared across the river, and then he began. He played the old favorites first, tunes to dance to on a Saturday night. Cleo tapped her foot, and yielding to the moment, jumped up to dance around him, holding her skirts above her ankles.

The sweat stood out on her upper lip when finally Phanor said, "Now you rest, Cleo, and I will play something sweet for you."

He began to bow the same minuet that Cleo had played for him yesterday. It wasn't exactly the same; a passage here and there was a variant of Haydn, but he remembered the melody and the mood beautifully. He played as she did, by ear.

As the last note faded away, the two sat in silence, savoring the experience.

"That was very beautiful, Phanor."

"*Merci*. Do you sing, Cleo?"

"I love to sing. Mostly when I'm in the quarters, though. Do you know this one?" She began an old French folk song everyone in the quarters knew.

> *Au clair de la lune*
> *Mon ami Pierrot*
> *Prête-moi ta plume*
> *Pour écrire un mot.*

Phanor nodded and picked up the tune on his fiddle. Cleo's voice was a full-bodied alto, clear and smooth and low. The two of them worked their way through the old tune twice, with as much depth and purity as any two musicians in Louisiana.

Cleo wished Remy were with them. He would have loved to play the fiddle, or a banjo, like Old Jean Pierre who played for the slaves when a big party was on. But Remy was a field hand, and he'd never had a chance to learn. He sang like the angels, though.

"You could play for money, Phanor," Cleo said. "That's what I'd like to do. Sing and play the piano, wear a pretty dress, everybody clapping and saying, 'Mademoiselle Cleo, encore, encore.'" She laughed at her own vanity. "Well. But you, Phanor, you could go all the way to New Orleans and be rich."

Phanor grinned at her. "You think so? I think I'd rather play on the levee with a pretty girl."

Cleo accepted the compliment with a smile, but she knew enough about boys to know an easy tongue didn't always reveal true feelings. She wished Remy had Phanor's ease with words. But she knew his heart without sweet, smooth speeches.

"Does your Josie play as well as you?" Phanor asked.

Cleo considered. "Josie tries too hard. She tries to play by thinking about the notes."

"Ah." Phanor nodded. "Not so well, then. When will she be back?"

"Saturday." *Josie's certainly on his mind,* Cleo noted.

"You can get away again tomorrow?" Phanor said.

"I think so. I'll try." Cleo stood up and brushed her dress off. "What if," she said, "what if you came after suppertime? Maybe Remy could meet us here. He sings better than anyone."

"All right. Tomorrow at dusk, then." He motioned toward the pattens. "You want me to help you put those things on?"

Cleo shook her head. She held the muddy shoe guards in one hand and her boots in the other. "You were right. It's easier to just wash your feet." She picked her way around a boggy puddle and turned to wave. "*Au revoir*, Phanor."

Chapter 10

Toulouse

The second day the sun reclaimed the sky, Mr. Gale withdrew all the little boys he'd posted along the levee. The sunshine convinced him the danger of a breach was over, but Mr. Gale had not lived his entire life along the Mississippi, and he did not understand the way her waters worked against the earth.

Emile, as usual, disengaged himself from the details of the plantation his mother and Mr. Gale contended with. He gathered his dogs for a morning grouse hunt, and he was a happy man as the hounds jumped and bayed around him.

Cleo sang through her chores anticipating the evening to come. Remy would be in the fields until nearly dark, but she would wrap a supper for him in her kerchief and he could meet her and Phanor on the levee.

In the garden, Cleo inhaled the rich steaming odors. The fragrance of roses floated above the heavier air scented with black earth and manure. She cut a bouquet of new red blossoms and imagined herself bedecked with flowers in her hair and on her bodice. She'd wear a dark blue dress, she decided, and wear her hair down on one side, pinned up on the other. She'd rouge her cheeks and redden her mouth, as red as the roses. She'd sing and play to a room full of fine ladies and gentlemen, and they would all admire her beauty and applaud her talent.

Because Cleo was humming as she climbed the stairs to the back gallery with her roses, she did not at first register the rumble coming from north of the plantation. She glanced to her left. The distant glint of sun on water held her. There should be no water there, west of the river. In the moments it took her to understand, the rumble became a thunderous roar.

Cleo could hardly hear her own voice, there was so little air behind it. She tried again. "Maman! Maman! Madame Emmeline!"

Bibi came frowning from the dining room. "What you so loud about, Cleo?" Bibi stopped. "What dat noise?"

"The river! Madame Emmeline!" Cleo rushed through the dining room to Madame's office. She banged the door open wide.

Emmeline shoved Cleo out of her way as she ran to the gallery to see, her little slave Laurie at her heels.

The torrent found the easiest path, following the lowest ground west of the big house toward the quarters. The house was in effect on an island now, with the main river to the east and this new Mississippi to the west. Cleo and Madame, stunned, watched uprooted trees, an outhouse, a cow surge along in the current a hundred yards away.

But Bibi—Bibi clattered down the stairs.

"Bibi, come back at once," Madame called.

"Maman!" Cleo cried.

Bibi ignored them both, running toward the pecan grove,

the cabins, and the flood. "Thibault!" she shouted with all the strength in her lungs.

"Maman!" Cleo moved toward the stairs, but Emmeline seized her. Cleo twisted free only to have little Laurie grab her knees and bring her to the floor. "Let go!" Cleo said. She beat at Laurie, who held on tight. "Maman!" Cleo screamed.

Emmeline threw herself on Cleo. "You can't save her!" Cleo writhed, but Emmeline was taller and heavier, stronger than she looked.

Laurie let go of Cleo's legs. Mutely, she pointed toward the pecan grove.

The three of them, dazed by the noise, gaped as the water roared through the quarters. They couldn't see Bibi. The pecan trees held fast, but the cabins broke apart in the furious sweep of the flood.

The current surged from the lowest ground up to Louella's cookhouse, and then to the brick piers supporting the gallery where Cleo and Madame and Laurie huddled together, clutching at each other, unable to look away from the furious water.

The roar of the torrent drowned out all other sounds. Though Cleo could see people flailing in the current, she could not hear their cries. She shivered with fear and cold as she watched the brown froth cover the plantation.

Cleo and Madame Emmeline and Laurie crouched close together on the gallery, well back from the railing. They were too frightened to sit in the rocking chairs. They pushed their backs against the wall, their legs folded under them. Emmeline grasped Cleo's hand with her left and clenched Laurie's in the other.

Their eyes never strayed from the scene below them. The cookhouse held, and they knew Louella was alive inside it by her frantic singing to the Lord for salvation. There were two cats on the cookhouse roof, and several chickens.

By noon, the boiling current subsided. The flow was still swift, but not so violent, and Cleo began to hope her people were safe. Remy might have been in the north field and missed the flood altogether. Grammy Tulia, Thibault, and Bibi might have been able to ride the stream. She'd heard tales about survivors being found on rooftops miles from the home ground.

Mr. Gale appeared in a rowboat with two slaves pulling on the oars. "Hello, the house," he hollered.

Emmeline crawled to the gallery rail and pulled herself up. "Have you seen my son?"

"No, ma'am. Not yet, but we're still looking for survivors." When Cleo appeared at Madame's elbow, he said, "Here, gal, take this rope." He tossed the painter to her to fasten to the railing.

"I haven't seen your people yet, either," he said to Cleo. "But we got plenty of time for hope yet."

"Your family," Madame said, her voice steadier now. Emile could be found yet, in a skiff, or on a knoll. "Your wife and children, Mr. Gale. Are they safe?"

"Yes, they's all safe, thank you kindly. They was visiting over to the Daniels' place upriver and didn't see the flood at all."

"How is it with the slaves, Mr. Gale?"

"They's mostly saved, Miss Emmeline. I had the crews out in the north fields, and they was above the breach when it happened."

Then Remy is safe, at least, Cleo thought.

"Most of our lost slaves will be from the homestead here," Mr. Gale said, "but some of them we'll find in trees or on roofs. Lots of them can swim, you know, spite of the law."

"Let me come with you, Mr. Gale," Cleo burst out. "Let me come, and I can help look for Maman."

"Certainly not," Madame said. "I will not have you in that

water for any amount of money. This house will hold, and you're safe here."

Ignoring Madame, Cleo scrambled into the boat, her haste rocking the skiff. She grabbed for the gunwale, but it was too late. Laurie screamed and Mr. Gale cursed. Cleo tumbled into the flood and under the muddy water.

One of the slaves in the boat slipped over the side without fuss and grabbed Cleo's dress at the back of the neck. He shoved her back into the boat, where Cleo gasped and coughed.

"Put her back up here immediately, Mr. Gale," Madame said.

The overseer grabbed her by the elbow and roughly pushed her back over the gallery railing. Cleo fell to the floor, still coughing up water.

"Mr. Gale," Madame said, "as soon as you find any of Cleo's family, you'll bring them here directly. In fact, bring anyone who needs tending. Cleo and I will prepare for them as well as we can."

"Yes, ma'am," Mr. Gale said. "You remember what I said, now, Miss Emmeline. We'll find Monsieur Emile. They's plenty of time yet for hoping."

Madame marched into the house, but Cleo stared after the boat as the men rowed away. Helplessness nearly choked her.

When she'd caught her breath, Cleo peered over the side of the railing trying to guess the depth of the flood. Laurie leaned over too, but she pulled back. "It scary, Cleo," she said.

The water lapped at the brick pillars only ten or twelve inches below the floor of the gallery. That meant even Elbow John, tall as he was, would be drowned if he couldn't swim. She took Laurie's hand. She was Elbow John's granddaughter. Laurie's whole family, her maman and papa, her brothers and sisters, all had been on the plantation somewhere. Laurie clung to Cleo and together they watched the water.

Madame appeared at the dining room door, herself again. No more cowering on the gallery floor. "Cleo, get up. Laurie, come with me. We'll need blankets and sheets first of all."

They gathered linens and wool blankets. They made bandages and lay pallets on the floors. Laurie collected what little drinking water there was in the house.

Throughout the afternoon, the boatmen rowed the poor souls they'd picked up back to the big house. They laid the dead ones on the front gallery, and Cleo wondered how long they could lie there before . . . She refused to think about it.

The slaves who still breathed docked at the back gallery, where Cleo helped them step onto the dry boards. Some of them were in shock and were as quiet as the dead. They lay themselves down and closed their eyes.

Those slaves whose wits were unaffected prayed, sang, or moaned. A woman with three children missing in the flood keened on a high piercing note, and an old grandmother rocked and shrilled in accompaniment.

With every rowboat—and there were four of them rescuing survivors—Cleo scanned the people, looking for her loved ones. As dusk began to darken the waters, Cleo peered into the eight or nine dark faces in the last boat.

"Grand-mère," she shouted. She didn't even realize what she'd called Madame Emmeline. "It's Thibault!"

Emmeline came running from the parlor. "Where is he?"

Cleo pointed. "There. In the back of the boat." She raised her voice and called, "Thibault!"

Thibault lifted his head. When he recognized Cleo, he started to stand, but someone held him back. As soon as the boat nudged the gallery stairs, Cleo reached for him and pulled him out of the boat. She wrapped her arms around him and rocked him back and forth.

Thibault tried to wiggle free, and still she couldn't let him go. "Cleo, I has to breathe," he told her.

She laughed and released him. She wiped the tears from her face, and Madame Emmeline stepped closer. Gently, she stroked the head of her son's son, and Thibault rewarded her with one of his smiles.

Cleo took her brother's shoulders and turned him to her. "Thibault, what happened to Maman and Grammy Tulia?" Still smiling, he looked at her blankly. "Did you see Maman and Grammy swimming, Thibault?"

"Grammy say she too old for swimming."

"Were you on the roof when they found you? In a tree?"

"I in a big ol' chinaberry tree. Me and a rooster. Erookaroo!"

"Was Maman in the tree with you? And Grammy? Did you see her in the water? Thibault, think."

"Maman helped that man push me up the tree. She say 'Hold on, Thibault,' so I holded on."

"What man?" Madame Emmeline said.

"M'sieur. The one bring me licorice, and whittling sticks."

Cleo met Madame's eyes over Thibault's head. He meant Emile. Emile had fought the river to save his son. But Emile knew how to swim. He would have kept Bibi afloat, the two of them riding the current, until they fetched up against a tree, or a roof.

Cleo tried to believe it, but she'd seen the violence of the water rushing by. She put a brave face on for Madame Emmeline. "They're waiting for rescue, that's all. Tomorrow. We'll see them tomorrow."

Mr. Gale climbed on to the gallery behind them. "Ma'am, it's gone too dark for us to see anybody else tonight. By first light, I'll have these four crews out looking for people. We'll find lots more yet. Some of them probably washed all the way down to the Cherleu place. One wet night won't kill nobody, and we'll pick them up in the morning."

"Thank you, Mr. Gale." Emmeline hesitantly kissed the top of Thibault's head. Then she went about the business of tending to the cuts and scrapes of her people.

Cleo took Thibault indoors, out of sight of the frightful water. She sat with him on the sofa and kept him close. The only blameless soul she'd ever known, simple, loving Thibault. He might have seen Maman's and their father's last moments.

Those first minutes of the flood—Cleo remembered the stupendous noise that was as total as silence. She could see Maman and M'sieu gasping, struggling in the roiling water, the panic on their faces as they were swept away from their child. She and Thibault, they were likely orphans now—and Josie too. She shivered in the heavy, sultry air.

Chapter 11

Johnston Plantation

Albany was quite solicitous after the incident on the horse path. Once Josie had cleaned the mud from her hair and changed her frock, he hovered at her side all through the afternoon. Sit here away from the sun's glare, he'd say, or perhaps she'd like a little brandy to ease her bruises.

Chamard absented himself the rest of that day touring the Johnston plantation, and Josie watched the door for his return. He was the most handsome man she'd ever seen, and so sophisticated. As Albany droned on about cane futures, Josie relived her cousin's kiss. She absently traced the shape of her lower lip, the memory of Bertrand Chamard's mouth on hers warming her whole body.

Josie became aware of Albany's eyes fastened on her mouth. She dropped her hand and valiantly pretended interest in the workings of the New Orleans market.

Abigail and Mrs. Johnston sat on either side of the tall window busying themselves with their embroidery. They were both uncharacteristically quiet, and Josie caught Mrs. Johnston peering at her and Albany over her sewing glasses. Judging by her encouraging nod and smile, Josie gauged she was meant to bear Albany's attentions quite alone.

Before supper, Mr. Johnston and Chamard joined them in the drawing room. At last, Josie thought. She hoped her cousin would sit next to her, but Albany diverted his guest by motioning Chamard toward the humidor across the room. "Have a cigar?"

Josie admired the obvious relish Chamard took in the first inhalation of the fine Cuban cigar.

"What did you think of the plantation, Mr. Chamard?"

He peered through the smoke at his hostess. "Very fine. You have some excellent bottomland on this side of the river. As dark a soil as I've seen hereabouts, and well drained."

Mr. Johnston changed the subject. "You'll be relieved, my dear," he said to his wife, "that the levees hold fast against the high water." He turned to Chamard. "Mrs. Johnston has been anxious about flooding. Someone in New Orleans told her the river can carve a path through a levee, and she has not slept well with this excessive rain we've had."

"Like a knife through butter. That's what Felicity LeRoy said."

"I told you, Mother," Albany said, "we fortified every foot of the levee. We are quite safe."

"Thank you, dear," she said, and put a hand to her heart. Josie wondered that Mrs. Johnston didn't seem to realize her neighbors' levees upstream were as crucial to her security as her own.

"You are quite recovered, Josephine?" Chamard said.

Josie thought she only barely blushed to have his eyes on her. "Completely," she said.

"I'm sure she suffers more than she lets on," Abigail said. "She has terrible bruises on . . . she's terribly bruised."

Bertrand's smile hinted at the indecent, and Josie knew

her face must now be in full flush. Phanor assumed that same teasing familiarity, she thought, but of course Phanor lacked the refinement of Bertrand Chamard. Bertrand oozed elegance; Phanor, for all his charm, was ignorant and immature.

But Phanor had dug the trench around Maman's grave. Would Bertrand have done that so kindly and simply?

When the party rose to go in to dinner, Josie found she was a little stiff from her fall. Albany too quickly offered his arm, and Bertrand, with an amused nod of his head, offered his to Abigail.

Over strawberry preserves and cream, Abigail asked, "Exactly how are you and Josephine related, Mr. Chamard?"

Bertrand put his spoon down and considered. "It's very complicated among us Creoles, Miss Johnston. We tend to have many children, and we count anyone with a tinge of family blood as close relations. Now Josephine and I. Let's see."

He turned to Josie. "Your mother Celine was René and Marie-Louise's next-to-youngest daughter. Yes?" Josie nodded. Chamard thought a moment. "That makes Josephine my second cousin once removed."

"Kissing cousins?" Abigail said. Josie played with her strawberries and cream.

"*Oui,* mademoiselle," Bertrand asserted. "Kissing cousins."

Josie glanced up and Bertrand winked at her.

"If I were a betting man—well, I am a betting man—I'd be willing to wager my young cousin and I share a certain birthmark." He looked directly at Abigail. "I don't wish to be indelicate, but it seems all of Grand-mère Helga's offspring carry her remembrance."

Josie twisted the napkin in her lap and felt the heat radiate from her face down past her bare shoulders. She did indeed have a patch of reddened skin, very like a rash, just at the small of her back, as had Maman. Josie had even seen it on her little cousin Jean Baptiste. But to mention it in company—Bertrand was coarse and crude. She noticed Abigail's face was ablush too. Who was he trying to embarrass? Her, or Abigail? He was insufferable.

"Ah, I see it's true, isn't it, Josephine? But I've distressed you. *J'en suis au regret, ma chérie.*"

The ladies rose, and Josie smiled sweetly at Albany as he held her chair for her; she pointedly ignored her cousin.

After supper, the party gathered in the music room. The Johnstons' piano was a Chickering like the one Josie had at home, but while the ivory keys had yellowed with age on hers, Abigail's keys were uniformly bright.

"Will you play for us, Josephine?" Mrs. Johnston asked.

Josie quit breathing. She touched the curls over her ear and ducked her head. The silence as Mrs. Johnston waited for a reply became impossible for Josie to break.

Albany came to her aid. "Perhaps you would play a duet with me? I am only a poor player, but if you will play slowly, I believe I can keep up."

What kindness, Josie thought. She arranged her skirts on the bench, and together they made their way through a Mozart sonatina arranged for two. They earned no accolades, but they had not disgraced themselves either. Josie touched Albany's hand in gratitude as they rose from the bench, and he led her to the blue damask chair near his mother.

Abigail played next. She had great facility. Her fingers flew over the keyboard, seemingly without thought. Bertrand sang a German melody with her, and they were a stunning pair. Abigail's blond hair reflected the candlelight; Bertrand's black hair, brushing the collar of his coat, seemed to absorb it.

When Abigail asked Josie to sing with her, Josie felt on safer ground. Her voice was pleasant enough, and she sang in tune at least.

"That was lovely, Josie," Albany whispered to her as she

sat down again. Josie knew her voice wasn't lovely, but she accepted the compliment very prettily, as she'd been taught. Believe every compliment is the absolute truth, Maman had preached, but receive it humbly.

Mr. Johnston dozed in his chair and Mrs. Johnston sat dreamily on her settee, embroidery in her lap. Abigail and Bertrand began another piece.

Josie admired Abigail's straight back as she sat at the piano. Monsieur Pierre had scolded Josie constantly about her posture on the bench. But whenever Josie sat at the piano, defeat sat with her. She simply couldn't bridge the gap between her feelings and her fingers. And here was Abigail, blue satin and golden curls, effortlessly infusing the room with music.

Bertrand shifted his stance so that Josie could see his face, and she forgot all about her poor musicality. His voice oozed seduction, and with a roguish smile on his lips, he sang just to her. Meeting his eyes, Josie found need of her fan.

Albany wandered over to stand behind his sister, as if to look over her shoulder at the music, but Josie saw clearly his protective instinct at work. For her or for his sister, she wasn't sure. He nearly blocked Josie's view of Bertrand, whose smile grew a little wider at the intrusion.

When Abigail finished the piece, she slammed the piano shut. Without looking at Josie or Bertrand, she excused herself and abruptly left the room.

The fourth day of Josie's visit, she pulled a long brown curl through her fingers. Honey brown. She puzzled over the fact that her nose was as freckled today as it had been a month ago, her lips as overplump, her eyebrows as thick. And yet, clearly Bertrand and Albany both found her attractive. How many beautiful women had Bertrand seen in Paris?

Today Albany planned to take them on a picnic. He had ridden out with the slaves after breakfast to oversee the picnic site. They would need cloths laid on the ground against the damp, and chairs, a table for the ham, the muffins, the pitchers of lemonade. Josie hoped he'd remember they would need some children to hold their parasols. She didn't want any more freckles.

Lingering over morning coffee, Bertrand promised to show Abigail where he'd seen hummingbirds in a stand of wild honeysuckle. Josie had recognized jealousy when she saw it the night before, and she watched over the rim of her cup as Abigail succumbed to Bertrand's charm. *How sensitive he is to notice Abigail needs her feelings soothed. He can be a perfect gentleman.*

Midmorning, Abigail and Josie donned their riding habits and chatted as they walked to the stables to meet Albany. Bertrand would join them later once he and Mr. Johnston had reviewed the property north of the Johnstons' land.

At Albany's insistence, Josie rode an old mare. She suspected the horse was near blind, and with no chance of riding faster than an amble, Josie opened her black ruffled parasol and tried to remember what her maman had told her about bleaching freckles. She hadn't been interested at the time.

Albany led her and Abigail across the eastern fields to the picnic site in a played-out orchard. Only a few peach trees remained, and they'd lived past their fruitfulness, but Charles had arranged a lovely welcome under the shade of a mossy live oak. White linen covered a folding table, cushions adorned the canvas chairs, and heavy blue cloths covered the ground in their picnic area. And yes, two little slave children stood ready to shade the ladies.

Albany helped Josie and his sister dismount. The air was still and warm, the droning of bees the only disturbance. Charles brought them lemonade in tall crystal glasses, and Josie sat back to enjoy herself.

Albany brought Josie a plate of ham and fresh peaches, but his pleasantries were drowned out by the sound of rapid hoofbeats. A horse with white froth on its flanks rushed into the clearing. The rider slid off and ran toward them, calling out, "Mas'ser Johnston."

Albany met the man and drew him several yards from the ladies. Josie watched them curiously, especially after Albany glanced at her and led the man further away.

"My apologies, ladies," Albany said when he returned to them. "I'm afraid we'll have to have our picnic another day."

"What on earth, Albany!" Abigail said. "We just got here."

"What's happened?" Josie asked.

"Nothing to worry about."

Josie didn't believe him. "Please, Mr. Johnston. Have you had a message from Toulouse?"

"No. Really, there's no need to concern yourself. The slaves reported a drop in the river, that's all, and that can mean a break in the levee upstream. But it could have happened fifty miles from here, or a hundred."

Abigail grabbed her brother's arm. "A levee break? Are we going to be flooded?"

"I told you, Abigail, not to worry. But it would be prudent to return to the house until we know where the break is and how far the new channel flows."

Albany put them on their mounts and escorted them to the stables. Charles stayed behind to dismantle the picnic, but Josie saw him urging the others to hurry. She didn't know which side of the river had broken through, but if it was on this side, Toulouse wouldn't be affected at all.

As soon as they dismounted, Josie hurried toward the dock. Surely a riverboat coming downstream would stop and tell them the news. But Mrs. Johnston, and Abigail too, feared irrationally that the river might suddenly swell and sweep her from the dock. They insisted she stay in the house.

Josie leaned against the gallery railing even though the afternoon sun hit her full force. She didn't give a thought to her complexion or the heat, but kept watch for a boat.

Before a boat showed itself, Albany, Bertrand, and Mr. Johnston brought the news. They had ridden north along the levee to look for evidence of a breach on either side. The levee had failed a half mile north of the Tassins' home, they reported, at the upper edge of Toulouse Plantation.

Mrs. Johnston began to shake. "Oh my God," she said.

"Now, Mary Ann," Mr. Johnston said sternly. He guided her to a chair and forced her to sit down. "The flood is on the other side of the river. We're perfectly safe, and I want you to settle down. Charles, bring Mrs. Johnston a sherry."

Josie had gone white and stood very still. Bertrand guided her to the opposite side of the room and sat with her on the satin sofa.

"Listen, *chérie*," he said. "Toulouse is flooded, but the break is far enough above the house that the first force was spent before it reached them. The house stands; I could see it across the river."

"I want to go home."

"Of course not, Josephine. You cannot go home. In a few days—"

"I have to know if they're all right." She clutched Bertrand's sleeve. "Papa—Bibi and Cleo. And Grand-mère."

Bertrand considered for a moment. "Can you ride? You're not too sore from your fall?"

"I can ride. We can get a boat upstream and cross over."

Albany stepped over to them. "Impossible. We can't allow you to cross the river now."

Josie looked to Bertrand to contradict Albany. He was family. He would understand.

Bertrand shook his head. "Johnston is right. You mustn't ford the river until the flood has ebbed. But I will take you up this bank to see across the river."

"That's foolish, Chamard. She has no business anywhere near the river."

Bertrand looked at Johnston coolly. "We'll be safe enough, I think."

"I'm going," Josie said.

The three of them rode along the top of the levee wherever they could to avoid the sucking mud of the river road. Twelve miles north of the Johnstons', Bertrand pulled up.

"We are directly across from Toulouse, Josephine. You see now, the dock, the alley of oaks? And beyond is the house."

The green shutters against the yellow boards showed clearly. Josie couldn't see the underhouse or the height of the water because of the opposite levee, but the second floor was clearly steady and dry.

"I see people on the gallery." Josie's distance vision was excellent. "Do you see them?"

Albany nodded. "I see movement."

"Your eyes are better than mine, then," Bertrand said. "The important thing, Josephine, is the house is intact. It couldn't have been hit by the force of the river. Your family will be safe, and in a week or ten days, we can take you upriver. We'll hire a boat to cross over."

Albany touched her elbow. "For now, Josephine, you must content yourself to stay with . . . with Abigail. Where you'll be safe." He urged her toward her horse. "My father has sent a team of workers upriver to see what needs to be done. The Metoyers and the Cummingses will do the same."

Riding back to the Johnstons', Josie gazed across the river until the levee took a turn and she could no longer see Toulouse. What had become of Maman's crypt? Surely it was high enough on the knoll to escape the water? Otherwise, Maman would have been caught in the flood, washed away. Josie pushed the image away and prayed to Mother Mary that the people on Toulouse had all survived.

At the stables, Bertrand helped her dismount. "This is not

the first flood your grand-mère has seen." He gently kissed her forehead. "You mustn't worry."

Albany rather abruptly took her arm to escort her to the house. Another time, she might have bridled at Albany's possessiveness, but now she hardly noticed the rivalry he seemed to be engaged in with her cousin. She looked over her shoulder at Bertrand, craving his reassurance. He nodded to her, and she allowed Albany to lead her away.

Chapter 12

Toulouse

The second day of the flood, Mr. Gale had the rescue boats out at first light. They found Elbow John and his woman Suzette a mile down from the quarters. They'd ridden their roof as far as the Cherleus' orchard before it lodged against the peach trees. Apparently the new current had commandeered a tributary, enlarged it, and then rejoined the main river just below the Cherleu place.

Mr. Gale left Elbow John, shaken as he was, in charge of rescuing people, then took two boats to pull against the current to the dry fields north of the house. He needed to organize his own crews as well as the slaves from the neighboring plantations sent to help, and he'd have to forage tools, logs, mules. Protecting the fields not six feet under water was up to him, he figured, since Emile Tassin had not yet been found and Madame had her hands full.

In the big house, Emmeline noted who among her slaves lived and who was unaccounted for. Most of the slaves had been safe in the fields above the breach. Everyone avoided the front gallery where the bodies lay, and Cleo made sure the front doors and windows were kept closed against the growing stench. There was nothing else to be done.

Cleo leaned over the railing to note the wet line on the brick pillars under the back gallery. The water had receded perhaps two feet since the height of the flood. Most of all, she watched for the rescue boats to return.

When she spotted the next incoming boat, she gripped the railing and strained to make out the figures in it. Everyone in the boat was colored. Emile was not among them, but maybe her maman . . .

Emmeline strode onto the gallery and peered into the skiff too.

"Not in this boat either, madame," Cleo said.

Madame straightened from her posture over the railing and called to Elbow John in the first boat. "Tie on to that dead sow and tow her downstream. She's been knocking against the house all day."

Emmeline, as she had after each boat had disappointed her, stepped back into the house without speaking of her son. Cleo knew her well enough to understand she would not share her anxiety. That would be a weakness, in Madame's mind.

Cleo watched Elbow John trying to lasso the bloated pig that had been pushed against a house piling by the current. *See?* she told herself. *Elbow John, with only one good arm, has survived.* Emile and Bibi were both younger and stronger than old John. They'd be perched in some high branches somewhere, Emile holding on to Maman and promising her there were no snakes in their tree. No reason not to hope.

At midday a boat arrived from the Cummings plantation. Two boys just strong enough to manage the skiff delivered food and water.

"Ev'body elfs be at the breach," the skinny one said.

He must be one of those Carolina coloreds, Cleo thought. She could barely understand him.

"We be back wit 'nother boatload vittles. Wha' else y'all need?" he asked Cleo.

She was staring at his skin. He was the blackest slave she'd ever seen.

"Are you from Africa?" she said.

The skinny boy's white teeth lit his face when he grinned at the other Cummings slave. "Dese yeller gals, dey tink dey don't got no Afric in dem." The second boy snickered, and they shoved off.

Angry and embarrassed, Cleo thought, *Those boys have no manners at all. That isn't what I meant. I only* . . . Cleo looked at her own brown skin. She'd made the kind of thoughtless comment M'sieu sometimes made, even Josie now and then. She should have known better.

Throughout the day, Cleo kept vigil. Maman would surely be in the next boat, or the next. Whenever Elbow John brought more survivors, she searched for her mother's face, then hiding her disappointment, she'd help the survivors on to the gallery and see they had food and water.

She dealt with her fear by making up her mind her mother and father would be found. All these other people had survived. They were hungry and thirsty, but they had lived through the flood. Maman and M'sieu would need water, but they'd be all right, even if they weren't found until tomorrow.

Cleo thought of Phanor and his family. Their house, she understood, was a good ways west of the river, almost in the swamp, and Phanor had said they'd built on tall pilings. They were surely safe with so much ground between them and the levee.

The day passed helping Madame Emmeline nurse the ones who'd been injured. The provisions the neighbors sent had to be meted out, the clean water rationed. The house was full of the plantation's people. They were careful to stay off the fine furniture, and they treated Cleo properly, with the respect a house girl merited. Thibault played contentedly with some of his cousins, all of them mindful to keep their voices low.

The sun set, and the longest day of Cleo's life closed with no word of Grammy or M'sieu or Maman.

The dawn light showed the water down another full foot or more. The break in the levee could have been much worse, Mr. Gale reported. They had a fair chance of filling in the breach. Logs and debris were already blocking the cut.

After Mr. Gale left the house, another boat approached. It was the narrow hollowed-log craft the Cajuns made, and a lone figure stood in it wielding a long oar. Cleo recognized Phanor. Thank God he was all right. She waved and hallooed.

As Phanor set his bare foot on the stairway, Cleo opened her arms to him. He rocked her for a moment, and then released her.

"*Mon père*, he say I should speak to Madame Emmeline."

Cleo took him into Madame's room, which was crowded with the bedding of displaced slaves. An old woman lay sleeping in the corner.

"Monsieur?" Madame greeted Phanor.

"Madame Emmeline, I have brought a message from my father."

Madame waited, but Phanor did not proceed. He twisted the hat in his hand and glanced at Cleo.

"Cleo, would you see that the children don't play on the gallery stairways?" Madame said. "I fear they might fall into the water. And mind the snakes don't climb the steps."

When Cleo had cleared two of the stairways of children and assigned the older boys to keep the snakes off the gallery, Phanor waited at his boat for her.

"Madame says you may come with me. It is your maman we have found, Cleo."

Cleo's hands flew to her face. Then she as quickly made the sign of the cross. "Thank our Blessed Mother."

"You'll see her soon." He helped Cleo into the boat and settled her on a bench.

Afraid to ask, but having to know, Cleo said, "Is she hurt, Phanor?"

"She is."

"How? How is she hurt?"

"We'll be there soon." Phanor turned his back on her as he oared the boat across what had been the slave quarters.

Cleo sat still and tried not to be afraid. No one had seen M'sieu Emile yet, but at least Maman was not in the water anymore. There were many people searching for survivors. Phanor's father and his brother-in-law had gone out again after they'd found Bibi, and other neighbors—Creole, Cajun, and American—searched the waters. Still time for hope, she told herself.

Nearer to the DeBlieux homestead, the trees grew close together, the moss hung heavily, and the mosquitoes buzzed mercilessly. "Phanor, did Maman say she'd seen Monsieur Emile?"

"*Non*. She's not talking much. She say 'Thibault' some-times, and once she say 'Tell Cleo.' That's all."

She's probably exhausted, Cleo thought. *She must have been so frightened—she just needs sleep.*

The water barely flowed as they approached Phanor's house. Even so, Cleo wished the boat rode higher in the water. Several rats and a cottonmouth swam nearby. Maman had been nearly three days in this black water, rats and snakes all around. How had she stood it, she who could not bear a little garden snake or a mouse in the linen cupboard?

"Hold that extra oar ready," Phanor said.

Half drowned, with yellow teeth and beady eyes just out

of the water, two of the rats paddled straight for the boat, intending to board. Phanor neatly batted one away with his paddle. Cleo slammed her oar again and again, smashing the other rat's head against the edge of the boat.

Cleo sobbed once. All those hours out in the flood, Maman could have been bitten in the dark, not even enough light to fight for herself. She could be swollen with venom, or—

Phanor took the oar from Cleo and helped her sit down. Her hands were shaking, and he took them in his own. "It's over now. They're gone."

Not much farther along, Cleo saw the weathered gray boards of Phanor's home through the mossy cypresses and tupelos. When the boat bumped gently against the gallery, Panor steadied the boat while she climbed out. A young woman with a babe on her hip opened the front door.

"My sister, Eulalie," Phanor said. "This is Cleo, Lalie."

"*Bonjour*, Cleo. Your maman is waiting for you."

Inside, Maman lay on her back. Straw was stuck in her hair, and the bedraggled dress was torn half away. She didn't turn her head when Cleo and Phanor came in, but she moved her eyes to follow Cleo across the room.

Cleo paled at sight of Maman's wide eyes. She knelt and caressed her mother's tangled hair. "Maman, it's me." She took her mother's hot, dry hand. *God, don't let her have fever.*

"Maman, where are you hurt?"

Bibi spoke in a whisper and gasped for every breath. "Thibault?"

"Thibault is safe, Maman. Not even a scratch." Cleo tried to pull aside the sheet to find where Maman was injured, but Bibi stopped her hands.

"Emile?" Her chest heaved with the effort. When Cleo hesitated, Bibi's eyes darkened.

"He's probably sitting on M'sieu Cherleu's gallery, Maman, sipping whiskey."

"He . . ." Bibi's every word cost her precious breath. "Saved . . . Thibault."

"I know, Maman. Elbow John will find M'sieu. He's a swimmer, remember?"

Bibi opened her mouth wide to pull in air, and Cleo saw her teeth were bloody. Oh God, she was bleeding inside somewhere.

"Take care . . . Thibault."

"Yes, Maman. I will take care of Thibault. Let me see where you're—"

"And Josie . . ."

"Take care of Josie?" Cleo tried to read Bibi's eyes.

"You . . . stronger."

"I will, Maman. I'll take care of Josie. Maman, don't talk. Just breathe. I'll take you to the big house, and Madame Emmeline will fetch the doctor."

Bibi shook her head once and closed her eyes.

"Please, open a window," Cleo said to Eulalie. The mosquitoes couldn't be worse than the smoky air from the smudge pot.

With the shutter opened, sunlight filtered through the tree branches to light the cot where Bibi lay. Cleo saw clearly now how pale her maman was. Bibi allowed her to pull back the sheet.

There was no blood on the dress. Cleo opened the top buttons and found a massive livid bruise covering Maman's breastbone. The color—black and deep purple—did not disguise the depression in the chest. Maman's breastbone caved inward. No wonder she couldn't breathe.

"Log . . . ram me."

Cleo began to cry, but Bibi reached for her hand and tried to squeeze it.

"Your father . . . loved you," Bibi managed to say. "And me."

"I know, Maman. Don't talk."

Maman could never make the trip to the big house. There would be no doctor for Maman. Nor sunrise either, Cleo was certain.

Maman closed her eyes. Cleo gripped her hand. During the hours the dappled sunlight retreated from the window, Cleo couldn't stop talking, couldn't let go of Maman's hand. If she just kept talking, Maman couldn't go.

She reminded her mother of all the happy times she could think of—how Maman had helped her and Josie make daisy chains in the summertime; how once she'd found the girls in Madame Celine's rouge pot, and how she'd spanked them, then cleaned them up and kissed them before Madame came home; how M'sieu always gave Cleo and Thibault special Christmas presents after everyone else had gone to bed.

Cleo found herself trying to breathe in rhythm with Maman's painful panting. A thin red trickle flowed from her mother's mouth. Cleo couldn't bear to have the blood stain her dress, and she blotted it with her handkerchief over and over.

Cleo borrowed Eulalie's rosary and helped Maman count the beads. How long could Maman keep breathing like this? *God help her.* Each gasp seemed more difficult, more desperate. *Maman, Maman, how can I let you go?*

As the last rays of the sun penetrated the shadows, Bibi signaled with her eyes. Cleo leaned close. "Sing for me?" Bibi whispered.

Cleo sang, fighting to keep her voice clear of tears. Phanor picked up his fiddle and played softly along with her.

Bibi's breathing grew shallower. Mercifully, she took her last rasping breath and lay still.

"Maman?" Cleo whispered. There was no mistaking it. She was gone.

Cleo wailed and threw herself over Maman's body. She pulled at her hair and wept. Maman hadn't deserved to die. The sin was Monsieur Emile's, not hers. All Maman had ever done was love them—Emile, Thibault, and her—and Josie, whom she'd owed nothing. She'd loved them all.

Cleo exhausted herself at last. She sat back from her maman, and Phanor helped her stand. By the lantern light, he tenderly wiped the blood from Cleo's scalp and led her to a chair. Eulalie handed him a cup of water, and he held it to her lips.

When she had recovered somewhat, Cleo kissed her mother and placed her hands across her chest. Maman seemed so much smaller now, and still, still beyond any stillness life could bring.

Phanor knelt with Cleo at the bedside to pray. Eulalie cried quietly on the other side of the room, her little one big-eyed in her lap.

It was full dark when the thunk of another boat hit the gallery post. "That'll be *mon père*." Phanor went outside, closing the door behind him. Cleo could hear their voices, but the words were indistinct.

It was unlikely, unreasonable to expect Monsieur DeBlieux to have found M'sieu as well as Maman. But she had to know, she had to see. Cleo opened the door onto the gallery and stepped out. The men stood in the yellow glow of lantern light, the blackness of the swamp all around. Phanor's papa and Eulalie's husband blocked her view of the pirogue.

". . . not twenty yards from where we found her," Monsieur was saying.

"Wait, Cleo." Phanor stepped to her side and took her arm. She brushed him off and pushed between the men to see into the boat. Her knees gave way and the men grabbed her to keep her from falling into the black water.

It was him. M'sieu Emile. Her papa.

Chapter 13

Johnston Plantation

At the Johnston plantation, Josie lived every hour in dread. She knew nothing of who died, who lived, and anxiety stole her appetite and her sleep.

The boats that stopped at the Johnston dock at last reported Madame Emmeline Tassin still reigned over Toulouse, but they knew nothing of all the other souls Josie yearned to hear of. She kept her rosary in her pocket and fingered it constantly.

Mixed with her fear, guilt and remorse weighed Josie down. She could see now that what Papa had done with Bibi had nothing to do with his love for her. She had been so hateful to him since Maman's funeral. What if she never saw him again? Or Cleo? She had not treated her sister kindly either, and oh, how she missed her. The hours, the days—time nearly stopped for her. She dressed, arranged her hair, sat at table with the Johnstons, but all the while her heart and mind were at Toulouse.

On the fourth day under a brilliant sky, Josie and Abigail sat on the upper gallery, Josie with her embroidery in her lap, the needle untouched in the last hour. She smelled the barge before she saw it round the bend and turn in to the dock. Josie assumed it was a load of guano for the fields until Mr. Johnston appeared on horseback below the gallery.

"Abigail," he called. "You and Miss Josephine go inside. Go to your room, fix your hair, whatever. Stay there until supper."

Abigail didn't argue, didn't ask why. "Yes, Father." With a hand at her nose, she gathered her sewing and her book. "Come on, Josie."

Josie lingered as she gathered the embroidery. It didn't smell right for guano. The barge nudged the dock, and Josie saw the white bundles on the deck were not bags of fertilizer. They were long bundles, long as a man or a woman. They were bodies.

Josie threw her embroidery bag on a chair and rushed through the house and out the front door. She ran toward the dock fifty yards away, her skirt flying above her knees.

Albany ran from the barge to meet her and caught her midway from the house. "Josephine!" He blocked her with his body and grabbed her into his arms. "You don't need to see this," he said. "Go back to the house."

"They're from Toulouse, aren't they? They're my people."

"Only the slaves, Josephine. Not your people."

"They are my people." Elbow John could be on that barge, or Grammy, or even little Laurie. "I have to see who they are." She tried to pull her arms from his grip. "Let go!"

"I won't, Josie." He tightened his hands on her. "Be sensible," he said. "They've been dead four days. You can't see them."

Her cousin stood on the barge, staring at them. "Bertrand!" she shouted.

He shook his head at her. "Go with Albany, Josephine," he called.

"Come to the house," Albany said. "I have news from Toulouse."

Josie quit pulling against him and searched his face. Albany's pale eyes told her the news wasn't good. "Who is it? Tell me now, Albany!"

"Come inside," Albany insisted and steered her by the elbow back to the house.

As they entered, Charles met them at the door, and Albany took him aside for a quiet word. Albany then led Josie to the parlor and sat with her on the horsehair settee.

"The news is not good, my dear." He took her hand, a very forward gesture, but Josie did not withdraw it.

"They've found your father, Josephine. The flood caught him."

Josie shook her head. "No. Papa can swim. He's a good swimmer. It's someone else they found."

"Your grandmother has seen his body."

Josie's breath came ragged and harsh. "Charles," Albany called, and the butler appeared with a vial of smelling salts. As Albany passed the vial under Josie's nose, she jerked her whole body away.

Josie seemed to gulp air rather than to breathe it. She stared at the carpet on the floor as she hugged her arms tight and swayed. As if from far away, she heard the tinny chime of the clock on the mantelpiece.

Mrs. Johnston took Albany's place on the settee and stroked Josie's back. "Your mother gone, and now this. God has sent you a terrible burden, child."

Josie's hands covered her face and she leaned over her knees. She'd never see him again.

Albany murmured, "I'll see to the burials, Mother. Excuse me."

Mrs. Johnston stood up and touched Josie's shoulder.

"Come, my dear. You must go to bed. I'll order you some tea, and Abigail and I will sit with you."

Josie allowed herself to be led up the staircase. Suzanne undressed her and Mrs. Johnston tucked her into bed. Josie didn't speak, neither did Abigail or Mrs. Johnston, who sat with her.

Josie kept picturing Papa on the dock at Toulouse, waving to her in the rain. And she hadn't even waved back to him.

A letter came from Grand-mère informing Josie that Bibi had died in the flood, and Josie grieved anew to have lost the woman who had mothered her far more than Maman ever had. Through the sticky heat of sleepless nights, Josie prayed fervent appeals to the Virgin to intercede for Papa's and Bibi's souls. Her faith shaken, she tried to add humility to the list of requests from the Blessed Mother, but for Him to have taken Maman, Bibi, and Papa from her—it was impossible not to be angry with God.

She ached to be home, but the Johnstons wouldn't hear of Josie leaving them before the land was unburdened. Even when they had word that most of the Toulouse fields were bared to the sun again, they tried to delay her.

"It won't be pleasant at Toulouse, Miss Josephine," Albany said. The household was gathered for morning coffee. "Some of it is still underwater, and the ground around the house will be deep mud. You'll be housebound for weeks if you go home now."

In this place, among near strangers, Josie had struggled to subdue her grief during the long, numbing days. Here she could not express her feelings, could not yield to the weeping or even the long silences her grief demanded. She had to go home. She had to be with those who shared her heartbreak, with Cleo and Grand-mére and Thibault. They needed her, and she needed them.

Josie shook her head vehemently. "I must go home. Whatever the difficulties. I appeal to you, Mr. Johnston," she said to Abigail's father. "You surely know how difficult it is to do nothing, to be idle, when there is so much to be done at home."

Mr. Johnston raised an eyebrow at his wife, waiting for her lead. Albany began to protest, "It simply won't be—"

"Safe? I'm sure I will be as safe as my grandmother or anyone else at Toulouse." Josie stood up. "Will you please put the flag up on the dock to let the next boat know to stop here? I'll be ready in half an hour."

Bertrand Chamard had not participated in this discussion, but now that Josie's assertion seemed to have settled the matter, he claimed a kinsman's familiarity. "You need not go alone, Josephine. I will escort you."

"I'll help you pack," Abigail said. Even in Josie's preoccupied state these last days, she had not missed the signs of her friend's jealousy. With Josie gone, Abigail would have Monsieur Chamard to herself. Poor Abigail. Bertrand, she thought, found Abigail's company tedious.

Early in the afternoon, a steamboat docked and took Josie and Chamard aboard. Albany touched his hand to his hat and Abigail waved as the boat fought against the current and found its channel.

On the way upstream, Josie and Bertrand stood on the upper deck in the sun. The breeze cooled them, and Bertrand leaned on the railing next to her. He was kind too, as kind as Phanor. Might he always be near, she prayed.

He spoke very little, leaving Josie to her thoughts. All these long days, in spite of her troubled soul, Josie had been alert to his presence, and now she memorized the look of his hands on the railing. They were tanned and broad, and his right hand carried a scar across the middle knuckle. Abigail said there had been a duel in Paris, that he'd fought a man in the Tuileries. Was it over a woman? she wondered.

Bertrand's musing cut in on her own. "The land," Bertrand said, "the land abides. You still have your land, Josie, and that is no small thing."

A memory of riding across Toulouse with Papa on his big horse came to her. Papa had loved the land. He didn't concern himself with running the plantation, but the woods and fields and bayous were dear to him. Josie gripped the railing. Oh God. Toulouse without Papa and Bibi.

The boat docked, and hot, humid air defeated the river's breeze. The captain indicated he would wait for Bertrand; Josie and her cousin disembarked to a deserted levee. She listened to the stillness. No one came to meet the boat, no birds sang.

The tree trunks shone yellow where the flood had scoured the bark away, but they stood stalwart, flanking the lane from the river to the house. The house itself was sunlit at the other end of the shaded drive, but the open shutters framed dark and silent windows.

The slaves had laid planks the length of the oak alley, and Bertrand held Josie's arm as they squished the planks into the muck on their way to the house. Instead of the midsummer scent of roses and magnolias, Josie smelled wet earth, moss, and decay.

Cleo opened the door to them. Josie stepped forward, arms raised. She had so wanted to be with Cleo, to embrace her, but Cleo's impassive face stopped her. Cleo had lost weight, and any hint of mischief or joy about her was erased.

"Hello, Mademoiselle Josephine," was all she said. She took Bertrand's hat and sent Laurie to call Madame Emmeline.

When Grand-mère Emmeline entered the room, her step was so frail and slow that Josie moved toward her, but a gesture from Grand-mère held her back.

"Josephine," Grand-mère said. A mere acknowledgement. "Monsieur Chamard. I am grateful to you for bringing my granddaughter home."

"I am glad to see you well, madame. I wish I might console you for your loss."

"Will you not sit down, monsieur?"

"If you will accept my thousand apologies, Madame Tassin, I may not keep the boat waiting. I go on to Baton Rouge, and the captain stopped here for a moment only in order that I might deliver Josephine to you safely."

"We are in your debt, monsieur."

"Please, we are cousins. I am Bertrand to you, and I hope you will allow me to call you Madame Emmeline."

Madame used her public smile and tilted her head to one side. "Of course."

He picked up his hat from the table where Cleo had set it. "Josephine, now you are home, I hope your mind will be at ease. *Au revoir*, ladies."

Now Josie was here, she wondered how she would bear the overwhelming aura of grief in this house when her spirit was already so burdened. She followed Bertrand to the gallery, unwilling to see him go. "Bertrand . . ." she said. He seemed the only spark of life in the house.

"Time will heal," he told her kindly. He glanced briefly back toward the shadowed parlor, then bent and kissed her tenderly on the lips. "Till we meet again, *chérie*."

Chapter 14

Toulouse

Toulouse was a house of lonely souls. Emmeline, Cleo, and Josephine walked through their days like ghosts, crossing paths without noticing one another. The water had receded, Mr. Gale had rebuilt the levee, and grass sprouted from the sodden land. But no roses bloomed and no cane grew in the fields.

Josie and Cleo still lived in the same house, slept in the same room, but in their grief, neither had the spirit to reach out to the other. They were as subdued as Grand-mère, and with so much between them, they had nothing to say.

Tendrils of vapor rose as the sun beat down on saturated ground. Whatever didn't flourish in the replenished soil rotted and stank. Standing water turned fetid. Hordes of flies flitted from filth to lukewarm dinners and water jugs.

Dr. Benet worried the cholera would strike after the flood. The people were weakened by stress and overwork, and whatever directly caused the disease, the doctor feared the conditions were ripe for it. He moved into the *garçonnière* and waited.

Old Ursaline, the midwife, was the first one stricken. Dr. Benet examined her in the dark little cabin, then returned to report to Madame and Josie.

"It's the cholera, all right. I'm sure of it."

Josie put a hand to her eyes. The newspaper had printed accounts of the Asian cholera, new to this continent in the last half decade, and she knew how lethal it was. *Dear God, not more deaths.*

Dr. Benet left them to prepare his defenses against the coming onslaught. Josie retired to her room with another of her headaches where she found Cleo changing into the dress she saved for her dirtiest chores.

"You still wearing that old thing?" Josie said, indifference flattening her voice.

"It's going to be messy, Dr. Benet says, nursing this cholera."

Josie turned to her, alarmed. "You're going down there?"

"They're my people. They'll need me." Cleo finished fastening the threadbare dress and looked under her cot for her oldest shoes.

Josie sat on her bed. "They're my people too," she said softly.

Cleo sat next to Josie and looked at her. "I suppose they are, in a way."

"I'm coming with you."

"Josie, you don't have to do that. Stay here, with Madame Emmeline."

"Grand-mère will have Laurie for company." Josie put on an old dress too, and then stood ready.

The two of them clasped hands for a moment, and then entered the field of contagion, together.

In the days to follow, Josie and Cleo followed Dr. Benet into the quarters, fed water to the growing number of the fallen, and stripped beds with their own hands. In addition, they mixed gallons of molasses and water according to Dr. Benet's direction. "Will it save them?" Josie asked.

"My dear, I know nothing of a cure. I only hope to hit upon a remedy that may help the body heal itself."

While Cleo tended to the stricken down the lane, Josie visited the cabin next to Ursaline's. Three little children— Tansy, her thumb ever in her mouth, Val jean, his knobby knees always scraped, and Josephine, named after her— lived there with their father Luc and their grandmother Bella. They were everybody's favorites as they skipped along with their Grammy Bella to the dairy, to the cookhouse, then back to the quarters to deliver the milk rations. Josie examined each of them, as Dr. Benet had taught her. If one of these children should die, Josie felt the blow would be greater than she could bear.

In spite of the doctor's molasses potion, the cholera strengthened. With every death, Josie felt her faith waning, her hopes more desperate. She hardly slept, keeping vigil by the bedsides of the stricken. If her will alone could save them, they would live. Cleo and Louella put food before her and she ate; they brought her draughts of the molasses and water she herself had mixed, and she drank, but she knew nothing of it. Once she focused on Cleo's gaunt face and ordered her back to the house, but she hardly noticed that Cleo too remained among the sick.

Josie took to looking for Grammy Bella and the children during the day, in the dairy, near the cookhouse, just to see that they were well. *Josephine, Tansy, Val jean*—it became a chant she invoked all through the day. In her sleepless state, she believed, somehow, that if only she kept up her chant, no harm could come to them.

But Tansy died. The cholera swept through her little body and nothing Josie or Cleo or Dr. Benet could do stopped it from ravaging her. Josie labored on as one whose wits were gone, and later she remembered nothing of the days after Tansy's small body was wrapped in its shroud.

Ursaline, the first stricken, was the first to show signs of revival. Josie, Cleo, and the doctor continued feeding the molasses mixture to everyone taken with the cholera. Some died, but some lived another day, and then another, until the sun set with no new cases, no new deaths. Of the twenty-six who came down with cholera, all of them slaves, only seven of them succumbed.

As the second day of reprieve closed, yet again no new cholera, no new deaths, Josie sat on the porch of Grammy Bella's cabin. Little Josephine was in her lap, Val jean leaning against his mam'zelle. He sang softly of Jesus and salvation, and Josie's head began to nod. She slipped into sleep without knowing.

Grammy Bella called her son out to the porch. "Luc, look at dis chile. You think you kin carry her up to de house?"

"She don' weigh nothin'. I get her to home."

Josie might have been a sleeping toddler for all she knew of Luc's carrying her through the pecan trees. When the sun woke her in the morning, she was in her own bed, and Cleo slept in the cot on the other side of the room.

The outbreak over, the plantation struggled to carry on. At her desk, Madame Emmeline, as drained as her granddaughter, struck the names of the dead from her roster. As she reviewed the demands of the coming year against the work force remaining, she despaired.

Albany Johnston came to call twice, but Josie had little to say to him. She had little to say to anyone. She and Grandmère Emmeline had neither the energy for small talk nor the intimacy for deeper connection. Cleo seemed to have her own life now; she continued to see Remy in the evenings and began to come back to the house later and later in the night-time. Josie slept a great deal, and she took long, lonely walks.

One afternoon, Josie sat at her writing desk trying to compose a letter to Tante Marguerite. Sweat trickled down her ribs and the sheen on her arms smudged the blotting paper. She continually flicked her wrist to discourage the flies attracted to the ink on her pen and ended up spattering ink across the page.

She stared at the tear-shaped drops on the creamy paper. The letter was ruined. Josie leaned her head on her arms and wept. She had no comfort, no reserves left.

Cleo looked in from the bedroom where she was folding laundry. She walked over to Josie and put a hand on her back. "Sit up," she said quietly.

Josie wiped her eyes and blew her nose. Cleo folded the spoiled paper and put it in her pocket. "Here," she said, and laid out a fresh sheet for Josie.

"Thank you." Josie began the letter anew, and Cleo returned to her work.

As the sun eased up that evening, Dr. Benet sat on the front gallery enjoying a cigar and the river breeze when he saw Josephine walk aimlessly through the oak alley toward the levee. *Her shoulders droop like an old woman's,* he thought, and even from the gallery he could see her hair was undressed. *Poor child. She's had too much.*

And so had her grandmother. Fatigue and worry and grief had aged Emmeline a dozen years. Dr. Benet prescribed a sleeping draught for her, hoping that might restore some of her energy, but her complexion turned ashy and her eyes lost the snapping quickness he had always admired.

The morning of Dr. Benet's departure, he knocked on the office door. "Good morning, Emmeline."

She gestured to the big leather chair at the window, and he settled himself in it. "Before I go, I want to discuss something with you."

"Very well." She motioned to Laurie to keep the flies away.

"It's you and Josephine, my dear. The melancholy in this house is overpowering."

Emmeline leaned her forehead against her hand and simply stared at the floor.

"I know," the doctor said gently. "How could it be otherwise? But I am concerned about Josephine. The child has had too much shock. Even when that young man, Johnston's boy, comes calling, she hardly loses her torpor."

"I'm afraid he's a dull young man."

"It's more than that. You must see it. Josephine is lost, she's floundering in so much grief."

Emmeline's face showed nothing. Her eyes, always alert, even predatory like the eyes of a hawk, were now flat and dull. "Everyone on Toulouse has lost someone, François."

"I know. I'm sorry, Emmeline."

The clock on the wall ticked loudly as Laurie gently fanned at her mistress to shoo the flies away. At last Emmeline said, "What would you have me do? I cannot bring my son back, nor the child's mother."

"I was thinking of sending her to New Orleans for the season," he said. "It would relieve her of the silence of this house, Emmeline. And it's past time Josie made her mark in society."

Emmeline's lack of response didn't deter him. "Your daughter-in-law's sister, Marguerite, will be in New Orleans for the winter. I'm sure she'd take her under her wing."

"Yes. All right," Emmeline said. Her gaze wandered to the window where the hot sun shone on the bare branches of the crepe myrtles. "No flowers of any kind in the garden now. Had you noticed, François?"

"Never mind. I'll send some camellias over, and the gardener can root some roses for you. This time next summer, you'll have a garden again."

"We likes the red roses," Laurie said.

"Well, then, I'll see to it you have red ones," Dr. Benet said. He let himself out of the house and crossed the make-do boardwalk to the levee where Elbow John and three other men waited to take him across the river.

At dinner, Madame told Josephine she would write to her aunt about spending the season with her. But Josie did not at first think of balls or beaus or concerts. "Leave Toulouse?" she said.

Grand-mère put her spoon down. "Dr. Benet is right. You've become dull and morose. You need to get away from here—unless you can tell me Toulouse holds more delights for you than New Orleans?"

Josie smiled for the first time in days and days. "No, Grand-mère. I'll be very happy to go to New Orleans."

Phanor rode his old mule Toine into the courtyard and dismounted. Madame had summoned him, so at the bottom of the gallery stairs, he wiped his bare feet and put on the dry socks and boots he carried across his shoulder.

Cleo met him at the top of the stairs. "Ah, Phanor. Your poor Toine. Should I have Thibault give him some feed?"

"Old Toine, he is always ready to eat," Phanor said. Once the cholera was over, he had met Cleo and Remy and sometimes one or two others with jaw harps on the levee for dancing and music. Now he pulled Cleo's arm through his until they reached the door into the house. "Cleo, I think you putting back some of that weight you lost from all your troubles."

"We're all beginning to eat again, I think. Even Josie."

Phanor asked about Josie every time he met Cleo. "Is she well? Do you think I could say *bonjour* to her?"

Cleo gave him a sly look, and Phanor's smile was his confession. When he had attended the mass for Monsieur Emile,

Josie's white face had pulled at his heart. He could well imagine how painful it must be to lose a second parent. As for their differing stations in life, well, he wanted only to comfort her. What would be so wrong with that? As the summer days wore on, though, he thought less about her grief and more about her hazel eyes and the way her hair caught the sunlight.

Cleo led him into the parlor where Josie sat gazing out at the river. As usual, her needlework covered her lap, but the needle was buried somewhere in the folds of the linen.

"Mademoiselle," Phanor said.

Josie jumped. "Oh, I didn't hear you come in." She wadded the linen up and stood to greet him. Josie's freckles had faded. She seemed thin and unhappy, and the black dress— Phanor noticed such things—hung on her and seemed to pull all the color from her face.

"I'm sorry for your father, Josie."

She bowed her head briefly. "Thank you, Phanor." The two months since Josie had seen Phanor had been a lifetime. Lost in his big dark eyes, she gazed at him almost as she had the first time she saw him. "Your family is well?"

"*Oui*, all of them." The moment dragged on until Phanor slapped his hat against his knee. "Well, I best see Madame." But still he stood there, and his next words came out in a rush. "Listen, Josie, sometimes Cleo and I, and some others, we make music in the evenings, on the levee. We could play for you, maybe, if you could come."

Her smile overpowered the gloomy dress, the pale skin. "I'd like that, Phanor."

The way the green in Josie's eyes deepened fascinated Phanor, but he made an attempt to pull his attention back to business. "Well, I better see Madame. Maybe tomorrow, eh, Cleo?" When Cleo nodded, he said, "Tomorrow, then, Josie."

Cleo let him into Madame's office and closed the door.

She lingered to hear what she could through the keyhole, one impish eye on Josie.

In a few minutes, Josie whispered, "What are they saying?"

Cleo held a finger up. "Wait a minute."

Finally, Cleo walked quietly and quickly to Josie. "Madame said something about Monsieur Cherleu. And New Orleans. Would she send Phanor all the way to New Orleans?"

The office door opened and Phanor emerged with a big smile on his face. He strode over to the girls and checked that Laurie had closed Madame's office door.

"What do you think?" He looked at both of them. "I'm to be old Monsieur Cherleu's wine merchant in New Orleans! Madame has arranged it. Me, Phanor DeBlieux."

"Congratulations, Phanor!" Cleo said. "I knew you would get to New Orleans."

Phanor glanced over his shoulder at the office door and lowered his voice. "Josie," he said, "this means I cannot play my fiddle for you tomorrow. Tonight, though . . ."

Madame Emmeline came out of her office. "Are you still here, Phanor DeBlieux?"

"I was just leaving, Madame." He looked at Cleo and winked, then bowed formally to Josie. "*Au revoir*, Mademoiselle Josephine."

When the door closed behind him, Josie looked an enquiry at her grandmother.

"Monsieur Cherleu grows old, Josephine. He's tired, too tired to begin anew after the flood." Grand-mère lowered herself wearily to the settee and motioned for Cleo to pour her a glass of water. "He depends on his wine import business now, and he needs someone to represent him in New Orleans. Young Phanor is an intelligent fellow. He'll learn quickly."

Phanor would be in New Orleans over the winter! Would

she see him there? He wouldn't be invited to the soirées, of course, but maybe on the street, in the square?

Supper over, the sun nearly below the tree line, Josie and Cleo slipped out of the house and collected Thibault from Louella's cabin. He was as good a chaperone as they could expect under the circumstances, but more important to them, Thibault's high, sweet singing voice promised joy and hope of heaven.

Thibault ran ahead to Phanor's mule grazing on the levee. He rubbed Toine's nose and pulled a patch of grass for him. "Toine, you a good mule. You my friend," he said.

Phanor stoked the beginnings of a fire in the center of the clearing. "Hey, Cleo. That Thibault, he sure love ol' Toine," he said. Then he grinned. "*Bon soir*, Josie."

Not so confident as he, Josie smiled back, unsure what to do. Phanor patted the log next to him, and she sat down. Not too close. She'd probably been invited only because of Cleo.

"Is Remy coming?" Phanor said.

Cleo held a hand against the sun. "He's still in the field. He'll be along once he's eaten and poured a bucket of water over himself."

Phanor launched into a country favorite and Cleo pulled Thibault away from the mule. "Dance with me." They linked hands and marched in time to the music, Cleo's skirt held daintily out with one hand.

Thibault called, "Dance with us, Josie."

Cleo held out a hand to her, Josie took it, and the three of them laughed their way through the intricate steps Monsieur Pierre had brought to Toulouse. God, it'd been so long since she'd felt so light, so free of her burdens.

She was still dancing to Phanor's fiddle when the sun reached its lowest, orangest point before dipping below the horizon, leaving a pink and lavender sky. Cleo's friend Remy emerged from the shadows.

"Look here what I got," he called. Then he saw Mademoiselle Josephine in the dusk. "'Scuse me, mam'zelle," he said, and began to back away. "I didn't know you wuz here. 'Scuse me."

Abigail would be appalled if she knew Josie spent the evening with a Cajun and a field hand. But what of it? Josie decided.

"Remy," she said, "Cleo says you have the best voice on the place." He still hesitated. "I'd like to hear you sing."

"Come on up here," Phanor said. Remy began to climb the levee. "What you bring in that sack?"

"Biled peanuts," Remy said. "We got 'em from dat fella over to de Cummins' place. Traded him a mess of catfish fo 'em."

"Josie and I love boiled peanuts," Cleo said.

The five of them gathered around the light of Phanor's small fire, eating peanuts and talking. Josie discovered Phanor was a storyteller and a wit and—as she'd known all along— a charming devil. She loved the way he kept a straight face while he told a joke, but as soon as he delivered the punch line, he'd allow the slightest hint of amusement to show around his mouth.

Josie watched discreetly as Cleo and Remy cuddled close on a scrap of canvas spread on the ground. Papa would certainly have wanted more for Cleo, would have found her a skilled hand, maybe a blacksmith, or even a freedman, yet she had taken up with a common slave. Here he was with the rough hands and the ignorant speech of a field hand, and here was Cleo, nearly humming with love for this boy. Josie's loneliness deepened at the sight of her leaning against Remy, touching his arm or his hair, always making contact.

Josie collected her peanut shells in a neat pile in her lap

till Thibault showed her how to spit them over her shoulder like everybody else. In the twilight, her inhibitions, and Remy's, were easier to lift, and the party grew merrier as it grew darker. Soon Phanor picked up his fiddle again.

He played a quick-step Cajun tune, and Josie and Thibault, Cleo and Remy paired off to dance in the firelight. When the music stopped, Thibault grabbed Josie around the waist and hugged her tight. "I love you, Josie," he said.

Tears sprang to Josie's eyes. In the light from the fire, she could see something of her papa in Thibault's face. She knelt down to hug him. "I love you too."

Over Josie's shoulder, Thibault said to Remy, "She my sister."

"Thibault!" Cleo said. "I told you—"

Josie stood up, embarrassed for all of them. "It's all right, Cleo," she said. "I know it."

The moment dragged on until Remy began to clap his hands in a complicated rhythm, then added a stomping foot. Phanor picked up the beat with his hands and began to move his feet over the ground, faster and faster, trying to keep up with Remy's mad syncopation.

In the light of the half-moon, the five of them passed another hour of singing and dancing and laughing. Then with a flourish Phanor pulled a reed flute from his fiddle case. He blew gently into the flute, and sweet, pure notes poured into the night. The others sat still and listened, their breath and pulses slowing. When he finished, Phanor handed the flute to Josie.

"Try it," he said.

"Oh, I can't play a flute. I've never—"

"Try it," he said again.

She put it to her mouth and blew, expecting a horrible croak, but she produced a round, clear tone.

"Not bad," Phanor said. "Use the finger holes."

Josie blew and ran her fingers up and down. Then she tried

a two-note trill that sounded as sweet as any bird. She experimented as the others ate the last of the peanuts. She could play this! Before the last shell hit the ground, she tried a minuet she'd been struggling with, and suddenly it was music. Not the lead-fingered rendition she generated on the piano, but flowing and joyful.

"I knew there was music in you," Phanor said. "You were born to play this flute."

She played another tune, with only a few misfingerings, and felt the melody flow from her heart into the flute. Music, without strain or tension.

Josie laughed. "I didn't know I could play like that." She handed the flute back to Phanor.

"Of course you can," Phanor said. "And the flute will fit in your pocket better than the piano."

He placed the flute firmly in her palm again. "This is yours, Josie."

"I can't take your flute, Phanor."

"It never was my flute. I carved it for you. And it took me fourteen reeds to get it right. It's yours."

"Take it, Josie," Cleo said, and it was settled.

The moon had moved enough to tell them the evening should end. Remy began to sing a slow spiritual. Cleo sat on the ground and leaned against his knees; Thibault drowsed with his head in her lap. The frogs, the crickets, the cicadas, the very wind stopped while Remy's sweet tenor filled the night. Each note a perfect bell tone, an encapsulation of longing and love and hope.

Josie again sat on the log next to Phanor. All through the evening, she'd been aware of him constantly, the way he moved his body, held his head when he talked, showed Thibault a dance step. Now, she was mindful of the way the fabric stretched over his thigh in the firelight, and his closeness enflamed every sense. She smelled the smoke in his hair, the sweat in his shirt, and breathed in deeply for more.

Phanor looked at her in the dying firelight. "Josie," he said. She leaned toward him. She wanted to kiss him, to feel his body under the thin shirt.

He leaned slightly toward her, too, but he stopped. He touched her lip with his finger. "Mademoiselle Josephine," he said softly.

Cleo's voice brought Josie back. "Wake up, Thibault. I can't carry you all that way," she said. Remy had already slipped into the darkness to find his way back to the quarters alone.

The next morning, as Josie lingered alone over breakfast and remembered Phanor's every move and word, music came to her through the windows. *It's him,* she thought. She hurried to the front gallery, and there below her was Phanor with his fiddle.

He swept his hat off in a grand bow. "What is your pleasure, mademoiselle?"

Josie leaned over the rail, her face alight, and commanded, "Something lively, if you please, sir."

Phanor launched into a gay Cajun stomping tune. Josie was about to dance down the stairs to join Phanor in the yard when the steamboat whistled on the river.

"That's the New Orleans boat," Phanor called up to her. "I have to go."

"Wait. I'll come down."

Phanor put his fiddle in its case. He picked up his valise and stood tall. No longer, Josie thought, would he spend his days fishing, hunting, telling tales, and listening to the mockingbirds. Today he became a man of business.

Josie walked with Phanor through the oak alley to the dock. Her steps matched his perfectly, though he was so tall. She congratulated him sincerely on this opportunity in New Orleans, but mostly she thought how sorry she was to see him go. Maybe, in New Orleans . . .

"Will you wish me luck, Josie?"

"Of course I do. But it'll be even quieter here. Now." She touched his sleeve shyly. "Will you play for me again some day?"

"I will. And you will play your flute for me."

The captain tooted the whistle for his passenger to hurry up. Phanor stole a squeeze of Josie's hand and hopped aboard. He stood on deck smiling at her as the boat turned into the current.

Josie waved until the trees and the curve of the Mississippi cut off her view of the boat. She stayed on the dock for a long time, admiring the blue dragonflies hovering over the lily pads at the river's edge and listening to the sleepy croak of a frog hiding in the reeds. Finally she strolled back to the house, humming one of Phanor's Cajun tunes.

In the days after Phanor's departure, the last summer days, hot and humid, followed one another in an indistinguishable monotony. The house was so quiet without Papa's comings and goings, without Maman's friends dropping by, without Bibi's quiet singing in the mornings. Now Toulouse was well again, Josie thought more and more about the coming season in the city.

Abigail called on her once or twice, accompanied by her brother. Albany would talk about business with Grand-mère; the two of them found the intricacies of the cane market fascinating. The girls would excuse themselves to Josie's room so they could look at the fashions in Abigail's latest magazine from New York.

Other times Albany Johnston came alone to call on Grand-mère, ostensibly, and then sat with Josie in the parlor, but Josie's and Albany's ideas of fun differed. He followed Washington politics closely and was sure the details of Van Buren's campaign against the Whigs would entertain her as much as they did him. And did she fully understand the consequences of that scoundrel Jackson's dismantling the Bank of the United States? Josie became adept at stifling sighs.

At last, fresh winds from the Gulf blew away the heavy, humid air, and Josie enthusiastically planned her winter wardrobe. She wrote to tell all her many cousins she would be in town for the season, and had they seen the latest style in sleeves?

Visions of balls and banquets occupied only a part of Josie's anticipations. Her daydreaming more often involved Phanor. Just remembering the moment his knee had accidentally touched hers that night on the log would reignite her body. But, she told herself, he could only be a friend. Yes, she enjoyed his company, and they shared this part of the river. But he was a Cajun. Still, those unkissed lips—

And what of her cousin, Bertrand Chamard? His kisses, the first one and the second—she relived those moments over and over. They had not roused cousinly feelings in her; how had they felt to him?

Comparing the sophisticated Chamard with the rough-hewn Cajun—well, they both had their charms. Bertrand no doubt would attend Tante Marguerite's evenings, might even know how to do this new dance, the waltz, that Abigail had told her about. Might he kiss her again?

Cleo's life, too, began to take a new shape.

All those long summer evenings, neither Josie nor Grand-mère complained that she left the house after supper. Sometimes she visited with Thibault and Louella in their cabin behind the cookhouse. But most often Cleo joined Remy in the quarters being built on new ground.

They'd meet after Remy had finished in the fields. He'd be hot and sore and tired. Cleo would rub grease on his scratches or pull the burrs from his pants as he ate his ration of cornbread and fatback. She often brought him treats from Madame's table—pickles, or even a leftover pork chop.

"What's dis, den?" Remy said.

"Marmalade." Remy sniffed it. "Just taste it," she said.

Remy rolled his eyes when he put a spoonful in his mouth. "Dat sweeter dan cane. You spoilin' me, Cleo."

Remy slept in the bachelor cabin, so there was no privacy for them there. They'd walk to the levee to catch the river breeze and light a smudge pot against the mosquitoes. Later they'd go to their hidden glade and make love on an old blanket. Afterwards, they'd watch the stars, fingers entwined.

"You gon' have a baby, we don' watch out," Remy told her.

"I know it. It's all right."

"No. It better we wait, Cleo, best we can. When I gets free, I get you free—den our babies be born free."

Chapter 15

Toulouse, November 1836

Cleo snuggled closer to Remy in their leafy bed under the trees. "I found a map in Monsieur Emile's room, Remy."

"What good dat do me? I cain't read, Cleo."

"I bet you could read a map. I'll show you how."

"Maybe."

"How else you going to know how to get to the free states?"

"Well, you bring me dat map, and I try it."

"It's cold up there now."

"Yeh, but nobody miss me I go at Christmas. Madame gone give us two days off, and dat's two days Mr. Gale don' look fo me."

They held each other close and watched the moon move through the tree branches. "I'll miss you," Cleo whispered.

Remy tightened his arms around her. "I know, *chérie*, but we got to try. Fo the chilluns we gone have, we got to get free."

"I have news from the house, Remy."

"Good news?"

"I don't know. Mr. Gale has bought a farm in Texas. Madame's hired a new man to be overseer."

Remy grunted. "I hear der others lots worse dan Gale."

"Anyway, Gale's leaving."

Remy thought for a while. "Den I best be going."

"Before Christmas?"

He nodded. "De new man, he gon' want to show Madame how tough he be. It be better I gone befo he know me."

All her life, Cleo had heard stories of slaves who'd tried to escape. So many of them got lost in the woods and swamps. They'd trail back into the quarters starved, fevered, and swollen all over from mosquito bites.

The stories about the ones who were caught were horrifying. Cleo knew tales of what some overseers did to runaways were meant to discourage the slaves, but they were nonetheless true. The beatings that tore the flesh down to the bone were not the worst punishments. Mr. Gale thought the lash was penalty enough, but some overseers, like the notorious Scotsman in the next parish, used an axe on a man's foot to keep him on the place.

"The new overseer, he might be a good man," Cleo said. "Maybe as good as Mr. Gale."

"More likely he be like dat man McGraw up de river, de one Old Sam say love his branding iron."

"Madame never had any branding on the place, Remy. She won't let you be burned."

Remy pulled away from her. "You talk like you tink I be caught."

Cleo sat up. "I know you can handle the swamp, Remy, but the patrols are out there looking day and night. You remember when they brought Old Sam back in chains, half dead?"

Remy put his hand under Cleo's chin and tilted her face to his. "I goin' to try, Cleo. You know dat."

"Yes. I know that."

They made love, safe in their bower in the dark. For a while, they shoved the vigilance required of slaves into the shadows and lived just for themselves.

Afterwards, Cleo stood on the moonlit gallery stairs and watched Remy disappear in the pecan trees as he cut around Mr. Gale's house to reach the quarters.

With Josie in New Orleans, Cleo sat alone in the bedroom with two candles lit to study Emile's map. The river itself would be the easiest way north, but the most dangerous. Slavers were ever on the lookout for runaways, and Remy wouldn't make it even to Iberville if he didn't leave the Mississippi as soon as possible.

Fleetingly, she wished she could talk it over with Josie. That was ridiculous, of course, but Cleo missed her. The luxury of having an entire room to herself didn't make up for the loneliness. She sometimes caught herself listening for M'sieu Emile's footsteps or imagining she smelled his cigar. She often talked to her maman, told her she was going to have to mend another sheet, or confided how much she loved Remy. But ghosts never answered.

If M'sieu Emile were alive, Cleo considered, she might have asked him if Remy could earn his freedom. It was a common enough arrangement. An able slave might hire himself out to another white man, the wages to be turned over to the owner with a small portion kept by the slave himself. But Madame would never consent. There had been no agreements like that on Toulouse since Monsieur Tassin died twenty years before, and since the flood and the cholera, the plantation was shorthanded.

Remy would have to take his chances. The cool weather would keep the snakes sleepy and the mosquitoes down. Cleo could slip him some decent clothes from Emile's wardrobe, and she could steal food for him from Louella's kitchen or from the table in the big house.

Most of all, Cleo would protect Remy with a forged pass. It was a terrible crime for a slave to write a false pass. It was even a crime for Cleo to know how to write. But she couldn't let Remy face the roving patrols or the itinerant slavers without it. He simply didn't have the glibness of tongue to convince them his business was legitimate if they caught him.

Dawn came grey and cool. Cleo put a shawl over her dress and stuck her feet in old stiffened leather boots of Josie's. She often wondered what Madame would have done for her if Josie's feet had not always been larger than hers. Some house slaves had good shoes, and some went barefoot year round. Now that Emile was gone, Cleo suspected Madame would be content with a barefoot maid.

When Cleo had ground the coffee beans and collected the hot breakfast from Louella, she called Madame to the table. Madame Emmeline's long, loping steps had lost half their length and all their spring since the flood. Her shoulders turned in slightly now, and the angles of her face had softened.

Cleo poured steaming coffee for Madame and then stood nearby while she ate.

"No marmalade?" Emmeline grumbled.

"No, ma'am." With a straight face, Cleo added, "Gone in the flood." Daily some minor lack would remind them of all that had been washed away. There was no butter on the place, and there would have been no coffee had not Tante Marguerite sent Madame five pounds of fresh beans.

When Madame Emmeline finished her blood sausage and corn cake, she motioned for Cleo to stand across the table where she could see her. Cleo waited while Madame eyed her over her coffee cup for a moment.

"You know, of course, that Mr. Gale is leaving." It was a statement. Cleo knew Madame only pretended not to know she listened at doors. "Monsieur LeBrec arrives today," she went on. "He will have a few days' overlap with Mr. Gale in order to become acquainted with our routines. Until Mr. Gale's family vacates the overseer's house, the LeBrecs will need lodging. The other slaves have too much to do right now to be taken away from their jobs. I want you to prepare the new carriage house for them."

"Shall I leave the carriages in the outdoors? What if it rains?"

"Then they will get wet."

"Yes, ma'am."

"Let Louella know the LeBrecs and the Gales will dine with me tonight. I'm tired of sitting at this table all alone."

"I'll tell her to come up to the house for the menu."

Madame Emmeline waved a dismissive hand. "Tell her to serve whatever she likes."

That evening, the two overseers and their wives sat down to supper at Madame's table. Mrs. Gale and Madame LeBrec each wore her best dress and spent the evening gauging how much superior she was to the other overseer's wife. Both were bathed and curled and rouged, and since each believed in her own supremacy, they were happy in each other's company.

As Cleo waited table, she closely observed Monsieur LeBrec. He was a Cajun and affected a gentleman's haircut with a pomaded wave of thick black hair. His brown jacket was well made, but Cleo noticed the fine darning stitches in each elbow.

"Me, I had no trouble with slackards at my last job," LeBrec was saying. "Punishment, swift and sure. A pocket knife, a quick notch in the ear. That's what keeps your slaves in line."

"You'll find, I believe," Mr. Gale answered, "we have good workers on Toulouse, Mr. LeBrec." Cleo heard a hard note in Mr. Gale's voice. "Take those fellows you watched building the cabins this afternoon. You didn't see no slackards among them, I'll warrant. Fair treatment, that's what it takes to get the most out of your slaves."

LeBrec smiled. Cleo read arrogance in the curve of his lips under the black mustache, its tapered points carefully waxed.

"Fair treatment? Your average slave don't know what fair is. That's when you get young bucks running off, thinking they're going to outsmart you."

Mr. Gale stiffened. "We haven't had a runaway in, what?" He looked to Madame Emmeline. In the past, she would not have tolerated talk of slaves at her table, but now she seemed indifferent to the increasing heat in the argument.

"Six years or so," she answered.

"You see. Six years!" Mr. Gale said.

Mrs. Gale touched her husband's sleeve. He was becoming excited. She smiled at Madame Emmeline in apology. "These two men spent the whole afternoon together," she said with a nervous laugh, "and they still haven't managed to get everything said."

Once the women had curtailed the men's discussion, Monsieur LeBrec lost interest in the pleasantries of trivial conversation. His eyes followed Cleo as she moved around the table pouring wine.

Occasionally, Emile had had a guest who did not grasp the relationships in this house, and the man would look at her much the same way as LeBrec did now. She understood that look, and her hands trembled.

When Cleo reached for his glass, LeBrec's right hand, hidden from the others by Cleo's body, slid up Cleo's leg under her skirt to caress her bottom. She jerked back and knocked the glass to the floor.

Quickly, she knelt to pick up the pieces of the broken goblet.

"Silly girl," Madame LeBrec shrilled. "It's so hard to train a slave to handle nice things."

Cleo looked up as she gathered the shards in her apron, and LeBrec's eyes moved from her cleavage to her face. His smile was a signal Cleo understood as well as if he'd spoken.

Cleo hurried from the room with the broken glass as if to fetch a new goblet from the pantry. Instead, she passed the pantry to slip into Emile's old sitting room. She closed the door behind her and pulled her legs up into his old leather chair. She hugged her knees and took in the lingering scent of his tobacco. Who would protect her now?

That evening LeBrec's wife kept Cleo running for first one thing and then another as she settled her family into the carriage house. Was there not another lantern? Little Yves required a pillow. Sylvie's cot was so hard; perhaps there was another mattress she could lie on. By the time Cleo had satisfied the LeBrecs, the quarters had been long dark.

The following morning Cleo gathered Madame Emmeline's linens to take to the wash house. She hoisted the basket to her head and crossed the yard, passing the new carriage house on the way. Madame LeBrec made a point of cutting Cleo's path.

"*Bonjour*, madame," Cleo said.

"Stand still a minute, girl."

Cleo waited, wondering if the woman expected her to turn the barn into a palace. But the mind of the overseer's wife was on her husband.

"Monsieur LeBrec is a handsome man," she said. "And a man of appetite."

Cleo held her breath.

"I saw you looking at him."

"No, ma'am," Cleo protested.

"The last girl, I had her branded. Among other things." The woman turned to go, but added over her shoulder. "Just so you know."

Back in the house, Cleo polished every piece of furniture.

Then she scrubbed the floor in the dining room on her hands and knees. She climbed on a stool and polished every facet of the chandelier in the parlor. She worked furiously all day, scared and desperate.

There was no one to help her. She couldn't tell Remy. What could a field hand do against an overseer? Madame might be made to understand, but not until too late, when LeBrec had already laid his hands on her.

As Cleo shook the tablecloth over the gallery rail, Mr. Gale emerged from Madame's office. Cleo took a step toward him, and he paused, his hat in his hand.

"Mr. Gale?" Cleo whispered. "This new overseer . . ."

He nodded once and put his hat on. "You best keep close to the house, gal," he said. "That's all I got to say to you. Stick close to the house."

But she had to see Remy. The moon was high when she arrived at their special place. She waited, and the moon moved a hand's breadth across the sky. Remy wasn't coming. Sometimes Mr. Gale was out and about until late into the night, and sometimes Remy fell asleep before Cleo could get loose from her chores. He was an eager lover, but a man who worked at hard labor twelve hours every day carried fatigue on his back.

Cleo followed the moonlit patches back toward the house. Her own steps dragged with exhaustion, but when she heard a noise in the shadows, she quickened her pace.

"Hey, there, girly." It was Monsieur LeBrec. "What you doing out here so late? Looking for trouble?"

He stepped close and she smelled liquor on his breath. He grabbed hold of her arm.

"You got yourself a buck sniffing around you? That why you out here? Want some of that buck, do you?"

"No, monsieur. Let me go, please."

"'No, monsieur.' Don't she talk pretty. Little gal got a

tongue on her. Setting yourself up with airs, ain't you? 'Please,' she says." He bent down till his breath was full in her face. "You a spoiled little nigger. But I can fix that."

Cleo twisted her arm free and ran for the house. LeBrec's low laugh followed her.

Cleo hardly slept all night. She heard Madame Emmeline get up, pace for an hour, then go back to bed. She was still awake when Madame rose and sat in a creaky rocker on the gallery to watch the sun rise.

Later that morning, Cleo watched Mr. Gale load his family on a wagon and leave Toulouse for a new life in Texas. She heeded his advice and kept to the house all day. After dinner, though, Monsieur LeBrec conferred with Madame Emmeline in her office. That was her opportunity to see Remy for a few minutes.

She hurried down to where the men were building a new sugar mill. Remy wasn't there. She tried the quarters where the new cabins were going up. Old Sam was hammering floor boards, and she asked him where Remy was working.

Sam leaned back on his heels and wiped the back of his neck with a kerchief. He took a long time to answer. Finally, he said, "Cleo, he gone."

"Gone? But . . ." Cleo gaped, her senses gone stupid. "But I had a bundle for him."

"He pick a good time, Cleo. Gale be on his way. Dis new man don't know who is who. It a good time."

Old Sam stood up. "Now don't you cry, honey." He hugged her and patted her back. "Worry don' fix nothin. You know dat. Remy a smart boy. He gon' be all right."

Cleo felt safe in Old Sam's arms, but she knew it was an illusion. He couldn't protect her from LeBrec, and he couldn't protect Remy either.

"Look dere, Cleo. See dat lil' cloud up dere? Don' it look like a white butterfly? De bestest sign a man kin have. Dat white butterfly be fo you and Remy. I's sure of it." He thumbed away the tears under her eyes. "You gon' put on de good show in de house. You don' let nobody see anyting diff'rent."

Cleo nodded. She stood on tiptoe to kiss Sam's leathery cheek and hurried back to the house. She wanted to be behind the closed door of Josie's room when LeBrec left Madame Emmeline's study.

Part II

Part I

Chapter 16

New Orleans, November 1836

New Orleans: City of music, dancing, dining. Josie reveled in a whirlwind of night life, loved being in Tante Marguerite's household. She adored the parties and the concerts. But the afternoon hours of dreary, rainy, winter days—Josie sighed and put her book away. The print was too small, and Cleo had already read it to her anyway.

The hall clock chimed three. Abigail had said she'd call at three, and as *une américaine*, she would actually arrive at that time. Josie had introduced Abigail to several of her Creole cousins, and they had adopted her into their circle. Still, Abigail continued to seek Josie's company, and Josie thought she knew why. If Abigail was to ever leave the house, she required a protector, of course, and Albany Johnston willingly attended her if Josie was included.

Josie heard her aunt's butler answer the knock on the door. She picked up her cape and bonnet and went to the parlor to meet her friends. However, Albany Johnston waited for her alone.

"Abigail sends her regrets," he said. "She's indisposed with a cold. But rather than disappoint you—I know you need to get out of the house now and then—I thought perhaps Madame Lambert might accompany us on a walk."

Always, Albany couched his invitations in terms of what would be good for her, Josie thought. Just one more of the little annoying ways he made her feel like a child. And was it quite proper he should come calling without Abigail? Still, she had looked forward to getting out.

Josie sent for her aunt's seamstress. Madame Lambert was an ancient widow, kept on for mending and for charity's sake, an excellent woman if a bit deaf. Yes, she said, she would be pleased to have a coffee with Monsieur and Mademoiselle, only give her a moment to fetch her bonnet.

Once outside, Albany offered Josie his arm. Madame Lambert trailed along behind them in her widow's weeds. Josie pitied the old woman's stale black dress, almost as faded as the one she'd had to wear at Maman's funeral. Josie's own wardrobe was brand new, though of course everything was still black.

Jackson Square bustled. Albany allowed Josie to stop to watch two little black boys singing and dancing. They had a ragged old hat on the ground with a lone penny in it to entice bystanders to drop a few coins in. The boys sang and clapped their hands in rhythm with their shuffling feet. They finished with a flourish and grinned at Josie.

"They're adorable," Josie said.

Albany tossed a coin in the hat and drew her away. "*Merci*, m'sieur," the boys called. "*Merci, jolie* mam'zelle."

The first weeks in New Orleans, Josie had looked for Bertrand Chamard at every event she attended. Disappointed, she learned he had not yet appeared in town. Other days her heart would leap at sight of a figure very like Phanor De-

Blieux's. Surely just in the next street, or around this corner, she would see him. She knew he was still in New Orleans because Grand-mère had relayed Monsieur Cherleu's praise of Phanor's good sense and reliability, qualities rare in a Cajun, Grand-mère added.

Between the two hoped-for sightings, she kept herself in a near-constant state of anticipation, yet neither handsome gentleman had appeared in front of her to sweep the hat from his black hair, brown eyes twinkling.

"I want to show you something, Josephine," Albany said. Her heart sank. He was leading her toward the levee. No doubt there were ships in the river, and she'd have to hear all about where they'd come from and what they carried. Albany was obsessed with the amount of commerce flowing through New Orleans.

"Wait, Albany," she said. They were passing a vendor slicing plantains into a cauldron of bubbling hot oil. "Madame Lambert perhaps would like a cone of fritters?"

"Of course," Albany said.

Josie touched his sleeve and smiled up at him. "Me too."

He laughed indulgently and bought them each a paper cone of plantains sprinkled with brown sugar. "You'll ruin your gloves," he said.

"No, I won't." She pulled her kidskin gloves off and handed them to him to put in his pocket.

Josie was right about the lecture on commerce. Albany pointed out the barges carrying cotton bales from upriver, the casks of molasses being loaded onto a ship, and the tuns of wine and beer off-loading at the dock. He seemed oblivious to the cold wind blowing up Josie's petticoats.

"Your grandmother's own molasses and sugar likely unloaded at this very dock last year," he said. Josie nodded and tried to be attentive. She knew exactly how many kegs her grandmother had sent downriver. Of course, Toulouse had produced neither molasses nor sugar this year.

Albany led Josie and Madame Lambert to the café, where the three of them had coffee. It was warm enough most days to sit outside, if one were sheltered from the wind, and the coffee was strong and hot. Albany entertained Madame Lambert while Josie sipped her *café au lait* and watched a juggler across the road. He wasn't very good at it. Only three balls, and he often dropped one, but he kept trying. He was one of the few redheads Josie had ever seen, one of the new Irish immigrants she'd heard about. They were all so poor. No better than darkies, really, Madame Lambert said behind her fan.

Albany led Josie and their chaperone along the Rue Esplanade back to Tante Marguerite's townhouse. Once inside, he recommended Josie take a rest before the supper bell rang. "You mustn't overtire yourself," he said.

Josie stifled a retort that she could have walked twice as far and twice as fast if only he hadn't insisted on watching the ships in the river.

"Thank you, Albany," she said. "It was lovely to be out today."

Pulling her bonnet off as she climbed the stairs to her room, Josie heard her aunt call to her from her bedchamber. "Josie? Come in here, dear."

Josie tossed her bonnet on Tante Marguerite's writing table.

"Did you have a nice walk with your *américain*? Such an imposing man. Very handsome, you lucky girl."

Josie sighed. "Would you have guessed there was a ship in the river all the way from Madagascar, an island off the east coast of Africa, exporter of such goods as cloves, coffee, vanilla, and sisal?"

Tante Marguerite smiled. "Don't be too hard on the man, Josie. They can't all be poets." She held an elaborate gown up in front of herself. "What do you think? Shall I wear the cream silk tomorrow night?"

Marguerite had invited a few friends over for a buffet, nothing elaborate. Still, candlelight and wine could only do so much for ladies of a certain age. She chose her gowns and jewelry with great care.

Josie wondered if Alphonse, Tante Marguerite's nephew on her husband's side, would be there again. Alphonse had been dashing in his buff trousers and bottle green waistcoat the last time she'd seen him. On the other hand, she hoped Oncle Sandrine's old bachelor brother Monsieur Breton would not be there. He had been all too attentive, and she disliked his yellow teeth and the smell of his *eau de toilette*.

The following evening, Josie donned her second-best party dress. It was necessarily black, but it was cut in the latest style and adorned with really lovely black satin ribbon. With her hair curled and her cheeks lightly rouged, she was every inch *la belle*.

Tante Marguerite's parlor glowed with candlelight. The second parlor had been cleared for dancing, and the musicians played quietly while Tante Marguerite welcomed her guests. The dining room was too small to seat so many friends; instead, delicacies were spread on the mahogany table for people to help themselves throughout the evening.

Josie sat on the yellow damask sofa with her skirts spread prettily around her. Cousin Violette kept her company. She was two years older and becoming a little desperate for a fiancé, Josie thought. Twenty, and still no suitor in sight. What was she doing wrong? The gentlemen hardly noticed her. Perhaps it was Violette's long nose, Josie thought, but other girls even less pretty than Violette found husbands.

Tante Marguerite's nephew Alphonse arrived. As soon as he saw her, he came to pay his respects. With a charming bow, he addressed her, and Violette, as was proper. Then he pulled a chair near Josie and began to tell them about the morning's horse racing. He made Josie laugh as he described his sure bet falling farther and farther behind in the second race.

Violette waved her fan as if she'd never been more bored. Perhaps that was the problem, Josie thought. Her cousin was dull because she found everyone else so.

Josie told Alphonse all about her gelding at home, and how she'd been thrown at Abigail's. He swore he'd have swooped her from the horse's rearing back before she could have hit the ground. The good humor in his eye cancelled the braggadocio; he was utterly charming.

Monsieur Breton of the yellow teeth hovered nearby, but Alphonse did not yield his hold on Josie's attention. Manners dictated that the fragrant gentleman instead engage Violette in conversation. Violette did her best to be entertaining, Josie thought. At least she didn't yawn, but her fluttering fan and shrill laugh at every remark Monsieur made were hardly more endearing.

The musicians broke through the hum of the busy room with the first notes of a quadrille. Alphonse stood. "Will you dance?" he said and held out his hand.

Then the magic of the evening began. The violins, the wavering candlelight, the scent of lemons from the courtyard—Josie floated over the polished floor, unmindful of the black dress among the swirl of green and blue and lavender skirts.

The heat of the dance drove the pair to the punch table, where a white-jacketed servant ladled sweet frothy wine punch into crystal cups. Behind her, Josie heard a whispered, "Disgraceful!" She idly wondered who had offended the old women of the party until a second voice said, "Hardly in mourning six months, and on the dance floor already."

She flushed to her very toes, and tears wet her lashes. Alphonse had heard them too. He leaned over. "I'm so sorry. I didn't think."

She shook her head to absolve him. "It's not your fault. I should have remembered."

He led her to a settee away from the dancing and sat with her. "You mustn't mind," he said. "Those two old biddies always criticize. I've heard them snipe on other occasions, believe me."

"But they're right." Josie felt deflated, the magic of the dance floor reduced to the realities of etiquette.

Tante Marguerite excused herself from a circle of guests and approached Josie. Alphonse stood and offered her his place on the sofa, then hesitated. Was he to excuse himself from Josie's censure, or remain to give her support?

Tante Marguerite settled herself and smiled at Alphonse. "Might I have a glass of wine, my dear?" she said.

With Alphonse disposed of, Marguerite patted Josie's hand. "Don't worry, *chérie*. My dear old friends—" She nodded to the stern ladies across the room. "They imagine they are the final word on propriety. But I know my sister would be happy to see you smiling again. And your papa never cared what anyone thought, did he?"

Alphonse returned with a flute of champagne, which Marguerite accepted with a wink. "Enjoy yourselves in my home," she said, and left them to smile awkwardly at each other.

Even with their hostess's blessing, however, Alphonse did not suggest another dance. Instead, they adjourned to the banquet table and filled their plates with shrimp, curried oysters, pickled okra, and ginger cake. They found a spot on the gallery overlooking the Rue Royale and dined with moon glow on their faces.

Another white-jacketed servant took their empty plates from them, and they leaned against the wrought-iron rail to watch the street life below them. Alphonse remarked on the drunken crew on their way to the bars on the riverfront, and

Josie wondered who the woman in the red hat might be waiting for as she stood under the torch lamp on the corner. Alphonse made no comment, but drew her attention to a fine pair of horses drawing a carriage up the street.

The carriage stopped just below them. A man in a black top hat stepped down. As he turned to speak to the driver, the scarlet lining of his cape caught the light. A very elegant gentleman, Josie thought. He tapped the carriage with the tip of his cane and entered Tante Marguerite's door.

Chapter 17

New Orleans, Tante Marguerite's Party

"Oh." Josie put her hand to her throat as she recognized the man in the satin-lined cape.

"Do you know him?" Alphonse said.

"It's my cousin."

Alphonse nodded to the parlor behind them. "Would you like to go in to speak to him?"

Josie opened her fan. "It's stuffy in there, don't you think?"

She continued to laugh in the right places as Alphonse entertained her with a story about getting lost in the cane when he was a youngster, but her mind was on Bertrand.

She'd so often relived the moments at the Johnstons' when Bertrand had smiled at her over his port, had sung to her heart alone. No one else had ever kissed her, and she'd filled lonely hours dreaming of his lips on hers.

But by now, Bertrand might have forgotten all about her. The kiss on the gallery stairs—it might have meant nothing to him.

Tante Marguerite stepped onto the gallery. She spoke a few words with the other guests enjoying the cool air and then sat down next to her niece. "Bertrand has arrived. Late, as always, but what can you do with these fascinating men? Alphonse, you must promise to be more punctual when you are an independent bachelor on the town."

"With such charming company, Tante, how could one not be?" he said.

"Ah, watch that Monsieur Alphonse doesn't sweep you away, Josephine. He has all the charm of Creole manhood, and none of its vices."

"Ah," Josie said. "Then he is the paragon we all seek."

"Yes, he is. But, nephew mine, paragon that you are, your father is complaining of his rheumatism again. Perhaps he is ready for his bed."

Alphonse rose and bowed to the ladies. "You will excuse me, Mademoiselle Josephine. *Mon père* has not been well. I hope to see you again, soon." He lingered over Josie's hand and took his leave.

Tante Marguerite pulled her chair closer to Josie's. "Your cousin has asked after you, *chérie*."

Josie felt the flush rising. "Bertrand?" she said.

"Yes, that cousin," Marguerite said with a wry smile. "Why don't you come inside and say good evening?"

Josie trailed Marguerite into the parlor, the band still playing in the other room. Bertrand stood with his back to them, talking with an old gentleman with white side whiskers. Now the moment had arrived, Josie's hands were damp.

"Here she is, Bertrand. I found my niece captivating young Alphonse on the gallery."

Bertrand broke off his remarks to the elderly man. When he turned his attention full on Josie, she forgot anyone else was in the room.

"Gabriel, perhaps you would sit with me on the gallery?" Marguerite said to the elderly guest. "It's just the remedy for this overheated parlor." She walked away with her arm on the old gentleman's, leaving Josie gazing into Bertrand's brandy-colored eyes.

Bertrand smiled at her. "Josephine," he said as he kissed her hand, "you look lovely." His eyes lingered on the creamy skin above the neckline of Josie's gown. She felt her breasts rise and her blood warm.

A couple rose to join the dancing in the other room and Bertrand nodded toward their chairs. "Will you sit with me a while?" From his breast pocket, Bertrand withdrew a letter and presented it to Josie. "From your grand-mère. Please, open it. I'll find us something to drink."

Grand-mère wrote that the peas and collards were growing well though the potatoes had all rotted. In the quarters, they'd lost a child to a bowel ailment, little Angelite that belonged to Louella's son, so Grand-mère had dosed all the other children with garlic and rue. The new overseer proposed a fish pond, but Grand-mère couldn't see the sense of it with the river at their front door. LeBrec had confiscated all the knives from the slaves. What they'd cut their meat with Grand-mère didn't know, but she supposed they'd manage.

Oh, and they'd had a runaway, that boy they call Remy. He was worth eight hundred dollars at least, but LeBrec had put out a hue and cry, and Grand-mère was confident the patrols would catch him.

Josie pictured Remy in the fire glow that night on the levee, heard his voice. How could he have left Cleo? She must be frantic now that Remy was in danger.

Bertrand appeared with two glasses of punch and studied Josie's face. "Not bad news, I hope?"

"We've had a runaway. I can't remember the last time a slave left Toulouse like that."

"They'll catch him, or he'll tire of the woods and drag himself back in, hungry and sick."

"It's just that . . . he's my maid's sweetheart."

Bertrand raised an eyebrow. "You're very attached to your servant."

"My father gave her to me. We grew up together, Cleo and I. Almost like sisters."

Bertrand watched the dancers in the other room. "Yes, I understand. I have a man like that. Been with me since we were tykes. But I haven't told you how I have your letter."

"You've been to Toulouse?" She admired the whiteness of his shirt, his carefully buffed nails. His scent, she couldn't describe it, but she would have liked to put her face next to his ear and inhale him.

He nodded. "I've bought the Cherleu place next to yours. We shall be neighbors."

"Then we can see each other every day," she said.

Bertrand's eyes continued to rove the party, and she'd have given anything to pull those words back into her mouth. Here she was in a party full of elegant women, two of whom had smiled at Bertrand from across the room. She was just another female cousin to him, and she felt like a fool.

Bertrand seemed to remember his manners. "Certainly, *chérie*. As duty allows. But Monsieur Cherleu has let his place run down these last years, and there was the flood, so there will be many days of work."

"Of course," she murmured.

Bertrand stood up. "My dear, let me return you to your aunt. I have another engagement this evening, but I am so glad to have seen you."

Josie felt abandoned. This was not the romantic encounter she'd imagined. Deflated, she took his arm. Again Bertrand's eyes ran over her bare shoulders and neck, and he led her across the room where Marguerite chatted with friends.

Josie's aunt held a hand out to her to sit on the sofa next to her. "Are you leaving us so soon?" Marguerite said to Bertrand.

"*Oui, a mon grand regret*. But perhaps you will ask me again when your lovely niece is with you?"

"I will do so," she said, accepting his kiss on her cheek. "Good night, Bertrand."

"Josephine," he said, and once again she felt the full force of his attention, however briefly. It was very confusing. A moment before she'd felt he had no interest in her after all, but when he looked into her eyes, she was certain they had a secret connection.

The music and the lamp glow lost their charm after Bertrand left. Josie wondered if she could decently excuse herself from the rest of the evening. She wanted to retire to her room upstairs, to write in the journal she had begun when she left home. She needed to sort out this frustrating encounter with Bertrand, and her diary was her only confidant.

In the next days, in the odd moments when Josie didn't dream of Bertrand, she worried about Cleo. Surely she hadn't been foolish enough to help Remy escape. That could put Cleo in jeopardy, especially with this unknown new overseer, and only Grand-mère there to protect her. Josie wished she could be certain Grand-mère would intercede if Cleo were accused of aiding a runaway, but she had never seen Grand-mère show any special attachment to Cleo.

Josie was seldom homesick, but thinking of Cleo's predicament troubled her, and she wished she were at Toulouse again. Cleo belonged to her, and no one could harm her if Josie asserted herself. But Josie was a day's journey from home.

Thinking of Toulouse reminded Josie of music on the levee, of Phanor's slow easy smile. Grand-mère hadn't mentioned him in this letter. He could still be in New Orleans.

As so often happens in life, thinking of Phanor seemed to conjure his actual presence. Abigail and Albany called for Josie on Sunday afternoon. The three of them strolled through

Le Vieux Carré enjoying the sunshine when a well-dressed young man presented himself in front of them.

Josie didn't recognize him for an instant, but even a well-cut jacket and new leather shoes did not disguise Phanor's easy grace.

"*Excusez moi*, monsieur," he said. He addressed Albany only, as if unaware of the two ladies present. "I am Phanor DeBlieux, an associate of Monsieur Cherleu's. Perhaps you know the gentleman?"

"Monsieur Cherleu? Yes," Albany said.

"I am known to Mademoiselle Josephine. Would you permit me to renew our acquaintance?"

Albany held Josie's elbow as if to protect her from the dangers of an encounter with a near stranger in a public place. "Very well," he said to Phanor.

Josie wanted to throw her arms around Phanor's neck, but she was as sly as he in manipulating the social intricacies. She merely held her hand out to Phanor, who performed the bowing and kissing ritual with aplomb. "How nice to see you, monsieur," she said.

"I am delighted to find you well, mademoiselle. Monsieur Cherleu has me in New Orleans for the winter, as you see."

"Then you are still selling wine?" Josie said.

"Oh, so you are the wine agent," Albany said. "I have heard Cherleu speak of you at the club. You seem to have a head for business, Monsieur DeBlieux."

Phanor tilted his head in acknowledgement of the compliment. "Monsieur and I, we have done well." He turned back to Josephine. "It is a pleasure to see you here. I am most often in the cathedral square on Sunday afternoons, so it is my good fortune to have been on the Rue Royale today."

There was a short moment of awkwardness. When Albany issued no invitation to join their party, Phanor raised his hat. "Mademoiselle Josephine," he said. He nodded to Albany and to Abigail. "Monsieur, mademoiselle."

Phanor strolled on, his ebony walking stick swinging in his hand.

Abigail leaned behind her brother's bulk to raise her eyebrows at Josie and purse her lips as if to whistle. Josie shared a quick grin with her, and then resumed the sober expression appropriate to one in the company of the august Albany Johnston.

In the cathedral square on Sunday afternoon, Josie thought. Perhaps she could find a way to meet him there. She wondered if Phanor played his fiddle anymore, now he was in New Orleans.

After a week of dreary gray days, a Sunday morning dawned bright and clear. It was cold, but at least it was bright and dry. Oncle Sandrine proposed they walk to mass on such a fine day. Josie looked up at the few leaves left on the trees and filled her eyes with yellow against blue sky.

Inside the cathedral, the candles burning in every nook did nothing to dispel the chill. Josie prayed to the Virgin for her maman and papa's souls, and she prayed Mary would protect everyone at Toulouse. Josie's feet were numb with cold by the time mass was over.

She blinked when she walked into the bright square outside the cathedral doors and then stood mutely as her aunt and uncle chatted with their friends. The square outside the church bustled with vendors selling hot chestnuts and pralines. The redheaded Irishman juggled in front of his upturned hat on the ground. He was much improved, Josie noted, as she saw him toss a fifth ball into the air.

Through the noise of people crying "Hot peanuts!" and "Me, I got cane here!" Josie heard a fiddle. She listened intently over the sounds of the crowd: it was the same melody Phanor had played for her the morning he left the plantation. She stood on her toes to see over the crowd, but there were so many people. He'd said Sunday afternoon, and it was only just after eleven, but it could still be Phanor.

Josie had to make up her mind. If she left with her aunt and uncle, she didn't see how she could get back to the square that afternoon.

Josie's enthusiasm joyfully routed reason. She slipped through the throng exiting the cathedral and hurried toward the sound of the fiddle. If her aunt fussed at her later, she'd tell her she'd been abducted by Portuguese sailors, and Tante Marguerite would smile and forgive her.

There he was, one foot propped on his fiddle case. Phanor's shock of black hair gleamed nearly blue in the sunlight as he bowed a tune. Josie could hardly wait until he finished playing. Then she would run to him, heedless of all these people, and they'd laugh to be together again.

Phanor didn't see her in the crowd, and so she studied him as he played. The fine wool coat he had worn when she last saw him was replaced by a simpler brown frock coat, a little threadbare, whose sleeves stopped short of his wrists. He was neat, but not so prosperous looking in his old clothes. In the straw hat at his feet, coins glinted in the sunlight. Phanor was playing for money!

The people grouped around Phanor were clapping their hands and tapping their feet; one elderly man with holes in the knees of his trousers found a little space in front and danced a spry jig to the music. Another man, standing just beside her, reeked of whiskey and urine.

No one among Phanor's audience seemed at all proper, not one of them. Josie edged behind a woman whose hair straggled from under her dirty gray cap, a baby on her hip. Josie raised a hand to her nose at the odor from the child's soiled pantaloons. She stepped back to keep her fine velvet cape from being touched by anyone in this grimy, squalid crowd.

She didn't belong here, with these people. She didn't belong with Phanor. She backed out of the circle and ran toward the doors to the cathedral, the music following her over the heads of all those unwashed people. She pushed through the crowd to find Tante Marguerite, who didn't seem to have missed her.

During the walk back to the townhouse, Josie lagged behind. Phanor was back there, in the square, in a world she didn't belong in. With a heavy heart, she trudged along behind her aunt and uncle, feeling she'd lost something precious.

Chapter 18

Toulouse

When the patrol turned into the gate at Toulouse, the coffle of slaves behind the white man's horse shuffled to keep up. The rattling of iron on iron had accompanied Remy's every step since the patrol had caught him eight days before.

Seeing the place of his birth again, Remy swallowed hard. His maman rested here in the cemetery behind the quarters, the smell of hickory smoke rose from the cabins, the new blacksmith shop Remy had helped build with his own hands shone with fresh timber. The place was home, and Cleo waited for him here. Yet Toulouse was the place of his bondage, and he was in chains.

For two months and eleven days, Remy had been a free man. He'd run and he'd hidden, he'd been struck at by a sleepy copperhead that was slower than he, he'd been chased by a pack of dogs, and he'd starved when he couldn't steal a pumpkin or corn out of some farmer's crib. But he'd never known such exhilaration. Every moment Remy breathed free air, he knew he was alive.

The runaways followed the slaver into the backyard. Remy heard Cleo's voice before he saw her. She was yelling "Madame," and then she came running down the gallery stairs and across the ground toward them.

He didn't call to her. He was so weak, and he was ashamed. But Cleo found him, grabbed him in her arms, and when he swayed on his feet, she held him steady. Infection oozed from the crusted blood on his brow, yet Cleo put her hand on his swollen face and whispered to him, "You'll be all right now."

With no warning, the white man's whip lashed into Cleo's back, cutting through her blouse and ripping the flesh. "Get away from there, gal," the man on the black mare said. No malice in his voice, just the assumption of obedience from a black slave.

Remy, though emaciated, his hands bound behind him, his ankles manacled, his neck circled by an iron collar attached to another man's collar with five feet of heavy chain— Remy drew himself up and blazed defiance.

"You, boy, what you looking at?" The slaver raised his arm to lash Remy with the whip, but Cleo hurled herself against the mare's side. The toe of the man's boot was in the stirrup and couldn't find Cleo's ribs, but he began to club her with the butt of the whip. The horse stepped back and Cleo hung on, absorbing the blows from the slaver.

Remy leapt, his only weapon his body as a ram against the flank of the horse. The black man chained to him fell to his knees and the man behind him staggered. The other slavers drove their horses into the chained men and women, wielding clubs and whips, the cursing and the cries commingling.

Remy pulled Cleo from her grip on the horse's mane and tried to shield her with his body.

LeBrec ran from the overseer's cabin, pistol in hand. Madame Emmeline intercepted him and took the pistol from him. No longer stoop shouldered, she stood erect and fired into the air.

The men and women jerked at the blast, a horse reared and neighed, and then it was over. Remy leaned over his knees, stunned from the blows the slaver had delivered. Cleo scrambled to her feet and helped to support him.

The plantation people nearby all came running when they heard the shot. Louella, her big bosom heaving as she ran, cried, "Wha's happ'ning? Who been shot?"

Madame Emmeline handed the gun back to LeBrec. "No one is shot. Bring water for these people." Then she turned her attention to the slaver on the black mare.

"I see you've found my boy, Mr. Hayes," she said.

"Yes'm. I reckon he's the one."

"Well, cut him loose. Monsieur LeBrec, you will put him out of this wind. The storehouse will do." She turned back to the patrol leader. "You may wait here until I return with the reward money."

The slaves, almost as one body, sat down. They were in the sun, and the cookhouse blocked some of the cold wind. Louella began ladling water for the poor souls who'd marched barefoot through icy mud puddles, their ankles and wrists bloodied from the manacles.

"Thibault," Louella said, "go get dem other ladles from de quarters. We needs to get some water in dese folks."

One of the white men unlocked the chains from Remy's throat, hands, and feet. He shoved him hard against Cleo, and both of them went down. The slaver laughed and idly kicked at Remy's bloody leg.

Remy struggled to his feet and extended a hand to Cleo to help her up. Then LeBrec roughly moved Cleo aside and pushed Remy toward the storehouse.

"M'sieu, you gon' let me give dis boy some water first?" Louella said.

"He's got plenty of sass in him without no water. Move on, boy," LeBrec said.

Madame Emmeline handed an envelope up to the slaver on the black mare, who hadn't the courtesy to dismount.

"I'd keep an eye on that one, Madame Tassin," he said. "He's a tough one. Don't got no respect for whip nor cane, neither one."

"I'm sure we know what to do with our own people, Mr. Hayes. Good day to you."

Hayes touched his hand to his hat, then flicked his whip over the heads of the seated slaves to get them on the move again.

"Madame," Cleo began. Her knees barely held her, she was so afraid for Remy. "Madame, you won't let Monsieur LeBrec . . ."

Remy heard her, and he turned back. He couldn't bear to see her beg for him. His voice hardly carried across the yard. "Don't, Cleo."

Madame Emmeline looked coldly at Remy. "Go to the house," she told Cleo.

LeBrec shoved him toward the storehouse, and Remy shuffled on, his gait awkward from the miles he'd walked in chains. *Why don' I run?* he thought. *I could take dat pistol 'way from him, knock him out, and be in de swamp 'fo dey call de slavers back.*

Remy swayed, feverish and dizzy. He was too weak. Beaten and starved as he was, he'd die before the day was out if he ran now.

Remy stepped into the dark storeroom. It was cold, but dry, and it smelled sweet from the grain sent by generous neighbors after the flood. When LeBrec put a hand in the middle of his back and shoved him toward the corner, Remy lost his balance and fell on the hard floor.

For light, LeBrec opened the six-inch window slit next to the door. When Remy rolled over to face the overseer, LeBrec stood above him with a knife in his hand. The sunlight glinted on it, but Remy barely saw it flash before LeBrec was on him.

The blade slashed into the gristle of his ear. Remy screamed, and then fainted.

Moments later, Remy roused, alone in the room, and Cleo was pounding on the locked door. "Remy," she shouted.

He put a hand to the bloody stump of his ear and nearly passed out again. Through the door, he heard LeBrec say, "Don't cross me, gal."

"Remy!" Cleo screamed. Remy knew what an overseer could do to a slave girl; LeBrec was out there with Cleo, and Remy was on the wrong side of the door.

"Cleo, I's all right," Remy called though the tiny window. "Go on 'way from here. Go on, 'fo you in trouble."

"This the one you sweet on, is it?" LeBrec growled.

Remy felt the impact as Cleo's back slammed against the wall. He pushed his face against the window slit to see LeBrec's tobacco-stained teeth grinning at Cleo.

"I guess you know how to keep him from the axe, don't you?" LeBrec said.

"Cleo, *non*. You don have to do dat. *Non*, Cleo."

Remy could smell LeBrec's stink, like mule piss steaming in the cold. He pounded his fist against the inside wall of the storehouse. "I kill you, LeBrec," Remy yelled as the overseer mashed his reeking mouth against Cleo's.

"Monsieur LeBrec."

LeBrec whirled around, and for a moment stood witless. Madame Emmeline's face was stiff, her black eyes hard. Then he tried to explain.

"This black gal trying to get in to the runaway. She don't hear 'no' lessen it's said with a couple of knocks."

Madame looked at Cleo. "I told you. In the house," she said.

Louella came up behind Madame carrying a pail of water and some cloths. Madame said, "I should like to tend to the boy, now, Monsieur LeBrec. Open the door and leave me the key. You may return to your work."

LeBrec surrendered the key and slunk off. Remy watched Cleo all the way to the gallery steps, the bloody blouse stuck to her back. Then Madame was inside with him and insisting he lie down against a rice sack.

Madame herself washed the wound where LeBrec had cut away half of Remy's ear. She stanched the flow with a medicinal paste she had concocted after years of trial and error. He remembered when he was a child, his maman had been so worried about the pain in his ear that she'd sent for Madame Emmeline. Then Madame had poured warm sweet oil in his ear, and he had been able to sleep at last. Now he closed his eyes and let her do what she would with his wounds.

In the big house, Cleo peeled the shirt from her back and peered over her shoulder in Josie's mirror. The gash was six inches long and deep, just between her shoulder blades. There would be a scar. The mark of slavery.

Cleo's hands trembled as she tried to wash the wound. When Louella came in with a basin and clean cloths, Cleo lay down on the floor and let Louella take over. Cleo clenched her fists at the vinegar wash, but the paste Louella applied soothed her.

"You don' be lifting not'ing, Cleo, chile. Dis here open up and spread, you be pulling at it. I bring in de dinner. You stay flat like dis."

"Louella, what's going to happen to Remy?"

"Law, chile, I not de one to know dat. Maybe dat LeBrec, he be happy wit cutting Remy's ear. Maybe dat be enough."

Cleo stayed in the bedroom while the moving shadows marked the passage of the day. *If only Josie were here,* Cleo thought for the hundredth time. Josie would save Remy from the axe on his foot. Josie would protect him, Cleo was sure of it.

Thibault crept in and lay down next to Cleo. She held his hand, and they were silent.

Late in the afternoon, Cleo heard LeBrec's heavy boots on the gallery stairs. Thibault had fallen asleep. She should go to the door to let LeBrec in, but she lay where she was.

Madame herself admitted the overseer and led him in to the office. Cleo eased herself from under Thibault's arm. The motion pulled at her wound and she gritted her teeth as she rose from the floor. She padded on bare feet to the office door and put her ear at the keyhole.

Madame was not happy with LeBrec. He had not only marked her property, he had risked the life of her slave with the additional wound to his ear in his weakened state. In the future, LeBrec was to consult with her before any punishment out of the ordinary was administered.

Cleo breathed easier. Madame would not allow Remy's foot to be maimed. That would further decrease his value, yes, but Cleo wanted to believe that Madame cared for her slave as well as for her purse.

"We got to do something to show the other slaves what happens to them if they run, ma'am," LeBrec said. "You know how one gets away with it, there'll be others try it."

"Yes. I am aware of the need for punishment. However, there will be no more maiming. And a slave beaten half to death at the whipping post is of no use in the fields. Devise a punishment that does not damage my property, Monsieur LeBrec."

Cleo put her eye to the keyhole. LeBrec had not been invited to sit down. He turned the hat in his hands nervously.

"I know what to do. Yes, ma'am."

"Then you may go about your business, monsieur."

Cleo hurried back to the bedroom and peeked from behind the drapes as LeBrec swaggered through the courtyard toward the smithy.

After dark, she slipped down the back stairs. She could take Remy some extra food left from Madame's table and talk to him, touch him through the little window.

At the stand of crepe myrtles, their bare limbs smooth as flesh, Cleo stopped to scan the grounds between her and the storehouse. As she was about to cross the yard, lantern light shone from around the corner of the building. LeBrec walked into view, carrying a shotgun, a hound at his heels.

He checked the lock on the storehouse door, shone the light through the slitted window, and seemed satisfied. For a moment he stood still and looked Cleo's way. He held the lantern high, but she was part of the tangle of shadows. If only the hound showed no interest in her, she would be safe.

LeBrec scratched his groin and spat on the ground. Then he headed back to his own house. Cleo watched him step onto his porch, extinguish the lantern, and hang it on a hook before he went inside. The hound crawled under the porch to make its bed.

Cleo scurried across the yard. "Remy," she whispered at the window. "Remy, are you awake?"

He put his hands through the little window, and Cleo grabbed them in both of hers. She kissed every finger, and he cupped her face.

"Cleo, you hurt bad?"

"It's just a welt. Don't worry about me." She pulled a napkin out of her pocket. "I brought you a chicken leg, Remy. I know you're hungry."

"I think I gon' be hungry de rest of my life." He took the chicken leg and ate it in three bites, gulping it down.

"Louella gave me this for you, too. She said drink it all at once and your ear won't pain you in the night."

"Dat be a blessing."

"How far did you get, Remy? Before they caught you."

"I hardly knows. Peoples was still blacks and whites, everywhere I seen. I don' reckon I make it as far as de North, but I musta been close."

"Madame told LeBrec no more cutting. He won't be marking you again, Remy."

Remy was quiet a moment. "A man like dat. He have other ways. It ain't over yet. But I take it. I ain't quitting."

"What do you mean? You aren't going to run again?"

"*Chérie*, I tole you. I goin' to be a free man. When I get my strength, I goin'."

Cleo held his hand tight. "Remy," she said.

"It fo us, Cleo. You know dat. We goin to have free chilrun."

She put her face to the little window and kissed his lips.

"You have to be strong, first, Remy. You have to eat, and you have to stay out of that man's way."

"You, Cleo. You stay out of dat man's way. You hear me?"

"I hear you, Remy."

"You go on in, Cleo. My legs say I got to set down, and I don' like you out here in de dark."

First thing the next morning, the blacksmith's boy fired up the box and manned the bellows. All through the morning and early afternoon, the smithy hammered and shaped and welded until he had executed the design LeBrec had given him. Before supper, he attached the final pieces, four bells, and sent the boy to tell LeBrec it was ready.

The overseer gathered every man, woman, and child in the quarters to witness Remy's humiliation. Dark came early this time of year, and he hurried them into the lane before dusk. Old Sam and his son were sent to bring Remy to the circle the people made among the cabins.

LeBrec forced Remy to his knees. "This is what we do to runaways on Toulouse," he announced.

He hoisted the heavy iron device the smith had made and

held it so everyone could see it. He gave it a shake so the bells would ring, and he laughed. Then he opened the hinged ring around the base and placed the device over Remy's head. The collar bit into his shoulders. Curved iron slats rose around his head to join at the top so that Remy's head was encased in an elongated basket, the bells suspended from the highest point.

"Now try to run with that on, nigger," LeBrec said. Remy didn't move. "Get up, I said, and let's see you try to run now."

He kicked Remy's leg, and Remy tried to stand. Old Sam and his son helped him lift himself and the weight of the basket. The device tilted forward, Remy swayed, and the bells rang. He reached his hands up to steady the iron casement and found his balance.

"Run, damn you," LeBrec demanded.

Remy staggered, then began to shuffle around the circle. The bells jangled with every step, and the weight of the cage dug into Remy's collarbones. He registered the presence of friends and relations—Old Sam's face was stony, Tante Liza wept, cousin Jean gazed on him with pity and fear—and then Remy looked only at the ground.

Remy's vision blurred as he pushed himself to jog round and round. He felt the weight of the iron on his shoulders all the way through his knees and feet. Worst of all, the bells mocked his pain, ringing and ringing and ringing.

Exhausted, Remy sagged to his knees, the bells still at last, but LeBrec yelled at him to get up, to run. Remy struggled to rise, the bells once again clanging, but he collapsed on the ground, panting, his shoulders raw where the iron collar rubbed him.

Satisfied, LeBrec spat into the dirt, turned his back on the people, and left them staring at Remy.

Old Sam and two others helped Remy up. They took him to his old place in the bachelors' cabin and put him in the

bed, the bells ringing with every movement. They folded up
an old quilt to try to cushion his head inside the iron cage,
and told him to try to sleep.

Remy listened to the night noises—a child crying before
it slept, men talking on a porch nearby, wind blowing
through the leaves of the live oaks. As long as Remy didn't
try to turn over, didn't move, the bells were silent.

I thanks de Lord Cleo wadn't in dat circle, he thought.
*When I sees her, I gon' stand straight. I show her dis cage ain't
nothing. I show her I a man.*

Chapter 19

New Orleans

New Year's Day, clouds from the Gulf of Mexico covered New Orleans. A cold, damp wind blew up the river, and the fireplace's warmth radiated only a few feet into the parlor. This had been a hard week for Josie, her first Christmas and New Year's without Maman and Papa. Tante Marguerite welcomed Josie into her family, but of course it wasn't the same. When Oncle Sandrine sang noels with the children at the piano, she remembered her papa's baritone, and it was as if she had lost him all over again.

In the parlor, the yellow glow from candles and fireplace countered the gray light coming through the windows; the relentless ticking of the clock on the mantel pushed the afternoon along. When would Abigail arrive?

When the doorbell rang, Josie rushed to the upper hallway and leaned over the balustrade ready with a cheery hello. Albany Johnston, handing his hat to the manservant, looked up in time to catch the last of Josie's dying smile. He had come alone.

"Is Abigail ill?" Josie called down.

Albany shook his head. "She's well." He began to climb the stairs to the sitting room, and Josie had an odd sense of trouble on its way.

Albany followed her into the parlor, the manservant behind him. "Please tell my aunt Mr. Johnston is here," Josie said. The servant left the parlor door ajar in spite of the draft, aware of the delicacy of a single young woman's position in the company of a gentleman.

Albany stood awkwardly in the center of the room until Josie said, "It's dreadfully cold today, isn't it?" She gestured to the chair nearest the fire.

"No, please," Albany said, and insisted Josie take the warmer chair.

"Abigail is well, then?" Josie began.

"Quite well. The fact is, Josephine, I asked her to permit me this visit alone. I've wanted to discuss something with you for some time, and today seemed—"

Tante Marguerite bustled in. "Mr. Johnston, how nice to see you." She held out her hand and Albany stood to greet her.

"You see I have taken your husband's encouragement to heart," he said.

Fully alerted now, Josie's unease grew. Surely Albany couldn't . . . She'd never led him to think . . .

"Oh," Marguerite said. She glanced at Josie. "Well. I'll just see to the tea, shall I?" She bustled out and closed the door behind her.

Albany ran a hand through his thinning hair and sat down again.

"Josephine," he began. "I've spoken to your uncle. Of course I will write to your grandmother." He stopped and looked at her. Josie gave him no help at all.

"I know you're young, Josephine. Too young, really, to become a wife. Not this year, anyway. At least I think you're too young. I know the Creoles marry younger than we Americans do, but . . ." He seemed to realize he was babbling and took a breath before he began again. "When you're older—twenty, I think, is ideal—then I will build you your own home on the plantation, and we can start our family."

Josie didn't move. This was awful. How could he think she wanted to marry him? She'd never, ever—

"There's a boom on, Josephine, and we're going to be very rich, the way cane sugar is in demand around the world. Naturally I will relieve you of the burden of running Toulouse. It will be no trouble, being so near, and the two plantations together will become a powerhouse in Louisiana."

Ah, Josie thought in a rush of resentment. No wonder he and Grand-mère had spent so many hours together in the summer. They were two of a kind. "So this is a business proposition?"

"Well . . ." Albany exhaled. "I assure you I will shepherd your fortune as vigilantly as my own. To that extent, business must be attended to. Of course, you will still have your **home at** Toulouse, but I will build you a bigger place, with the latest innovations. You can furnish it as you please." Albany stood abruptly and began to pace. "You'll have Abigail right next door to you, at least until she marries. My parents will be a mother and a father to you."

Josie seethed. An unwanted proposal was bad enough, but that he should turn it into an economic transaction, as if she were no more than an extension of her plantation . . . There was an edge to her voice when she said, "If it's a business partnership you're interested in, Mr. Johnston, I'm sure we can arrange that without marriage."

He looked at her bleakly. How had this gone so wrong? "Josephine, I assure you, I did not mean to imply this was a monetary proposal. My dear Josephine, surely you must know how I feel about you."

Before she could think, she spouted, "Feel? I have not discerned any great feeling on either of our parts."

Albany's stricken face showed she'd hurt him. He turned his back to her and, with one arm braced against the mantel, gazed into the fire.

Oh dear Mother Mary, I didn't realize. Had she been so absorbed in her own sentiments, she'd failed to perceive Albany's? All those afternoons he'd chaperoned her and Abigail, she'd thought he was simply dutiful. She'd been willfully, foolishly blind.

Josie softened her tone. "It's just that . . ." He wouldn't look at her. She really had been unforgivably selfish not to have seen. With genuine contrition, she said, "You do me a great honor, and I do thank you humbly for it."

"But?" he said, his eyes on the flames.

"I'm sorry, Albany. I don't want to marry you."

Albany looked at her over his shoulder. In a husky voice, he said, "And why is that, Josephine?"

Her temper flared again and overcame her moment of conscience. He had no business to press her. What could she tell him? That she did not desire him, did not want to ever kiss him or have children with him? That he was more boring than needlework, more fleshy than Louella's prize pig, that he seldom joked and had no wit whatsoever? She struggled with herself. As infuriating as this conversation was, Albany deserved a civil answer.

"Because, Albany, I don't love you." There. That was as kindly put as she knew how to say it.

Somehow, her assertion only animated him once again. Albany stepped away from the fireplace eagerly. "But, Josephine, it's only natural at your age that you know nothing of love. It shows you come from a good family who has protected you," he said. "Love will come in time, and I can wait."

"Albany, I know my own mind." She spoke sharply, and Albany drew back as if she'd slapped him.

She put a hand to her forehead. She wasn't handling this any better than he was. "Forgive me. I value our friendship, truly, Albany. But I do not wish to marry you."

He walked to the window and looked out at the leaves blowing in the street. "I see I have spoken too soon, Josephine," he said at last, his face turned from her. "You have so recently lost your parents, have no father to guide you. When you have consulted with your grandmother and your Oncle Sandrine, I hope you will in time reconsider."

No, Josie thought. *I do know what love is—and desire—and I will not live my life without it.* "Perhaps you mistake my youth for being of weak mind," she snapped, "but I assure you—"

The parlor door opened and Tante Marguerite breezed into the room. "I've brought us a pot of chocolate," she said. "I know, I know, I'm interrupting, but I have already allowed you two more time alone than the gossips would approve." She set the silver tray on a side table and began to pour. "We'll have our chocolate to celebrate until your uncle comes in. Then we'll open a bottle of champagne!"

The rustle of her taffeta skirts had at first filled the silence, but now Marguerite felt the tension in the room. The very air between Josie and Albany seemed weighed down with it. She looked from one flushed face to the other. "Oh dear," she murmured.

"Excuse me, madame," Albany said. "I must take my leave." Stiffly, he kissed Josie's hand with his heavy moist lips. "*Adieu,*" he said to both ladies and, without further pleasantries, departed.

As soon as Josie heard the downstairs door close, she

turned on her heel to leave the room, but her aunt would not allow it. "Josephine, what does this mean?"

Josie stood with her chin set. "I have declined Mr. Johnston's proposal."

With her eyes on Josie, Tante Marguerite sat down heavily. "What on earth? Why would you do such a thing?"

"I don't wish to marry him."

"Oh, for heaven's sake, Josephine, you're not going to tell me you don't love him," Marguerite said with a dismissive wave. "Even at your age, you must know these notions of romance are nonsense. Marriage is not about love and kisses and poetry in the moonlight."

"But it should be," Josie retorted. Yes, marriage was a contract, but there must be room for love. She would have a man who roused her passions, a man like—she dared to say it to herself—like Bertrand Chamard.

"Listen to me," her aunt said. "Albany Johnston is nice to look at. He has fine manners, a nice family, a good fortune. And"—here she insisted Josie heed her—"Josephine, he is willing to overlook the losses Toulouse has incurred this past year. It will be no quick or certain matter to make Toulouse profitable again."

Oh yes, money. This is the answer Josie would have expected from Grand-mère, but Tante Marguerite? Josie didn't even try to keep the anger from her voice. "My grand-mère will bring Toulouse into full production as well as any man can. I won't be held hostage to fields of cane and corn."

Josie rushed from the parlor and up the stairs to her room. She paced, muttering and fuming that her aunt and uncle, and no doubt her grandmother too, would expect her to marry a man just for his wealth. Heartless, that's what they were.

Late that night, Josie wrote pages and pages about why she didn't want Albany Johnston. In the privacy of the diary, she noted his fleshy chin and neck, how his hair was so thin and light that in the wind you could see his pink scalp. No doubt he was a fine man, kind and decent. And yes, he would provide a house as grand as Mrs. Johnston's, and Josie could be as idle and useless as she was too. But she didn't want him. It was that simple.

What Josie wanted was breathlessness, arousal, fire.

Two men stirred her, Phanor DeBlieux and Bertrand Chamard. She'd covered page after page about each of them, but rereading her account of Phanor playing his fiddle for those poor people in the park shamed her. Sheltered on Toulouse, she'd not fully realized how her station was so far above Phanor's, but her first weeks in New Orleans had brought home to her the difference in her life and a poor Cajun's. She'd written, "They were awful. Dirty, smelly, unrefined, unwashed, uncouth beings. And Phanor so at ease among them. How could I ever have thought of being with him?"

But the initial dazzle of the sophisticated Creole social whirl faded, and more recently Josie had come to see that as rigid as society was, not all of its strictures were just. She was ashamed she'd been such a snob. Phanor was a poor Cajun, it was true, but he was a man of ambition and energy.

And whether it was acceptable or not, Josie felt Phanor's pull. What a fool she'd been to deprive herself of his company that day in the square. His black eyes and ready smile, the way his shoulders tapered to narrow hips came to her mind's eye. And of course his humor, his talent . . . his *élan*. Regardless of their different spheres, she felt connected to him, and yes, she admitted, she wanted him.

And what was she to do about that? Even now, with Phanor's allure freshly recalled, she knew the convention she scorned could not be ignored. No, she would not allow anyone to force her into a marriage she did not want; however, her family would certainly prevent her from marrying a man of Phanor's station. *There is no future for me with Phanor, a poor man, and a Cajun at that. No, Phanor is true of heart, and I hope a friend forever, but we will never be more than friends.*

It's Bertrand whom I'm meant to be with. Sophisticated, worldly, mature Bertrand.

Sorting through these conflicting, confusing feelings put Josie's mind more at ease. She blew out the candle and lay back on her pillows. Poor Albany, but in truth she could not blame herself. She had not encouraged him, indeed she had not.

Her mind drifted and she imagined herself at a grand ball. She's in a green satin gown that shows off her eyes. The door opens, Bertrand steps in. The women in the room take note of his figure behind their fans and watch him as he crosses the room to Mademoiselle Josephine Tassin.

She and Bertrand speak only with their eyes. He takes her arm, leads her to the dance floor. The band is playing the new waltz. Bertrand places his hand on her waist, she rests hers on his shoulder. He guides her in sensual circles around the dance floor.

My skirt will swirl, touching his legs and then mine. His eyes will never leave my face, and even when the music stops, we'll waltz on and on.

But, she recalled, the last time she'd seen him, he'd made her feel like a child. *That will not happen again. Next time, his eyes will not roam the room gazing at other women.*

She knew now she was a woman, woman enough to have had a marriage proposal, and she intended Bertrand Chamard should succumb to her charms as she had to his.

Chapter 20

Cherleu

The Cherleu plantation had been badly run the last dozen years. The old man had lost the will and the strength to keep it up. That made it a good buy for someone willing to put in the work to bring it back to full production. Bertrand put aside his tailored shirts, donned coarse trousers and rough boots, and strode into the fields.

The soil was black and loamy, and the new overlay of silt from the flood increased the depth of topsoil in the northern half of the plantation. The experienced man Bertrand hired to oversee the slaves and advise him about cane taught him to taste the dirt as they moved to different parts of the plantation. This, the overseer explained, is the ground your cane will love best. And that is where they planted the first shoots.

Too much good food and wine in New Orleans had left Bertrand feeling slow and restless. Now he relished his muscles straining to handle the hundred-pound bags of cane

stalks the slaves would chop into sections for planting. He
lent a hand in burning out a stump and in disentangling an
ox from a briar patch. He harnessed the mules to pull the
wagons from the delivery dock on the river, and learned the
name and gauged the stamina of each of his slaves.

At the end of the day, he returned to the big house dirty
and tired and happy. He washed in the basin, not overly concerned if his nails were still black when he went to bed. His
house slave Cora, an older woman, had been brought to
Louisiana directly from the west coast of Africa as a young
girl. Toothless and wrinkled as she was, she'd been a bargain
at seventy-five dollars when he stocked his new plantation
from the slave market. She worked as hard as she was able,
and she cooked Bertrand's meals and washed the mud from
his clothes with good cheer.

Cora was a talker, chatting at him as he ate his supper or
talking full-voiced to herself if he was in another room of the
old mansion. He could have told her to hush, but he didn't.
The house was empty and silent but for the two of them, and
gradually, he learned to decipher her thick and broken speech.

"Misshie got ting aday," Cora said.

"Thing? What kind of thing?" Bertrand said.

"Ting folded up. Ink on it. I get it fo you."

She came back into the dining room where Bertrand ate
his solitary dinner at the stained mahogany table. The Cherleu
daughter had taken all her china and linens when her papa
sold him the place, and Bertrand ate on the same wooden
platters as the slaves did.

"Here tis," Cora said. "See, it got ink."

"A letter, Cora. That's called a letter."

"I know dat's a letter, Misshie."

Bertrand tore the heavy paper open to read an invitation
from Madame Emmeline Tassin of Toulouse. Would he care
to dine with her on Thursday? Nothing formal, just the two
of them, neighbors now with their cane fields abutting.

"Tomorrow you can take an answer back to Toulouse. Do you think you can do that? Can you find it?"

"Yes, Misshie, I do dat. I do dat in de mawnin after yo eats, and be back to cook yo dinner 'fo noon. I likes de walkin and I likes seeing de river move on along 'side me. I do dat, shore."

On Thursday, Bertrand rode his stallion down to Toulouse. He was dressed once again in fine linen and wool, and though his velvet collar was in need of pressing, he was a handsome figure. He expected Josie's favorite—was her name Cleo?— to open the door when he arrived. The girl had been solemn and rather unresponsive the day he'd brought Josie back from the Johnstons, but then she'd just lost her people in the flood. Her big almond-shaped eyes, the curve of her long neck, the smooth, creamy brown skin—she was a striking girl.

Instead, it was Madame's little favorite who opened the door to him. Laurie took his hat very properly and asked him to sit in the parlor while she fetched her mistress. Bertrand idly examined the stereoscope on the table until Madame entered, then he stood and bent over her hand. "Madame Emmeline," he said.

"Bertrand, I'm so happy you could come."

Emmeline rang a silver bell before she sat down. They would enjoy a glass of sherry before dinner.

Bertrand was discussing the Louisiana winter, so much warmer but damper than Paris, when Cleo brought in a tray with the sherry decanter and two crystal glasses. He eyed her absently as she poured the wine, taking in the well-made dress she wore, the leather shoes. No doubt hand-me-downs from Josephine, he thought.

The evening passed pleasantly. Madame Emmeline and Bertrand had so much in common, working the slaves, planting the crops, caring for the land itself. Emmeline freely shared her knowledge and experience, and he was impressed with her business sense.

Cleo waited table mutely and efficiently, giving Bertrand ample time to observe her. The faded dress did Cleo's figure justice, he thought, cinched in at the waist, swelling tightly over her bosom. She seemed different somehow, less girlish. No doubt she'd taken a lover by now and was a woman. It became her.

When Bertrand spoke of having seen Josie in town, Cleo stood behind Madame Emmeline and openly listened. He felt the power of her deep eyes on him, and smiled inwardly at himself to be so distracted by this girl.

In the following days, Bertrand and Madame Emmeline fell into the habit of dining together at one o'clock twice a week. He admired her shrewd intellect and listened attentively to all her advice. She even knew how much water the hive-shaped cisterns held and how long the water in it could be expected to last in the dry season. He learned from her mistake in trusting too much to her overseer, resulting in the breached levee and all the devastation from the flood.

"You must ride out on the property yourself, Bertrand," she told him. "That was my mistake, staying too much in this house instead of seeing the plantation for myself."

Bertrand continued to labor on his land, his afternoons with Madame Emmeline his only concession to the life of a gentleman. By the end of January, the cane cuttings had all been planted and they needed only to be left alone to sprout when the ground began to warm. Bertrand pulled his slaves from the fields and put them to work on the outbuildings. They tore down the old smithy and built a new one, repaired the brick cisterns, built a dovecote and new chicken coops, and then made their own cabins more habitable.

On the first Sunday morning in February, Bertrand sat at his desk figuring costs and assets, pleased with the way the plantation was beginning to function. Cora shuffled into the room, her hands already talking before she spoke.

"Misshie, Misshie, der a man comin up to de do'! I seen him slide off a horse dat big, and he comin in here."

"Cora, you can manage this. Simply open the door and ask him in. Then take his hat for him and let him sit in the parlor."

"Sure, I do dat. I let him in." She shuffled as quickly as she could back to the front door.

Bertrand ran a comb through his overlong hair and tied it back with a leather string. He congratulated himself that at least his hands were clean and checked that his shirt was fresh. It would have to do.

He heard Cora admitting the visitor two rooms away and took the time to button his collar. Then he proceeded to see who had come to call.

"Albany, my friend!" Bertrand held his hand out as he crossed the room, remembering how uncomfortable Americans were with the Creole habit of kissing cheeks. Albany met him halfway to shake hands with enthusiasm.

"Cora, light us a fire," Bertrand said. "Sit down, Albany. Mind the furniture, though. What's left in here threatens to give way under me every time I sit down."

Albany laughed and lowered himself carefully onto the ancient settee, which creaked a little as it accepted his weight.

"You'll find the rest of the house is much the same," Bertrand explained. "The whole place needs painting and updating, but the prettifying can wait until I've a crop in the field and promise of some return on the initial investment."

"I understand completely. Indeed, you do look the part of the old-time planter, Bertrand, just as Madame Emmeline has told me you would. I've just come from Toulouse, in fact."

"And then back to New Orleans?"

"Yes. I've taken care of business on this end for Father, and later today I hope to catch the steamboat from your dock. Will it stop here, do you think?"

"Certainly. I'll have the flag put out for you."

The two men spent the morning riding over the plantation, discussing the merits of giving slaves an extra half day off on Saturdays, the advantages of allowing the slaves to go to church on Sundays, the expectation of losses during yellow fever season. They returned to the house for a late dinner.

Cora, who'd been trained as a cook for field hands, had scrubbed the polish off the old mahogany table till it was as smooth and dull as the table in the cookhouse. She served up collard greens and pork chops, stewed apples and sweet potatoes to the men, chatting all the while about how good her collards and turnip greens were because she picked them first thing in the morning.

Bertrand smiled and shrugged a shoulder when Albany caught his eye. He imagined his friend must think him hopelessly lax, but that was all right. Bertrand liked old Cora just as she was, and someday, when he had a wife and a table to impress people, he'd bring Valentine in from the stables, and Cora could put her feet up in the cookhouse and relax. Meantime, she'd do fine, and his longtime valet was of more use tending the horses and mules. Valentine made no secret that he preferred running a household to a stable, but it was only for a year or two.

Over their cigars, Bertrand said, "So you've been to Toulouse. I'd say Madame Emmeline must be one of the best planters on the river. This new overseer she has, LeBrec's his name, has nearly got the fields in order and they have most of the cane planted. She'll soon have Toulouse making a profit again. A flood won't stop that lady."

"Yes, it's a good property. I hear in the city, though, that Madame Tassin has had to mortgage it. Too many expenses in rebuilding for out-of-pocket resources. But even under debt as it is, I'd be interested in adding it to my own. I've been to speak to Madame Tassin about her granddaughter."

"Have you?" Bertrand narrowed his eyes at Albany through his cigar smoke.

"With disappointing results, I'm sorry to say, with Madame and Mademoiselle." Albany relit his cigar. "But I'm a patient man. I can wait. In fact, if Madame Tassin has her way, I may wait quite some time."

"Holding you off, is she?"

"She expects Josephine to succeed her in running Toulouse. There's really no one else, now, and she intends that Josephine be thoroughly capable of running the plantation. I gather Madame Tassin has had her disappointments depending on the men of the family, and she will have Josephine an independent woman."

Bertrand held up his hands in mock horror. "Lord spare me from an independent woman."

Albany laughed. He tapped the ash from his cigar, and then confided, "And of course, I am not Creole."

Bertrand smiled. He knew exactly what that meant. Doing business with Americans was one thing, but accepting them into the family was another.

Late in the afternoon the river channeled cold damp air over the Cherleu dock. Bertrand and Albany pulled their collars up around their necks while they watched the steamboat close the gap. As the boatmen shuttled the ramp out for Albany to board, the two friends shook hands.

"I'll see you in town, then," Albany said.

"Yes, in a few weeks. Give my regards to Cousin Josephine."

Bertrand watched the huge red paddle wheel churn the muddy water, waved to Albany, and then headed back to the house. Cora had promised him a supper of beans and rice with red peppers and onions on top.

A cold drizzle set in and Bertrand hoped heavy rain would hold off a few more days until he could get the roof patched. The big house was in worse shape than some of the cabins in the quarters, but there were at least a couple of habitable rooms, and those two, his and Cora's, had working fireplaces, so he'd held off with repairs until the cane was in the ground. Tomorrow he would get a few men up there to replace the rotten struts and missing shingles.

On Thursday, as usual, Bertrand cleaned himself up to spend the afternoon with Madame Emmeline. Her grief over Emile's death seemed to have run its course, though Bertrand understood the depths of her heart would not be apparent. At any rate, he'd come to look forward to her company. He heeded her counsel on curing the slaves' bodily complaints, rationing their victuals during the winter, and balancing discipline with kindly treatment. What he hadn't expected was that when they tired of talking business, Emmeline proved to be witty and charming. She read widely and kept up with the news from New Orleans, and even from Paris. They often laughed over foolishness they'd read about in the New Orleans papers and speculated about what the scoundrels in Washington would do next.

As Bertrand rode through the wintry late morning on the way to Toulouse, his mind was not on running his plantation nor on Madame Emmeline. He anticipated seeing the lustrous brown eyes of Emmeline's girl Cleo. He no longer associated her with Josephine. Now, somehow, she seemed to be at Toulouse just for him. She always met him at the door to take his hat and coat, to ask him if he'd like a sherry while he waited for Madame. She poured his wine and served his dinner to him. And all the while she openly listened to the conversation. Her intelligence wasn't hidden by the prescribed calico *tignon* on her head nor by a slave's usual lowered eyes. In fact, he often caught the curve of her lips or the sparkle in her eye when he made some jest with Emmeline.

When Bertrand dismounted at Toulouse, he handed the reins to Elbow John, who this time was accompanied by the little simpleton who looked so much like Cleo. Bertrand had concluded they must be siblings.

"*Bonjour,* m'sieu."

"*Bonjour,* John. Tell me again what this fine fellow's name is."

"Dis here is Thibault."

Thibault's wide grin charmed Bertrand. "Think you can take care of my horse, Thibault?"

"I do a good job, m'sieu. I love dis horse."

"That's fine, then," Bertrand said.

He mounted the stairs and before he knocked, Cleo opened the door to him. "*Bonjour*, monsieur," she said and held her hand out for his hat.

"*Bonjour*, Cleo." He touched her hand and watched her face. Was she an innocent who would be surprised at his deliberate touch, or had she understood his gaze on her these last weeks?

Cleo raised her head and looked directly into Bertrand's face.

Perhaps he'd hoped for blushes or parted lips, but what he saw in her eyes was acknowledgment, nothing more. No smoldering welcome of his attention, no quickening of her desire. No ignorance of his own, either. She returned his smile with simple, but firm, friendliness. She was no easy target, this Cleo.

Emmeline welcomed him in the parlor and they had a glass of sherry while Cleo finished arranging the table. When Cleo stood in the doorway to the parlor to indicate dinner was ready, Emmeline raised herself from the velvet chair and Bertrand offered his arm. They seated themselves near one another at the big table, and Cleo served the turtle soup.

This was their first meeting since Albany Johnston had been to Toulouse. When they finished their meal and were sitting in the parlor again, Emmeline raised the subject of the American's visit.

"The Johnstons appear to have settled into river life. I understand you know them well?"

"Yes, I do. I met Mr. Johnston in New York when I returned from Paris, and we found ourselves both Louisianans. His son Albany showed me around and introduced me to his friends at the Atheneum Club."

"And do you approve of this Albany? As a man, I mean?"

"Oh, indeed. He's a straight shooter. A little proper, sometimes, but a dependable, honest fellow. You might not expect it, but a good man in a poker game."

"He's asked to marry Josephine. Did he tell you?"

Bertrand nodded. He touched the cigar in his pocket, but didn't take it out.

"I've had a letter from Josephine," Emmeline went on. "She says she does not wish to marry Mr. Johnston. I'm inclined to agree, for the time being."

"You mean for her to take over the plantation before she marries?"

Emmeline gazed at him. "Not necessarily."

Bertrand's hand was on his pocket again without his realizing it. He brushed a fleck off his jacket as if that had been his intention.

"Oh, for heaven's sake, Bertrand, smoke your cigar."

He grinned at her and pulled a Havana from his pocket. "Thank you, Emmeline. I am in your debt."

As Bertrand clipped the end off the cigar and prepared to light it, Emmeline said, "I've been thinking about Josephine and this place since Albany Johnston was here. I do want her to be able to run Toulouse if she needs to. The Lord knows not every husband, nor every son, is an able manager."

Bertrand drew on the cigar and the tip flamed red. He sighed in deep contentment. "I can understand that. But I think I can assure you Albany is a competent businessman. He and his father are already looking for additional acreage."

"I would not have him marry Josephine just for her land."

"Of course not. I didn't mean to imply that. Back in the

summer at the Johnstons, when Josie and I were both guests, Albany seemed quite taken with her."

"And how about you? Are you taken with her?'

Bertrand looked at her through his smoke. "What are you getting at, Emmeline?"

"If you were interested in Josephine, I would find it a desirable match. Your family is Creole and well known to me. I believe I understand you. So I ask, are you taken with my granddaughter?"

Bertrand stared at the low fire burning yellow and orange across the room. "I find her very appealing. But I had thought of her as hardly more than a child, lovely as she is."

"Josie will be nineteen next August. Two months before Cleo," Emmeline said.

Bertrand glanced at her, and she held his eyes. She didn't miss much, he thought. He looked back at the fire and smoked his cigar.

"There's plenty of time," Emmeline said. "Josephine will come home in May. There will be long summer days for getting better acquainted."

Chapter 21

Toulouse

From the bedroom window, Cleo watched the overseer's house go dark. Then she waited. Sometimes LeBrec slipped out of the house to prowl the grounds. She knew what would happen to her if he caught her alone in the dark.

She made her mind go blank as she waited. There was no moon and only a dusting of stars across the sky. Cleo focused on the outline of the big bell hung next to the overseer's house so as to see LeBrec's door more clearly from the corner of her eyes. Half an hour, and she couldn't bear the waiting any longer.

Cleo picked up her bundle, closed the door of the house silently behind her, and crept down the stairs. She shivered and pulled her shawl tighter, glad for the shoes on her feet as she trod the wet grass, finding her way by the faint gleam of the oyster gravel path.

At Remy's cabin she pushed the unlatched door open.

Old Sam and two of his grandsons slept in here too; Cleo felt her way to the cot nearest the door.

"Cleo?" Remy whispered. He shifted and the bells of his cage tinkled.

"It's me," she said.

Remy turned himself a little, the bells signaling the shift. His cabin mates were inured to the sounds by now, and they slept the sleep of men worked hard too many hours of the day.

Cleo stretched a hand out and found Remy's reaching for her. She knelt by his cot and kissed his hand. Then she reached through the cage and touched his face. They sat in the dark holding on to each other, not talking.

Finally Cleo unwrapped the bundle she'd brought. "I have a chunk of ham for you, and a pot of marmalade. The bottle is full of buttermilk."

"I eat it in de mawnin," Remy said. "It help. I already feelin' stronger. By warm weather, I gon' be ready again."

Cleo touched the cage with her fingertips. "What about this?" she said.

"I's studying on it. When de time come, I get it off."

Cleo opened her hand and held it against his face. She didn't argue with him anymore. If he was caught a second time, they might sell him to the slavers, and she would never even know where they took him. But she and Remy had said it all, the what ifs and the buts and the musts. She was scared, but she loved him all the more for his grit.

She pushed her face to the bars around his head and they kissed until Remy's hands made her forget the cold floor under her knees. She pulled his blanket back, hiked her skirt up and climbed on top of him. "Be still," she whispered.

"I cain't be still."

She caught the gleam of his smile and grinned back at him. "I'll do all the moving. You just keep still."

The ropes of the cot groaned, and the bells rang. Cleo stifled a laugh and wrapped the blanket around the bells. She straddled Remy once more, and they made as little noise as they could. When they were tranquil, one of Old Sam's grandsons sighed in his sleep, and the cabin was quiet again.

"You be careful getting back to de house," Remy whispered.

"I will. I know how to go in the dark."

When Cleo left the cabin, Old Sam's yellow dog sniffed at her and followed her a few steps. She rubbed his ears and whispered, "Stay here, Boots." He sat back and wagged his tail, but he stayed.

Cleo moved in to the deeper darkness under the bare pecan trees. When she heard a rustling behind her, she turned and said, "Stay, Boots. Go on back."

Silence again. "Boots?" she said. She peered back toward the cabins, and then the darker shape of a man appeared between her and the clearing.

Cleo turned to run to the big house, but he was on her. She smelled his alcohol breath and knew it was LeBrec. She struggled, kicking and scratching, but she had to keep quiet. If Remy heard her scream, he'd come running, and then LeBrec would punish him again.

LeBrec knocked her to the ground and fell on her. Cleo twisted to squirm from under his weight, but he was too heavy. He grabbed both her wrists and held them over her head. His three-day beard scratched her face as she turned her head back and forth, trying to avoid his wet mouth.

"Let go," she hissed. "I'll tell Madame."

"And I'll tell her you was sneakin out here to be with that runaway. You think you too good for me? I'll make you know what a man can do."

He released one of her hands to fumble with his pants, and Cleo pounded him on the head, shoved against him, scratched his face and neck. Her legs were trapped under him, but she arched her back to try to throw him off.

LeBrec pulled his arm back and smashed her face with his heavy fist. Then he hit her again. Her senses stunned, Cleo's body went limp. She felt him enter her and cried out. He slapped her and clamped his hand over her mouth.

Cleo struggled to breathe with LeBrec's calloused hand mashing her mouth, his greasy hair at her nose. LeBrec's pelvis ground into her, and she groaned in pain.

Suddenly LeBrec jerked and pulled his head up at Boots's low growl. Cleo wrenched her mouth free and cried, "Boots, get him!"

The dog weighed enough to knock LeBrec off Cleo. She began to crawl away and then found her feet. She ran through the pecan trees toward the house, the sounds of LeBrec's curses and Boots's growls behind her.

As Cleo gained the stairs, Boots yelped once, and then the night was silent. *Blessed Mother, he's killed Boots.*

Cleo closed the door to Josie's room behind her and sank to the floor. She didn't cry. Crying wouldn't do any good. She worried about what would happen if Remy found out. He would go after LeBrec, and the overseer would surely kill him.

She'd have to make sure Remy never knew—but she couldn't avoid Louella, Thibault, and Elbow John, and they would have no trouble figuring out why she was bruised. They would have to be made to understand they must not talk in the quarters about what had happened. And she couldn't see Remy again until her face had healed.

She grew cold and stiff on the floor and roused herself to light a candle. She filled the basin from her pitcher and washed her aching face, wincing when the cold water touched the scratches. There was only a little blood between her legs, but she washed herself over and over. Then she brushed the leaves and dirt from her hair. She dressed herself in a soft pair of Josie's old pantaloons and put on a fresh gown.

She crawled into Josie's bed and huddled under the covers. Cleo hadn't slept in Josie's bed since the summertime, when Josie was visiting Abigail Johnston. But now she needed comfort, and she felt closer to Josie with her head on Josie's pillow.

Cleo stared big-eyed into the dark until daylight crept through the window. Then she got up and twisted the crystal knob of the door to Madame Celine's room. She hesitated in the doorway. The quiet seemed heavier in there. The room smelled of dust, and a black drape still covered the big mirror. In the dim grayness, the four-poster bed, covered by the gossamer of mosquito netting, seemed to hover in the shadows.

This was the bed Celine Tassin had died in. Cleo stared at the faint outline of pillows on the bed. Was there an indentation on the pillow where the dead woman's head had lain?

Cleo breathed deeply. She mustn't let her imagination pull her into the mumbo jumbo of the slaves. Most of them were ignorant and foolish, and they saw evil and dread everywhere. Ursaline, fully recovered from the cholera, continued to feed them *vodou* tales and kept them on the lookout for signs from the other world. Cleo knew the tales, but she knew enough, too, that they were mostly just that. Stories and nonsense. Cleo was confident God didn't hold with messages that depended on chicken feet and fresh blood.

She touched the *benitier* on the doorjamb and crossed herself, then entered the room and walked softly to Madame Celine's dresser. She found a dried-up pot of rouge, a jar of rancid face cream, and a box of pale ivory powder. The spoiled cream turned her stomach, but she took the box of powder back to Josie's room.

Cleo's skin was lighter than any other slave's on the place, even lighter than Thibault's, but her *café au lait* color was far darker than Celine's fair skin had been. The powder did nothing to conceal the black bruises and the red abrasions. The light dusting made her swollen nose look even bigger, and in the end, she washed it off. There would be no disguising the beating she'd taken.

At breakfast, Madame Emmeline sat down at the table, accepted her coffee from Cleo and reached for the cream. She stirred the cup absently as Cleo served her the blood pudding and sausage Louella had brought over. Presently, Emmeline asked for the jelly. When Cleo set it down at her elbow, Emmeline glanced up.

Madame put both hands on the table and stared at Cleo's battered face. Cleo dropped her eyes and endured the inspection, waiting to hear what Madame would say. Madame might demand an explanation, might punish her. That she should punish LeBrec occurred to Cleo, but she knew it would not happen.

After a very long moment, Madame finally spoke. "I told you to stay in the house."

Cleo nodded and kept her eyes down.

Madame Emmeline shoved her breakfast away. She shook her head. "Stay in the house, Cleo."

"Yes, Madame. I will." Cleo looked into Madame's face. The only other time she'd seen pain in her grandmother's eyes was during the days after the flood, when they had both lost their loved ones. Yes, Madame did care for her; it was there, in her eyes.

The moment was short. Madame Emmeline stood up. "I'll have my coffee in the office."

Cleo spent the morning cleaning the same floors she'd cleaned yesterday. With only little Laurie, Madame, and herself in the house, there was not much work to be done. Today, though, the routine was soothing, and Cleo gladly dusted the parlor and swept the galleries front and back. She asked Madame's permission, and then let in the midday light to dust and polish Madame Celine's bedroom. There was no indentation on the pillow, no eeriness with the fresh wind blowing in from the open window. Cleo tied the mosquito nettings up from around the bed and ran her hand over the satin coverlet. No trace of Celine in the room at all, only what one's mind put there.

Late that morning, at the expected time, Monsieur Bertrand Chamard rode up the alley of oaks from the river road. Cleo saw him from the window as she was closing up Madame Celine's room. Monsieur was an observant man, and he would notice her bruises immediately.

She retreated to Josie's room and hoped Madame would not send for her. Surely Laurie was old enough to help in the dining room. She listened to Elbow John and Thibault greet Monsieur in the courtyard below her windows. Then, when he climbed the back gallery stairs, she waited to see if Laurie would answer his knock.

At last Laurie opened the door to him and invited him inside. A little later, Cleo heard Louella in the dining room with Laurie preparing to serve dinner. Madame had excused her, then.

She lay down on Josie's bed. As long as she had stayed busy, the pain had been bearable, but now her face—eye, nose, and jaw—throbbed. After Madame and Monsieur had dined, she would ask Louella for some of the *tafia* she kept in the cookhouse. It was rough spirits, nothing like as smooth as the wine she served Madame, but it would dull the pain.

When she heard Madame and Monsieur settling in the parlor after dinner, she opened the bedroom door that opened into the dining room. Louella was clearing the dishes from the table when Cleo entered.

"Law, *chérie*, you no need to be up. You get back in de bed."

"It hurts, Louella. Will you bring me some *tafia?*"

"I tole you dis mawnin you need a piece o' beefsteak on dat bruise, Cleo. De sooner you get de swelling down, the sooner you can see dat Remy. He already know 'bout Boots lying dead in the grove. Won't do no good me keeping my mout shut, you don't get dat face looking right."

"They gave Boots a good burial? A real grave?"

"Elbow John see to it hisself, Old Sam bein' in de field already."

Louella maneuvered Cleo into the chair in the corner next to the big buffet. She took a glass down from the cabinet and filled it from the decanter. "You drink dis. You don' want no *tafia* when you got de good wine right here. Madame don' care and won't know neither. I comin' back wif de beefsteak, and you gon' sit right dere."

Louella left with a tray of dishes, and Cleo leaned her head against the chair back. She closed her eyes for a moment, but then the door from the parlor opened and Bertrand Chamard stepped in to fetch the wine decanter.

Cleo stood up quickly to leave, but when Chamard saw her, he stopped dead in front of her chair. She could only stand there.

"My God, Cleo."

He touched her swollen cheek with his finger. The compassion in his eyes nearly undid her, and tears welled. She dropped her eyes so he couldn't see her embarrassment, or how moved she was at his kindness.

Chamard glanced over his shoulder toward the parlor and spoke quietly.

"Who did this to you?"

Cleo shook her head. She moved to get past him, but Bertrand blocked her way.

He stood very close. The scent of his wool jacket, of his tobacco, of the man himself seemed to pull her to him.

"Please, monsieur," she said.

Bertrand hesitated. He touched her face again very gently; then he stepped aside. Cleo brushed past him and hurried back to the bedroom.

When Bertrand returned to Madame Emmeline with the decanter, he poured them each another glass of wine. He pondered whether to mention Cleo's evident beating, and decided he would be straining their friendship to intrude into Emmeline's household affairs.

They talked instead of the market activity and the reputations of several brokers in New Orleans they both knew. But Bertrand was unsettled. He couldn't forget Cleo's poor discolored face or the look of resignation in her eyes. He wanted to smash whoever had done this to her.

He considered for a moment that it might have been Emmeline herself who had beaten Cleo, but these were not the marks from a woman, however furious she might have been. It had been a man who attacked Cleo. There were precedents enough in cane country for Bertrand to realize it must have been the overseer. His hands itched to give LeBrec back what he'd done to Cleo.

He excused himself early from Emmeline's parlor, pleading the threatening clouds in the west.

"Laurie," Madame said, "go tell Elbow John to bring Monsieur's horse from the barn."

"No need, Emmeline. I'll get it myself."

"Of course not, Bertrand. Laurie is to go out to bring LeBrec to me anyway. I sent word to him that I would see him this afternoon. Run along, Laurie."

"Trouble?" Bertrand ventured.

Emmeline looked at him. "I believe you saw Cleo in the dining room after dinner."

"I did. She's had a very bad beating."

"Yes, she has. But she knew to stay out of his way. She didn't listen to me."

"Can I help in any—"

"That won't be necessary," Emmeline said and handed him his hat.

As Bertrand crossed the yard to mount his horse, LeBrec sauntered toward him on his way to the house. Bertrand took the reins from Thibault and said, "Run on, now, Tio."

LeBrec's left hand was bandaged tightly, the whole hand. Red scratches ran the length of one cheek, and there was a deep gouge near his eye. Every mark proved Cleo had not yielded submissively, and Bertrand applauded her.

"How do you do, Monsieur Chamard," LeBrec said.

Bertrand reached a hand out and grabbed the man's arm. "I have an interest in this girl, LeBrec," he said. "If I see another mark on her . . ."

There was no conviction in LeBrec's voice when he spoke. "What are you talking about?"

"You know what I'm talking about." Bertrand saw fear in the overseer's eyes. It was no surprise the man was a coward. "Don't touch her again," Bertrand said. He turned his back on the overseer and mounted his horse.

As Bertrand rode past the house, he looked up at the bedroom Cleo had retreated to. The curtains moved, and he knew she'd watched him with LeBrec.

Chapter 22

New Orleans

Phanor's new life presented him with long hours and new challenges, but he greeted each day with a happy heart. Being Monsieur Cherleu's wine merchant meant he had to learn which ships traversed the Atlantic the quickest, which captains could be trusted to deliver a shipment intact, which season roiled the ocean and thus the wine. He introduced himself to the bosses on the wharves, to majordomos in the best restaurants and clubs, and to riverboat entrepreneurs who delivered to the plantations along the Mississippi.

Phanor's palate was innocent, and at first he hardly discerned the difference between a sweet white wine and a dry one. When he met with his customers at the various restaurants and clubs, the buyers inevitably wanted to discuss the bouquet, the body, the length of the wine. Phanor felt they were speaking another language, and he determined to cure his ignorance.

At the famous restaurant Les Trois Frères on the Rue

Dauphine, Phanor cultivated the friendship of Jean Paul Rouquier, the chief wine steward. Jean Paul loved wine, and he loved to talk about it.

"This now, Phanor, observe. You see the wine's robe is very pale."

"Its robe?"

"*Oui*. Its robe is rather a golden hue. Before we even inhale its bouquet, we expect an older, fuller flavor. The deeper the color of the *vin blanc*, the more it has aged. Now, my friend, gently move your glass, like so."

Phanor swirled the wine in the fine crystal glass as Jean Paul demonstrated. Then he sipped.

"*Non, non*. Not yet. You must not hurry it. This is not a young wine to be guzzled with one's sausage and rice. Now. Breathe in the bouquet." Jean Paul closed his eyes and inhaled. "Ah. Tell me, Phanor, what do you smell?"

"Flowers," he said.

"Very good, Phanor," Jean Paul said. "Now we will explore the *arome de bouche*. Take only a sip, that's right. Now purse your lips together, like so. Breathe a little air over your tongue and roll the wine around in your mouth."

After several weeks of tutelage, Jean Paul said, "Soon, my friend, you will be a *connoisseur* of wine, and you will be after my job."

Phanor raised his glass to Jean Paul. "You have nothing to fear from me. I am only a country Cajun, and I always will be. But I thank you for making me less the bumpkin I was. *A votre santé*."

Those first months in New Orleans, Phanor relished the city's hustle and bustle, every corner offering new sights and sounds. Phanor was conscious of a new life with new possibilities. He would not have to be a poor man living on the edge of the swamps. He might be a man of New Orleans, a man of taste and fashion.

With his first earnings, more money than he or his papa

had ever seen at one time, Phanor bought bolts of cotton to send to his sister. She would make clothes for herself and little Nicholas. For his father and brother-in-law, he bought tobacco and pipes of polished briar.

Then Phanor began to think of his own appearance. He met with respectable merchants nearly every day, and he had become aware of how rough he looked. So it was that when he met Josie in the park with the *américains*, he was dressed in a fine bottle green jacket and buff trousers. His hat sported a green ribbon, and his black boots shone.

He hadn't been surprised to see Josie in Jackson Square. He had looked for her on every street every day since he had learned she was in New Orleans. Phanor's sister Lalie could read and write a little, and she had sent him a letter. Nicholas had taken his first steps alone, Papa had the rheumatism, the neighbors on Toulouse had nearly rebuilt everything swept away by the flood.

"They caught that runaway," Lalie wrote, "the one you know." *Worse luck, Remy,* Phanor thought. *I hope they go easy on you.*

"Oh, and Mademoiselle Josephine," Lalie continued, "is in New Orleans too, staying with her maman's sister."

After the letter, Phanor constantly thought, *Surely I'll see her today. She'll be promenading, or riding in a surrey. She'll be very grand in her town clothes, and she'll be happy to see me.* After all, he looked rather grand himself in his stylish hat and coat.

On the day Phanor at last spotted Josie in the square with the *américains*, he'd had a moment to look at her before he approached her party. She was even prettier than he'd remembered. The pallor of last summer was gone, and Josie's cheeks were rosy. He thought he might be able to reach all the way around her waist with his two hands, and he longed to finger one of the curls peeping out from her black bonnet.

When she recognized him, Phanor watched the light in

her green eyes. She was glad to see him too, but he knew better than to rush to her and grab her hands. He had acquired enough polish to approach the gentleman who escorted her first, and with the restraint the *américains* preferred.

"I am always in the square on Sunday afternoons," he'd told her. Josie had smiled and he knew she'd understood. After that, Phanor appeared in the square in front of the cathedral, rain or shine. But she didn't come.

He began to habit the square earlier and earlier, and he took his fiddle along for company. He wore his old clothes, patched and mended as they were, so that his new suit might be cleaned and pressed by his landlady to be ready for the work week. He'd play his old favorites, easing the loneliness and passing the time. The people seemed to enjoy it, and he enjoyed having an audience to play for. The money they threw in his hat meant nothing to him; Monsieur Cherleu paid him more than he ever dreamed he'd have. But the men and women, however poor they were, seemed to want to pay him. They expected to, and they valued him the more for having paid for his music.

When the worst of the winter was over, but spring had not yet announced herself, Phanor took a steamboat upriver. He hadn't been home since late last August.

Phanor hopped from the steamboat onto the dock at Toulouse. He turned and waved to the captain once, and then climbed the levee. Before him lay the rows of oaks and Josie's house clearly visible through the bare trees. The bright yellow walls with the green shutters, the long row of windows, the expanse of gallery and roof—the house seemed the same, yet somehow smaller than he'd remembered.

He recollected Cleo slogging through the mud on those silly pattens the first time he'd played the fiddle for her. His keenest memory, though, was the night on the levee when he'd played while Cleo and Remy, Josie and Thibault sang around the fire. Their knees touching, Josie had sat on the log next to him. He'd wanted to kiss her, had nearly done it. How many times he wished he had.

Phanor walked through the corridor of trees and stood at the front gallery steps. He was no longer the barefoot Cajun boy come to sell eggs or hickory nuts. He was a man of business. Surely this time he should announce himself at the front door.

He raised his hand to pull the bell chain, but before the first ring, Cleo opened the big cypress door. "Monsieur DeBlieux, I believe." Cleo said. "Won't you come in, monsieur? Let me take your hat."

He laughed at her overplay of propriety, then caught her in his arms and whirled her around.

When she stepped back, Cleo said, "Let's see how fine you look." She touched the velvet collar and the linen cravat. "You the same boy I know?" she teased.

Phanor straightened his jacket. "You mean that boy, the one who play for you on the levee? That's me, sure. But I don't plan to be barefoot no more, Cleo, *non*."

"I've missed you, Phanor. Lalie brought a letter over to send with Madame's dispatches. Did she tell you about Remy?"

"*Oui*, I know Remy is back."

Cleo looked toward Madame Emmeline's office door. "I'll tell you about it later. First I better let Madame know you're here."

Phanor spent more than an hour with Madame Emmeline. She had taken an interest in his new life, and not just for her old friend Cherleu's sake; she'd even written Phanor a letter suggesting he let her review his records. They went over his book, and she showed him a better method of accounting for the cases of wine he brokered. He told her how he had been investigating warehouses to find the best prices for storing

Monsieur Cherleu's wine shipments, and she suggested he include in his comparisons which companies included the cost of stevedores in their figures.

"Me, I can do that, Madame Emmeline," Phanor said. "I know many of these men, now, and others will do business for the price of a bottle of ordinary Bordeaux."

"Well worth the persuasion, I'm sure," Madame said. "You've done well, Phanor. You may stay for supper, if you like."

"Thank you, Madame. But I have not seen my papa or my sister since August. I will go home."

"Of course. Before you go back to New Orleans, then."

"*Merci*. I will come another day, if you wish, before I leave."

Phanor said good-bye and found his hat on the parlor table. He heard Cleo sweeping on the back gallery. When she saw him, she leaned her straw broom against the wall.

"Do you have time to see something before you go home?" Cleo asked.

Phanor glanced at the weak sun in the west. He'd need to be at the house on the swamp's edge before dark, and the winter sun set early. "I have a little time."

"We have to walk out to the fields. If we find Elbow John, he can bring me back."

Phanor looked at her. Since when had Cleo needed any kind of escort? She was the most fearless girl he knew.

"Never mind about why," Cleo said. "That's not important now. Let me get my shawl, and we'll go."

Phanor followed Cleo through the pecan grove and to the south fields where the slaves were planting the last of the cane in the reclaimed land. When Cleo stopped abruptly and held up her hand, he was silent. He looked around, but all he saw were the usual men and women laboring over the soil and a white man on horseback nearby.

Cleo motioned for Phanor to go with her back among the trees that skirted the field. "We can see well enough from here," Cleo said.

"See what? Are you afraid of the overseer?"

Cleo's face distorted into a sneer. "He can't hurt me any more than he has." She showed him the folded razor in her pocket. "I'll take care of myself if he tries me again. But it's better for Remy this way. If he knew what LeBrec did . . ."

Phanor looked at Cleo closely. Her eyes were hard, and he understood.

"Listen," Cleo said. "You hear?"

A tinkling of bells came to Phanor across the field. He nodded and looked at the people bent over punching cane sections into the black earth.

Cleo pointed. "See Remy in the last row?"

"What is that thing on his head?" Phanor squinted his eyes to make out the contours of the head cage Remy wore strapped on his shoulders.

"It's to humiliate him. And to keep him from running again. Every movement he makes, those bells on the top of the cage ring. All day, those bells clang in his ears. And when he bends over, the cage slaps him in the back of the head. You should see the scars on his shoulders where it cuts into the flesh."

Phanor stared at Remy. How the man could bend over and keep his balance Phanor couldn't imagine. It was inhuman.

"How long?" Phanor said. "How long does he have to wear it?"

"As long as it pleases Monsieur LeBrec."

Phanor gazed at the white man on the horse. LeBrec sat lazily, one arm propping his body up against the saddle horn, his hat pushed back, his eyes on the slaves.

"Remy is going to try again," Cleo said.

"Run away? With that thing on his head?"

Cleo's face was turned to the scene in the cane field. "He

said he's thinking about how to get it off. But I don't see what he can do without the blacksmith to help him. And Smithy can't risk it. Or anyway, he says he won't." She looked at Phanor. "LeBrec loves the whip."

Phanor grimaced when Remy bent over to his task and the weight of the cage caused him to misstep. A man should not have to live like that. Not any man.

Phanor watched LeBrec spit over his horse's shoulder. The man's build was powerful. Phanor guessed he was short in the leg, but even from where he watched with Cleo, he could see the thigh muscles tight against LeBrec's trousers. Sometimes short men, his papa had always said, were the meanest. Like God had cheated them of the stature that fit their opinion of themselves, and they could not rest without punishing God's other people. Even the slaves. No, Phanor amended to himself, especially the slaves.

"I'll think about it," Phanor said.

Chapter 23

In the back country

Yellow light glowed from the windows of the little gray house as Phanor walked up the path among the moss-draped tupelos. Fog was moving in from the bayou, and the house of his birth seemed to float on the mist.

The weathered boards of the porch were warped, and the floor sagged on one end. Light seeped from the roof where the winter had claimed a shingle. If the pneumonia had not filled her lungs, Phanor's maman would have been stirring a pot of rice and beans on the woodstove. It seemed so long ago, and Phanor wondered that he had never noticed how shabby the place was.

But the chimney smoke carried the aroma of sizzling bacon, notes from Papa's dulcimer penetrated the thickening air, and Phanor heard little Nicholas let out a shout and a peal of laughter. Phanor hurried to immerse himself in his family.

The days that followed were filled with music and singing and storytelling. Phanor, his father, and his brother-in-law Louis sat up late into the night talking and drinking Papa's 'shine. Phanor had brought them two bottles of good Burgundy, but his Papa said, "It's mighty fine going down, son, but I tell you true, it lacks the kick of my corn."

Phanor carried Lalie's little Nicholas around on his shoulders, showed him the hollow tree where the bees lived, and handed him back to his mother when he became odorous or fussy. Louis and Phanor took the pirogue out and gigged for frogs at twilight. It was good to be home, but before long, Phanor grew restless. He missed the hum and buzz of New Orleans.

Throughout the days, Phanor thought about Remy. It was dangerous to help a slave escape. It was grand theft. And Phanor depended on Madame Tassin's goodwill for the future he had glimpsed for himself.

But Remy had to be freed from that cage.

Papa would not want to make an enemy of his old friend Madame Emmeline. They were not in truth equals, but there was friendship of a kind, based on long association between their families over three generations. Phanor didn't want to place his father in a position of having to lie. He was not good at it anyway. But Louis might help him.

Louis owed nothing to Remy, and Phanor didn't remember his ever having spoken against slavery. But his brother-in-law was a fair man, and in Remy's favor, not above raiding a neighbor's fish pond or log pile.

When Phanor explained Remy's situation to Louis while they were out in the pirogue, Louis presented the obvious arguments. Remy was property, after all. Phanor had to think of himself first.

"What you want to get messed up in that for?" Louis said. "He belong to that Madame Tassin. He no concern to you."

"Maybe."

"Sure, this slave, he not your problem, Phanor."

"If you could see what they've put on his head, Louis. And Cleo, she wants her babies to be free. You remember Cleo."

"Sure, me, I know Cleo. We find her maman and her papa in the flood. That girl, she have a hard time." They listened to the frogs' chorus while they drifted in the boat. "So this Remy, he Cleo's man, eh?"

Phanor nodded. He told Louis about the overseer being after Cleo, and how that made it even more dangerous for Remy to be on the place.

"Sound like Cleo, she the one need to get off Toulouse," Louis said.

"Cleo can take care of herself, I think. Until Mademoiselle Josephine comes home."

The moon had risen and lit the edge of the shallows. Louis stood up and poised with one foot on the gunwale. He stabbed his gig into the water and raised up a writhing frog on the barbs. "Lalie, she fix us a late supper, we catch a mess of these."

Phanor stood too and searched the night for the eye gleam of bullfrogs. He gigged an old bull bigger than his two hands together, and the men frogged for another half hour without talking. Even in the cool darkness, the teeming bayou smelled of the living and the dead—birds, reptiles, fish, trees, and vines—and of ripe, rich earth.

When the men gutted the frogs and threw the offal back in, the splashes attracted a silent gator. Its body glided under the water, but its eyes caught the moonlight and gave it away. Louis thwacked it on the head with the gaff. It retreated, and they sat down again and picked up their oars.

As they pulled back toward the house, Louis said, "So, Phanor, how we gon' do this?"

Timing was the most important part of the plan. Remy needed help to remove the cage. Phanor needed to be seen boarding the steamboat at the Toulouse dock alone. Louis would take Remy through the bayous to a point downstream where the two of them would board a boat for New Orleans. No one knew Louis on the boats, and no one would question a white man traveling with his slave. If they planned carefully, the hue and cry would not have reached the settlements downriver.

Once in New Orleans, Louis would turn Remy over to Phanor, who would find him a safe place, and Louis would return home to Papa, Lalie, and Nicholas. If anyone asked where he'd been, he would say he'd been hunting gators in the swamp.

Wednesday night, two days before Phanor was due to return to New Orleans, he accepted Madame Emmeline's invitation to dinner. He tied his hair neatly at the nape of his neck and wore his best shirt and jacket. His pants were fashionably long. He'd seen older gentlemen in New Orleans who still wore silk stockings and pants that stopped just below the knee, but with an eye for style, he'd chosen the more elegant trousers that reached all the way to the ankle.

When Cleo admitted him to the parlor, she said, "And who shall I tell Madame is calling?"

Phanor held his arms out and turned around for her. "Me, I am very fine, it's true."

Then he lowered his voice. "I leave on Friday, and you must have Remy ready before that."

"I'll meet you in the pecan grove later."

"No. In the underhouse. We'll be quiet enough. There's no need for you to risk being out."

Madame Emmeline's office door opened and Cleo stepped away.

"Good evening, Phanor," Madame said.

"Madame." Phanor bowed over her hand with the grace of one who was born to a life of gentility.

The two passed an amiable evening talking of New Orleans and riverboats, sailing ships and wine. Phanor listened carefully to Madame Emmeline's tutorial on the intricacies of finance and markets.

Over their last glass of wine, Madame said, "Now I must speak plainly, Phanor. Your writing, as evidenced in your ledger, is appalling. Not only your penmanship, but also your spelling and diction. If you are to be a man of the world, of which I believe you are quite capable, then you must master the written language. I advise you to embark on a course of study while you are in the city."

Phanor acknowledged the truth of it. His mother had taught him his letters, and he had been a willing pupil, but she could not teach him what she did not know.

"I will give you a *grammaire française* for your study."

"You are very kind, Madame. I will learn it page by page, I promise you."

"And you will have to learn English," she told him.

"*Oui*, Madame. I have made a beginning on *l'anglais*."

"*C'est bon*. I expected you would."

The evening over, the grammar book in his pocket, Phanor took his leave. Cleo handed him his hat and opened the double doors onto the front gallery for him.

"Five minutes," she whispered.

Phanor waited on a stool among the wine racks. When he saw Cleo's silhouette against the night sky, he whispered, "Over here."

She stubbed her foot against a barrel and reached a hand out for him. He took it and guided her to the casks to sit next to him.

"You'll help Remy?"

"Louis and I, and you. Louis will have most of the risk,

but he has agreed to it. I believe he loves the possibility of danger as much as the idea of helping Remy."

"And you? I think you like it, too?"

"You know us Cajuns, Cleo. We take joy in a little peril."

"How will we do it?"

Phanor explained the parts he and Louis and she would play. Cleo had one suggestion. "Forgive me, Phanor, I don't mean to offend. But Louis must not look like a poor Cajun if he is to be Remy's master."

"I intended for him to wear one of my new shirts."

"You don't have to give up yours, Phanor. Monsieur Emile left a dozen shirts moldering in the wardrobe. I'll take one for Louis, and maybe Louis will have an old blouse that Remy could wear, to better cover the mess the cage has made of his shoulders."

"And what about LeBrec?" Phanor said. "You'll be able to get to Remy in the night?"

"I'm ready for LeBrec. He won't hurt me again."

That sounded like the Cleo Phanor knew, but that didn't mean she could handle a man of LeBrec's size. "I better come with you," he said.

"No. That's my risk, not yours," she said. "First we have to get the cage off Remy."

Phanor did not want to tell her he had no idea how to get the contraption off Remy. He'd not had a close look at it, and all his imaginings had been disastrous. He'd thought of padding Remy's neck and then taking a hammer and chisel to the neck piece. But if the chisel slipped, or if the hammer missed and hit his skull . . . Cleo had said there was a locking mechanism on the base, and maybe he could smash it. Or maybe he couldn't.

"We'll get it off," he said.

For weeks, Cleo had thought of nothing else but getting the cage off Remy's head. In desperation, she had gone again to the smithy. "You don't have to do anything, don't have to ever touch the cage again," she'd told him. "Just show me how you made the lock."

Smithy's arm muscles bulged through his thin shirt, and his black skin glistened with sweat from his furnace. But strong as he was, he was afraid of LeBrec. Cleo offered inducements, but Smithy shook his head.

Through the days, Cleo wore him down. Smithy agreed to teach her how the mechanism worked in exchange for various provisions Cleo would steal a little at a time from the big house—oil, cotton cloth, candles, extra meals.

Now she was ready. "I know how the lock works," she said.

Phanor tried to see her face in the dark. "You know how the lock works?"

"Yes. I can open it. But getting the cage off isn't enough. Remy has to have help getting away this time. If he's caught again, well, he must not be caught again. So I've waited."

Phanor breathed in relief. "Well. That was the hard part, the damn cage."

Thursday night, Cleo found her way through the dark by starlight. She carried a ball of wax from a honeycomb in her pocket to pack into the bells on Remy's cage. This she did while Old Sam and his grandsons slept, or seemed to. She wondered about Old Sam. He lay very still on his cot, but his breathing was not audible. It didn't matter. Sam would never tell LeBrec Remy was gone.

Once she was sure the bells would not ring in their wax packing, she and Remy stepped from the cabin into the cold, damp night. They crept through the sleeping quarters toward the western edge of the plantation where Phanor and Louis waited for them in the woods.

"No one saw you?"

"I don' tink so," Remy said. "Least not de overseer. He de one dat matter."

"All right then. We'll follow Louis."

Light from the evening star and a sliver of moon filtered through the canopy, but it was not enough to keep them from stumbling on tree roots. Remy repeatedly was thrown off balance by branches that snagged his cage, and Phanor kept a hand on his shoulder in readiness.

As they approached the swamp, the cicadas and the frogs hushed. The only sounds were the migratory birds overhead and their own hesitant steps on the overgrown path. Now and then a creature rustled in the undergrowth, and once Cleo was startled by the shining eyes of a raccoon not six feet away. She was glad they hadn't roused a skunk.

Louis led them to a hummock raised above the surrounding swampland. Three miles and thousands of live oak, tupelo, cypress, and sweet gum trees lay between them and Toulouse. Louis lit a lantern and held it high. It was his first look at the iron monstrosity Remy carried on his shoulders, and Louis was shocked.

"*C'est inhumaine,*" he said.

"Yes, it is," Phanor answered. "Cleo, get your tools."

Remy sat on the ground and Phanor held the lantern near, creating an oasis of light in the midst of the dark wet woods. Cleo pulled a thin blade of metal from her pocket. It was not a key, but Smithy had explained how the blade on which he'd welded a small nub near the tip could spring the catch in the lock.

Cleo said a quick prayer and crossed herself. Then she began. She inserted the slender tool into the keyhole and gently twisted. Nothing happened. She twisted it the other direction, but still nothing in the lock gave way.

Smithy had told her if she twisted too hard, tried to force

it, the nub on the blade could break off. Patience, she reminded herself. She sat back and breathed. Then she tried again, feeling for the catch, imagining the blade as an extension of her fingers.

"We may have to use the mallet," Louis said.

"Give her time," Phanor answered.

A mother possum waddled through their island of light, two babies on her back. She ignored the humans and the lantern and chose a tree to climb into.

Cleo looked up at Phanor, worried. He nodded to give her confidence, and she reinserted the blade. She pulled it back a sixteenth of an inch so that the tip did not touch the back wall of the chamber, then twisted it. There—she felt the nub fit into the notch. She held her breath and turned the blade slowly and carefully. A little more.

In the silence and tension, the click inside the lock startled all of them. Then Cleo laughed out loud.

"Well done!" Phanor said. He handed the lantern to Louis and knelt down next to Remy to open the neck piece. Phanor held the weight of the cage, and Remy undid the straps he'd devised to help balance the weight. He shrugged out of the fastenings and pulled his head backward out of the cage. For the first time in months, he was free of the weight, the indignation, the horror of the iron trap.

He leapt to his feet and raised his hands as far overhead as he could stretch them. He twisted his shoulders and rotated his head. "My God, dat feel good! I tink I could run all de way to New Orleans."

"No need for running, *non*," Louis said. "We go to my pirogue now, and the dogs not be able to follow us."

Remy held his arms out to Cleo and whirled her around the glade. "I gon' be free, a free man, Cleo."

She held him tight, afraid to let him go.

"Don' you worry," Remy said. "I send for you. You know dat."

With one arm around Cleo, Remy held his hand out to Phanor. "My friend, I thank you."

"I'll see you in New Orleans. Remember to play the part, Remy. You still have to look like a slave, act like a slave when you're on the boat."

"I know how to do dat, fo sho."

Cleo handed him the bag with a washcloth, soap, a razor, and clean shirts. She kissed him and clung to him.

"They have to go, Cleo," Phanor said. "The farther down the swamp and into the bayous before sunrise, the better."

Louis and Remy left them on the hummock and quickly disappeared into the forest. They had only a quarter mile, Louis had figured, to where he left his boat. They would hide themselves among the maze of streams and lagoons in the daytime, and at night they would paddle toward the river, where they would catch a steamboat. Louis had Phanor's last month's earnings in his pocket, enough for their tickets, food, and a smoke or two.

On the hummock, Cleo stared into the dark long after she could no longer hear their passage through the trees. Phanor picked up the hateful cage and its straps. With all his might, he heaved the monstrosity into the swamp. With any luck, the mud would suck it beneath the black water before morning.

Cleo was shivering. "Are you cold?" he asked her.

"It doesn't matter," she said. "We'd better go."

Without Louis as their guide, they kept the lantern alight until they were sure of their terrain. Then Phanor extinguished the lamp and they stumbled on through the fields of Toulouse.

The quarters were silent and still, no lights in the overseer's window nor in the big house. Phanor guessed it must be near four o'clock in the morning. He watched Cleo's shadowy figure climb the back stairs and cross the gallery. If she waved to him then, he couldn't see her.

Then he hurried back home. He had to clean the mud off, say farewell to Lalie, Papa, and Nicholas, and present himself at the dock for the riverboat to pick him up. By that time, it would be well into the morning, and no doubt LeBrec would have discovered Remy was gone.

Chapter 24

Bertrand Chamard fidgeted as his man Valentine buffed his nails.

"That'll do," Bertrand said. "I'm shaved and barbered and trimmed. That's enough fussing for one day."

Valentine didn't release the hand, however, until he'd finished the last nail to his satisfaction. "Tomorrow I have to get at that callus again."

"Yes, Monsieur Valentine, sir."

Bertrand and Valentine had been together since early childhood, and their bond was easy and comfortable. It was true, Valentine had borne his months in the stables at Cherleu with ill grace, freely reminding his master he much preferred polishing silver to rubbing oil into leather. But, Bertrand noted, Valentine had worked hard mucking out stalls and repairing harnesses and trying his hand at shoeing till Val's hands were as rough as Bertrand's. One difference between them, though, was that Bertrand truly didn't mind the calluses.

Bertrand glanced in the mirror and pronounced himself ready for the evening. He tossed the cape with the red satin lining over his shoulder and accepted his hat and cane from Valentine.

"Don't bother to wait up for me," he said. "It may be dawn before the game is over."

"Then don't come in here banging around and waking me up," Valentine said.

Bertrand smiled and planned to do just that. The ebony stick he carried made a wonderful racket if he dropped it on the hard floor.

The gaming room at the Blue Ribbon was already smoky when Bertrand arrived. He knew nearly everyone at the tables, most of them Creoles from the lower Mississippi or from the Cane River farther north. In recent years, however, a prosperous Acadian or two and a handful of *américains* would join the gentlemen at the roulette table.

Bertrand sat down with his friends, two of them cousins, and lit the first cigar of the evening. Young LaSalle dealt the cards, and each man scrutinized his hand with an assumed air of indifference.

Toward midnight, the gentlemen took a respite to stretch their legs. Bertrand carried his tumbler of whiskey onto the balcony to breathe in some fresh air. He had never put much stock in the womanish worry about night vapors or poisonous miasmas. He'd enjoyed all that Paris had to offer in the small hours of the night, had often adjourned to the rooftop of his friend Lafrènniére to gaze at Venus through the telescope. He had discovered no substantial difference in the sunless air of the night. Why should it be any different half a world away from Paris, here in New Orleans?

"Is that you, Chamard?"

Bertrand squinted to identify the man who was backlit by the chandeliers inside.

"Johnston? Come join me, my friend."

Albany stepped onto the balcony, and the men shook hands. "When did you get to town?" Albany said.

"Three days ago. I'm just getting loose from my business calls and I'm ready for some relaxation. How are your mother and your sister?"

"They're well."

The two leaned against the railing, companionably blowing smoke into the night.

"Josephine?" Bertrand asked.

Albany puffed on his cigar. "A bit difficult, I would say. As women are apt to be."

Bertrand looked at the stars, reluctant to pry. If Albany wanted to discuss it, he would.

"So this is where they hold the famous balls?" Albany said.

The Blue Ribbon was a notorious establishment which every Creole boy looked forward to visiting on his maturity. The balls held there employed the best musicians in New Orleans, and the best caterers. But most important, here one found the most beautiful women in Louisiana displayed for the pleasure of the white planters. The ladies were quadroons, for the most part, and their futures were made by becoming mistresses to Creole gentlemen. Once a man had his heart pierced by a quadroon beauty, he often kept her, and their children, all his life.

"Upstairs," Bertrand answered. "There'll be a ball next week. I could bring you as my guest."

"Actually, I'm already invited. Your cousin Marguerite's friend Achille Dumont insists I accompany him. Apparently one has not experienced Louisiana if one has not seen the womanhood at these affairs."

"I would have to agree with that."

"But I take it this is not a brothel."

"Don't let the good mothers of these ladies hear you say the word!" Bertrand said with a laugh. "No, these girls are career mistresses, and their virtue, within their own bounds, is legendary."

"They're all virgins, then?"

"Not at all. Their gentlemen die, or tire of them, and they reenter the ballroom with an enticing air of maturity."

Bertrand thought of Philomene. She and his father had been lovers for twenty years before his death, and even yet, she was a handsome woman. When Monsieur Chamard had passed away, he left her a generous legacy, and she chose not to reenter the Blue Ribbon.

A man stepped onto the balcony where they stood. "There you are, Johnston," Achille said. "We're ready to play. Hello, Chamard."

"Dumont," Bertrand said. "How are you?"

"Well, thank you. So you know Johnston, here. Did he tell you he's going to risk enchantment by the lovely ladies of the Blue Ribbon? My plan is to introduce him to the most tempting girl in the room. He'll be a real Louisianan once he's found himself a fancy gal in a satin *tignon*."

Bertrand had always found Achille Dumont slight in character, though he admitted he could be amusing company. As friendly as his cousin Marguerite was with Achille, Bertrand wondered if she was playing a game, having Achille distract Albany with the beauties at the Blue Ribbon. Perhaps Marguerite's favorite niece was sincerely reluctant to marry Albany. Bertrand pursued that thought.

Not many streets over, Josie peeked in at the children on her way upstairs. Pierre snored softly in his bed. André still slept with his thumb in his mouth. Josie gazed longest at little Jean Baptiste and remembered what Grammy Tulia always said: Dere's nuttin sweeter dan a sleepin' chile. Jean Baptiste's lashes curled against his cheek, and tiny pearl teeth glistened between his pink lips. Josie hoped she would have a little boy as perfect as Jean someday. She tucked a bare foot back under the covers, kissed Jean's forehead, and thought how rich and wonderful to have a family of one's own.

Next day, Josie sat down with Tante Marguerite in the parlor. Her aunt was in a dither about the preparations for her final entertainment at the end of Lent. After that, everyone left New Orleans to avoid the fever season, and Marguerite had so much to do and had had a bad throat for days.

Marguerite sipped hot tea with lemon and honey. "Well," she rasped, "you have no idea how much work there is yet to be done. I've been running myself ragged for weeks and even now I don't see how we shall be ready by the eighteenth. I shall have to rely on you, Josephine."

"What would you like me to do? I could oversee the housekeeping, or the children. Or would you like me to help with the food?"

"Oh, do you feel you could take over the kitchen? Yes, of course you can," Marguerite said. "Your grand-mère keeps an old-fashioned house, doesn't she? She must have had you cooking cakes and pastries before you could read, and now you could probably cook the whole menu yourself."

"No, of course I can't," Josie said and laughed. "But I will do what I can. The ordering, the planning—"

"And then there's the wine," Marguerite rasped. "With this dreadful cough"—and then she coughed—"I have allowed the days to go by and have not even ordered the wine!"

"I know a wine merchant," Josie said. "Phanor DeBlieux." Marguerite raised her eyebrows that her niece should be acquainted with a merchant she herself didn't know.

"He is Monsieur Cherleu's agent, and Grand-mère approves of him thoroughly."

"Does she?"

"I could send for him through Monsieur Cherleu. Grand-mère wrote me Monsieur keeps rooms on the Rue Dauphine, in case I ever needed an escort home."

"Already you are making my life easier, *chérie*. Send for your Phanor DeBlieux immediately."

Josie rummaged in her letter box upstairs to find the reference her grandmother had made to Monsieur Cherleu's lodging. Tante's butler could get Phanor's address from him and then deliver the note. She rattled back down the stairs with a note for Thomas to deliver.

While they waited for an answer to their note, Josie and her aunt considered the menu. They decided on tournedos of beef, pork medallions in wine sauce, and both boiled and sautéed shrimp. Raw oysters and fried oysters too, Josie suggested. The markets were short of fresh vegetables this time of year, but they could have buttery potatoes, both white and yellow, and tiny creamed spinach pies. Jam crêpes, apple tarts, and candied oranges and lemons would fill the dessert table. For those who remained as dawn approached, there would be hot gumbo and fresh bread.

Thomas returned with a neatly written note on heavy cream paper. Phanor DeBlieux would call on them at four o'clock that afternoon with a complete list of the wines available in his warehouse.

"Excellent," Marguerite said. "Now you must excuse me, Josephine. The dressmaker is fitting my gown yet again. It is very tiresome, but one does want it done right." Marguerite was nearly to the door when she turned back. "And what shall you be wearing to the party?"

Josie shrugged. "The same black gown I wore in the fall, I suppose."

"Don't worry, *ma petite*. Only a few more months and you can shed your mourning weeds. I'll treat you to something bright, perhaps a new pink gown, or, no, a pale green to bring out your eyes."

Marguerite patted her perfectly curled coiffure. "Now let me run on to the dressmaker's. You'll speak to Cook about seeing the butcher, won't you?"

Josie checked the tall clock in the foyer. Two hours until Phanor would arrive. She rushed upstairs to brush out her hair and start over with the pinning and curling. The honey-colored highlights seemed to darken with every month between washings, and it was her opinion that hair was prettiest when lightest, but washing would have to wait. In only three weeks, she'd be home and Cleo could help her.

Curled, powdered, and rouged, Josie surveyed the effect in her aunt's cheval glass. She placed her hands at her tiny waist with satisfaction. Josie practiced a sideways smile, looking out from under her eyelashes. The beauty spot she had painted just to the left of her mouth was a nice touch.

Beware, she told herself. *You are becoming vain, Josephine Tassin.*

She returned to the parlor, ready to dazzle. Phanor almost certainly would not be punctual, but it was of small importance. Only the *américains* made a fuss over the hands of the clock. She picked up her crochet bag. Unlike embroidery, crochet did not necessitate actually seeing each stitch.

She opened the balcony doors and kept an ear tuned to the street sounds. Would Phanor knock at the front door? At Toulouse, when Phanor had arrived barefoot with a basket of this or that, he had not climbed the front steps. But now he was a city merchant, dressed in polished boots and fine wool. She decided she would receive him in the parlor rather than in the cramped little room Tante used as an office downstairs. And she would have tea served. Or maybe coffee. She'd noticed most men seemed to prefer coffee.

Only ten minutes after the grandfather clock struck four, someone knocked at the street door. Josie couldn't restrain herself. She rushed on to the balcony and peered over.

"Phanor," she called.

He removed his hat and made a sweeping bow. They grinned at each other as if they shared a great secret: they were only playacting in their fine clothes, and in truth were still Phanor and Josie of the night on the levee.

Thomas opened the double doors and Phanor disappeared into the foyer. In the parlor, Josie arranged herself to best advantage and waited. When Thomas admitted Monsieur DeBlieux, she stood and offered her hand in her grandest manner.

Unsmiling now, Phanor made a leg, took Josie's hand and kissed it. She loved the brush of his lips on her hand. "Mademoiselle," he said.

The courtesies perfectly observed, they shed the formality. "You look wonderful," Phanor said.

Josie twirled around. "Am I not a fine lady?" she said with a laugh. "It takes me twice as long to dress now, so it must be true."

Josie rang the little silver bell for coffee and the two of them sat near the balcony doors for the sunshine.

"I had hoped to see you in Jackson Square some Sunday afternoon," Phanor said.

Had he seen her that day? No, she saw no trace of knowingness in his face. Ashamed of the lie she was about to tell, and of the need for it, Josie blushed. "I'm sorry," she said. "I couldn't get away."

"I've been to Toulouse, you know," Phanor said. He told her how her grandmother had been three weeks before and how the fields were greening.

"Did you know Remy has run away again?" Josie asked.

Phanor barely hesitated. "Remy? I saw him in the fields when I was there. Wearing that monstrous cage on his head."

"A cage?"

Phanor described the device LeBrec had designed and how the bells jangled with every movement.

"That's dreadful. And my grandmother approved of this?"

"According to Cleo," Phanor said, "she insisted LeBrec not injure her slaves with beatings or any kind of maiming. This was LeBrec's answer."

"Poor Cleo. She must be sick with worry."

"Josie, I think I should tell you something. I know it is not my place, but I think you will want to know."

"What is it? If it's about Toulouse, I need to know."

"It's the new overseer, this LeBrec. He is a cruel man. And he's after Cleo."

"No, Phanor. Don't worry. My grandmother would never allow a man to bother one of her house slaves. Especially not her own . . . especially not Cleo."

Phanor did not reply. He thought he understood Madame Tassin's pragmatism better than Josie did.

"Well," he said. "Lent will be over soon. You'll be going home?"

"After Easter, they say the city is quite deserted."

Josie caught Phanor staring at her beauty mark again. He'd focused on it repeatedly as they talked. It made her self-conscious. She wasn't entirely sure he admired it.

"Are you going home, too?" she said.

"Not for a while. We expect a ship in June. Maybe after I've warehoused the cases and made my inventory, I can come home for a visit."

"Oh, your inventory. We have to talk business, Phanor. Just like old times."

He smiled, pulled the list from his pocket, and they proceeded to discuss the menu and the wines to accompany the evening. Champagne, of course, and several cases of whites and reds.

"I have a Chenin Blanc that tastes like a fresh, crisp apple," Phanor said. "And you'll want a softer, honeyed demi-sec as well, I think." For the red, Phanor suggested she include a Bourgueil from the Cabernet Franc grapes in the Loire region.

"You have ordered ice?" Phanor asked.

"Oh, ice! I have not. I hope it's not too late?"

"Smithfield is still receiving shipments from the lakes up north. I trade with them for two of the restaurants I sell to. Would you like me to see to the ice?"

"Yes, please."

He was looking at her mouth again. She didn't find it at all flattering. Abruptly, Phanor reached out and smudged her carefully blackened beauty mark.

"What is that?" he said.

He looked at the smear on his thumb. "Oh."

Josie put her finger to the mark and knew it was ruined.

"I'm sorry," he said. "I thought it was maybe a fleck of . . . I didn't realize."

Josie was stiff with embarrassment. She stood up as if to formally end the interview.

"Josie, don't be mad at me," Phanor said. "You're always so pretty, I didn't know it was make-up."

Josie was quite offended, even deflated, and yet here was Phanor, handsome and winning, telling her she was pretty. In her confusion, she didn't know what to say and she kept her head turned away.

Phanor tipped his head to the side and bent over a little to see her face. "*Je suis désolé*, mademoiselle."

Josie kept her eyes averted.

"Josie?" Phanor said. "Mademoiselle Josephine?" he sang sweetly.

Against her will, Josie's mouth began to pull up on one side.

"I see that," Phanor said. "Josie's going to smile."

She looked at him then, and she did smile.

Having won her over, Phanor turned serious. "Forgive me, Josie. I'm still just a Cajun country boy, but I meant what I said. About your being pretty."

They shared a sweet moment holding one another's eyes. Josie felt she could forgive Phanor anything at that moment.

Voices and footsteps in the foyer downstairs reached them. "That'll be my Tante Marguerite. Stay a moment so she can meet you, Phanor." Josie quickly wiped at the beauty mark with her handkerchief before her aunt entered.

Marguerite bustled in, as she always did, and greeted Phanor cordially. More than cordially, Josie thought. Marguerite allowed her hand to linger just a bit too long in Phanor's, and her color was suddenly quite high.

"So you're from Toulouse," Marguerite said.

"A mile or two behind the plantation, madame," he said.

Josie eyed her aunt's transformation from busy matron to flirtatious coquette with disdain. She must be close to thirty, her aunt. Josie glanced at Phanor. He would surely be ill at ease from such brazen attention.

If he was uncomfortable, however, it certainly didn't show. His beautiful smile on display, Phanor returned her aunt's witticisms with the ease of a courtier. Josie felt like a shadow in the room.

"Well, monsieur, it is a great pleasure to make your acquaintance," Marguerite said. "And I'm so glad you will be on hand the night of the party. I don't know how we could manage the wines without you."

"You needn't worry, madame. I will take care of everything." He turned to Josie. "Mademoiselle Josephine," he said formally. "Madame." He bowed to each of them and left the room.

The door closed, Marguerite turned a bright face to Josie. "What a lovely young man," she said. "So handsome and well made. Those shoulders! And charming too. He'll go far, this Monsieur DeBlieux, Cajun or no."

Josie found her aunt's attraction to Phanor distasteful. She was practically gushing. Most unbecoming, Josie thought.

She returned the coffee cups to the tray and gathered her crochet bag. "I'm going upstairs, Tante. I promised to read to André and Pierre."

Upstairs, she found Tante's three boys, Jean Baptiste, André, and Pierre, eating an early supper. She joined them at their small table, and Jean Baptiste climbed down from his chair to sit in her lap. Then he stretched his arms for his plate and continued to stuff bread into his mouth. Josie held him steady and ignored the crumbs he scattered over her skirts as the two older boys proudly explained how they had made little sailboats with paper and sticks.

Josie spent a happy hour with the children. When their nanny announced it was time to wash faces and get ready for bed, Josie gave Jean Baptiste a squeeze. He put his little hands on her face and said, "Jophine." Then Josie kissed André good night. The eldest, Pierre, declared, "I am too old for kisses, cousin." He solemnly held his hand out, and Josie shook it just as gravely.

In her room next to the nursery, Josie listened to the children's voices as their nanny helped them put their toys away and change into their night shirts. What a fine thing, she thought, to have a house full of little boys. And what a delight it must be to have a little girl whose hair you could fix and who would wear pretty dresses and ribbons.

Josie lit the oil lamp and set it in front of the mirror on the dresser. There was still a slight smudge from the beauty mark. She moistened her handkerchief and rubbed the rest of it off. *I suppose it was silly,* she thought. Phanor hadn't liked it at all. But he had said she was pretty. She gazed at herself a while. Not a beauty, she could see that, but fairly pretty. And when she was with Phanor, she felt pretty.

Bertrand would never have been so gauche as to wipe it off with his thumb, like Phanor had done, but he might have thought how foolish she was, all the while he was being charming. Thank goodness Phanor had saved her from that.

Since the moment she'd read Tante Marguerite's invitation list, Josie had been picturing the evening. Bertrand would arrive in his red-lined cape. She would be aware of Bertrand's entrance, but too engaged with the several gentlemen who surrounded her to greet him. He would look for her and spot her immediately. When he saw his chance, he would approach her, a little taken aback at how she had matured these last months.

"Josephine," he'd say, "you are absolutely enchanting."

Josie would employ her fan and murmur, "*Merci*," and she would contrive to blush just a little. He would want to kiss her again; she would see it in his eyes.

The musicians would begin playing a waltz, and Bertrand would say, "Will you dance with me?"

She would place her hand on his arm, her dainty lace-clad hand—and then the fantasy fell apart. The lace was black, and she would invite censure yet again if she danced in her mourning silks. And her hands weren't dainty either. Her fingers were quite long, really, like her long arms and legs. Elegant, she thought, rather than dainty.

Dainty or not, she was not the girl Bertrand had last seen in the fall. Now that she had had a season's worth of parties and practice, Josie felt quite capable of entertaining several men, the handsome Alphonse among them, and Bertrand would see she was ready for him.

Chapter 25

New Orleans

For the first time in his life, Remy had enough to eat. Every coin he earned, he spent on food those first days. And he earned more than he had ever thought possible. However, Remy had no notion of what things cost, and so he spent his earnings carelessly. A plate of beans and rice might be two pesetas at one establishment, and six at another, but Remy simply paid whatever he was asked.

The escape had gone flawlessly. Louis had advised Remy to change his name before they reached the river, and no one questioned the Cajun gentleman and his slave Alain. Once in New Orleans, they found Phanor waiting for them. He had met every steamboat for three days, taking care that his presence was unremarked, but growing increasingly anxious. Phanor greeted Louis warmly with kisses on both cheeks, but quite properly ignored Louis's man Alain.

Phanor led them through the lower streets of New Orleans, past the warehouses full of imported French silks, satins, wines, furniture, china, crystal, and books. They picked their way through the working district watching out for manure and other filth in the unpaved streets. They passed noisy grog shops that catered to sailors, cheap brothels where a skinny woman with unbelievable red hair beckoned to them, and on to the Rue Boucher where they were assaulted by the smell of butchered beef and the drone of black flies dining on offal and blood.

The following morning, Louis caught a boat going upstream. Remy remained out of sight in Phanor's rented room, a sparsely furnished chamber above one of the many butcher shops in the lane. Phanor went in search of the kind of paper a statement of ownership might be written on. He had seen such a document when he struck up a conversation with two slaves working on the docks. Their arrangement with their master was that they brought him 60 percent of their wages and were then allowed to support themselves as they wished with the remaining 40 percent. The two slaves had been challenged so many times by white troublemakers that their owner had allowed them to carry a copy of their papers.

Were Phanor to create papers showing Remy was a freed man, then Remy would be at the mercy of any white slaver unscrupulous enough to steal him back into slavery. There were enough of these men in the cities to make it a real risk for black men, especially one like Remy with no experience of urban life. It was safer to present himself as the property of a white man and thus under his owner's protection. Freedman papers could come later.

At the stationers, Phanor chose three sheets of official-looking paper and bought a fresh nib for his pen. Back in his room, he used a scrap sheet to draft and redraft the forgery. When he was satisfied with the wording and the arrangement of the heading, he wrote a certificate of ownership: One Phanor DeBlieux had purchased one Alain for the sum of $800 in the year of our Lord 1832. He then experimented with one of the extra sheets to make it seem worn and old. A wash of weak tea on both sides of the paper was very effective, but it made the ink run, so he started over on the remaining sheet. Using fine blotting sand, he was able to distress the paper to a realistically worn look, and then he folded and refolded it until it was soft and creased.

With this document safely tucked into a wallet in his pocket, Remy presented himself at the docks to hire on as a stevedore. The head man asked a question or two, glanced at the proof Remy was no runaway, and put him to work loading bales of cotton in a ship bound for New York.

At night he returned to the Rue Boucher. Under Phanor's tutelage, he learned to handle his wages from the docks and found he could save nearly a fourth of what he earned. Someday he would have enough to buy Cleo's freedom.

Phanor bought chalk and a slate. In the evenings, he began teaching Remy to read and write. While Remy practiced making letters on the slate, Phanor studied the French grammar Madame Emmeline had loaned him. The first time he opened it, he had found Josie's childish scrawl on the inside cover: first name, middle names, and last. He had run his finger over the rounded loops and smiled. It would amuse her to know he had her old grammar. Someday he would show it to her, and they would look at the page in the first chapter that was stained with something that looked suspiciously like chocolate.

When Phanor received the note from Josephine to call on her aunt, he had had three weeks with the grammar book. He took his time, tore up the first attempt, and finally produced a respectable note in return. He used the two hours before the appointed time to brush his coat, shine his boots, and scrub himself from a small basin on the floor.

He had arrived at Madame Marguerite Sandrine's block half an hour early, so he walked back toward the river and sat on the levee a while. The Mississippi was hopelessly fouled at this point. Logs always rode the current, but so did carcasses and all the filth of the city. If it had been a narrower river, Phanor thought, the air near the water would be unbreatheable. As it was, the view of ships pulling in and out of the docks was not sufficient reward for the stink. Phanor retreated to the streets, bought a coffee, and watched the people passing. New Orleans never lacked for diversion. Phanor had even seen Chinamen hurrying along in their funny baggy clothes and the wide conical hats they made for themselves.

Phanor had returned to Josie's aunt's and knocked on the door. When Josie herself called to him from the balcony overhead, his uneasiness vanished. She looked wonderful, and she was smiling at him. Of course, later in the day as he reflected on how he had smudged the spot next to her mouth, he cringed at his gaucherie. How was he to have known she would put a black spot on her face—on purpose?

He had the menu and the number of guests. He spent the evening calculating how many bottles of which wines to deliver. Josie's aunt had left it all up to him, and it would present a very nice profit for Monsieur Cherleu. And for him. He was now to take a commission from the sales, to encourage him, Monsieur had said.

That aunt, Marguerite, her name was. She was a handsome woman. And very charming. She'd liked him, clearly, but Phanor remembered Josie's face as Marguerite had flirted with him. Her blank expression was as clear as a scowl to Phanor. Josie was not pleased. He smiled a little at that. *Good, let her be jealous.* He'd certainly be jealous if he were in her place, some man flirting with her while he stood by helplessly.

Remy's footsteps on the stairs announced he was back from his labor on the wharves. Phanor put his papers aside to hear how Remy's day was. Often he came back to the room with questions about how he should handle this or that situation. Once he had been watched by two grungy white men as he rolled kegs of beer up a gangplank. One of them shifted his coat and Remy caught the gleam of metal handcuffs hanging from his belt. The other man gestured toward Remy, and Remy feared they'd noticed his maimed ear. But, he reminded himself, lots of slaves had notched ears. He touched the pocket in his rough pants for reassurance. He was not a runaway: his name was Alain, and he had paper to prove he belonged to Monsieur Phanor DeBlieux of the Rue Boucher.

The two men approached the head man and nodded toward him. Remy was trapped on the long gangplank. He considered diving in the water, even though he couldn't swim. Or he could push the other stevedores aside and make a run for it. But the headman saved him, whether he knew it or not. He shook his head once, then gestured toward the city behind him. The meaning was clear. The slavers were not welcome on the docks, and they'd do well to make their exit.

Since that day, he wore a red plaid kerchief on his head. Phanor had bought it for him at one of the open-air shops near the levee, and he tied it so that it covered his ruined ear. Someday, he would repay Phanor for everything. The escape, the reading lessons, the help in every way. Someday he would be independent, and he would be Phanor's devoted friend until death.

The eighteenth of April arrived, and Phanor rose early. He double-checked that the ice would be delivered to the Sandrine house after the sun went down. Next he oversaw the transport of the cases of wine before the day heated up. The cases filled a large wagon, and he hired two horses to pull it from the warehouse to the back courtyard. Once there, he supervised the unloading of the cases and sorted them according to when he expected them to be served during the evening. Then he helped the hired men set up a loose canopy to shield the wine from the sun during the day. By the time everything was ready, he had sweated through his white shirt, and still the household upstairs slept.

Phanor conducted his usual business throughout the afternoon, calling on his customers and tempting them with samples of his better wines. Before sunset, he hurried back to his rooms to wash and change into a clean shirt. He would be working in the courtyard while his betters enjoyed the party upstairs, but that didn't mean he shouldn't be presentable. Josie might come downstairs to say hello, if she could.

He arrived at the Sandrine's just as the ice wagon did. He supervised the shaving of the ice into vats and the packing of the remaining chunks in sawdust boxes. He layered the bottles of champagne in the loose ice. They would have over an hour to chill before the first corks were pulled.

Liza, the cook, joined him in the circle of the oil lamp set on a wrought-iron table. She was a big woman, testament to her own cooking, and the lamp cast shadows under each of her chins. Even so, her queenly air and bright eyes made her a handsome woman, Phanor thought.

"M'sieu, you best set awhile now. It gon' get busy when all Madame's friends come in. Can I bring you a plate of supper?"

"Liza, you are my angel. I'm a hungry man, I am."

Phanor uncorked a bottle of Cabernet and poured the wine into a tin cup. He noted the taste of the cup first of all, but it was a generous wine, full-flavored, and the feel of it along his palate was a delight. Liza rolled across the courtyard with a tray loaded with shrimp, beef, potatoes, cornbread, and her own special plum preserves.

"A feast!" Phanor said. "You, Liza, you think my legs both hollow?"

Liza laughed from deep in her belly. "You gone need yo

strength, you work long fo Madame Sandrine. You eat dat, I bring you some oysters later." She winked at him, and Phanor laughed heartily. He dug in and ate nearly everything until he thought he might have to unbutton the top of his trousers.

The musicians began tuning their instruments upstairs, and Phanor had a pang of regret that he was not among them. He had hardly played his fiddle at all these last weeks, he'd been so tied up with business, Remy, and his own studies. The coming Sunday, he resolved, he would take his fiddle to Jackson Square and play all day. He had an idle moment wishing Josie would come with her flute and Remy would sing as they played. Foolish thought. He stood up and gathered a basket full of bottles to take upstairs to the serving pantry.

Once the party was well under way, Phanor found Liza was right. Acting as wine steward, he was on the run from the cache in the courtyard to the pantry, orchestrating the type and number of bottles open and flowing as the evening wore on. The butler kept him apprised of hot dishes arriving from the kitchen and of the progress of the party, so Phanor did not actually see the whirl of satin skirts. He had an ear for the orchestra, though, and he found time to wonder who Josie might be dancing with, and whether she had painted another spot on her face.

Not long after midnight, the pantry door swung open and Marguerite Sandrine sauntered in. She wore an emerald green gown with enormous puffed sleeves. The neckline revealed a smooth white bosom generously plumped by her bodice so that Phanor barely registered the emerald pendant nestled just at the hollow between her breasts.

"Monsieur DeBlieux," she said. "I've come to tell you how much I appreciate your efforts tonight." His eyes were on her bosom, and she folded her fan. "I've never seen a party go so well, and I'm sure it's because of the flow of just the right wines."

Phanor raised his eyes. She was a beautiful woman tonight, he thought as he admired her deep brown eyes, and she knew it. That knowingness did not detract from her charms, however. On the contrary.

When Phanor did not respond, at least not verbally, Marguerite said, "May I call you Phanor? My niece and you, you are quite good friends, I gather. From childhood?"

Phanor recovered himself. "Mademoiselle Josephine and I are friends, yes. We share our home place, and we have music between us too."

"Music? I had never thought of Josephine as being particularly musical."

Phanor detected just a hint of malice. It made Marguerite only slightly less alluring.

"I'd like us to be friends too," she said. She opened her fan and moved the black lace across her reddened mouth. The green silk rustled as she took a step farther into the pantry.

Phanor glanced at the closed door, a crowd of people just on the other side, their voices and laughter loud and gay. He stood very still as Marguerite advanced closer.

"I hope we are friends," he managed to say.

Marguerite was very close now. The hem of her gown brushed against his boots. Her expensive Paris perfume wafted over him, and he knew he'd never been so close to divinity in his life.

She traced the line of his jaw with the edge of her fan. "You are a handsome man, Phanor DeBlieux."

Phanor's breathing came shallow and rapid. Her perfume was intoxicating, the strains of the waltz sensual and compelling. He hardly knew his own hand when he saw it on her waist.

He bent his head to meet her upturned face, and he tasted her lips. As their kiss deepened, Phanor slid his hand around to the small of her back and pulled her to him.

The door opened.

"Thomas, have you seen my—" Josephine stood in the doorway.

Phanor froze. Marguerite, however, pulled away slowly and turned to her niece. No blush, no hint of shame or guilt, but perhaps a glint of triumph in her eyes.

"Yes, Josephine?"

Phanor stared into Josie's wide eyes. She mustn't think he . . . Well, what could she think?

"Josie," he said.

Josie slowly backed out, her eyes still on his, and allowed the door to close.

When Marguerite turned back to Phanor, so close that her bosom brushed against his chest, she smiled and reached an arm up to his neck. But Phanor did not respond. He stood stiffly and gently pulled her arm down.

"I have to see to the wine," he said.

Marguerite stepped back. Her expression hardened, and the expanse of chest and bosom reddened. "You're still a boy, I see," she said. She gathered her skirts and stepped quickly through the pantry and out into the din of the party.

Phanor ran his hands through his hair. What had he been thinking? Hell, thinking hadn't been any part of it. Marguerite's perfume still filled the little pantry, but it wasn't Marguerite's face in his mind's eye.

Chapter 26

Earlier the evening of the party

As Josie checked her hemline one last time in her aunt's mirror, Marguerite stood behind her.

"You look quite the young lady, Josephine. No wonder your Mr. Johnston does not forget you, in spite of my friend Achille's efforts." She smoothed a bit of lace at Josie's neckline and said, "Hold still a moment." Marguerite chose a crystal atomizer from her dresser and sprayed her best perfume on Josie's shoulders.

Josie inhaled deeply. "That is the most wonderful scent."

"Of course, now you will have to work even harder to keep Mr. Johnston at bay," Marguerite said.

"I wish he'd follow you around all night instead," Josie said.

"Not an unpleasant prospect, *chérie*, in spite of your assessment of his charms." She adjusted her bosom in the push-up bodice of her gown. "Those wonderful big hands of his," she said.

Josie had never noticed Albany's hands. If pressed for a compliment, she might have mentioned that he always seemed very clean.

"Shall we go down?" Marguerite said.

As the guests mingled, Josie kept her eye on the door for Bertrand's arrival. The orchestra played for the few who were ready to dance so early in the evening, and Josie's foot tapped as she sat on a sofa. There'd be no forgetting she was in mourning this time, but next season in New Orleans, she meant to make up for the dancing she'd missed.

Her companion of the last party, Alphonse Bardot, came in with his old father on his arm. Alphonse nodded and smiled at Josie before he settled the old man on a sofa with his friends, then came to her and bowed.

"Mademoiselle Josephine, I'm happy to see you again."

She held out her hand and asked, "Will you sit with me, monsieur?"

He spread the tails of his coat and took the yellow silk chair next to her. "You look lovely tonight."

She put her fan in her lap and smiled. "Have you been following the horses this season?"

As amusing as Alphonse was, Josie kept an eye on the door. Bertrand was late, as always. Now and then, when Thomas the butler emerged from the pantry, she would catch sight of Phanor uncorking bottles of wine. She wanted to show him she had not worn the beauty spot. And she wanted to tell him his fiddle playing was at least as good as these New Orleans musicians'.

Albany Johnston arrived with his sister Abigail on his arm. He had continued to attend Josie at every occasion since she'd turned him down. Josie wondered how he could bear the awkwardness, but he made no further mention of his suit—perhaps he was a patient man. They had become almost comfortable with one another again.

When Albany and Abigail joined Josie in her corner of

the room, she introduced them. "Do you know Alphonse Bardot?" Alphonse stood and bowed to Abigail, then held out his hand to the American gentleman. *Interesting,* Josie thought, *how we Creoles are adopting the* américain *handshake rather than the* américains *learning to kiss.*

Abigail, in a blue gown with yards and yards of ruffles, fluttered her blue eyes at Alphonse. When the orchestra resumed, he invited Abigail to dance, and Josie was left with her suitor.

Josie struggled for a suitable topic of conversation. "How do you think the cane will sell this year?" she said.

Albany's small smile was pained. "I don't believe you are really interested in cane, Josephine."

She forced a laugh. "Well, I know I should be."

"Very well. I'll tell you what the brokers are saying," and he launched into a technical discussion of futures and markets. Josie really did listen the first ten minutes, but her attention drifted to the door every time it opened. Wasn't Bertrand coming?

Alphonse's father interrupted Albany's discourse. "My son is enjoying himself, mademoiselle," the old man said, "and I leave him in your delightful company. Perhaps, however, you could find your aunt for me to bid her good night."

"Of course, monsieur. I'll bring her to you."

Marguerite should be easy to spot in her green gown, Josie thought, a jewel among the partiers, but she wasn't on the dance floor, or in the parlor, or on the balcony. Maybe she was consulting with Thomas in the pantry.

When Josie swung the pantry door inward, she said, "Thomas, have you seen my—" But it wasn't Thomas she saw.

The heat between Marguerite and Phanor was unmistakable, even to one so inexperienced as Josie, and the guilt in Phanor's eyes gave him away even if his mouth on her aunt's had not.

Josie closed the pantry door and stood trembling, her whole body aflame with indignation, and with something else. She was aroused, though she would have scoffed at the idea.

How could he? she fumed. Marguerite was a married woman. With three children. And old. It was true, then, what they said about Cajuns and women. She blinked back hot tears. Well. Well, it was nothing to her what Phanor DeBlieux did.

She wouldn't think of it again. Not now, anyway. With a shake of her head, as if she could clear it of the image of Phanor's hand pressing her aunt's back, she took a breath and reentered the party. She had duties to perform.

Josie made her aunt's excuses to Monsieur Bardot, and she and Albany walked with him to the door. Turning back into the party, Josie saw her drab cousin Violette, she of the long nose and discontented expression, sitting alone and forlorn.

With a hostess's mindfulness, Josie led Albany to Violette's seat. "Mademoiselle Violette, Mr. Albany Johnston. Violette is my cousin, Albany. You two have a lot in common, you know. Her father spent several years in New York, and he is now a broker here in New Orleans."

"Indeed?" Albany sat down next to Violette without ceremony. "New York is my home. Or rather it was. I am a Louisianan, now. And your father, he deals in cane?"

Violette found her tongue, and the two of them launched into a knowledgeable discussion of the business world in New Orleans. Josie wondered if her plain cousin appealed to Albany more than the beauties at the Blue Ribbon. He certainly seemed interested in her remarks about the inner workings of finance.

The parlor door opened. Surely this time it would be Bertrand.

He entered the party as if he owned the room, aware he

commanded the attention of every female eye. His mouth drew up on one side in a slightly amused smile at the momentary stillness of the party. Oncle Sandrine offered him a flute of champagne and the two of them joined a group of men who shared their love of gaming, men who thought nothing of tossing the deed to some lesser property on the table to cover a bet.

Josie circled the room, speaking to this guest and that, but watching Bertrand every moment. He stood in the gallery door, the breeze hardly ruffling his thick hair tied in the back with a black satin ribbon. He'd lost weight, and his face showed the vitality of days spent in the sun. Here was a *man*, not a groping boy raw from the bayous.

Josie stood with Oncle Sandrine's aging brother, but she focused on Chamard. The noises of the party receded into a silvery blur as the voices, even the orchestra's strains, became muted. Every one of the hundred candles in the room became a golden shimmer.

She willed him to look at her. She let her desire fuel her concentration as she fixed her gaze on the arch of his brow, the fullness of his dark lashes. He had to feel her heat.

He raised his eyes, absorbed her gaze, took in her whole being. Even across the room she caught the color of his eyes, like fine brandy in candlelight. Josie felt her soul might leave her body to enter those eyes.

He left his companions and moved sinuously through the crowd, the grace of his body seducing every woman he passed. Josie heard the silk skirts rustle as the ladies turned in his wake, but she never released him from her gaze.

"Cousin Josephine."

Josie held out her hand. Chamard took it in his, and her whole body vibrated at his touch. When he brushed his lips across the back of her hand, pressing his thumb into her palm, the sudden response of her most private place astonished her. What did he do to her? Was this love, then?

Neither of them aware of the speechless and forgotten elder man, Bertrand took her elbow and guided her away from the current of guests moving in and out of the ballroom. Under the fronds of a palm in the corner of the room, Bertrand inspected her openly, brazenly, and she didn't falter in his steady gaze. "How are you, *ma chérie*?" he said.

Bold and reckless, full of champagne, Josie said, "Very happy to see you."

Bertrand raised an eyebrow. "The lovely mademoiselle surrounded by eligible young men? You're glad to see your old cousin?"

Josie leaned her head back. She refused to be condescended to. "You are not so very old, nor am I so very young." She held his eyes and forced him to recognize the challenge in hers. He did want her. She could feel it.

"Not too young to marry Albany Johnston?" Bertrand said.

"Not too young, no." Did she detect disappointment in her cousin's eye?

"So it's settled."

"Indeed it is. I will not be Mr. Johnston's wife."

Josie kept her chin tilted up and smiled. She had a hook in Bertrand Chamard, she was sure of it.

Part III

Chapter 27

Toulouse, June 1837

"Ready?" Bertrand said.

Josie's hands were on his shoulders, her foot in his cupped palms. "Ready."

Bertrand lifted Josie into her saddle effortlessly. She laughed at the moment of weightlessness, nearly giddy with Bertrand's touch.

Bertrand mounted his big roan and led the way out the lane to the river road. The morning dew softened the summer greens and a light fog hung in the treetops. Josie eyed Bertrand's legs astride the saddle. She imagined running her hands over those taut muscles, entangling her fingers in the mane of black hair tied at his neck.

Once on the main road, Bertrand picked up the pace. They loped along for a quarter of a mile side by side, neither disturbing the quiet air with idle chatter. Then Bertrand said, "Shall we run?"

Josie gave Beau the whip and she was off. She leaned forward, clamped her knee tight around the pommel, and pressed her left foot hard into the stirrup. She looked back over her shoulder and grinned at Bertrand. She'd got the jump on him, but the stallion would easily overtake her if he let it. She spurred Beau on.

They galloped full tilt under the overhanging live oaks, their horses throwing clods up behind them. Josie's hat flew off and soon she was streaming honey brown hair behind her, the pins fallen somewhere in the dust. She stole a glance at Bertrand. He must surely be holding the roan back, but even so, his face showed the same joy she felt. Release and exhilaration all in one. They were two of a kind, she and Bertrand. They were meant for each other.

Bertrand pointed to the peach orchard that grew between their two properties. Josie slowed Beau and directed him into the shade where the golden peaches were swelling with every new day of sunshine. Josie inhaled the scent of horse and grass and rich black dirt. The sensual earth breathed in rhythm with Josie's own breast, heightened her senses, smell and sight, and most of all, touch.

Bertrand dropped his reins to let his horse browse among the trees. Before he helped Josie from her saddle, he took hold of her booted ankle and gazed into her face. "Such a proper young lady, one might think, until one sees you on a horse." He tilted his head to consider her. "Are you brave enough to walk with me in the orchard, no chaperone, no spying eyes to keep you safe?"

Josie's breath caught, and she held the pommel to keep her hands from trembling. "I will walk with you anywhere, Bertrand. You know that."

He smiled and held his hands up to her. When he had her feet on the ground, he lingered close to her and then stepped back. He took her hand and they strolled under the peach trees. The grass, sprinkled with tiny white wild flowers, grew lush and green. Each blade, each leaf, was distinct. Each peach, perfect and round and golden, promised pleasure. A mockingbird flitted along ahead of them, and every note, every flap of its wings impressed itself on Josie's senses. The very air, heavy on her skin, excited her.

Bertrand picked a peach, yellow and red and ripe. He held it for her to take a bite, and the juices filled her mouth, ran down her chin and into her bodice. She wiped her mouth but his eyes were on her lips, and she yearned for him to taste her. Instead, he took her hand again and drew her further into the orchard.

Josie's skirts swept the remaining dew from the tall grass, but she didn't notice. Her heart beat hard enough to flutter the ruffle on her bodice. At the same time, she felt deeply content and calm. It was time. That was all. It was time, and she was ready. Bertrand would never need another woman. She would be everything he desired because she desired him in return.

Deep into the orchard stood a massive live oak, dripping with moss, its branches drooping down to create a shadowy chamber cut off from the rest of the world. Here Bertrand turned. He touched her windblown hair and pulled a tangled curl from her forehead.

Now, she thought. Now.

His first kiss was tender. If flesh could melt, her lips would surely melt into his. Josie swayed on her feet, and Bertrand's arms held her closer. As he kissed her with more ardor, she felt his body harden and lost all awareness of the world outside the two of them.

When Josie felt his tongue against her lips, she opened her mouth, yearning to take all of him in. He pressed the small of her back against him, and through her summer skirt she felt the hardness of his manhood.

Josie shifted and placed her palm over his swelling. He trembled, then pulled his head back from her and breathed deeply. Again he questioned her with his eyes, and Josie smiled. Why should they wait? She reached her arms around his neck and kissed him as he'd kissed her.

Bertrand swept her into his arms and carried her deeper into the grassy shade. He laid her down and knelt beside her. "You're not afraid?"

She answered him with her mouth on his. Bertrand slipped a hand into her bodice, felt the weight of her breast. When he flicked his thumb over her nipple, Josie nearly cried out. She reached for his swollen groin, but he held her hand. "Not today," he murmured.

Bertrand lay beside her in the grass and reached down to her hemline. He ran his hand up her leg, and through her pantaloons found her secret pleasure. Josie gasped and he smiled at her, his beautiful eyes on hers. He kissed her mouth, her neck, tasted the hollow at the base of her throat, all the while stroking and caressing. The exquisite tension grew until Josie moaned and her breath came ragged.

Bertrand broke their kiss and held her tight until her shuddering stopped. He kissed the top of her head and let her rest in his arms.

The world came slowly into focus again—the grass tickling her skin, the bees buzzing among the peaches, the dappling of the sun through the oak leaves. Such peace. Such completeness. Was not this a promise? Did they not belong to each other now?

Josie opened Bertrand's shirt at the neck and kissed the sweetness there. His voice roughened by desire, Bertrand said, "I'd better take you home."

They brushed the grass from their clothes. "Should you fix your hair?"

"I've lost all the pins, I'm afraid."

Bertrand pulled a twig from her curls. "You'll have to do, then. Surely your grandmother has lost her hairpins in a gallop or two."

Josie laughed and took his hand. They found their horses

grazing among the trees and rode them slowly back to Toulouse.

At the stables, Elbow John took the horses. Josie slipped into her room to repair the damage to hair and face and dress. In the mirror, she saw a new Josie, lips swollen, cheeks chafed by his whiskers. What she'd shared with Bertrand was not consummation, she understood that, but she didn't feel like a virgin anymore, either. She was his woman. She would be the mother of his children, all of his children.

Bertrand had ambled on to the front gallery where Emmeline was reading a two-day-old *New Orleans Picayune*.

"Have you seen this, Bertrand?" she said, snapping the paper in agitation.

He leaned against a gallery post. "Not yet. What has you so stirred up?"

"It can't last. An acre of off-river land goes for three times what it did two years ago. Fools borrow to grab what they can, and the banks feed the frenzy. There will come a reckoning."

"It's a boom time, Emmeline." He searched his pocket and pulled out a cigar. "May I? It's a new era. As long as Europe continues to buy more and more cotton and sugar, the market will expand." He inhaled the smoke gratefully and blew it toward the ceiling.

Josie stepped onto the gallery, her hair properly dressed, her face washed. Bertrand straightened from his slouch against the gallery post. "Josephine," he said in his courtly manner.

Emmeline cast a shrewd eye on each of them. Yes, she believed, there would be a wedding in the fall. She had been scandalously negligent in not insisting the pair were chaperoned at all times. But she was in a hurry. Bertrand wouldn't remain a bachelor for long.

Bertrand held his hand against the sky to measure the sun's progress. "I must be on my way. Work awaits."

Josie could hardly bear for him to leave her. She wanted

only to be in his arms, but she behaved as a young lady ought. His warm eyes looking into hers suffused her heart, and she let him go.

On the way to the stable, Bertrand spotted Cleo cutting flowers in the garden. He'd hardly seen her these last weeks. She had been avoiding him, he realized. He willed her to look up, and as if his stare penetrated her skin, Cleo raised her head and returned his gaze. Then she lowered her eyes and turned away.

Cleo filled her flower basket before she went inside. In the parlor, she arranged a vase of roses and baby's breath, saving the camellias for the dining table. The transplants from Dr. Benet's garden thrived in the renewed soil, and Cleo had taken it on herself, since now the reduced number of hands were all needed in the fields, to revive the garden. She had a new callus on her palm from wielding the hoe, but she welcomed the mindless work. Her body and her heart ached for Remy, and with every message Phanor brought, her patience wore thinner.

Cleo carried the three secret letters in her bodice, each of them worn from opening and reopening. Remy's first effort was a mere three words, scrawled slant-wise across the page, and he wrote as he spoke: *I workin hard.* With Phanor's tutelage and practice, though, the lines had become level, the letters more precise. *I save ever week. I got four silver dollar put by. I gon' kiss the paper where I make the X. Keep waiting. I working hard for us.*

Four dollars. How could Remy ever earn enough to buy her freedom?

Josie entered the room and paused to admire the bouquet for a moment. "Those are pretty," she said, and then she walked on.

Cleo felt Josie's absence even now she was home from

New Orleans. Josie was abstracted, sat for long periods staring at the river from the gallery or out her bedroom window at the stump where the lightning had burned down the old oak.

Even when Phanor came home to visit his family. Cleo had expected Josie to be at least pleased to see Phanor. Phanor would have hoped for that too, Cleo was sure. He'd made no secret of his attraction to her, for all her being the daughter of a planter. And that night on the levee, hadn't Josie sat as close as possible to Phanor on the log in the firelight? Yet Josie had greeted him rather coolly, even with a bit of hauteur, and Cleo had seen Phanor's face droop. It was odd, his reaction. He was disappointed, but didn't seem surprised.

It was no mystery where Josie's mind and heart were—she was bewitched by her Monsieur Chamard, he of the seductive, enchanting eyes.

And did Josie think this Chamard was any different from her beloved papa? Did she think he would love only her forever and ever, would never hurt her as Emile had hurt Josie's maman Celine? Cleo knew better.

Chapter 28

Toulouse

"Mam'zelle," Laurie said, "Madame say you come now. And don' forget dem spectacles neither."

The dreaded spectacles. Josie kept them in a drawer wrapped in a handkerchief. She'd rather not be able to read than to be seen wearing spectacles. Bertrand certainly had never seen her in them. If Grand-mère required them, that meant she was in for a session with the account books.

"Sit down, Josephine." Grand-mère had covered the green-clothed table with ledgers, and a cup of freshly sharpened pencils stood at the ready.

"Did you read the newspaper this morning as I asked you to?"

"Yes, Grand-mère," Josie lied. Well, she had read a little of it, but her eyes had begun to hurt and her glasses were in the other room. And it was deadly boring, those pages about President Van Buren, Congress, and the economy. She much preferred to sit unseen in her window seat, glasses on, reading Victor Hugo.

"Then you know Monsieur Beaufort insists the economy is healthy, and people who say otherwise are foolish doomsayers. What is your opinion, Josephine?"

Josie swallowed. How was she supposed to know? And who cared, anyway? Grand-mère ran Toulouse, and Bertrand would take over when they were married. "Grand-mère, I—"

"You didn't read the financial page, did you?"

"No, but—"

"Laurie, we'll have a pot of tea," Grand-mère interrupted again. "Meanwhile, Josephine, I will try to impress upon you yet again the importance of reading the financial news. We'll begin with the ledger for three years ago. Find the one for 1834 and look up the figures for the year's expenses."

Josie perched her spectacles on her nose and read off the costs for feeding and clothing the slaves, for fertilizer, for repairs to the roof, for Monsieur Gale's salary, wine, provisions, Dr. Benet's fees, gifts to the church, and so on.

"And the total?" Grand-mère said. "Write it in the appropriate column on this sheet. We're going to compare the last three years."

Josie grudgingly began filling in the assets and debits on the chart for each year. Naturally there had been little income the previous year because of the flood. They'd lost most of the crop, and there was the rebuilding and replanting to pay for. Papa's gambling losses had also been substantial. Still, she'd had no idea. They were deeply in debt.

"What is your conclusion, Josephine?"

Josie peered at the chart. "Well, we seemed to be doing quite well before the flood," Josie said. She looked at Grand-mère. "Is that right?"

"Yes, you are correct. And now?"

"We're in debt. But surely that's just until the next crop comes in. Isn't it?"

"Did you compare the cash realized from the cane crop before the flood with debt we now carry?"

Josie ran her finger across the page. It would take four or five good years to erase their debt, even once the new refinery was up and running.

"But—"

"No foolish optimism, Josephine. Debt grows. You realize that, don't you?"

Josie remembered an earlier lecture about interest rates. She began to wish she'd listened more carefully.

"Which brings us back to the financial pages. Will the bank hold our paper, or will it not? That depends on the economy. Do you begin to see?"

Josie hoped Grand-mère would not again fix her with steely eyes and remind her how much like her father she was, how irresponsible, how likely to go to ruin if she depended on others to look after her interests.

"Grand-mère, why don't you just tell me what's going to happen?"

"If I had the Sight, you would have known it before now. I speak of possibilities, that's all, but I don't like this heated economy. Too many people are overextended—as we are."

"And what am I do to about it?" Josie said as mildly as she could.

"Do?" Grand-mère snapped. "There is nothing either of us can do, Josephine. But you must at least be aware of what can happen. Use the brain God has given you."

"When I am married to—"

"No one has asked me for your hand, Josephine, not since you turned down the rich *americain*. What is certain is you will be responsible for Toulouse and all the souls who labor on it. Married or not."

Josie flushed. Grand-mère had as usual rubbed her most

sensitive spot. Josie was not engaged. As good as, she thought, but in truth Bertrand had not spoken of marriage. Not yet.

"You realize, Josephine, your Monsieur Chamard is likely burdened with large debts himself. He's bought more slaves, cleared more ground, replanted old fields. Bertrand reads the financial pages, I assure you. However starry-eyed you may be, he has a clear eye on the final figures in his ledger."

Josie straightened in her chair. Grand-mère might believe Bertrand was as mercenary as she was, Josie thought, but Josie knew better. Josie had felt the promise in his kisses. Bertrand wanted her, with or without debts.

"Is that all?" Josie said coolly. "I need to dress before Bertrand arrives."

"You may go. But I shall expect you to have read the financial news when next we talk of business, Josephine."

Cleo smoothed her dress when she heard Monsieur Chamard's horse in the courtyard. She did not encourage his attention—she would not be so bold, nor so hateful to Josie. But Cleo admitted to the pleasure of his glance.

During noon dinner, Cleo served the baked hen, the fried okra, and the fresh rolls Louella had baked. Now that Josie was in love, Cleo thought, she might realize how badly she suffered without Remy. Then again, Josie had likely forgotten all about Remy. Josie could afford to think only of herself, to anticipate hopes fulfilled. A slave had no such luxury.

Monsieur divided his attention between Madame Emmeline and Josie during dinner. He spoke with Josie about horses and manners on the Continent, with Madame about the latest fluctuations in the market. All three women in the room, Cleo realized, craved his notice. Madame was lonely since Celine, Emile, and even Bibi had died. Few people matched her quick mind, but Monsieur apparently did. And Cleo herself felt his presence, even when he seemed to ignore her.

But Cleo had resolved long before to have her own life with Remy. She did not wish to repeat the role her mother had played in this house, sharing another woman's husband, no right to his love nor to his protection. She was honest with herself about her attraction to Monsieur, and about his obvious appreciation of her, but she would not seek his attentions—or accept them, if it came to that.

As the three rose from the table, Madame put a hand to her throat. "It is exceptionally warm today. I hope you will excuse me, Bertrand. I believe I will lie down."

Bertrand hastened to take her arm. "Are you all right? Should you like the doctor?"

"No, no. I'm simply tired, and I foolishly ate too much of Louella's sponge cake. You and Josephine enjoy the breeze in the parlor. Josephine, have Louella make you some lemonade."

Bertrand handed Madame off to Cleo, who walked her into the bedroom. Cleo unbuttoned the stifling dress and poured water into the basin to bathe Madame's face and neck. "The heat has put me down, I'm afraid," Madame said. "Thank you, Cleo."

As Cleo prepared to leave Madame in order to wait on Josie and her guest, Madame said, "Perhaps it would be as well if Laurie served Josephine and Monsieur."

Cleo avoided the piercing look, understanding its meaning, and dipped her head. "Yes, Madame."

She found Laurie wiping the dining table and informed her she was to serve lemonade in the parlor. Laurie must be mindful not to address either Mam'zelle or the gentleman, but simply to hand them a glass without spilling a drop.

"You think I stupid? I know dat," Laurie said.

Madame had spoiled this child beyond enduring. She grabbed a pinch of flesh above Laurie's skinny elbow and twisted it. "Not a sound out of you, Laurie. Madame's resting, and you better get to it." Laurie stuck her tongue out at Cleo, but she hushed.

While Bertrand entertained Josie in the parlor with stories of his schooldays in Paris, the mail boat tooted, and Elbow John hustled to the dock. When all went as planned, the boat slowed enough to catch the mail bag onto the hook hanging out over the river, but if the boy missed the hook, he'd try to toss it to John on the dock. More than once John had had to slip into the river to fish the bag out.

In fact, though, the boy heaved the bag onto the hook with perfect timing and waved to John as the boat veered back into the current. Madame Emmeline had heard the boat whistle too, and roused herself from bed to watch Elbow John take his time sauntering back from the levee. "Up here, John," she called when he came close.

She was vaguely aware of the murmur of Josie and Bertrand's voices in the parlor as she impatiently dealt with the knot on the mail bag. She left the several letters for later and unfolded the *New Orleans Picayune*. She did not need to turn to the back to find the financial news. The editors had emblazoned the state of the economy in huge black type across the front page: FIRST BANK OF NEW ORLEANS CLOSES ITS DOORS, she read. Below that, another headline: NEW YORK IN PANIC AS INVESTORS RIOT IN THE STREET.

It had happened. Even sooner than she'd feared, the boom time had collapsed. She had lived through the depression of 1792 when she was a girl, and she knew what lay ahead. Her father had lost half of his estate before the economy righted itself. Toulouse was at terrible risk.

Emmeline swayed a little as she stood. She walked lead-footed into the parlor and, without preamble, handed the paper to Bertrand. At sight of her face, he yielded his seat to her immediately and looked to Josie to pour her a lemonade.

Emmeline waved the glass away and said, "Read it."

Bertrand scanned the headlines and sat heavily in the chair next to Emmeline. "You were right all along."

Josie took the paper from his hand and read the news. She raised her head to find Bertrand looking at her curiously.

"Do you know what a panic is, Josephine?" he asked.

"Grand-mère has told me. We won't be able to borrow any more money, I think."

Bertrand looked to Emmeline, who met his eyes and confirmed what he suspected. Josie had no idea how bad things could get. Nor how the crash might affect her personally.

Josie looked from Bertrand to Grand-mère. Neither offered her any reassurance, and their silence frightened her as much as the pallor of their faces. Bertrand's gaze seemed to her to be heavy with a meaning she could not read.

Formal now, as he had not been in all these last glorious weeks of courting, Bertrand stood. "I must go to New Orleans," he said.

He picked up his hat from the side table where Cleo had left it. "Madame," he said, and, "Mademoiselle."

"How long will you be gone?" Josie said.

He looked at his hat a moment before he answered her. "I don't know when I will see you again, Josephine."

She followed him to the front gallery hoping for a moment alone with him, a touch of his hand, some gesture of closeness, but he didn't turn to her at the top of the steps. Standing on the gallery, Josie watched him cinch the saddle on the big roan grazing in the shade. She waited for him to turn and wave, but without looking back, he quickly rode away from her down the alley of oaks.

Chapter 29

Toulouse

The house was quiet the rest of the day as if there had been another death in the family. Cleo sent Laurie to the gallery to fan the flies away from Madame. Madame Emmeline hadn't spoken since Monsieur Chamard left the house. She sat on the shady side of the gallery and stared out at the oaks and the levee and the glint of the river on the other side of it.

Supper was cold meat and bread, eaten in silence. Cleo attended the table unobtrusively. She had read the paper discarded on the sofa, and though she understood the news imperfectly, she knew Toulouse had to be in debt, and that even Josie wore a frightened pinched look.

Did it mean Remy would not be able to save as much money? Would he still find work on the docks in New Orleans? Phanor would know, if only he would come home to visit, bring her another note from Remy. The longing and loneliness sometimes swelled inside her until she thought she'd burst.

When the summer sun at last began to sink, Madame called for Cleo to light the oil lamp in her office. The cheese-cloth over the windows kept out most of the mosquitoes and flies in this room, and Madame said, "I won't need Laurie anymore tonight. Send her to bed." Cleo delivered a pitcher of cool water and a crystal goblet to the office and left Madame with her ledgers.

In the bedroom, Cleo found Josie writing in her diary by candlelight. After the afternoon and evening in a silent house, Cleo wanted to talk, but Josie didn't look up from her page.

From the steps of the back gallery, Cleo peered into the early darkness and listened for the overseer's step. His snarly dog never left his side since Old Sam's dog Boots had at-tacked him, and Cleo feared this dog as much as she did LeBrec. Satisfied they were not about, Cleo crossed the thirty yards to the cookhouse.

A single candle lit the back room where Louella and Thibault slept. Thibault lay on his cot in blissful oblivion. Louella rested in the cowhide chair leaned back against the wall. "Come in, *chérie*," she called when Cleo appeared at the door.

"Whas goin' on over dere?" Louella said as Cleo lowered herself into the other chair. "I hear not a sound all day from de house. Madame got one of dose headaches?"

Cleo shook her head. "It's bad news from New Orleans. The banks are closing, and people are worried about their money."

"Dat's one worry I don' never have. Me, nor you neither."

"Madame is worried enough for all of us, I think."

"I got me two lemons left in de kitchen. We have us some lemonade, just like de white folks. You fetch us some cool water from de cistern while I cuts de lemons."

Cleo stepped out into the yard and took a deep breath of the cooler air. She filled Louella's water jug, swatting at mosquitoes the whole time. As she turned to cover the twenty feet to the cookhouse, she smelled the ripe odors of whiskey, man, and dog.

"You s'posed to be out here, gal?" LeBrec said.

The dog's low growl froze Cleo's steps. She touched the folding razor in her pocket, the one she had taken from Monsieur Emile's drawer. He would have wanted her to have it, she'd reasoned, now that he could not protect her.

"I'm fetching water for Louella," she said. The edge of defiance in her voice was stronger than her fear.

"I might like me some of what you got there." LeBrec, and the dog, stepped toward her. "You probably as cool and sweet as that water, ain't you."

"Don't come any closer, monsieur," Cleo said. She pulled the razor from her pocket and hoped he'd see a glint of light on the blade.

"You little bitch," LeBrec said and lurched toward her.

A candle held high at the cookhouse door lit the tableau of Cleo at the ready, Lebrec swaying in his drunkenness, the dog holding its head low.

"*Bonsoir*, monsieur," Louella said. Her tone was calm, but it hinted at deadly assurance. "Maybe I give you a cup for some of dat cool water."

In the candlelight, LeBrec considered Louella's bulk, half a hand taller than he was and forty pounds heavier. "Keep your damn water," he slurred. The dog growled once and followed its master into the darkness.

"Come on in here, sugar," Louella said to Cleo. "Let's us make dat lemonade."

An hour later, Cleo headed back to the house, Louella walking her halfway and then watching her climb the gallery steps in the light from the new moon. In the house, Cleo saw Madame's lamp glow under the doorway to the office. She tapped on the door to see if Madame wanted anything, but there was no answer.

Cleo opened the door, assuming Madame had fallen asleep over her ledgers. She would be stiff and cantankerous in the morning if Cleo didn't get her into the bed. For a moment, Cleo admired Madame's silvery hair in the lamp's glow, but then her awkward posture registered. The slump of her body was rigid, not relaxed in sleep.

"Madame?"

A muted cry came from deep in Madame's throat and Cleo rushed to her. Madame's face pulled down on the left side, that eye nearly closed.

"Madame, what's happened?"

Madame Emmeline fixed Cleo with her one good eye in fearful appeal. A whimper escaped her twisted mouth, and Cleo grabbed her arms to steady her.

"I'll be right back. I'll be back." Cleo ran from the room and at the top of the stairs began calling, "Louella, Louella!"

At the third cry, Louella appeared at her door with the candle in hand. Cleo called her again, and the big woman came running. She thundered up the stairs and ran to the only room in the house that wasn't dark.

Cleo knelt at Madame's chair. "She can't talk, Louella. Look at her face."

"Lor' amighty! I seen dis afore. You go get Mam'zelle, den we put Madame in de bed."

Cleo ran to the bedroom and pulled aside the stifling mosquito netting. "Josie," she said. Josie slept in a sleeveless shift, and when Cleo shook her she felt the sheen of sweat on Josie's skin. "Josie, wake up."

Josie sat up, startled. "What is it?"

"Grand-mère's had a stroke."

The two hurried back to the office where Louella was unbuttoning Madame's neckline. "Grand-mère?" Josie cried. When she saw her mouth pulled down on one side, her eye drooping, Josie drew back.

"Let's get her in de bed, fust ting," Louella said.

Josie's trembling roused Cleo. "Can you turn the bed down?" she said to Josie, hoping something to do would calm her.

Cleo and Louella pulled the hot dress off Madame and carried her into the bed. She whimpered when they lay her down, and she raised her right hand toward Josie.

"I'm here, Grand-mère," Josie said.

Cleo watched Madame struggle to speak, but the sounds were garbled. The hand pointed vaguely to the back of the house, and the three women could not understand. "Do you want water?" Josie asked and rushed to fill a glass from the ewer.

Madame's voice raised in frustration. She didn't want water.

"Cleo, go get Ursaline," Josie said. "And rouse Elbow John. If he starts now, he might find Dr. Benet at home first thing in the morning." In a lower voice, she added, "And the priest."

Cleo, forgetful of the menace waiting for her in the dark, turned for the door, but Louella stopped her. "I'll do dat," she said to Cleo. To Josie, she said, "Cleo don' know where Ursaline be in de new quarters. And Cleo gots to bring you paper fo' Elbow John's pass."

"Just hurry," Josie said. "And tell him not to take the mule. Tell him to take Beau; he'll be faster." She squeezed out a cloth from the basin and bathed Grand-mère's face with it.

Cleo came back to the room with paper and pen. "You write it," Josie said.

Elbow John appeared at the doorway, the sleep still in his eyes. Cleo handed him the permit to leave the plantation and urged him to hurry.

When Louella returned with Ursaline, the midwife, Josie moved from her perch on the side of Grand-mère's bed. "Can you help her?"

Ursaline leaned over Madame and peered into her good eye. Madame stared back at her. "I hep her, I do dat. I gon' need hot water for de herbs."

Louella left them to stir the embers in her cook fire. Ursaline brought forth from a burlap bag a rattle decorated with feathers. She began to chant and shake the rattle over Madame's body. Cleo looked wide-eyed at the *vodou* priestess. She'd heard the talk all her life about Ursaline's powers, but she'd never witnessed the magic herself.

"What are you doing?" Josie demanded. "Stop it. We won't have that superstitious nonsense in this house."

Ursaline looked at Josie with hooded eyes. In the dim light, Cleo thought of a copperhead, full of secret venom.

"I thought you would have medicine, some herbs to help her," Josie said. "Take your things and get out of here."

Ursaline nodded her head toward Madame. "You ask your Grand-mère, mam'zelle. She don' send me 'way. She know de power of de Loa."

Madame's good hand moved toward Ursaline in a come-here gesture. Cleo had had no idea Madame knew of Ursaline's dark powers. The woman who never passed a *ben-itier* on a doorjamb without dipping a finger into the holy water and crossing herself, the woman who said her rosary morning and night, who sent money to the Church every quarter—this woman would allow *vodou* over her injured body?

Cleo touched Josie's arm. "It's only feathers and herbs, Josie. What can it hurt?"

Josie crossed her arms, her mouth tight.

"If it's what Madame wants," Cleo said.

Josie marched from the room. Cleo nodded to Ursaline to continue. Over the next hour, Cleo stood aside and watched the *vodou* rites of healing as Josie paced the gallery outside the bedroom.

The old woman tied a *gris-gris*, a red flannel bag of herbs, around Madame's neck. Then she held a small dried alligator head in her palm for Madame to see. She placed it in Madame's good hand, and Cleo leaned forward to see her grasp it tightly. The *juju* would keep evil away while Madame's *ti bon ange* was vulnerable.

Madame's eyes slowly closed as Ursaline rummaged in her burlap bag. She pulled out a smaller bag of cornmeal and began to sprinkle a pattern on the floor. Cleo crossed herself, but continued to watch Ursaline's hands deftly create the *veve* for Ghede, a benevolent Loa powerful in healing. A coffin with a star above it flanked both sides of a large cross on a three tiered pedestal. Xs and arcs adorned the cross.

Ursaline spoke to the Loa as she worked. Cleo's beloved Grammy Tulia had believed in *vodou*, but Cleo herself had been raised alongside Josie as a Catholic. She said a silent prayer to Blessed Mother Mary—*please ask God to forgive her for allowing this paganism in the house.* She promised she would say ten rosaries in atonement, then wondered if that would be enough. She would confess to the priest when he came, and he could tell her the appropriate punishment.

Ursaline finished her ministrations and pulled the drawstring on her burlap bag. She looked at Cleo expectantly.

Cleo took one of the candles back into the office and opened the drawer where the household purse was kept. She chose a coin, and then returned to the bedroom to press it in Ursaline's palm.

When the old woman left, Cleo opened the bedroom door onto the front gallery where Josie had paced for the last hour. "She's gone," Cleo said.

Josie came into the room and paused as if she thought she could feel the *vodou* in the air. She crossed herself.

"You see. Madame is asleep. No harm is done, Josie."

Josie arranged the mosquito bar around the bed. "I'll stay

with her," she said to Cleo. Josie climbed under the netting and lay down beside her grandmother on the big bed. She held the crippled hand in both of her own.

Cleo began to blow out the candles. "Leave one burning, please," Josie said.

In the morning, Louella brought strong tea for Madame. Josie tried holding the cup for her, but Grand-mère couldn't manage to drink that way. Josie reached for a spoon and fed her the sweet black tea a little at a time. When Josie offered her a spoonful of cornmeal mush, Grand-mère pushed it away roughly and spilled it on the bedding. Tears came to Josie's eyes, but she didn't let her grandmother see them.

Late in the morning, Josie heard Dr. Benet's carriage in the front alley. She left Cleo sitting with Grand-mère and ran downstairs to greet him. His clothes were rumpled and dusty, and the red of his eyes showed he hadn't slept, but he held an arm out for Josie and hugged her close.

"How is she, my dear?" he said.

"She can't talk, Dr. Benet. I don't think she can walk, either. Her left side seems frozen, from her face to her feet."

"Let me see her, Josephine. Then we'll talk."

Josie led him to the bedroom. "Grand-mère, Dr. Benet is here."

"Emmeline, my dear friend," he said as he advanced to the bed. "You are laid low, Josephine tells me."

Emmeline held up her good hand to the doctor, and he took it warmly. "Let me see how you are," he said.

Dr. Benet walked around to the other side of the bed to set his medical bag on the table. When he saw the cornmeal *veve* on the floor, he stopped.

"You've had the *vodou* in here?" He looked accusingly at Josephine. He angrily smeared the drawing with his boot and then spied the *gris-gris* around Emmeline's neck. He fetched his scalpel from his bag and cut the string, marched to the gallery doors, and threw the flannel bag into the yard.

Josie saw a furtive movement of Grand-mère's good hand. She had shoved the dried baby alligator head under her hip where Dr. Benet wouldn't see it. Cleo quickly arranged the bedclothes to help her hide it. Josie stared at her grandmother, this pious Catholic woman, as if she didn't know her, but Grand-mère's silent appeal moved her. She said nothing to the doctor.

Dr. Benet calmed himself. He sat on the bed next to his old friend and took her good hand in his. He felt of the pulse in her neck and examined the droopy eye. He squeezed her frozen left hand and said, "Can you move these fingers, Emmeline?"

She grimaced with effort, but there was no movement. Dr. Benet held her ankle through the covers. "And your foot? Can you move it?" She could not.

He felt the lack of tension in the sagging muscles of her face. "Do you feel my hand on your cheek, Emmeline?"

She answered with a garbled sound. Yes, then.

To Josie, he said, "Has she eaten anything?"

"No, not yet. She's had some tea," Josie said.

"I'm going to bleed her now, and later we'll see if she'll take some broth."

Cleo had a basin ready in expectation he would open Madame's vein. After a quick swipe of the blade against his pants leg to clean it, Dr. Benet nicked the blue line on the inside of Grand-mère's elbow.

As the ribbon of red flowed into the basin, Josie put a hand out to the wall to steady herself. The coppery scent of blood, the dark red pool under Maman in the moment she died—all those smells and images came back to her, and she thought she would be sick.

"Josephine, go in the other room, child," Dr. Benet said. "I will come to you when I'm done here." The doctor checked the color in Cleo's face as well, but she was focused on Madame, a cool cloth at the ready. A born nurse, this one, he thought.

When he'd given Cleo a sedative to spoon into Madame's mouth, he left his patient in good hands. In the parlor he found Josie fanning herself, still pale, with beads of sweat over her lip. She had taken the deaths of the previous summer hard, and now this. The cares of adulthood would wait no longer for Josephine Tassin.

"Your grandmother has had a stroke. As you said, her left side is paralyzed."

"But she'll get over it, won't she?"

Dr. Benet sat down heavily. "Josephine, sometimes a stroke patient improves amazingly. The brain heals itself and the paralysis lifts. Other times, there is little change. We shall have to wait and see."

"It's because of the crash," Josie said. "She was upset about the crash."

"No doubt the shock affected her. But Emmeline is a strong woman. Strong of will and mind. I believe we may hope for a degree of recuperation."

The sounds of crockery and flatware on the dining table reached them. "Ah, I smell dinner," the doctor said.

"You must be so tired, Dr. Benet. After you've eaten, you can rest. I hope you will stay with us a few days."

"Until tomorrow, at least. Then we shall see, Josephine."

After his dinner, Dr. Benet looked in on his patient, who was sleeping, and then retired to the *garçonnière* for a nap.

Josie pulled a rocking chair into Grand-mère's bedroom to keep watch while Cleo worked in the dining room. The sounds of the plates and glasses being cleared faded, and Josie fell asleep in her chair.

Laurie tugged at her sleeve. "Wake up, mam'zelle," she whispered. "Mam'zelle, you gots to wake up."

Josie straightened in her chair. "What is it?"

"Cleo say M'sieur LeBrec at the door. She say should he come in?"

"I'll see him in the parlor," Josie said.

The overseer stood in the middle of the room, his rough work boots planted awkwardly on the woven mats that covered the cypress floor in the summers. He held his hat in his hand and looked out of place among the fine furnishings of the parlor.

"Monsieur LeBrec," Josie said.

"I got word about Madame Tassin. How is she?"

"Not well, thank you, but we hope she will improve."

"Well, it's just, we got this building going on. The new sugar refinery, you know. And we're going to need more timber."

The man twisted his hat, and Josie waited. What did he want her to do about timber? The woods were full of trees. *Take some men and cut them down,* she thought.

"Madame said cut down them two acres, but she didn't say cut no more than that. Maybe she rather buy timber from somebody else's woods and keep hers growing."

"I see." Did she detect a whiff of alcohol? It was hard to tell when the man had been working in the sun all day and stank of sweat and horse.

"I thought maybe you might ask her what she want me to do. Cut, or buy?"

"Can't this wait until my grandmother is well?"

"I don't know, mademoiselle. She want this refinery finished in good time for the cane harvest this fall. We got a lot of building to do yet."

Josie considered the figures she'd added in the ledger. She didn't dare incur more debt, but she would have to make a decision.

"Then, monsieur, I want you to harvest the timber you need from the back acres," she said.

"All right, then. I'll get a crew out there this afternoon. Good day to you, mademoiselle."

He clomped out of the parlor and through the dining room to leave by the back gallery. Josie followed in his odorous wake to the water carafe in the dining room, and so she saw through the French doors when LeBrec veered from the gallery stairs to where Cleo was shaking out the tablecloth over the railing.

When Cleo whipped around to face him, LeBrec reached a hand out and grabbed her breast. Cleo dropped the cloth and was reaching into her pocket with one hand and shoving his arm away with the other.

Josie stepped onto the gallery. At sound of her footsteps, LeBrec backed off. Cleo's face was flushed and hard. Josie had never seen a face so furious.

"You got a sassy girl here, mademoiselle. She need taking down," LeBrec said.

Did he think she had not understood what she'd seen? Josie hoped he could read the contempt she felt for him. She spoke firmly and surely. "Monsieur LeBrec, you will not touch my house slave again."

LeBrec held both palms out, as if to soften her temper. "I was just trying to have a little discipline around here, mademoiselle, but if that's the way you want it." He backed toward the staircase, his hands still up. "So be it."

He turned and clattered down the stairs and swaggered across the courtyard without looking back.

The two young women stood very still and quiet, and then Josie said, "This has happened before?"

Cleo looked at her a moment before she answered. Would Josie really help her, more than to just say "Stay in the house"?

"It's happened before."

"He can't treat you like that," Josie said.

Did Josie think she'd be safe now, just because she had

told LeBrec to leave her alone? *And if he doesn't? What will you do, Josie? Will you fire him? Will you have him cut, the way he cut Remy?* Much as she wanted to believe Josie could protect her, she knew what LeBrec would think of a young mistress's warning.

Josie saw the doubt in Cleo's eyes. She remembered when Phanor had told her LeBrec was after Cleo. She hadn't listened. She hadn't believed such an awful thing could go on under her grandmother's watchful eyes. But Grand-mère had not been herself since Papa died. *I should have listened. I should have paid more attention.*

"I'm not going to let him hurt you, Cleo," Josie said.

Cleo nodded. At least Josie cared. "Louella killed a chicken. She has a pot of broth ready for Madame."

Josie nodded and returned to her grandmother's bedside.

That evening, the priest showed up at last, travel worn and weary. He had been on the mule most of the day, and welcomed the tall drink of water Cleo fetched him. Thank heavens all signs of Ursaline's *vodou* had been swept up. Grand-mère still held the baby gator head, but she again slipped it under her hip out of the priest's notice.

Father Philippe put on his dirty wrinkled surplice and performed the last rites for Madame Emmeline. Just in case.

Chapter 30

Toulouse

Josie prayed earnestly for her grandmother's recovery, and though her condition changed very little over the next three weeks, Grand-mère held on. Dr. Benet visited as he was able, and one afternoon he arrived with a rolling chair tied to the back of his carriage.

He and Elbow John toted it to the bedroom. Josie, Cleo, and Laurie gathered round to admire the new chair.

"Here we are, Emmeline," the doctor said. "It doesn't do for you to lie abed day and night. You need to get the blood moving."

Grand-mère eyed the contraption with a frown pulling down both sides of her twisted mouth. She uttered a string of garbled words and gestured emphatically. Not even Cleo, who understood Grand-mère better than anyone else, caught all the words, but her tone sufficiently carried her intent.

"Now, no fussing," Dr. Benet said. "Cleo, hold the brake. John, you take her good side, and I'll support the left. Ready?"

Before Grand-mère could protest further, they had her in the chair. She immediately slumped to the left.

"We'll need to tie her in, I think, Josephine."

"Of course." Josie quickly brought a broad blue satin sash from her chifferobe. "Will this do?"

Once Josie had secured her grandmother with the sash, Dr. Benet said, "Emmeline, you've been in this room too long. It would oppress anyone's spirits. We'll take the air on the gallery, if you please, John."

John rolled the chair, and Dr. Benet showed him and Cleo how to set the brake. Josie fussed at Grand-mère's neckline, adjusting the muslin scarf around her neck.

"Get your fan, Laurie," Josie directed.

Amid all the ado, the steamboat whistle from down river announced the mail boat's approach. Elbow John hurried down to the dock to collect it.

Every day Josie had waited for the mail boat. She'd had no word, no word at all, from Bertrand these three weeks. He'd not returned to Cherleu, she'd heard that from Elbow John. She'd taken to watching the river anxiously, listening for the mail whistle. Even if it wasn't proper, Josie had determined she would write to him if he didn't come back to her soon.

Cleo left them to retrieve the mailbag from Elbow John, and Josie brought the little fold-down table from the parlor to set next to Grand-mère's chair. When Cleo returned, Josie opened the mail bag and sorted through the letters from Tante Marguerite, Abigail Johnston, their solicitor in New Orleans, even one from her cousin Violette.

"Oh, Grand-mère," Josie said. "At last. Here's a letter from Bertrand." She looked at it a moment longer, puzzled. "It's addressed only to you."

Grand-mère spoke and nodded her head. Cleo interpreted. "Open it, she said."

Josie released the wax seal with her thumbnail and opened

the letter. "'July 14, 1837,'" Josie read. "'My dear Emmeline, I know you are as aware as anyone in Louisiana what the situation here in New Orleans is. I count on your understanding, though I do not hope for your approval, when I tell you I have had to make certain sacrifices to maintain my solvency. It pains me to injure our friendship, and to deprive myself of your granddaughter's companionship, but there is no other way to save Cherleu. I am . . .'" Josie dropped the letter.

Cleo picked it up and continued: "'I am to wed Abigail Johnston at the end of the month. Please explain this to Josephine. I am too much the coward to see her again. Yours with great regret, Bertrand Chamard.'"

Josie sat numbly in her chair staring at nothing. Dr. Benet touched his pocket where he kept a vial of smelling salts, expecting Josie to erupt, or cry, or collapse—something besides this silent stillness.

Josie stood up as if unsure of her footing, but still she made no sound. She barely registered the tear trickling down her grandmother's cheek; her own eyes were dry. With quiet dignity, she left everyone on the gallery and retired to her room.

The following days, Josie rarely spoke. Cleo urged her to eat and persistently set a cup of tea at her elbow. Dr. Benet recommended several glasses of wine before retiring each night, but even that did not keep Josie from wandering through the house in the dark.

Josie fulfilled her responsibilities in sitting with Grandmère and in consulting her, with Cleo's help, about orders for Monsieur LeBrec. Otherwise, she might have been a ghost.

She abandoned her diary. She avoided speaking with Cleo about anything more personal than whether to kill another chicken for supper. Her clothes began to hang on her,

her complexion paled, and her eyes became deep and secretive.

Josie's entire comprehension of the world shifted. The aunts had gossiped with great relish about men and women who had been unfaithful, and Josie had not forgotten her father's sin with Bibi while still visiting her mother's bed. But to be betrayed herself—that had not been in Josie's future. She had expected nothing but joy and fulfillment with a man who loved her and wanted her. Had Bertrand ever loved her at all? Or had he merely wanted to add Toulouse to his own plantation, to double the size of his acreage?

She relived every moment they had been together since the night the lightning struck the tree outside her bedroom window. She remembered now how, in the light from the flaming tree, he had looked at her, and at Cleo, two girls in their nightgowns. She should have realized that look was not one a gentleman would allow himself.

And yet each time he had touched her, kissed her, she was sure she'd known his heart. She saw the color of his eyes everywhere, in the brandy Dr. Benet drank in the evening, in the tea in her cup, in the polished mahogany of the dining table. His laugh came to her in the river breeze. The dress she'd worn when last she'd seen him still hinted at the scent of his cigar.

How many breaths must she draw, how many beats of her heart must she endure in this pain? Long lonely years stretched ahead of her. She saw herself brittle, dry, barren, and old. Life would be too long.

Chapter 31

Toulouse

"Them two young 'uns aren't much use as yet, anyway," LeBrec said. "But I figured you'd want to know we got sickness in the quarters."

"Whose children are they?" Josie asked.

LeBrec smirked. "They's too many of the little bastards running loose for me to pay mind to whose is whose. Begging your pardon, mademoiselle."

Josie bristled. "Mr. Gale knew every soul on this plantation, and managed to know who belonged to whom, monsieur. If you wish to manage as successfully as he did, I suggest you do 'pay mind to whose is whose.'"

The smile lingered on LeBrec's red lips, though his eyes narrowed. Josie suspected he'd thought life would be easier with Grand-mère laid low, but he was finding out otherwise.

Josie's encounters with LeBrec in the weeks after Bertrand's letter were the only moments that roused her. Her dreams of love and marriage shattered, Josie encased her inner life in a bitter, brittle shell. She spent her hours in isolation, however many people were in the house with her. She sat with her grandmother, spoke with Cleo about her care, with Louella about the menu, but she was only vaguely aware that the cane continued to grow in the fields, that life moved on around her.

LeBrec, however, stretched her awareness to include the rest of the plantation. The man himself disgusted Josie, though he made a good appearance, she'd give him that. He evidently pleased his wife, for she kept his coat brushed and provided a fresh shirt each morning. Still, however much he might satisfy Madame LeBrec, Josie found his arrogance unfounded and irritating. She had observed a man's pride was often disproportional to his feeling of self-worth, and she found his posturing ridiculous.

It seemed, too, that the peace of Toulouse had vanished under LeBrec's direction. When Mr. Gale had been overseer, lashings were rare. Now, Cleo insisted on telling her, this one had been whipped, and on another day, that one had had the lash. The new stocks, Cleo reported, had someone fastened in, head, hands, and feet, every day.

Josie had to wake up. She had to take control of Toulouse.

Her first action was to have the stocks destroyed. LeBrec had scorned her for coddling the slackers, but Josie knew they had not been slackers before LeBrec arrived. She forbade any lashings until he had consulted with her, and then she found less drastic, painful repercussions for the slaves who had offended LeBrec, especially the young girls whom she suspected had run from his attentions.

So, for the sake of her people, Josie became the mistress of Toulouse in more than name.

She excused LeBrec from her parlor and went to her grandmother's room to rummage for the book on remedies. Long ago, Grand-mère had learned every infusion and salve the book described, and had even concocted her own remedies. Josie would find a potion to fight the fever in the quarters, and she would administer it to the children herself, as her grandmother always had.

Josie took the book of remedies to the gallery where Laurie sat fanning Grand-mère. She polished her spectacles on her skirt and told Grand-mère what she was looking for. The children were fevered and complained of earache, she said. No rash, no runny nose.

Grand-mère indicated Josie should put the book on the table next to her. Her good hand, though not paralyzed, trembled so that she could not hold a pen or a teacup, but she was able to fumble with the book until she found the right page. It was stained with traces of the medicines she had brewed in years past, and in the margin were notes in her handwriting.

"This one?" Josie said. She considered it miraculous that Cleo had no difficulty understanding Grand-mère, but the emphatic grunt was clear.

"Willow bark tea for the fever," Josie read aloud. "Sweet oil, just warmed, for the earache." Next to the recipe Grand-mère had jotted down where she'd gathered the herbs and the willow bark. "Do you use olive oil?" Josie asked. Grand-mère nodded yes.

Josie thumbed through the worn pages. "You know all these remedies, Grand-mère?"

Grand-mère's fierce eye gleamed. She let forth a long string of words and stabbed a finger in the air toward Josie.

"She says it's the mistress of a plantation's responsibility," Cleo said. She had walked up silently behind Josie with a pitcher of cool water. "She says you're the mistress now."

Yes, I am. Josie looked at Grand-mère's drooping left eye, the twisted mouth, the sash that held her upright in the rolling chair. Josie had to do it. She would not spend the coming season attending parties in New Orleans. She would not be a wife. She would run Toulouse. There was no one else to do it.

Josie stuck a marker in the book and stood up with purpose. "I'll see to these earaches."

In the nights, long after everyone in the house had gone to sleep, Josie lay awake, allowing herself to feel, trying to make sense of what had happened to her. *Couldn't Bertrand have found another way to save Cherleu if he really loved me? Why did he let me go so easily?*

She reviewed all the betrayals she'd endured, including her own father's insistence on having both Bibi and his wife. Intolerable. Unforgivable. And his divided love extended to her as well. She knew her papa had loved her, but he'd loved Cleo more.

Were there men who were faithful? Tante Marguerite admitted her husband, Oncle Sandrine, had a woman from the Blue Ribbon. How is it Marguerite could smile when she told her that? But Marguerite herself was faithless—she had kissed Phanor in her husband's own house.

Phanor—his fickleness burned even now. She had thought there was a connection between the two of them. Yes, he was poor, and just a Cajun, but . . . somehow, she'd felt he was hers. That was nonsense, of course. She had no claim on him. But to make love to her aunt—even Phanor had hurt her.

The morning found Josie hollow-eyed from lack of sleep, but she did what needed to be done. With so many pressing tasks, she put her wounded feelings aside, and the days of sticky heat rolled on. She read the letters from the bankers in New Orleans. She pored over the accounts books. And with Cleo helping her understand Grand-mère's advice, she wrote back to the creditors asking for extensions on the loans, taking care the perspiration of her hands didn't smear the ink.

She watched for the mail boat, hoping and yet dreading the answering mail. One after another, the faceless men who held the fate of Toulouse in their hands turned her down. And then the letter from Monsieur Moncrieff, who held the largest loan, arrived.

Josie wadded up the letter and tossed it in the corner. "That's what I think of your offer, monsieur."

The banker had refused to extend her loans another quarter. Instead, Monsieur Moncrieff had offered to buy a parcel of Toulouse's acreage for a fraction of what it was worth. That sum would have reduced the plantation's debt by an even smaller fraction. She would have to raise the money some other way.

She'd already appealed to Tante Marguerite and Oncle Sandrine, but they were as short of cash as everyone else. The only ones who seemed to have prepared for the crash were some of the Americans. The Johnstons, rather than being in debt themselves, held paper on half a dozen planters in the area. But Josie would rather die than humble herself to Albany Johnston.

While Josie struggled to figure out how much cane Toulouse might reasonably produce in the fall, Cleo watched a steamboat churn up the river and then veer for the dock, its big paddle wheel backing water long enough for a passenger to disembark. It was Phanor, Cleo was certain. She called Laurie to sit with Madame, and then she ran down the stairs to meet him.

Under the oak canopy of the alley, Cleo hurried to him, her face alight with hope. Phanor would carry another letter from Remy.

As she approached him, though, she slowed her steps. Something was wrong. Phanor did not answer the smile on her face, didn't answer her call. As he closed the distance between them, the sense of foreboding built in Cleo until she could hardly breathe.

"What's happened?" she said.

Phanor took her elbow and guided her toward the wrought-iron seat under one of the ancient oaks.

"Tell me now," Cleo demanded.

He led her to the bench and insisted she sit down. "It's bad news," he said.

"Remy . . . ?"

"On the docks. There was a fight," Phanor said. He took Cleo's cold hand. "Between the Irish workers and the free blacks, over who would keep the jobs. Someone pulled a knife, and then others pulled theirs too. Remy was stabbed, Cleo."

"How bad is it? Does he need a doctor?"

Phanor shook his head. "He died on the docks."

Cleo rocked back and forth on the bench, a low sound coming from deep in her chest. Her body shook. She began to keen and pull at her hair.

Phanor's own grief was still sharp, yet there was nothing he could do but sit close to Cleo, his arm around her shoulders. When the shock eased, Cleo buried her face in his chest and sobbed like a child.

Phanor held her close and considered how Cleo would be able to hide her grief from her madame and mademoiselle. They had no idea she knew where their runaway had gone, much less that she had corresponded with him. They would want to know what was wrong with her, what Phanor had said to her.

He offered her his handkerchief. "Cleo," he said. "You can't let them see you like this."

Cleo wiped her face with the handkerchief and shook her head. "It doesn't matter," she said. "Madame Emmeline has had a stroke. No one will notice me."

Phanor looked up at the house as if he could see Madame lying in her bed. She had been good to him. His eyes fell on Josie standing at the gallery rail, watching them. On the trip upriver, Phanor hadn't known whether he would see Josie at all. She had been so cold, so superior, the last time he'd come. He'd had no opportunity to try to excuse himself, to explain to her about being in the pantry with Marguerite. What could he have said, anyway? He had kissed her aunt, had kissed her heatedly. Even now, her perfume lingered in his mind.

Even if Josie didn't want to see him, he would at least go to the house to enquire about Madame Tassin. He owed her that much, and maybe there was something he could do for her. But first, he supported Cleo to the cookhouse. The grief poured out of her all over again as Phanor explained to Louella that Remy had been killed. Louella handed her a glass of *tafia*, the rough spirits the cook made herself.

"You go on, m'sieu. I feed her dis till she sleep."

Phanor climbed the back gallery steps and tapped on the dining room door. Josie herself took him inside.

"What's wrong with Cleo?" she said without greeting him.

"Remy is dead."

Josie eyes were blank for a moment. "Remy?" Then he saw recognition dawn on her. "But Remy ran away months ago. How does she know?"

Phanor let the obvious answer sink in. He had committed a crime when he helped Remy escape, and had compounded it all these months by keeping his whereabouts secret.

"You've known all along where he'd run to?" Josie said.

"Yes."

Josie's posture stiffened. "But you knew he was a run-away."

"Josie—"

"You knew he belonged to my grandmother. After she's been such a help to you. How could you?"

"Josie, you don't understand. You were in New Orleans. You didn't see what he endured."

"Endured? No more than any other field hand, and . . ." She faltered. She didn't know what had gone on while she was in New Orleans, and Grand-mère had not been herself.

Phanor ran a hand through his hair. "Let me show you," he pleaded.

He stepped over to the little rosewood desk and helped himself to a sheet of paper. In quick strokes, he sketched the cage the overseer had locked on Remy's head.

"The bells rang, day and night, with every movement. Remember, I told you in New Orleans? If he shifted in his cot, if he took a deep breath, the bells jangled. And it was heavy, Josie. It was iron. He had to do a full day's work with that on, trying to keep his balance, to carry its weight, and still wield a hoe in the fields."

"We've never done anything like that to a slave," Josie said. She gazed at the drawing, and her shoulders slumped.

Phanor lowered his voice, sure the cruelty had touched her. "Your Monsieur LeBrec did this. After he cut off half of Remy's ear."

"My God," she whispered. Her eyes teared and she bowed her head. Phanor wanted take her in his arms, to comfort her, to kiss the tears from her cheeks.

Suddenly, Josie stiffened her spine, ignoring the tears on her face. "Nothing like that will ever happen again on Toulouse." Her eyes blazed with anger, and for the first time Phanor could see the resemblance to her grandmother.

"And the fact remains," Josie said, "Remy belonged to Toulouse." She tilted her chin up. Phanor had no right to criticize what went on here.

Phanor met her eyes and saw no hope of forgiveness. Blazing with indignation, she'd never looked more alluring, nor more distant, and Phanor's heart ached.

He put his hat on his head. "Mademoiselle," he said, and left her.

Phanor gone, Josie paced the parlor, her skirts sweeping roughly against the horsehair settee with every turn. *How dare he collude in helping an escaped slave?*

No matter how angry she tried to be with Phanor, though,

her mind returned to the drawing of the cage, to the image of LeBrec cutting Remy's ear.

Abruptly, sobs erupted and Josie's steps faltered. She fell onto the settee and cried out all the hurt she'd been carrying since Bertrand's betrayal.

And through her own heartache, she felt the suffering that seemed to permeate the world. Was there a soul living that wasn't burdened with pain? *Blessed Mother, how are we to bear it? A mother loses a child, a child her father, her mother.* Injustice and loss all around her.

Mother Mary, take pity on your poor children. Blessed Mother, take Remy's soul, for Cleo's sake.

In the following days, Josie and Louella took over Cleo's duties. They bathed and fed Grand-mère while Cleo slept or stared at her hands idle in her lap. Finally she bestirred herself and began to take long walks in and around the plantation. Josie imagined she revisited every place she had been with Remy, relived every moment they'd spent together. She knew about that kind of remembering.

Finally one morning as Josie helped Grand-mère with her breakfast in the dining room, Cleo appeared. Her face had a little color in it, Josie thought. Maybe she'd slept last night.

"I'll do it," Cleo said. "I'll take care of her."

Josie vacated her seat next to the rolling chair.

Cleo picked up the teacup and held it steady for her, but Grand-mère pushed it away.

"What's wrong?" Josie said. Grand-mère had taken the tea readily enough from her.

Grand-mère said something like "oo eet." Josie was about to ask her to repeat herself, which always made her furious, but Cleo had understood.

"It's too sweet?"

Grand-mère nodded. "Ooeet." Cleo smiled, and Josie re-

alized she hadn't seen her smile in a very long time, long before the news about Remy. Josie had just been too happy,
and then too miserable, to notice.

"Josie likes sugar," Cleo said, including Josie in her smile.

"Well, I never," Josie said.

"I'll fix you a cup the way you like it," she said to Grand-
mère. "After breakfast, I'm going to get to work on this floor.
It's past due a good scrub. You can sit in here, Madame, and
tell me not to scrub the roses off the paintwork." For the first
time since her stroke, Grand-mère tried to chuckle, and Josie
felt her burdens lighten.

Cleo took over most of Grand-mère's care and rolled her
from room to room with her as she did her housework. The
few and intermittent hours that the old woman was awake,
her mood brightened to be moved about and to have Cleo,
who understood her better than anyone else, include her in
the busyness of the house.

Josie began to ride out in the late mornings. The days
were cooler now, and both rider and horse breathed easier in
the autumn air. Josie only once directed Beau south on the
river road. She thought she might ride as far as the Cherleu/
Toulouse border, just for a change of scene. When she
reached the peach orchard, no longer fragrant and fecund as
it had been when Bertrand kissed her under the live oak, she
pulled Beau up in the middle of the road. She gazed at the
orchard, then focused on the oak on the far side. So much
more than a kiss, she remembered.

He had loved her that day. She knew he had.

She turned Beau around and rode home. Back at the
house, Josie untied her bonnet. "Laurie?" she called.

The little girl, grown so much that her feedsack dress
skimmed her knees, came padding barefoot into the parlor.
"Here I is," she said.

"How is Madame? Did she eat her lunch?"

"She jest like when you left dis mornin'. She don' do

nothing 'cept sleep all de time. Seem like even her good eye don' hardly open no more."

"Have Cleo bring me a plate, and you stay with Madame."

"Cleo not gon' want to bring you no lunch plate, mam'zelle."

Josie raised an eyebrow at her.

"Well, I's jus' tellin' you. She laid up."

"Cleo's sick? She's never sick."

"Dis not no regular sickness. Dis here from what dat ugly LeBrec do to her."

Josie hurried to the bedroom and flung open the door. Cleo lay on her cot against the wall, her knees drawn up and a sheet pulled over her head.

Josie knelt and eased the cover down. Cleo's lip was split and trickling blood. Her left eye was swelled nearly shut and her eyes were unfocused. Fine dots of blood oozed where a patch of hair at her temple had been pulled out. Josie's throat swelled with rage. She would see that man paid for this!

Cleo shrank away when Josie put her hand on her shoulder. "Cleo, it's me."

"Josie?" Cleo's eyes cleared for a moment. "Josie, he hurt me bad."

When Cleo began to cry, Josie fought back her own tears. "You'll never see him again, Cleo. Never. I promise."

Over her shoulder, Josie told Laurie to go to Louella. "Tell her we need hot water, right away. Wait, bring me the brandy first."

Josie pulled the sheet back up to Cleo's chin. She lay down on the cot next to her, wrapped her arms around her, and held Cleo tight while she cried. "We'll wash all the filth off you, Cleo," she told her. "You're going to be all right."

This is my fault. I should have gotten rid of that man weeks ago, Josie thought. She took a glass of brandy from Laurie. "Sit up a little and drink this."

Louella rushed in with a kettle and a basin. "Cleo, why you don' tell me you hurt?"

Cleo coughed and then managed another swallow. "I cut him, Josie."

"You cut dat debil? Good fo' yo, chile," Louella said. To Josie, she explained, "She kep' yo papa's razor in her pocket."

Oh, how Papa would grieve to see Cleo hurt. *I'm sorry, Papa.* Josie swallowed her tears. She would cry later, but now Cleo needed her to be strong. *I'm so sorry.*

Josie, with Louella's help, bathed Cleo and put a soft, clean shift on her. She brushed the dirt and debris out of the long black curls. Then as Cleo became light-headed and drowsy from the brandy, Josie began to dress her injuries. She consulted the book of remedies and with trembling fingers applied a poultice to the bruises, a salve to the cuts and abrasions.

While Cleo slept, Josie searched through Grand-mère's book. Near the back she found the recipes for terminating pregnancies. Turpentine, quinine water in which a rusty nail had been soaked, ginger, or even horseradish reputedly aborted an early fetus. But according to the book, pregnancy did not occur instantaneously. It took time for the "miracle" to occur, and Cleo had been raped only a few hours before.

Prevention. Here it was, in the pages after the abortifacients. Douching. One could use a vinegar mixture, or a syrup made of boiled ants. Grand-mère had marked a check next to the vinegar-and-water formula. In the margin, she had also noted a tea made from the root of worm fern to be drunk prior to douching. Josie wondered whom she had dosed, perhaps herself?

Ursaline would know what worm fern was. When Cleo had had her sleep, they would do what they had to to protect her from LeBrec's foul seed.

* * *

With Cleo safe in bed and the plans made for dosing her with worm fern later, Josie allowed her anger to take over. She left Louella sitting with Cleo and strode across the back courtyard to the overseer's house.

Madame LeBrec met her at the door. The children, a boy of six and a girl about two, clung to their mother's skirts and peered at the Mademoiselle. "*Bonjour*, Mademoiselle Tassin," she simpered. "How kind of you to come calling."

Josie read fear in the woman's eyes. Then she knew.

"I've come for your husband, madame."

"Likely you heard about that gal cutting my husband this morning. She cut him bad, she did." Madame LeBrec hurried on. "He's had trouble with that one before, he told me he did. She's a sassy one, always unsettling them others and thinking she can flirt her way out of trouble."

Josie looked at her coldly. How many times had this woman covered up for LeBrec?

"I seen her myself," the woman said. "Swaying her hips at my husband. She's a bad one."

"Where is he working today?"

"He's a good man, my husband is. You won't find a better overseer anywhere. It's just the girls are after him all the time. You seen yourself what a fine-looking man he is."

Josie eyed the two children. Yves and Sylvie, she remembered. And Bettina, the mother. The children both looked like their father, handsome children, whose big eyes took her in as if she were an avenging goddess. She was sorry to frighten them, but she meant to see their father as soon as possible. Kindly, she asked the boy, "Do you know where your father is working today?"

"He said at breakfast he's gone be down in the south fields, at Coon Corner. Another day, he said, I can go with him."

Madame LeBrec changed her tone. "That's a long walk, mademoiselle," she warned, her tone pitched to be intimidating. "Too far for you to go. Why don't you wait until this evening? My husband can come see you at the house after supper."

Josie didn't bother to answer. As she marched toward the stable, Madame LeBrec called after her, "You can't believe nothing that slut says."

Josie told the stable boy to saddle Beau and sent another child to find Elbow John. With John trailing behind her on a mule, Josie rode out to Coon Corner.

When she spotted LeBrec sitting on his horse, watching the slaves work the cane, her anger burned. He'd never touch another girl on Toulouse. She only wished she could cut off the offending member so that he never touched another woman anywhere.

White hot in her anger, Josie remained in control. She spurred Beau into a gallop and charged at LeBrec. At the last second, she reined Beau in sharply, spooking both LeBrec and his horse. While LeBrec pulled on his horse's reins, Josie sat her saddle in regal composure.

The razor slash crossed LeBrec's cheek from nose to ear. As LeBrec cursed his horse and whipped him across the face, Josie noted with satisfaction that the wound had bled through the clumsy bandage.

"What the hell did you do that for?" LeBrec said angrily.

"To get your attention, monsieur."

He glared at her. "What kind of game you playing?"

His surly manners wouldn't matter after today, Josie thought. "You will pack your things and be off this property by nightfall, monsieur."

"The devil you say. I don't take my orders from no gal. I'll straighten this out with Madame Tassin."

He whirled his horse and whipped its flanks. Josie's impulse was to race him back to the house, to beat him to her grandmother. But she didn't. She nodded to the slaves who had stopped to gape at the scene. Then she trotted Beau back toward the house, Elbow John following behind.

When she rode into the back courtyard, LeBrec's lathered horse stood in the sun near the back stairs. "A disgraceful way to treat an animal," she said to Elbow John. "Tie him in the shade and give him some water. Then come to me in the house."

Inside, Grand-mère had LeBrec pinned to a chair with her gaze. Her speech was excited and she jabbed her finger at him. Neither Laurie nor LeBrec could understand her, but Josie didn't need to.

She put her hand on Grand-mère's shoulder, quieting her. "Don't concern yourself, Grand-mère," she said. "Monsieur LeBrec is under the impression I have no authority. Now he will understand otherwise.

"Monsieur, I tell you once more. Collect your belongings and your family. I will write you a draft for the money owed you, and you will leave Toulouse before nightfall."

"Now see here . . ." LeBrec began and looked to Madame. She said nothing, but the look of glee in her eye told him he needn't appeal to her.

"John," Josie said as he came up beside her, "if Monsieur does not leave willingly, you will have Old Sam and his sons ready to help him on his way."

She held LeBrec's furious eyes until he backed down. He slapped his filthy hat against his leg and stomped through the parlor and out the back way.

Only then did Josie allow her knees to tremble. She walked around the rolling chair and sank onto the settee. Now she would have to face Grand-mère's scolding. What did she think she was doing? Grand-mère would say. What were they supposed to do without an overseer, and the cane nearly ready for harvest?

Josie braced herself and looked at her grandmother, resolved to hear her out before she explained. But instead of scowling, Grand-mère's crooked mouth pulled up and her eyes gleamed approval.

She pointed her hand at Josie and, distorted as her speech was, managed to make herself understood. "Mistress . . . Toulouse," she said.

As the sun sank to the treetops, LeBrec crossed the rope over and through the chairs, beds, and boxes in the wagon and then pulled it taut. His movements were efficient and unhurried. The only sign of the fury inside him was in the depths of his dark eyes. He ignored the cluster of colored men with Elbow John who looked on in silence.

On the porch, Madame LeBrec stood straight with tears streaming over her cheeks. Yves held himself like a little soldier next to her; Sylvie clung to her skirt, her thumb in her mouth.

His wife and the children would have to sleep out of doors in the cold tonight, like vagrants, LeBrec fumed. The miasma of the evening air, who knew what that might do to Sylvie, and her just getting over a cough. That bitch, Josephine. Not even to give them till morning. If Sylvie got sick again . . .

He touched the fresh bandage Bettina had put on the slash. It had bled through again, and it hurt worse than the toothache. He needed stitches, but that would have to wait.

LeBrec pulled the oat bag off his horse's nose and tossed it in the wagon. It belonged to Toulouse, but so what. She'd paid him his wages, but money didn't begin to cover what she was doing to his family. They were likely to be homeless for days, at the least. He'd find work in Baton Rouge—they'd never go hungry, he'd take care of that. But they were scared, and that was her fault.

Hers and that high-toned colored girl. Cleo, Cleo with her uppity airs. For all her better-than-you looks, she was nothing but a slave. And she wanted it, just like the rest of them.

He cinched the saddle on his horse too tight and the mare shuffled its feet and grunted. LeBrec hadn't had a drink all day, not even for the pain in his face, and the top of his head felt as though it might erupt. Controlling his frustration, he loosened the cinch and started over. He'd set up camp, build a fire an hour or two up the river. Once the kids were settled in, then he'd have a drink.

LeBrec loaded his family into the wagon. "You first, son," he said. He put a hand on the boy's shoulder. "You'll help your maman with the mules. Climb on up there."

He held a hand out to his wife. "Bettina."

She wiped her eyes and took Sylvie's hand. "I'm coming," she said.

Le Brec lifted Sylvie in to sit next to her brother. Then he helped his wife climb up and handed her the reins. "That mule's too old to give you any trouble, Bett. Just let him follow me on the mare."

All this time, Elbow John, Old Sam and his sons Etienne and Laurent stood nearby, their arms folded. They offered no assistance, and LeBrec added their witnessing of his disgrace to his list of grievances.

LeBrec mounted the mare, clucked to the mule, and pulled out. He felt the slaves' eyes on his back, and shame and rage boiled within him.

"She'll pay for this," he muttered.

Three nights later, in the dark of the moon, LeBrec rode the mare back downriver to Toulouse. He hitched the mare to a bare hickory tree and spoke soothingly to her. As he made his way on foot through Sugar Hollow, the prime field on the north side of Toulouse, the chorus of crickets resumed. The cane waved over his head, nearly ready for harvest, but LeBrec had a better target in mind.

At the edge of the quarter, he stopped and listened. No child crying in the night, no low chuckles from the porches. Everyone slept.

The near-finished refinery loomed darker than the night sky. A pile of boards lay nearby, cut and ready for Old Sam to have the crew lay on the roof in the morning.

LeBrec collected kindling from under the saw pen, pulled moss from the nearest oak, and built a pile against the sugar refinery's wall. He pulled his flints from a pocket and struck a spark in the moss. He nurtured the small flame and fed it more kindling.

The fire grew and glowed, its orange light gleaming on the three-day beard, the dirty bandage, and LeBrec's mad black eyes.

He crept back to the north field and disappeared among the cane to the sounds of the refinery crackling, smoking, burning.

Chapter 32

Toulouse

The timbers of the burned refinery still smoldered as Josie rode Beau out to inspect the cane. With LeBrec gone, she meant to ride the plantation every day, to be her own overseer. Beau snorted at the smoke and Josie let him circle well away from the blackened ruin.

A knot of young men who should have been hoeing weeds in the cane gathered around the smithy's forge. Struck by their somber mood, Josie dismounted. They stood aside for her to see Old Sam's son Laurent wielding a huge hammer on an iron contraption.

He'd smashed the bells and one of the supporting struts, but Josie recognized the cage Phanor had drawn for her. Laurent stopped, a question in his eyes.

Josie reached a hand to judge the heft of the thing. She would need both arms to lift it, and Remy, who had held Cleo so tenderly at the campfire on the levee, whose singing had been full of moonlight and love, had had to wear this thing. The flattened bells, though they would never ring again, jangled in Josie's mind.

I was too harsh with Phanor, Josie thought. *My pride, that's what I was thinking about. Someday, maybe, I can tell Phanor I was wrong.*

Josie nodded to Laurent. "Carry on." *Let them melt it down,* she thought. *Toulouse will never use it again.*

Josie suspected LeBrec had set the fire, but she had no way of proving it. No one saw or heard anything that night. Old Sam had smelled the smoke and raised the alarm only after the flames had already engulfed the refinery, and the buckets of water the slaves threw on it did no good at all. Josie had stood as close as the heat would allow, the light from the fire glistening on the sweating backs of men laboring futilely to put it out, the smoke roiling into the black sky.

Now that Cleo was recovered, from the rape and then from the remedy that had prevented conception, Josie concentrated on saving Toulouse. Not on revenge. And not on her broken heart or her wounded pride. With no refinery of their own, profits this season would be even slimmer—and the debt would grow. She'd have to go to Albany Johnston.

The next morning, Josie caught a steamer at Toulouse's dock. Elbow John hovered nearby, a fretful escort. The river scared him, and Josie had told him to stand behind her, well back from the railing. The trees showed the first signs of fall, their leaves worn and dry. Here and there was a maple tossing yellow flags into the wind. The fine spray from the paddle wheel chilled Josie, but she couldn't bear to sit inside.

She wore her best dress, a grayish green just the shade of her eyes, and she'd taken extra care with her make-up and hair. She couldn't expect Albany to still be in love with her after the way she'd flaunted her interest in Bertrand Chamard in New Orleans. Still, it couldn't hurt to look her best.

The boat let them off at the Johnstons' dock, and Elbow John settled himself out of the wind. Charles the butler escorted Josie to the house and into the imposing hallway. She regarded the expensive furnishings and found herself just as impressed as she'd been the first time she visited the Johnstons. All this opulence—and security—could have been hers. She ran her finger over the curve of a Limoges vase on the hall table.

In the sitting room, the ticking of the clock grew louder the longer Josie sat in suspense. The house might have been deserted for all the sounds she could hear. Not even the birds twittered outside. Josie had sent a note the day before asking if she might call, and Albany's mother had answered immediately: Abigail and Bertrand were in Paris, but of course she should come. Until Josie saw Albany in person, though, she wouldn't know what kind of welcome to expect from him.

Footsteps in the hallway at last. Josie stood, smoothed her bodice, and steeled herself for a cold reception.

The door burst open, and her long-nosed cousin Violette hurried in. "Josephine! How wonderful to see you," she said as she crossed the room, one hand held out. The moment reminded Josie of her first visit to this house, when Abigail had rushed in with an exuberant welcome.

Her cousin kissed both her cheeks and laughed. "You didn't expect to find me here, did you?"

"I hadn't thought of it, Violette. I didn't realize you were acquainted with the Johnstons."

"Oh, but you introduced me to Mr. Johnston yourself. Don't you remember?"

"At Tante Marguerite's party, of course."

Violette's pale lips pursed into a simpering smile, and her eyes signaled a wordless message. "Can't you guess, cousin?"

It came to her then, and Josie said, "You and Albany Johnston?"

"Isn't it romantic? There was another young man, of

course, but, well, you can understand how a girl would prefer Albany."

"Congratulations, Violette. I hope you'll be very happy." Two dull people, Josie thought, fortunate to find each other.

Mrs. Johnston joined them, and the ladies exchanged family news, Abigail's wedding trip with Bertrand the foremost topic. Josie bore it all with a fixed smile. After a respectable interval, she said, "I had hoped to speak to Mr. Johnston this morning. On business."

"Yes, so I understood," Mrs. Johnston said. "My husband is in New Orleans, but Albany should be home momentarily. He has been out for a grouse shoot, and I expect him to come clomping in with his muddy boots any time. Can I pour you another cup of coffee?"

Violette resumed the recitation of every garment and hat her dressmakers were constructing for the coming season. Josie obligingly inquired about the bows, ribbons, flounces, and ruffles to be employed, and the morning dragged on with that ridiculously tinny clock chiming the quarter hours.

The doors from the patio were open for the air, and that was how Josie first heard Albany's approach. They hadn't seen each other since early the previous spring. She readied herself, and in that she had the advantage.

"I smell coffee," Albany boomed. He hardly scraped his shoes on the mat before he entered the dimmer light of the sitting room. "I'll have a pot of that, if you please."

Josie stood up to greet him. Albany stopped when he saw her. His hair was mussed, his face tanned, and he'd lost the fleshiness that had been so distasteful to Josie. He looked very fine, in fact. Nevertheless, it was an awkward moment. The light was behind him, and Josie couldn't say whether there was gladness in his eyes.

"My cousin has come to call, Albany," Violette said. "Isn't that lovely?"

"Miss Tassin," Albany said. "How do you do?"

"Those disgraceful boots, son," Mrs. Johnston said. "Well, you're in now. Come and sit with us while I ring for another pot."

Albany put his hands in his lap. Josie fiddled with an embroidered flower on her skirt, and Violette's eyes jumped between her and Albany.

Josie drew a deep breath. "Mr. Johnston," she began. "I've actually come on business. I hope you can spare me a few minutes this morning."

Albany stood abruptly. "Certainly," he said. "Have the coffee sent to my study, Mother. Miss Tassin."

Josie followed his boot prints over the cream-colored rug and across polished floors to the back of the house. Albany's office looked out over the new pecan orchard swaying in the wind. Nearby a gardener whistled while he hoed the beds. Everything was in order here, everything thriving, Josie noted, while Toulouse struggled to survive.

Albany invited Josie to sit in his deep leather chair. He paced for a moment, and then brought himself back to composure. "I had not thought to see you here," he said, and looked her full in the face for the first time.

"Your mother didn't tell you I was coming?"

He shook his head. "She is not so fond of Violette, I'm afraid."

"Congratulations on your engagement."

"Is that what Violette told you?"

"Yes. Are you not betrothed?"

He ran a hand through his pale hair. "I suppose. As good as." He sat heavily in a swivel chair behind his desk and stared at Josie. "You're looking well," he said. "I was afraid, when Chamard . . . Well, I believe he behaved rather badly toward you. People talk, you know."

Josie held her chin up. "Not at all," she said. "We're merely neighbors. He and my grandmother are great friends, you see, so I saw him when he came to visit her. For the few months before his marriage to Abigail. How is she?"

Albany huffed. "Ecstatic, for the moment."

The whistling from the garden filled the quiet space until Josie mustered her courage.

"Albany?" She spoke softly. "Are you willing to do business with me?"

With one look, Albany revealed that his heart was still hers. "Of course," he said quietly. Josie dropped her eyes.

"It's the crash," she said. "After the flood, we borrowed to rebuild. And now, I must repay the loans."

Albany nodded. "And you can't make the payments."

"But I haven't come to ask for a handout," Josie hurried to explain. "I wouldn't have you think that."

"What do you propose?"

"A limited partnership."

"And what do you understand that to mean, Josephine?"

"You would finance the rebuilding of the sugar refinery, pay the interest on the loans, and share in the profits until conditions improve. At that time, I would buy out your interest in Toulouse. You would have made money on Toulouse's cane crops and the refinery, and I will regain full ownership."

A small smile came to Albany's lips. "Is this the same girl who so poorly concealed her disdain of markets and banks?"

Josie could only smile in return. "As my Grand-mère tried to tell me so often, necessity is a fine tutor."

"I heard she's had a stroke. Will she recover, do you think?"

Josie shook her head. "It doesn't seem likely."

"So you have become the manager of Toulouse."

Josie knew he had a poor opinion of her business sense, and rightly so. "I've changed, Albany. I've had to."

"Yes," he said. "I believe you have." He walked to the window and stood looking out at the whistler with the hoe. "Josephine, your proposal is valid. However, I haven't the cash to do all you suggest. I've similar arrangements with three other plantations at the moment, none of which can bring a profit for some time."

"I see." Josie lowered her face in embarrassment. She stood up, the rustle of her skirts loud in the little room. "I'll take no more of your time, Albany. Thank you for hearing me out."

"Please. Sit down, Josephine." Albany turned from the window, the light behind him again so that Josie found it hard to read his face. "I haven't finished."

"There's another way?"

He looked at her a long moment. "If you were my wife, I could save Toulouse. I couldn't bring it back to full productivity right away, but I could keep it for you."

"You mean, if I married you now?"

Albany strode the three steps to Josie and knelt down with his hands on the arms of her chair. "Will you marry me, Josephine?"

"But . . . Albany, you're engaged, or at least you have an understanding with Violette."

"I am yet a free man. And understandings can be broken, as you well know."

Josie flushed as she gazed into Albany's face. He was in earnest, she could see that. He was kind. And he was rich.

"I've changed too, Josephine. I won't treat you like a child again."

Albany's bulk dwarfed her. Even his head seemed too large, and his big hands and blunt fingers covered the arms of her chair.

"Albany, it's not that."

He read her answer in her face. "Is it Chamard? Still Chamard?"

Josie dropped her eyes. It was more than that, but how could she tell Albany she simply didn't want to spend her days, or nights, with him. She couldn't.

Albany stood up. "You live in a fantasy world, Josephine," he said bitterly. "You could have my fortune, my love . . ."

"I'm sorry, Albany. I really am."

Josie quietly closed the door of the study behind her. Violette and Mrs. Johnston's voices came to her from the sitting room. She walked to the front door and let herself out.

Chapter 33

Toulouse

October's shorter days and cooler nights signaled the ripening of the cane. Without an overseer on the place, Josie relied on Old Sam to organize the work crews for harvesting. Late into the night, she heard men spinning the grindstone to sharpen the machetes. Before light, she got up to ring the big work bell herself, and she stood near Old Sam in the dawn as he assigned the slaves to their jobs for the day.

Josie had made up several large jars of ointment according to the instructions in the book of remedies, and she had Louella keep water simmering on the stove all day, ready for the inevitable machete mis-strokes. She had snakebite remedy on hand too: aloe vera for both a strong drink and an aid to healing the wound; echinacea from among Grand-mère's stock of herbs, and a salve made of castor oil and papaya juice to press on the bite itself.

The cane towered over the slaves' heads, nine feet tall in

the best field, so close packed that a man could hardly stick an arm through the canes. With the warming of the morning air, the mass of towering stalks rustled and groaned in counterpoint to the thwack of machetes into the crisp stalks. The more staccato sounds of coughing completed the symphony as the wind carried black smoke from fields already cleared and set afire.

As the slaves filled wagon after wagon with cane to be taken to another planter's refinery downriver, Josie watched anxiously. In her notebook, she tallied each wagon that passed her on the way to the docks. After paying for processing the cane into sugar, there should be enough profit to at least pay the interest on the loans.

In the house, Cleo tended to Madame. She wondered if she had had another stroke, for Madame seldom bothered to try to speak anymore, and the light in her eyes seemed to dim with every passing week. Cleo resumed her long walks while her patient slept the afternoons away, Laurie sitting nearby with mending in her lap.

The smoke from Cherleu indicated Monsieur Chamard's cane was cut. He hadn't visited Toulouse since June when the financial world, and Josie's hopes, had collapsed. Today, as Cleo walked along a winding path through the plantation, she pictured the warm brown eyes that had looked into hers after LeBrec assaulted her the first time. A fork in the path veered south toward Cherleu, and Cleo took it.

The smell of scorched sugar spread through the wooded strip between Toulouse and Cherleu. Cleo could see the flickering orange of low flames in the nearest field, and the fire drew her to it. She stopped at the edge of the trees to watch the burning, and on the other side of the fire, perhaps fifty yards from her, sat Monsieur Chamard on his roan stallion.

He seemed bemused as he watched the flames, and she

stared at him. Cleo wondered if he had forgotten Josie already. *And what of me,* she thought. *Has he lost interest in me as well?*

Bertrand wakened from his reverie, raised his head and looked directly at Cleo across the burning field. She held his eyes a moment, and then she turned back into the woods.

The days of harvest passed. Josie met the interest payments, but Monsieur Moncrieff sent word she would have to begin paying toward the principal or he would be forced to foreclose. "Never," Josie breathed. "I'll find a way." In the late hours, she concocted scheme after scheme to raise money only to see them as pointless, even absurd, in the morning.

Cleo felt shut out from the business of the plantation. She might have been some help to Josie, but Josie didn't confide in her, didn't ask her to share the burden of worry. Instead, Cleo mourned Remy, cared for Grand-mère, and ran the house. Toulouse belonged to Josie, not to a bastard slave girl.

Cleo bore her grief differently than Josie had. She knew the peace of having been loved, entirely and surely. She had no doubts, no torments of there being something intrinsically unworthy about her. Her dream of a life with Remy, as free man and free woman, seemed very distant, and she had not found the heart to dream another dream. But the sap ran strong in her, and she felt herself ready, waiting, for life to begin again.

An hour before sunset, a shawl over her shoulders, Cleo wandered along the levee, watching the dark water flowing. All those months when fear of LeBrec had kept her housebound, Cleo had yearned for the solitude and solace of the outdoors.

A riverboat churned past, and Cleo waved to one of the colored men, an old man with white hair, who'd shouted a cheery hello. The noise of the paddle wheel covered the clomp of horse hooves on the road until a dark horse and rider emerged from the shadows. Cleo recognized Monsieur Chamard's roan and then the man himself.

When he drew near, he pulled the horse over and stopped. On the raised ground of the levee, Cleo stood perhaps three feet higher than Chamard, and he had to remove his hat to look up at her.

Neither spoke for a moment. Then Chamard said softly, "*Bonsoir*, Cleo."

When he had been Josie's suitor, Cleo had avoided eye contact with him, but not any longer. "*Bonsoir*, monsieur."

Chamard dismounted, climbed to where Cleo stood. The two spoke only with their eyes, and it was enough. He put his hand behind her waist and drew her to him.

A cold winter wind blew the day Cleo first experienced morning sickness. Josie might have known nothing of it except that it took Cleo by surprise as she rose from her low bed in Josie's room. She barely made it to the wash basin, and Josie hurried to hold Cleo's hair back as she heaved.

Maybe Cleo had eaten something that disagreed with her, Josie suggested. But then it happened again the next morning, and the next. Cleo was pregnant.

"So the worm fern didn't work." Josie slapped her hand on the table. "And now you carry that man's child." She reached for the medical book. "Cleo, there are other remedies in here. You won't have to have this baby."

Cleo didn't want any of Josie's remedies. She had nothing of her own in this life, and even if it had been LeBrec's offspring, she would want it. But she had counted the days. It wasn't LeBrec's.

"A sin. You know it'd be a sin," Cleo said.

"Not when it was rape. Father Philippe will ask God to forgive us."

Cleo shook her head. *If it's a boy,* she thought, *I'll name him Gabriel, like Remy and I had planned.*

"Cleo, you can't want that man's child."

"It's my child. This is my baby, Josie. Just mine."

And so the months went by, Cleo taking on that distracted air of mothers-to-be, as of someone listening to a small voice no one else can hear. She met Chamard often in a small cabin at the back of Cherleu, and he delighted in pressing his ear against her swollen belly to hear the faint heartbeat. However much he might accept the child, though, Cleo secretly claimed it wholly for herself.

Winter passed, and spring. The scent of magnolia blossoms weighted the air, the bees buzzed around the roses, and the cane grew in the fields.

Josie made the minimum payments to satisfy Monsieur Moncrieff by selling much of the timber in the back woods of the plantation. There was a limit to how much could be cut, however, and so Josie still paced and schemed.

Rain and sun favored the lower Mississippi day after day. Without the fear and dread LeBrec had inspired, the slaves followed Old Sam and labored heartily in the communal garden. They had corn enough for the coming year as well as a little surplus to sell. They had beans to dry, peaches and guavas, berries and cucumbers to preserve.

In mid-June, Josie observed the anniversary of the last time she'd seen Bertrand. She was quiet all morning. At noon, she wandered out to the river road, not even a hat to shelter her from the freckling sun, and stared southward toward Cherleu. The road might have been a path of briars and thorns for all she would have traveled it. And yet, she thought. After a moment, she shook her head and returned to the house.

Josie expected Cleo to birth her baby any day. It had been ten months since LeBrec had left the place, yet she showed no signs of imminent delivery. Josie perused the worn book of remedies for encouraging the onset of labor, but when she broached the idea to Louella, the cook only laughed. "Dem chil'rens come when dey's ready. Sometimes dey's born wid long fingernails and hair enough to tie in rags. No need fo' us to do nothin'."

Cleo herself seemed unconcerned. She moved more awkwardly, had more trouble getting out of a chair, and she minded the heat terribly, but she sang under her breath through the long days. She loved to take Laurie's or Louella's hand and lay it on her belly to feel the baby kick. Once she'd done the same with Grand-mère.

She laid her dust cloth down and smiled. "Here, Madame. Feel this."

She watched the old woman's twisted face and kept Grand-mère's hand on her tight abdomen to feel a kick, and then another.

"Louella says it's sure to be a boy, he kicks so hard," Cleo said.

Grand-mère agreed. "Sss boy," she said. Then Grand-mère sat back in her chair, her eyes hard and shrewd.

"Ooos?" she said.

Cleo stood very still.

Grand-mère pointed at Cleo's belly and said again, "Ooos?"

"You remember, Madame," Cleo said, as if Madame ever forgot anything. "In the fall—the overseer? That's why Josie told him to get off the place."

"I . . . mem . . . ber," Grand-mère said. "Ver . . . well."

She knows, Cleo thought. She picked up her dust cloth and busied herself.

It was late in August when Cleo swayed out to the front gallery after lunch with a tray of lemonade for Josie and Madame. She stopped suddenly, her eyes wide, and water gushed from between her legs. Josie jumped up and took the tray.

Cleo's face went pale with the first contraction. "God, that hurts," she breathed when it eased.

"Laurie, go tell Louella it's time," Josie said. "Then run on for Ursaline."

Josie sat Cleo in a chair and then hurried to her room to strip the sheets off her own bed. Over the mattress she laid the oiled canvas she'd put by for this moment and spread old sheets over it for comfort. She tied the braided cloth rope to the bedstead for Cleo to pull on, then rushed back to the porch to fetch her.

"Did you have another contraction?"

"Not yet."

"It's so late, I thought it might come fast," Josie said.

Grand-mère pointed to Cleo's belly and said something about "late," but Josie didn't understand her, and Cleo didn't explain.

Josie helped Cleo into the bed. She'd hardly lain back when the next contraction rolled over her. She groaned.

Josie looked out the window, hoping to see Ursaline on her way. She'd read the pages on birthing babies, but book learning didn't seem enough. She wanted Ursaline here, and fast.

Louella hustled in first, a big smile on her face. "We gon' have us a baby in de house again. Nothin' livens up a house like a baby."

Ursaline arrived at last, her bag of herbs in hand. She had Louella brew a tea to ease Cleo's pain, arranged the sheets for easy access to the baby, and periodically prodded and poked. Josie, she insisted, might stay if she wished, but she would sit in the corner out of the way. Josie sat.

Cleo labored through the afternoon. As the sun went down, the pains came faster and harder. Her hair hung in sweat-soaked tendrils around her face, and she began to pant with every contraction.

"It's a-comin'," Ursaline said. "Louella, you keep dat blanket at de ready."

Josie hovered at the head of the bedstead, too excited to sit in the corner. She wiped Cleo's face and made soothing sounds as Cleo gave another mighty push.

"It's a boy," Ursaline announced, and held him up for all to see.

The baby let out an indignant wail, and Cleo laughed and cried at once. Ursaline handed him to Louella to wipe clean and swaddle while she tended to Cleo.

Josie plumped Cleo's pillows so she could see better, and then Cleo said, "Give him to me, Louella."

Cleo unwrapped the swaddling enough to hold one tiny hand in her own. A perfect little hand, five perfect fingers curling around hers. "Gabriel," she said softly.

The baby had a fine thatch of straight black hair on his head, and Josie leaned in for a better look. "He's so red," she said. "But look at his eyes. He's looking right at me." She laughed and ran a finger over the soft cheek.

Ursaline mixed another potion to curb Cleo's bleeding and fed it to her by the spoonful over the next hour. Cleo finally fell asleep, and after Louella had given Gabriel a better washing, Josie held her arms out for him. There hadn't been a happy day in that household for a long time. Josie rocked and sang to Cleo's baby, his hand curled around her finger this time.

In the next weeks, Josie fell in love again. Gabriel smiled when she rocked him, she was sure of it. Louella always said, "Dat's jus' gas, mam'zelle. Dat baby don' know nothin bout smiling yet." But Josie knew he smiled for her.

Cleo regained her strength quickly. She was generous in her happiness, and often laid Gabriel in Grand-mère's lap, careful to support his head herself. Grand-mère patted his little tummy and cooed to him. As soon as she was on her feet, Cleo resumed her chores and cared for little Gabriel as well. When he wasn't feeding at her breast, she carried him in a sling across her back or in the front if her task allowed it. When Josie wanted to hold him, Cleo regretted letting him go, but not because she begrudged Josie his company. She simply hated to be without him for a moment.

She learned to share him gladly, though, as Josie clearly loved him too. Who else would listen when Cleo wanted to describe the moment when Gabriel discovered his thumb, how he shook his rattle, how he turned his head to listen to the mockingbird outside the window? And Josie exclaimed, too, when she had had him for an hour, over the miracles Gabriel had accomplished.

Cleo felt she had a friend, and a sister, again. She and Josie spoke more often now of Grand-mère than they had, of Toulouse, of the garden, and of how Gabriel would grow tall and handsome.

Josie spent most of the day dealing with the plantation, consulting with Old Sam about the work to be done, keeping the accounts, watching the weather. Cleo began to take an interest in the nursing to be done among the slaves. She studied the old book of medicinals and relieved Josie of seeing to the sickness in the quarters. All the coldness, the distance between them, seemed to have never been.

When the September heat peaked, everyone moved as little as possible. In the fields, men and women still toiled to keep the weeds out of the cane, but in the house, they kept all the windows and doors open for the river breeze to sweep through.

Josie had spent the day on her horse, reviewing the fields, checking the progress of each crew at work in the hot sun. Another bill was due the bank in ten days, and Josie had yet to accumulate the full amount. In the afternoon, her eyes strained from squinting in the bright light, her head aching, Josie retreated to the house.

"Come catch the river breeze on the front gallery," Cleo told her. "I've got a pitcher of water out here; that's what you need."

No, what I need is the next payment to Monsieur Moncrieff, she thought, but she kept that burden to herself. She carried all the weight of Toulouse now, all by herself. Always, whether she played with Gabriel, rode her horse in the cool of the evening—whatever else she did, Josie worried. She found few occasions to smile or relax. When she did, it was because of Gabriel.

In the shade of the front gallery, Gabriel lay on his back, watching his own legs and arms wave about. Josie picked him up and pulled the muslin dress over Gabriel's head, then laid him across her lap. She dipped her handkerchief in the water and wiped his chest to cool him. Cleo sat nearby stitching another gown for him, her skirt hiked up to her knees for the coolness.

Josie kissed his face and turned him over. She gently wiped the cloth across his back and shoulders, then unpinned the heavy diaper to cool the small of his back.

"Heat rash is back," she told Cleo. There was a faint patch of red skin, just at the base of his spine. Josie pulled her reading glasses from her pocket for a better look.

With her glasses on, this time she could see clearly. It wasn't a rash. It was the same birthmark she had herself. The same one her mother carried, as did Maman's sisters, her cousins, her nephews and nieces. Everyone, it seemed, who descended from Great Grand-mère Helga.

Josie looked at Cleo. How could this be?

"What's the matter?" Cleo said.

Josie hugged Gabriel to her. "You . . ." she said. She stood up and backed away. Gabriel could only be Bertrand's baby, Bertrand with the same birthmark . . . "Cleo, you—"

Cleo dropped her sewing and met Josie's staring eyes.

Blessed Mother, Josie knows. She'd never thought, never dreamed Josie would know. How could she know?

"Oh, Josie," Cleo said.

"He's Bertrand's, isn't he?" She backed all the way to the door.

"Josie," Cleo said. "Wait."

Josie ran from the gallery, Gabriel clutched to her. She slammed the door of her room and locked it. On the edge of her bed, Josie rocked back and forth, Gabriel held close. All these months, more than a year, Josie had schooled herself not to think of what might have been. But Cleo, Cleo had lain with Bertrand, had felt the strength of his body as he entered hers. All those lonely nights, aching for him, yearning for his touch—and Cleo was in his arms.

The bile of jealousy flowed into her mouth until she thought she would choke. First Papa, and now Bertrand—they loved Cleo.

How could she do it? Bertrand had abandoned her, Cleo had betrayed her. Her own blood. Self-pity flooded her soul. Loneliness deeper than she had ever known pierced her heart.

"Josie. Josie, let me in," Cleo pleaded and rattled the doorknob.

And here was Gabriel, Bertrand's beautiful child. *It should be my breast he suckles, my arms he sleeps in.*

"Josie!"

Gabriel fussed at the tension in Josie's arms, and she kissed his face, soothed him through her tears. *He should be mine!*

Gabriel started wailing. On her side of the door, Cleo's breasts ached and the milk began to flow. "Josie, open the door. You're scaring him." Gabriel cried furiously, hungry and hearing his maman's voice through the door.

Cleo pounded once, then again. "Let me in, Josie!"

When finally Josie unlocked the door, Cleo rushed in, her arms out to take her baby. But Josie held him against her shoulder, her hand on his head as he screamed.

"Let me have him," Cleo said.

Josie didn't answer, and she didn't release the baby. She strode out of the room to the back gallery and down the stairs.

"Where are you going? Josie, give him to me." Cleo followed her across the courtyard, panic rising, pleading for Josie to give Gabriel to her. "Josie!" At last, she grabbed Josie's shoulder. "Give me my baby!" she screamed.

Josie slapped her. In all their lives, Josie had never hit her. Cleo drew back, her hand covering the red print of Josie's hand on her face. They stared at each other, both of them stunned.

What am I doing? "Oh God. Cleo. I'm sorry." *What have I done?* Josie began to sob. She felt her very bones weaken, and she sank to her knees, baby Gabriel cradled on her shoulder.

Cleo stepped forward and took her baby. She left Josie on the ground, her face in her hands, weeping as if all the babies in the world had been taken from her.

Elbow John found her there, hardly conscious from the heat of the sun bearing down on her. "Get up, now, mam'zelle. You don' go making yoself sick out here like dis." He raised her up and half carried her into the house. Only Laurie was there to help him get her to bed. He fed her a glass of water and made her lie back. "You get cooled off, you feel better."

Josie began to weep again. "Go on, now, Laurie," John said. "You tend to Madame. I stay here."

She was too wrung out from the sun to shed tears; Josie's weak sobs were dry and heaving. Elbow John sat on the floor next to her and took her hand. Josie gripped his as if he were her only hope of staying in this world.

When she ceased to sob, John got another glass of water in her, and then another. Then he put her head back on the pillow.

"You don' ought'n to taken Cleo's baby that away, sugar. Where was you going wid dat boy?"

"I don't know, John. I don't know what I was doing." She reached for his hand. She began to cry again, tears flowing from her eyes now. "Cleo won't ever forgive me, John. How could she, after what I did?"

He couldn't answer that. He patted her hand and let her cry.

Elbow John still sat with Josie when the sun went down. Louella crept in with a pitcher of water cool from the cistern. She laid a bowl of grapes on the table too, to tempt her. John went out to his supper, and Louella took his place at Josie's bedside.

When Josie dozed, Louella relaxed in the chair she'd pulled up, but her mam'zelle began to moan and cry in her sleep. Louella wakened her, and Josie sobbed again as if her misery would never end.

"Here, now," Louella said. "You got to stop dis. You be sick wid all dis crying."

"I did a terrible thing. I did an awful thing. I don't know what I was thinking. Louella, tell Cleo. Tell her I didn't know what I was doing."

During the night, Josie developed a fever. Louella mopped her brow and tried to get more water in her, but Josie hardly knew where she was. She twisted her bedclothes and cried out. "Forgive me," she said, over and over.

By noon, Josie broke into a sweat, after which she fell into a deep sleep. Louella kept the house quiet, and stayed by her side all through the afternoon. When Josie woke at sunset, Louella washed her face and neck and helped her into a fresh nightgown. She opened the shutters to the evening breeze, and handed Josie a glass of wine.

"You drink dat, mam'zelle. Den maybe you feel like eating a little something."

"Thank you, Louella." Josie felt weak and subdued. She'd cried out all her pain. What remained was only remorse. And the need to put things right.

"Where's Cleo? Will you ask her to come see me?"

Louella busied herself with the damp linens. "Maybe after you eat something."

"I will eat, Louella, but bring Cleo, please." Tears welled in Josie's eyes, and Louella took her hand.

"You not seen de end o yo troubles yet, chile. You got to get a hold of yoself."

Josie stared into Louella's kind old eyes. "What?" she whispered. A cold tightness crept across her chest. She knew the answer before Louella said the words.

"Cleo done gone from here. She took her baby and she gone."

One shred of hope: "To Cherleu?"

"*Non*, John done been over dere. She gone."

Chapter 34

New Orleans

Not once in the two days it took Cleo to get to New Orleans did anyone ask her who she belonged to, where she was going, or if she had a pass from her owner. She had enough coins in her pocket, stolen from Madame's painted tin box in the desk, to pay her passage on a freight barge and buy a little to eat along the way. She carried only the clothes on her back and a sack of nappies for little Gabriel.

Once in New Orleans, she asked someone how to get to Butcher Lane, where she knew Phanor, and Remy, had kept a room. She walked through the filthy streets, watching where she placed her feet, the sun pulling out and mixing the scents of dog waste, horse droppings, garbage, and even the rotted carcass of a cat. She found the row of butcher shops soon enough and covered the baby's nose with her shawl.

She had no idea which shop Phanor lived above. She asked a kindly looking man if he knew Phanor DeBlieux, but after he peered at the baby's light skin, he pulled back abruptly. "You best get on from here, girl."

Cleo knew what he thought—that she was after the baby's father, a white man who'd left her to fend for herself. Likely all the white men would think the same. She tried a dark woman shucking corn in front of her gumbo stand.

"Sho, I know dat man," the woman said. She grinned and showed an inch-wide gap in her upper teeth. "He a good-lookin' fella, come in here sometime fo' a bowl of gumbo. Try dat place up de road. De one wit de pig sign over de door."

The pig butcher stopped his chopping when Cleo came in the shop. She felt her gorge rise when her eyes adjusted to the light. He had bits of blood and gristle in his beard, and his arms were bloody up to the elbow.

He wiped his hands on his apron. "What you need today, girl?" he said. "Give you a good price on trotters."

"I'm looking for Monsieur DeBlieux. My mistress has a message for him," she lied.

The butcher glanced at the baby and smirked. "Does she, now?"

A large black woman with a basket over her arm marched in, and the butcher's attention immediately shifted to her. "Emily Jane," he said. "What you need today?"

The woman nodded at Cleo. "She first, I reckon, massa."

All business now, the butcher dismissed Cleo with a tilt of his head toward the stairs in the back of the shop. "Up there," he told her.

At the top of the stairs was one door. Cleo knocked gently, then tried the knob. It was locked. She sat down and leaned against the door. She was out of the blazing sun, but the alcove was hot and airless. She dozed and waited.

Long after the shop had closed, the sun had set, and Cleo's hunger had come and gone, she heard a step at the bottom of the stairs. Cleo scrambled to her feet. "Phanor?"

The footsteps halted. "Who's there?"

"Phanor, it's me. Cleo."

He didn't answer.

"Phanor, is that you?"

Phanor took the remaining steps two at a time. Cleo's outstretched hand found him in the dark.

"Cleo. What are you doing here?" Phanor said.

"Can I come in?"

"Of course you can come in. Wait a minute." He fumbled in his pocket for the key, and then opened the door to his room. There was just enough moonlight coming in through the one window to show him the candlestick on the table. He quickly lit the candle and took in the bundled baby asleep in Cleo's arms and the circles of fatigue under her eyes.

"I call him Gabriel," Cleo said.

Phanor moved a chair behind her. "Sit down. Are you hungry? I have some bread and sausage, if the mice didn't find it."

"Hungry and thirsty."

He opened a bottle of wine and unwrapped the canvas sack to produce half a loaf of bread and a length of sausage. He set it in front of Cleo and let her eat.

When she sat back, satisfied, he said, "Now. Tell me."

Cleo told him everything that had happened since he'd brought the news Remy was dead. Everything.

"Josie wouldn't . . ." he said. "I mean, Josie isn't . . . She couldn't do that to you. Could she?"

"I don't know, Phanor. She was like a crazy woman. I was so scared, I just took Gabriel and ran all night."

Phanor paced the little room. "She was in love with that fellow Chamard, wasn't she?"

"Yes." Cleo felt the full weight of her guilt at that reminder. She'd been reckless with Josie's feelings, as Josie had been with hers. "She was in love with him."

Phanor sat down heavily and stared at the floor.

"I know you were sweet on Josie," Cleo said.

With a rueful, mocking laugh, Phanor said, "That's one way to put it." He shook his head, gulped down the remainder of the wine straight from the bottle, and then thumped it on the table. The candle flame through the curve of the bottle caught his eye and he gazed into the distortion. "She's not the girl I thought I knew," he said.

"She's had a hard year," Cleo offered. Josie really had not been herself, Cleo could acknowledge that now. But she did not regret taking Gabriel and running. Who knew if Josie would ever again be the Josie they'd known.

"You look like you haven't slept in days, Cleo." Phanor gestured to the bed. "Why don't you turn in?"

Cleo looked longingly at the bed. "Where will you sleep?"

Phanor surveyed the hard floor and then the inviting bed. He managed a lopsided smile. "I won't bother you if you won't bother me."

Cleo laughed. "Can Gabriel sleep in that box?"

"Sure." Phanor pulled out several books and his best hat, lined the box with his extra shirts, and presented it to Cleo. She gently placed Gabriel in it to sleep until he woke up hungry again.

Phanor and Cleo climbed in the bed and adjusted their elbows and knees to keep from poking one another. Not long after cock's crow, the butcher opened up his shop downstairs, Phanor dressed quietly, and Cleo and Gabriel slept on.

Midmorning, Cleo made a breakfast of the remaining sausage and watched the street from Phanor's front window. Everyone seemed so busy, and most people ignored everyone they passed. A city of strangers, she mused. If Josie had sent out a hue and cry for slavers to search for her, she didn't see how they could find her in this place.

At noon, Phanor came in carrying a mattress over his back. He tossed it on the floor and avoided Cleo's eyes.

"Did I elbow you last night, hog the covers, snore?" Cleo teased.

"Yeah, all those things." He gave her a sheepish smile. "We're good friends, Cleo. I don't want to change that."

"Thank you," she said. "For everything."

"Let's go eat some gumbo."

Cleo pulled the remaining coins out of her pocket. "I'll pay for it," she said.

Phanor shook his head. "You keep what you have. I make plenty of money to take care of you and Gabriel for a while." He looked around, suddenly realizing how shabby his room was. "I just haven't gotten around to moving yet."

The woman who'd directed Cleo to Phanor's lodging greeted them with her big gap-toothed smile. "It dat pretty girl and de handsome m'sieu. You gon' have my gumbo?" she said.

"Two bowls, Madame Flora," Phanor said. "And a pan of cornbread."

Cleo and Phanor retreated from the bustle of Butcher's Lane to sit on a bench behind Flora's stand. They ate gumbo thick with okra, corn, shrimp, and rice, and they wiped the bowls clean with the last of the bread.

Cleo watched Flora bustle from her cook fire to the wash-up bucket, all the while taking care of customers and calling out to passersby, "Hey, mista, come on over here and get you a bowl of gumbo. You know you hungry. Don't it smell good? Gumbo here!"

"Flora?" Cleo said.

"What, chile?"

"Do you need a helper? I could do the washing up, cut the corn."

Flora laughed from deep in her belly. "Honey, I don' hardly make 'nuff to feed myself. No, you don' find much work dis time of de year." She wiped the sweat from her face with a dirty gray cloth. "All the fine folks what hire girls be gone till the fever season over. Dey be back in a few weeks when de weather turn cool. Den dey be lookin' for kitchen girls, housemaids, and de like. De only other ting I know fo' you, maybe you get some work at de fever hospitals. Dey always needin' nurses."

"No," Phanor said. "It's too dangerous, Cleo. We'll find something, and like I told you, there's no hurry."

Cleo didn't say anything. She appreciated Phanor's generosity, but she meant to make her own way.

Phanor escorted Cleo and the baby back to his room. "I have a man I need to see tonight, Cleo. I'll try not to wake you when I come in."

The next morning, after a breakfast of muscadine grapes and cold cornpone, Phanor dressed in his business clothes. "I'll be back after lunch, Cleo. You and Gabriel be ready to go out."

"Where are we going?"

He paused to heighten the drama, then leaned over the table. "I've persuaded my friend Jean Paul to hear you sing. He's at Les Trois Frères—it's a supper club. You sing for him this afternoon, and maybe he'll let you perform in the evenings. What you think?"

Cleo put a hand to her throat. "Sing for a stranger? Phanor, I've never done that. I don't think—"

"Don't think, Cleo. Just be ready to sing for Jean Paul at two o'clock."

After Phanor left, Cleo fretted for a quarter of an hour. She'd always imagined herself singing in some grand club in New Orleans, but that had just been pretend. Now that the prospect actually presented itself, she wondered if anything would come out of her mouth when the moment came. Finally, she left Gabriel asleep in his box and went to the pump in the back courtyard for water. Back in the room, she bathed and cleaned her clothes the best she could. She combed out her hair and tried to tie her *tignon* just so, but with no mirror in the room, she had no idea if it even sat straight on her head.

She heard Phanor on the staircase and quickly cleaned her teeth one last time on the hem of her dress. It was an old one of Josie's, and though it was a cast-off, it was in good condition. Cleo had let the bosom out all it would go and tied a white lacy drape over the bodice. It was all she had, but she looked quite presentable, she thought. Not like a runaway.

She carried Gabriel through the streets, following Phanor several feet behind to look like his property. When they reached Les Trois Frères, Cleo drew a deep breath. Grand, ornate, and huge, the club intimidated her, but Phanor took her elbow reassuringly.

"His name, it's Jean Paul Rouquier, remember? Just sing for him like you would with me. He's a nice fellow, a Creole, and he needs you as much as you need him. Keep telling yourself that." He put his hand on the knob of the side door. "Ready?"

Cleo nodded. "I can do this, Phanor."

"I know you can."

They entered the cooler, dimmer rooms in the back of the club where they found Jean Paul. "*Mon ami*," he said. "And this is the songbird?"

Gabriel snuffled and fretted in Cleo's arms. "Here, let me have him," Phanor said.

Jean Paul eyed Cleo frankly. "She's very pretty, Phanor, just as you said." He tilted her chin toward the window. "More than pretty. If she sings as well as she looks, we will do business. Come, Cleo. The dining room is empty at this hour, and you can sing for me and me alone."

Cleo threw one last look at Phanor sitting near the window, but Phanor's attention was captured by Gabriel's coos. She followed Jean Paul into the main dining room where silver candlesticks glowed softly on snowy table linens.

Chandeliers sparkled in the light from the floor-to-ceiling windows on the north wall, and below them dark velvet cushions swallowed the light.

"Up there," Jean Paul said. He waved to a small stage against the inner wall where there was a piano and a few chairs for the musicians.

Jean Paul took a seat in the middle of the room. "Begin."

Cleo began to sing a cappella.

"Project, honey, project," Jean Paul demanded.

Cleo flinched at his irritation. She began again, all her breath behind her voice.

"Not bad," he said. "Now on the edge of the stage, and imagine you have two or three men playing along with you." He left his chair and stood at the far side of the room.

Cleo's voice quavered the first few words of the song, but she drew herself up and pushed the nervousness away. She sang to the back tables, imagining Phanor sitting there, or Bertrand. He loved it when she sang for him.

"That'll do," Jean Paul said. He stood up and Cleo followed him back to where Phanor walked the floor with Gabriel. The baby's angry little fists flailed at Phanor's chest.

"Could he be hungry again already?" Phanor said when she hurried to take him.

"If he's awake, he's hungry," Cleo said.

"Let's talk, my friend," Jean Paul said and gestured toward his office.

The men left Cleo to feed the baby. Nursing Gabriel calmed her. She felt she'd sung well, as well as she could anyway. She wanted the job, wanted to sing, but if it wasn't to be, then she would find something else.

When Phanor returned, he winked at her.

"I believe we have an arrangement, then," Jean Paul said. "We'll try her out on the early crowd Thursday night, to begin with. Let her get some confidence."

Jean Paul turned to Cleo. "You have an evening gown."

Phanor didn't hesitate. "Of course she has," he said.

Les Trois Frères behind them, Cleo hissed, "Why did you tell him I have a gown, Phanor? Do you have any idea how much a fancy dress costs?"

"We'll get a dress. I know someone, Cleo."

"A seamstress?"

Phanor laughed. "Not a seamstress. She's Russian, can you imagine? A Russian in New Orleans."

Madame Kirasov's establishment was several streets away from Les Trois Frères, and its dirt lane carried more refuse and more potholes. However, the doorway into Madame's home promised opulence and a particular comfort. A carved and enameled red rose graced the upper panel of the door just over the large brass knocker, and gilt filigree framed the narrow beveled glass set in its center. A small Negro boy dressed in purple with a red satin sash answered Phanor's knock.

The child smiled broadly when he saw Phanor. "M'sieu," he said.

"*Bonjour*, Narcisse," Phanor said, and placed his big hand on the boy's shoulder.

"Will you tell Madame I'm here?"

The boy left them in a lavishly appointed sitting room. Cleo sat down with Gabriel on a scarlet settee furnished with deep purple pillows. Everywhere there were reds and purples—the drapery, the carpet, the lamps. Cleo decided the effect was tasteless, even garish, but there was no denying the luxuriousness.

Madame Kirasov floated into the room in a red dressing gown, trailing ruffles and the scent of expensive perfume. She was a tiny woman, but she somehow seemed to fill the room. "Phanor, darling."

Phanor leaned over to kiss her cheek, but Natasha insisted on a fervent kiss on the mouth. Phanor came up grinning and turned to introduce her to Cleo. Natasha's feigned surprise at her presence in the room didn't fool Cleo. She knew the woman had been fully conscious of her from the moment she entered.

Cleo had no doubt Natasha's shrewd gaze assessed her relationship to Phanor correctly. Cleo assessed Natasha and her business accurately as well. That Phanor was obviously a familiar caller here gave Cleo something to think about. She offered a small curtsy, and Natasha assumed a friendly face.

"Does your friend need a job?" Natasha asked. She looked Cleo and the baby over with a practiced eye. "She would do well here, I think."

"She has a job, in fact. That's why we're here. I hoped you could help her with a dress. Maybe one of the girls could loan her one, or rent it to her?"

"Perhaps. What is this job?"

As Phanor explained, Cleo wondered if the women who worked here wore only purple and red gowns. She'd sometimes imagined herself in a scarlet dress when she'd fantasized about singing in New Orleans.

"And you are a free woman?" Natasha asked.

With conviction and without hesitation, Cleo said, "Yes, I am a free woman."

"With papers to prove it?"

"Certainly."

Cleo held Natasha's gaze. She could make papers the way Phanor had for Remy. If Natasha wanted to see papers, she would produce them.

Natasha smiled slightly. "That won't be necessary," she said.

A clever woman, Cleo thought. *She knows what I am.*

To Phanor Natasha turned a business eye. "I would so love another dozen cases of the Chenin Blanc, Phanor." She tilted her head down and looked up at him with soulful eyes. Her reddened lips assumed a pout. "But it is so dreadfully expensive, *mon chér.*"

Phanor smiled and glanced at Cleo. "Perhaps a discount could be arranged."

"Oh, could you, my darling? Perhaps a dollar a case less than my last order?"

"I think I could deliver a dozen at a half-dollar discount."

Natasha smiled prettily and actually batted her eyelashes. "You are my treasure, Phanor. Cleo . . . Is that your name? Come with me and we'll see what we have. Oh, dear. The child. Phanor, would you?"

Phanor held his arms out for Gabriel, and Cleo followed the red silk train across the floor.

Half an hour later, Cleo emerged with a glowing face. She carried a large soft bundle under her arm and a pair of black satin slippers in her hand.

"It's beautiful, Phanor," Cleo whispered. "And she said I can keep it. It's only a little soiled, and it has a frayed hem, but it's too long anyway."

"Is it purple, or red?" he teased.

"It's red. Red velvet."

Chapter 35

Toulouse

"You gots to eat dis," Laurie said. Grand-mère, slumped in her rolling chair, shoved Laurie's hand away and spilled the mush on Laurie's clean skirt. "Now look what you did, you mean old biddy."

"Laurie!" Josie gathered a handful of Laurie's pigtails and gave them a yank. "I've a good mind to take a switch to you. Now get on to the cookhouse and see if you can help Louella."

Josie sat down with her grandmother and stirred the bowl of mush. "Mémère, if you don't like this, I can get you some jam and toast. You can eat the toast by yourself, if that's what you want."

Grand-mère tried to speak, but it came out something like "ack ra."

"Okra? You want Louella to fix you some okra?"

Grand-mère raised her voice and waved her hand around.

"Ack ra ah san!" She let out a stream of angry words, one of which Josie thought might have been an actual swear word. But who could tell? Since Cleo left, no one understood Grand-mère, and her temper had become shorter and hotter.

Josie sat it out. She was so tired. She spent the early mornings riding the plantation and the afternoons consulting the logs Grand-mère and her father and his father had kept. They had recorded the dates they'd fertilized the fields, where they'd bought the fertilizer and how much they'd paid, how many hands it took to put in a field of corn. And then there were the thousand other details to keep track of, like whether there was sufficient charcoal made to last through the winter. Should she have the crews harvesting the vegetable gardens or hoeing weeds in the cane? If she had another twenty slaves, she wouldn't have to worry about juggling all the tasks to be done.

And she missed Cleo and the baby terribly. Remorse, guilt, shame, loneliness, and fatigue wore her down—on top of which, Grand-mère spent half her waking time in a fury. If only Josie could tap into all her years of experience, could ask her advice, but she couldn't understand one word in ten. The last time she had tried to ask her about which bills to pay first, Grand-mère grew so impatient they were both in tears before Josie gave up.

Josie saw to it that Laurie, respectfully, served her grandmother toast and jam. Then she returned to the office to ponder the accounts. She now kept the hated glasses on a ribbon around her neck. She needed them too often to be searching for them on mantels or in pockets these days, and it no longer mattered to her whether they were becoming or not.

It's time to do something drastic, Josie thought. *It's no good making payments just to keep the interest up. I've got to think bigger.*

The creak of a wagon and harness came to her through the window, and Elbow John's hearty shout of welcome announced it wasn't just a tradesman. Josie tossed the pencil on the desk, glad to be distracted.

From the front gallery, Josie looked down on Mr. Gale climbing out of his overloaded wagon. His two little tow-headed boys sat on top of a tarp-covered mound. They must be twice as big as they had been when they'd left for Texas. Where were the rest of the Gales?

Josie met Mr. Gale at the top of the gallery stairs. "Come in, please, Mr. Gale. I'm very happy to see you."

Mr. Gale was begrimed with road dust and he held his hat nervously. When he hesitated to sit on the horsehide sofa for fear of dirtying it, Josie insisted. "It'll brush right off," she said. "Please sit down. Give me just a moment, and we'll have some refreshment."

She called Laurie to ask Louella for lemonade. "And take the children to the cookhouse. They need a drink and maybe some of Louella's corncakes. Take good care of them, Laurie."

Josie sat down across from the former overseer. "Now, Mr. Gale, I want to hear all about Texas."

He shook his head. "It don't bear telling, the half of it, mam'zelle." He set his hat on the floor next to his down-at-heel boots. "It's a harsh country, no mistaking. The sun pulls the water right out of the soil, and the soil ain't but half a hand deep most places. First crop I planted withered 'fore it was full growed."

Josie waited while Mr. Gale collected himself. "They got bad sickness out there, too. Diphtheria, they said it was. I lost my wife and Roseanne. You remember Mrs. Gale and little Roseanne?"

"Of course I do, Mr. Gale. I'm so sorry. Your wife always had a handful of cracked nuts or a gingersnap for Cleo and me."

Mr. Gale wiped a hand across his stubbly jaw. "She were a good woman," he said.

Josie didn't know what to say, and Mr. Gale seemed to have told all he was going to. "Roseanne was the prettiest little girl," she said. "All rosy cheeks and smiles."

"Yes, she were a pretty child."

Laurie carried in a tray of lemonade in tall glasses. Josie nodded to her to serve Mr. Gale first.

"You're welcome to stay here, Mr. Gale. You're on your way back home? Alabama, was it?"

"Yes, Alabama. But my kinfolk there are all gone. This is home to me and my boys now." He drained his glass and set it on the side table. "That's what I come to talk about, mam'zelle. Back in Donaldsonville, I heard you got rid of that man LeBrec. I come to see if I can have my place back."

"Mr. Gale, I don't know what to say. Things have changed since you left. The crash, and—do you know about my grandmother?"

Josie told him about grandmother's stroke, about their inability to understand her, how she slept most of the day and railed the rest. She told him how she had been trying to do the overseer's job, and last of all, she told him that however much she wanted to, she couldn't afford to pay an overseer now.

Mr. Gale thought it over. "I have a proposal, Mam'zelle Josephine. You need an overseer, and my boys need a home. You let me move back in the old house, you pay for vittles and lamp oil and such, and I'll forgo my salary until such time as we've got Toulouse making a profit again."

Josie wanted to hug Mr. Gale, dusty jacket, stubbled chin and all. "Mr. Gale, you don't know what this means to me. I'll make it up to you, I promise I will." Impulsively, she left her chair to sit next to Mr. Gale on the sofa. "I have so much to tell you. And I want to show you what Old Sam has had the hands working on, all the building we've done since you left."

Mr. Gale stood up. "I'm eager to see the place, I can tell

you. You won't mind if I pay my respects to Madame Tassin? Her and me go back a long way."

"Of course. You're tired, and you want to get the children settled in. I'll tell Louella to fix your dinner, and Elbow John can help you unload."

"Thank you, ma'am. I know we got business to talk, and I'll be ready first thing in the morning, if that'll be all right."

"I'll have everything arranged, the accounts I mean. And after breakfast, we can ride out to see the fields." Josie grabbed Mr. Gale's rough hand. "Thank you, Mr. Gale."

"And I thank you, too, Mam'zelle Josephine. I'm glad to be back."

With Mr. Gale in charge again, Josie began sleeping past sunrise. Her mood lifted to have someone share the load of running the place, and she began to think in earnest about more drastic plans to rescue their finances. She had already looked over Maman's jewelry, trying to guess what each piece might bring. There was a pearl encrusted broach, a large sapphire pendant, several rings with semiprecious stones, and one moderate-sized diamond. Not likely enough for the coming quarterly payment of interest on the loans, but she'd see what they'd bring in New Orleans.

Josie carried the jewelry box to Grand-mère when she woke up from one of her naps. Grand-mère couldn't talk, and she could no longer hold a pen, but she could still think, and she might know how much to expect from the jewels.

"What about this one?" Josie said. "You think it's worth maybe fifty dollars?"

Grand-mère spoke; Josie questioned her. "More? Seventy-five?"

Grand-mère nodded, and so they went through Josie's mother's things until Josie had a good idea of how much to ask for them. She began putting the jewelry away when Grand-mère became agitated. She gestured toward her room and tried to tell Josie something.

"All right, Mémère. I'll roll you in there, just a minute." In the bedroom, Grand-mère indicated Josie should reach for the black lacquered box on the top shelf of her chiffer-obe. Josie placed it in her grandmother's lap and helped her open it. Inside was an assortment of rings and necklaces, worth at least as much as Josie's mother's collection. But that was not what interested Grand-mère. In the bottom of the box was a tiny concealed compartment. Resting on the black velvet lining was a large diamond pendant surrounded by smaller diamonds.

Josie was stunned. "Grand-mère, I've never seen such a beautiful necklace. You've never worn it, not in my whole life."

Trying to understand her grandmother, Josie said, "You want me to sell it too?"

Grand-mère became upset, and the more upset she was, the harder she was to understand. "Slow down, Mémère."

Very slowly, each syllable as distinct as she could make it, Grand-mère said, "Not for interest."

"You don't want me to spend the money on interest pay-ments."

Grand-mère nodded vigorously. With further effort, Josie finally understood. Her grandmother intended her to use the diamond to finance a business investment, something that would produce money rather than just stave off the bankers until the next installment was due.

The old woman was exhausted. Josie called Laurie to help put her to bed. Then she had Beau saddled. She needed to think. The diamonds meant opportunity, but she had no idea what kind of opportunity.

She gave Beau his head and ambled along the river road, musing on the ways people made money in the city. The streets of New Orleans had always been full of vendors sell-ing fruit or pies or gumbo. Even water, if the weather was warm.

What could she sell? She couldn't walk the streets like the low class did, but she could have a shop. She imagined herself in a storefront selling merchandise to strangers. At least she hoped they would be strangers. She wouldn't want her friends from society to see her.

Beau had trotted all the way to Cherleu while Josie was preoccupied. When she caught sight of the old house, she drew up. No longer gray and ramshackle, the mansion gleamed with a coat of white paint. The roof shingles shone blond, they were so new. The gardens were tamed, and the whole effect was of prosperity.

If Abigail Johnston—no, Abigail Chamard—knew I was thinking of opening a shop, of selling merchandise myself, she would be horrified. Women do not dirty their hands in Abigail's world.

Well, I don't live in Abigail's world. I'll never sit idle, be some man's ornament. Not now that I know what I'm capable of.

By the time Josie had ridden Beau back to Toulouse, he was lathered and she had a plan. She would take Louella with her to New Orleans. They would rent a kitchen, and they would bake pies. All kinds of pies—blackberry and apple, pork and chicken. She left her horse with the stable boy and hurried to her desk to figure out the cost of making a pie. Flour, fruit, meat, lard, salt, sugar. She tried to account for everything, even the cost of running an oven.

Diamonds into pies, she thought. She could do it. She could be in New Orleans within the month. For a moment, she wondered if Cleo had gone to New Orleans, if she'd gone to Phanor the way Remy had. Neither of them would want anything to do with her, though. Not after what she'd done.

Josie shook her head to dispel the image of Cleo's panic-stricken face. *I did an awful thing that day.* She put a hand to her forehead as if she could ward off the melancholia she'd suffered after Cleo left.

I have to stop this—I can't let myself think about what I did to Cleo now. I have to keep going. I have to save Toulouse.

Chapter 36

New Orleans, 1839

The wind off the river sucked the warmth right out of Josie's bones. She hurried through the dawn light to the gray board shack she'd rented not far from Jackson Square. The neighborhood changed quickly between the cathedral and her little kitchen, but Josie had seen far worse streets when she searched for a place to set up business. At least here the shopkeepers occasionally paid a crew to pick up litter and dung and dead animals.

Josie fought the wind to pull the door open and let it slam behind her. Louella already had a fire going under the brick oven. "It's a cold one, sho' nuff," Louella said. "Stand over here by de fire a minute 'fore you take off yo coat."

The kitchen measured twelve feet on a side with a large window and counter built into the street wall. The wind snuck in through every crack, and until later in the morning when Josie would open the counter window, it was dim and smoky inside. After the other places she'd looked at, though,

Josie knew enough to be glad of the board floor and a chimney that worked. Josie rubbed her hands together and drank a cup of hot coffee. Louella's forehead was already beaded with sweat, and Josie too would soon be grateful for the fresh air blowing in under the door.

Their early morning customers preferred fruit pies, so Josie got to work peeling apples. The noontime crowd bought mostly meat pies, and there were two pork butts on a spit over the fire.

Josie and Louella had developed an efficient routine. Each morning, Josie stayed behind in the rented room to count the previous day's receipts and keep the accounts by candlelight. Meanwhile, Louella walked alone through dark streets to the kitchen to get the oven and the fireplace going. She rolled out extra-thick bottom crusts and lined the small deep pans with the dough. When Josie arrived, she prepared the fruit with sugar, salt, cinnamon, and butter, filled the crusts, topped the pie with a thinner crust, and pricked an apple shape on top. By the time the scent of hot apple pie filled the little shop, the first customers would be at the window.

It hadn't taken long for the men who worked along the levee to discover Josie's shop. The first ones told their friends they could get a cup of hot coffee and a pie wrapped in paper at a reasonable price, and the pies were the best you could get on that stretch of the river. They paid in various coins, and Josie learned to make change in English shillings and pence, American half-dimes and bungtown coppers, Spanish reales, fips, medios, and pistareens.

Josie's strategy quickly began to yield a profit. She and Louella baked as many pies, both fruit and meat, as they could until midafternoon. Then they let the fires go out. Louella took whatever pies had not yet sold to the square and hawked them to the passersby. Josie remained in the kitchen to clean the work table, the grates, the floor. She took stock of what they'd need for the next day and then shopped for flour, lard, fruit, onions, garlic, and meat. On Butcher Lane she found the best prices for pork and beef, but it was an unsavory place. She tried to manage the buying so that she only had to smell the raw and sometimes rotting meat only two or three times a week.

Josie wanted to be back at the boarding house before the sun went down, and this time of year darkness came early. Though the room was in a safer neighborhood than the kitchen, it was foolish to be on the streets after dark. Besides, it was cold, she was tired, and her feet hurt. The lack of Toulouse's crystal vases, cut-glass lamps, and velvet upholstery didn't trouble her. She needed only a place for Louella and her to sleep, and a table and chair for keeping the accounts. They were both exhausted by nightfall anyway; they'd fall into their beds, indifferent to the bare walls and sparse furnishings.

As Josie turned into Butcher Lane, she met the wind off the river face-on. She pulled the wool scarf tighter around her neck and because she was watching her step in the nasty muck of the street, she nearly collided with another young woman carrying a bundled baby.

"*Excusez-moi*," Josie said and looked up into Cleo's startled face.

A medley of surprise, affection, mistrust, resentment, and guilt afflicted both their faces. Neither spoke as they read each other's feelings and tried to accept the improbable event of their meeting here, in a backstreet of New Orleans.

Josie looked at the bundle of blankets on Cleo's shoulder. "That's Gabriel," she said. Cleo took a step back and held Gabriel tighter against her chest. A mule and wagon rattled by, and tradesmen jostled them in the busy street.

Cleo's suspicion nearly crushed Josie. "I won't try to take him," she said. "I won't even ask to hold him."

Cleo took another step back, her eyes locked on Josie's.

"I'm so sorry, Cleo." Josie's breath seized in her chest. "Forgive me. Please forgive me, Cleo," she managed.

Cleo's eyes filled, but Josie read fear and mistrust behind the blur of tears. As Cleo backed away, Josie sobbed. "I'm sorry," she said.

"Good bye, Josie," Cleo whispered. She turned and quickly lost herself in the throng of people.

Josie leaned against a storefront and buried her face in her scarf until her breathing eased. She wiped her eyes and moved through the crowd Cleo had disappeared into, her whole heart yearning for her sister.

It was nearly dark. Josie put her handkerchief away and hurried to buy two butts from the pork butcher. She carried the heavy basket through the fading light back to the kitchen. Louella's basket was on the table; she'd already be resting in their room. Josie put the meat in a tin box to keep the rats out and locked the kitchen.

The moon had not risen and the streets were dark as Josie made her way to bed and rest. She was too tired and too pre-occupied to be afraid. She passed through the square where Phanor had played his fiddle that Sunday. *Likely to the same people who now buy my pies,* Josie thought. *Cleo looked good. Her cape was new, and now that I think of it, her boots were good too. She probably found Phanor, and he's helped her. He's a good man, Phanor is.*

Josie climbed the stairs to her room. *If only I'd seen Gabriel's face.*

Louella was snoring softly when Josie entered. She undressed by herself and climbed into the cold bed. She got up and found a pair of socks and climbed back in. She felt emptied and light. Even though sobs still threatened, she had told Cleo she was sorry. There was that, at least.

* * *

While Josie slept, Cleo sang at Les Trois Frères. She wore a new gown, blue satin trimmed in black lace. Her voice was low and intimate, and the diners quieted when she began. The gentlemen and ladies at the back tables felt the same warm caress in her full-throated voice as the admirers who made a point of sitting near the stage to see her.

Bertrand Chamard was the only admirer Cleo encouraged. He came alone, drank his brandy, and gazed at Cleo as she sang. Afterward, he would take Cleo home to the little house in the Vieux Carre where Gabriel and his nanny slept. He never stayed more than an hour or two, and after gazing on his son in the crib, he'd kiss Cleo once again and go home to his wife.

Chamard had discovered Cleo when he'd first come to town in the fall. He, his wife Abigail, her brother Albany, and his wife Violette had dined at Les Trois Frères for a quiet evening's reunion.

Cleo had noticed him immediately, and her whole body remembered the warmth of his bed. He'd stared at her for one intense quick moment, and then had looked away. She'd had no fear he would betray her, and when the club closed late that night, she wasn't surprised to see him waiting for her in his carriage.

Cleo wondered if she should tell Chamard she'd seen Josie. Would he help Josie if she needed it? She hadn't looked well. The familiar dark green dress and jacket hung on her, and her face was thin. Her hair straggled from the cap she wore, and her presence in Butcher Lane was unexplainable. Unless she had guessed Cleo would be in touch with Phanor. He was easy enough to find.

As she snuggled against Chamard under the warm quilt, Cleo realized she had overreacted. She'd been afraid Josie would take her back. It would have taken only a holler to commandeer several white men to seize her. But Josie's tears had been real. Her apology was real.

"I saw Josie today," she said.

Chamard shifted his weight. "Did you?"

"In Butcher Lane. I'd left a bag of lemons for Phanor and was coming back here when we practically ran into each other."

"What was she doing in Butcher Lane?"

"At first I thought she was searching for me, but now I think she was as surprised as I was. She's thin, and a little haggard."

Chamard was quiet, and Cleo let him think. He took her hand and held it against his chest. "I'll look into it."

Cleo kissed him, and in a minute he threw the heavy quilt off the bed.

Josie's Tante Marguerite had not invited Chamard to her home since his marriage to Abigail Johnston. He didn't blame her for excluding him, and at their mutual friends' *soirée*, she was her usual coquettish self. She fluttered her fan at him, and he bowed deeply.

"Would you care to dance, madame?"

She spread her fan over the lower half of her face, which emphasized her merry, dark eyes.

"I'd be delighted," she said.

Chamard whirled her into the crowd of dancers, and the two of them waltzed splendidly around the room. He was aware Abigail watched them from her seat next to her mother, but he refused to bow to her childish jealousy. He would dance with every woman in the room, if he pleased. Abigail needed to relax, have some fun on her own. There were plenty of young men in the room who would love to dance with her. She only needed to give them the slightest encouragement.

The orchestra took a break, and Chamard escorted Marguerite to the refreshment table. As he helped her to a plate of oysters, he said, "I understand your niece is in town."

"Josephine?" Marguerite said. She avoided his eyes, not her usual bold style at all. "I'm sure she decided to stay on Toulouse with her grandmother," she said.

"How is Emmeline?"

"Much the same, I hear. Josephine runs Toulouse now."

"They are much alike, I think," Chamard said. "Both strong women."

Marguerite rather abruptly hailed her friend Achille. She clearly did not wish to discuss her niece. Chamard bowed slightly and returned to the dance floor with an elegant woman dressed all in creamy satin. If Abigail continued to sit there with a long, dull face, he would send her home with the Johnstons and meet Cleo when she finished at Les Trois Frères.

The next morning, Chamard charged his man Valentine with sleuthing out Josephine's whereabouts. It would please Cleo, and he too would like to know that Josephine was well. From the way Marguerite had avoided him the rest of last evening, he felt something must be amiss.

Valentine had sources Chamard did not. He stopped in at the kitchen behind Marguerite's townhouse. Liza, the cook, welcomed him with a big hug and an amorous kiss. "Where you been, you sweet thing?" she said. "It been a month of Sundays since you been by."

Valentine did his duty. He pretended to try to seduce Liza, and she pretended to be just about to yield, but it was only sport.

Liza herself didn't often go in the living quarters of the family, but she got the news from the house slaves. "You right," she told Valentine. "Dere been whispering bout dat niece, Josephine. Somethin 'bout being common, like a tradesman, and her a girl and just grown. It's dis crash dey talks about, I reckon," Liza said. "Likely dat girl need de money."

"You know where she is?" Valentine asked.

"She got a place down on de levee, I think. I don' know no mo' dan dat."

Valentine spent the next several afternoons strolling along the river road, looking for any sign of a genteel lady out of her natural element. He'd been disappointed when his master married *l'américaine*. Mademoiselle Josephine would not have plagued him day and night like this Madame Abigail did. *Valentine, do this. Valentine do that,* he groused. *That woman too damn lazy to scratch her own head.*

He bought a pie from a slave woman in Jackson Square and moseyed again down Rue Chartres. He left the busy street to explore the alleys along the levee, and there he got lucky. Mademoiselle Josephine was locking the door to a weathered board house. She strode off with a large basket on her arm. Valentine followed at a distance, but he soon learned he needn't be particularly careful. The lady had no notion of being followed.

She bought produce in the farmer's market and returned to the kitchen near the levee. Shortly she emerged again, and Valentine followed her to her lodging. It was nearly dark by then, and he stayed in the street long enough to see her light a candle in the window above the doorway.

The following evening, Josie arrived at the little room just at sunset. Louella hadn't come in yet, and the room was cold and dark. Josie struck a match to the candle and shucked her shoes off. The soles had worn thin, but she didn't want to spend her hard-earned profits on shoes. Not yet, anyway. When the rain started soaking her stockings, then she might replace them with the brogans she saw the other working women wear. She'd completely abandoned her pride in such trivial matters. The girls she knew from last winter had never crossed her path, and they certainly would never be seen at her shop. Anyway, who cared if they saw her earning a living in clodhoppers and mob cap? She needed something to keep the hair out of her eyes while she cooked, and the delicate slippers of high fashion were of no use to a woman on her feet all day.

Someone tapped on her door. Louella never knocked.

"Who is it?"

The door opened.

Josie sat with a shoe in her hand, gaping. "Bertrand? What are you doing here?"

"May I come in?"

Josie stood up. "What do you want?"

"I heard you were in town, yet you haven't been at any of your friends' parties. I wanted to assure myself you are all right."

"I am well, thank you. You need not concern yourself."

"Josephine, please. You have every right to be angry with me, but . . . I want to know if you need some assistance."

"I do not."

Chamard looked around the room. Two cots, two chairs, a table. No rug on the floor. A shabby curtain at the window. The grate had only a few coals in it.

"Who stays here with you?"

"What difference does it make to you?"

"Please, Josephine. What are you doing here?"

Josie lifted her chin. "I'm making money. Isn't that what counts in this world? Money?"

He ignored the barb. "How are you making money?"

"With the work of my own hands. I have a kitchen. We make pies. We sell them."

Chamard sat on one of the hard chairs, his hat held between his knees.

"Are you making a profit? Truly?"

"Even more than I'd hoped. So you see, you need not concern yourself. You may leave in good conscience."

Chamard studied her in the candlelight. Josie's dress bore a streak of flour across one breast, and her hair was mussed from pulling off the white cap. "You're a beautiful woman, Josie. Not just a pretty girl. And tough, like your grandmother."

Josie held the door open. "I don't want you here, Bertrand. I don't need you." Would he say he was sorry? Sorry he broke her heart? Sorry he'd been more interested in money than he had been in her?

Bertrand stood and put his hat on. "I made a bad bargain, Josephine. I'm the poorer for losing you."

Josie closed the door behind him. *I told the truth*, she thought. *I don't need him. I don't need anyone.*

Chapter 37

New Orleans

As the winter weeks passed, Josie found bitter amusement in the irony of so many people, poor and rich alike, being in desperate circumstances while she, the spoiled and delicate mademoiselle, made money in a humble kitchen baking pies. The laborers at her counter sometimes lined up all the way to the corner, and she and Louella had all they could do to keep up with the orders. She hired an Irish girl, not much younger than herself, to help, but there was a limit to how many pies one oven could bake, no matter how fast they were put together.

Josie visited Monsieur Moncrieff at his bank. She paid him the interest for the quarter, but instead of also reducing the principal as she'd planned, she persuaded Monsieur to be patient a little longer. She would use the capital she'd earned to good effect. She would open another kitchen, closer to the docks, and by this time next year, she would be in a position to make regular reductions in the debt.

Monsieur gazed at her over the glasses on his nose. Josie knew he would be thinking she was too young to trust in financial matters, but she'd brought her account book. She laid out the figures for him and answered all his queries.

"Very well," Moncrieff said. "You must still make your interest payments, of course, but I will continue to hold your debt. I confess, Mademoiselle Tassin, your success so far is impressive. I will follow your enterprise with great interest, and you must feel free to come to me for consultation whenever you like."

"Thank you so much, monsieur," she said, smiling sweetly, the little woman grateful to the big smart man. What she thought, however, was, *Consultation my foot. I doubt you know very much about the price of lard or what my customers will pay for breakfast. Pompous ass.*

Josie quickly opened up the second kitchen and hired another Irish girl, one to help Louella and one to help her in the new business. As soon as it was running efficiently, and profitably, she began to think of setting up a third kitchen that would sell better pastries to the restaurants in the Vieux Carré. Louella baked a fine custard cake, and her crème puffs were as good as any cook's in New Orleans. But Josie would have to hire more help, and Louella would have to train them. One step at a time, Josie thought.

She bought Louella a new dress and a pair of sturdy shoes like the ones on her own feet. What Louella needed most, though, was rest. She was not so young anymore, and Josie saw to it that Molly, the Irish girl, took over the afternoon street vending. Instead of Louella struggling with a basket heavy with pies, Molly slung the same basket on her hip and sang all the way to Jackson Square to hawk them. With her red curls escaping from her cap and her merry smile, Molly quickly sold out of pies in the afternoons and would come back to the kitchen for more.

On a Sunday gray with springtime rain, Josie and Louella slogged through the mushy streets to the kitchen. Sundays were their only days of rest, but today Louella was to make a tray of cakes and pastries for Josie to use as samples. She'd made a list of the best supper clubs in the Vieux Carré, and she planned to dress in the best dress she had with her in New Orleans and present herself to the managers. If even one of them bought from her, she was sure more would follow.

Josie checked that the rain clouds were blowing over, covered the basket of samples, and set out to try her luck. At the first club, Le Petit Jardin, the manager, a corpulent gentleman with stains on his vest, gobbled the sample pastries Josie offered, then told her no, so sorry, no need for her services. At La Pêche d'Or, the gentleman in charge ate a crème puff and kissed his fingers in appreciation. "Most excellent, mademoiselle. However, you must realize my clientele will soon be leaving New Orleans. Before the heat strikes and the miasma poisons us, everyone who can leaves the city. But you know this."

"Yes, of course," Josie said. "But surely there are many people who must come to town on business through the summer months."

"Not enough. Not nearly enough. I believe this summer we will close our doors altogether until the fall. If you will come see me then, perhaps in late September, we will talk."

Josie still had a third layer of samples in her basket. She would try another club before she gave up for the day. The side door to Les Trois Frères stood open and Josie went in.

She followed the sound of voices down a short corridor to the back of the club. A tall, slim gentleman with wavy black hair stood with his back to her. A much shorter man, in his vest and shirtsleeves, held a bottle of wine up to the light. "I agree, *mon ami*, it has a beautiful hue," he was saying. "The color of a Swedish girl's hair."

Josie caught his eye as she entered the room. "Mademoiselle?" he said.

"Monsieur. Are you the manager?"

The tall man turned around. Phanor DeBlieux registered surprise at least as great as hers. "Josephine?" he said.

Josie heard the blood roaring in her ears. The last time she'd seen him, she'd been arrogant and harsh and unfeeling because he'd help Remy escape. And because he'd kissed her aunt. But she'd done worse than that—did he know how horrible she'd been to Cleo?

She tried to appear unruffled, but she couldn't keep her voice from betraying her. "*Bonjour*, Phanor." She cleared her throat. "I hope I see you well."

"Cleo told me you were in New Orleans," Phanor said.

So he did know. All the times she had been cold or unkind—Phanor knew the worst of all her faults. He must despise her. She looked at her wet shoes. Had she left muddy prints across the floor?

"This is *mon ami*, Jean Paul Roquier," Phanor said. "He's the one you want, if you want the manager." He looked at his friend. "Mademoiselle Josephine Tassin."

Josie wanted to run from the contempt Phanor must feel for her, but her feet seemed stuck to the bricks.

"How may I help you, mademoiselle?" Jean Paul said.

Josie swallowed and withdrew the linen covering the pastries. "Monsieur, perhaps you would taste a coconut cake?"

"*Avec plaisir*," he exclaimed and accepted a small cake. "Hmm. Wonderful," he said. "Did you bake this yourself, mademoiselle?"

"No, but it is from my kitchen." Josie kept her face averted from Phanor. "If we can do business, I will cater all the desserts you serve in your dining room."

Not a stupid man by any means, Jean Paul read the disturbance in his friend and in this lovely young woman. He licked his fingers and contemplated what history brought them to such an awkward moment.

Waving his hand toward Phanor, Jean Paul said, "So you are a friend of my friend, eh?"

"Monsieur DeBlieux and I . . ." Josie faltered. She still could not look at him, couldn't bear the dislike she would see in his eyes. "We are from the same part of the river," she finished.

"Not one of Phanor's lovely Irish girls, then. Phanor, you never told me about your Mademoiselle Josephine."

Phanor muttered, "*Non*, not this one."

Jean Paul's keen eyes examined him. "So am I to do business with mademoiselle? You would vouch for her?"

Silence hung in the room, and Josie felt Phanor would never answer. She gripped the handle of her basket and finally raised her eyes to his.

"I believe she is a good person," Phanor said.

Josie's chest swelled and she struggled not to cry. "*Merci*, Phanor," she whispered.

Phanor picked up his hat. "I must go," he said. "I have an appointment." He stared at Josie. "Do you . . . ?" he began, but he didn't finish.

Abruptly, he nodded to Jean Paul and left without looking at Josie again. She didn't mind the brusque leave-taking. In fact, she was joyful, gladsome, blessed. He knew, and he'd forgiven her. Josie looked at Phanor's friend Jean Paul and beamed through the tears on her cheeks.

Jean Paul pulled a chair out for her. "Sit down, my dear," Jean Paul said. "Let me pour you a glass of wine." He busied himself with the bottle and the glasses while she collected herself. "This is a delightful Sauvignon, if the golden hue lives up to its promise."

Josie drank a glass of wine with Jean Paul. He put her at ease, drew her out, and soon knew all about her two kitchens and the plan for a third.

"You are quite a shrewd businesswoman, *ma chérie*," he said. "Your part of the river apparently abounds in sharp wits. Phanor will go far, I have no doubt, and here you are, well on your way to being an entrepreneur as well." He raised his glass. "To your success."

"Does this mean you will buy your pastries from me?" Josie said.

"Well, I'll tell you. You do not yet have this third kitchen running, as I understand. And it is late in the season. I propose this. You have your bakery ready by September, and I will be your first client. I can tell you now, the coconut cake will be in great demand."

A soft rain fell as Josie left Les Trois Frères. She lifted her face to the sky for its benediction and let the drops fall on her eyes and in her hair. All these months of despising herself, and she had been forgiven. She gloried in Phanor's declaration—a good person, that's what he'd said.

With a healing heart, Josie attacked each day with new vigor. She ran both kitchens and proceeded with plans to open the third. She wrote her Grand-mére long letters with the details of her business activities, with amusing accounts of Moncrieff's unsought advice at the bank, and with scenes of a New Orleans that ladies like her grandmother never saw. As for Phanor, she mentioned she had seen him by chance and that he prospered.

"I will not be coming home for the summer," she wrote. "You are not to worry, Grand-mére. We Creoles have great resistance to the miasma, you know—it's mostly *les américains* who are at risk. I need to be here. The people who buy my pies don't leave in the summertime; the work of the city goes on, and they'll continue to spend their money at my kitchens."

Josie regretted she would get no reply from her grandmother. The only one left on Toulouse who could write was Mr. Gale, and she didn't believe Grand-mére could make herself understood to him. Josie suppressed a wave of home-sickness and began a new letter to Mr. Gale. They exchanged regular notes about the business of Toulouse, and Mr. Gale reported all was going well. Another blessing, Josie said to herself, to have Mr. Gale running the plantation.

In the weeks that followed Josie's encounter with Phanor at Les Trois Frères, she approached every corner convinced she would meet him coming the other way. She looked for him among the men lined up at her counter, she scanned the heads in the pews of the church at morning mass, she held imaginary conversations with him. But Phanor in the flesh did not appear. Josie tried to tell herself it was enough, the absolution she'd felt when he spoke kindly, but she yearned for his familiar face.

Easter passed, the sun grew hotter, and the city emptied itself of everyone who could afford refuge at the cooler, healthier resorts on the lakes. Josie had been right about her clientele, though. The men and women who worked in the lower parts of town had nowhere to go, and the loading and unloading of boats and ships continued. Josie and Louella and the two Irish girls, Molly and Kathleen, kept both kitchens going even as the flies and mosquitoes renewed their numbers and the stink of the river grew.

Josie had extra windows cut into each of the kitchens to make the heat bearable. Louella covered them with cheese-cloth, but that only ensured that the most enterprising of the flies swarmed around her sweaty forearms. With the long summer days, fortunately, the four cooks managed to finish their work before sunset, when the night air became threatening. Many of the people left in New Orleans did the same as Josie and Louella. They retired to their homes and hid from the dangerous miasma of the night.

After suffering through several sweltering nights in their airless room, Josie and Louella decided to risk the evening air. They tacked a double layer of cheesecloth over the single window and managed to sleep most of the night in their sweat-soaked beds. They'd awake in the morning unre-freshed and irritable.

"I's thinking I might sleep on de river, mam'zelle," Louella declared. "Dey's a world o' folks do dat, to get some breeze. I wrap myself up wit de 'squita net, and I get some sleep dat way."

"What about the night air? You'll catch the Yellow Jack out in the open all night."

"I don't see how dat can be. I breathes the same air at night whether I be in de house or under de stars. It don' make no sense to me."

"Please, Louella. I can't let you risk it."

Resigned, Louella said, "Yes'm," and continued to toss through the night on clammy sheets.

Every year, the Yellow Jack crept through New Orleans. Every year, the city fathers called for greater cleanliness, closer inspection of ships from the West Indies, stricter quar-antines, yet the mysterious fever continued to claim its vic-tims. It was well known that the new people on the river—the Americans, the Irish, the newly immigrated Frenchmen—were the first to fall to it, and that fact reassured Josie that she and Louella would be safe enough in the city. After all, every year the people upriver accused the steamboats of bringing the disease to them, and so even the plantations were not entirely immune.

On the way to the kitchen early in the morning, Josie saw a body fallen in the gutter. Blood smeared the man's yel-lowed face, and black vomit covered his shirt. Josie crossed herself and ran the rest of the way. The Yellow Jack, Bronze John—the fever—had arrived, and Josie worried about Molly and Kathleen. She'd warned them about the night air, but she knew they went to the taverns in the evenings to earn a few more picayunes serving beer and wine. She'd tell them about the man in the gutter and remind them they should stay indoors after dark.

The body wagons began to rattle through the streets in the early mornings. "Bring out yo' dead," the men would call, and families would open their doors to deliver their beloved one wrapped in soiled sheets. The wagon men, mostly toothless, filthy, and half drunk, would toss the body into the wagon like one more piece of cordwood and roll on.

After seeing yet another poor soul's swollen body lying in the gutter before the wagon men cleared her street, Josie went to the church instead of to work. She pulled a few coins from her pocket to pay for candles to light beneath the Virgin's statue. On her knees, Josie prayed for Cleo and Gabriel. "Wherever they are, Holy Mother, protect them from the Yellow Jack." She prayed for Phanor, and Louella and Molly and Kathleen. As for herself, she had had a jaundice when she was a child. She would not get it again.

In the kitchen, Josie rolled up her sleeves to pare the first bushel of apples. A mosquito floated in through the open counter window with the slight breeze. It lit on Josie's hand, but she waved it off. Then the tiny vessel of death lit on the fair, freckled arm of Kathleen. She held a heavy, hot pan of roast pork in her hands, and so merely endured yet another mosquito bite.

Three days later, Kathleen did not come to work. Two days after that, she was dead.

Chapter 38

New Orleans

"Cleo, this is foolish," Chamard said. "You and Gabriel would be much safer at the lake than in New Orleans."

"We're native born. We'll be fine. And I can't leave Les Trois Frères now. I'm the only singer they have for the summer." This was an old argument. However ardently Cleo enjoyed Chamard as her lover, she resisted becoming his *plaçée*, and she paid her own rent on the tiny cottage she and Gabriel and his nanny lived in.

"I'm going to be at the Hotel Milneburgh all month," he said. "If you change your mind, I'll come fetch you with the carriage." He nuzzled her neck. "Promise me you'll think about it."

Even in the heavy, humid heat, Cleo thrilled at his touch. The last months with Chamard had somehow been both serene and exhilarating. She wondered if she loved him. Her feelings for him were different from the way she'd felt about Remy. Remy had been sweet and vulnerable, for all his pride. He'd needed her, and she'd wanted to take care of him always. Chamard wanted to take care of her, but she didn't see that they needed each other.

She kissed the salty dew in the hollow at the base of his throat. He slipped his hand under her chemise, and another hour passed before he dressed to return to the resort on Lake Pontchartrain.

"I'll see you in a week," he said. "I don't think I can stay away from you longer than that."

Cleo straightened his collar. "Gabriel is awake. Hear him?"

Chamard opened the door into the nursery and peeked at Gabriel. He had one foot on the bar of the crib, escape clearly on his mind if only he could get some leverage. "Aha," Chamard said. "So it's come to this, has it?"

Gabriel beamed a guiltless smile and put his foot down. With both arms held up, he appealed to Chamard. "Up," he said.

"Did you hear that?" Chamard said to Cleo. "He said 'up' as clear as day. Come here, my little man. Papa will rescue you."

Chamard spent another half hour playing with Gabriel before he left the house. He kissed Cleo good-bye and warned her, "Don't neglect the mosquito netting, and wear your veil when you ride through the streets after dark."

"I will."

Cleo stood on the doorstep with Gabriel. "See?" she said, and pointed to the big stallion in the shade of the oak. "See Papa's big horse?"

Chamard swung into the saddle, disturbing a cloud of mosquitoes that had been sharing the shade. He dispersed them with a flap of his hat and waved good-bye to Cleo and his son.

As Cleo turned to go back inside, she slapped at a mosquito on the back of her neck.

* * *

The streets of New Orleans were almost deserted in the middle of the day as Phanor rode through town on the way to Cleo's cottage. Jean Paul had asked if he could let Cleo know not to come in to Les Trois Frères—they were closing their doors until the Yellow Jack ran its course for the year.

Phanor's path led him by the fever hospital. The sight of bodies laid out in rows to await the burial wagon, the howls of fever-mad patients, and the stench of death overwhelmed him. He covered his nose with his kerchief and spurred his horse to hurry on.

Phanor heard Gabriel's cries a block before he reached Cleo's house. *Poor little tyke,* he thought. *I bet Cleo made him lie down for a nap, and he doesn't have time for that. If she'll let me get him up, I'll take him for a ride.*

Phanor became uneasy as he tied his horse to the rail. There was a note in Gabriel's cry that didn't sound right. He knocked, and without waiting, shoved the door open. The smell sickened him, but he hurried to the bedroom and found Cleo barely conscious, her chemise blackened with bloody vomit. He touched her forehead—it was hot. She was still alive. He moved quickly into the nursery and found Gabriel standing in his crib, red faced, screaming.

"It's okay, Gabe. Shh." Phanor pushed aside the mosquito netting and lifted Gabriel out of the crib. His clothes were sodden and foul, and he'd cried so much the tears no longer flowed. Phanor held him close and rubbed his back. "It's all right now. Everything will be all right. Shh."

As soon as Gabriel released his grip around Phanor's neck, Phanor stripped him and took him to the well for a bucket of water. He helped him drink from his own tiny cup until he'd had his fill, then found him a peach and a scrap of bread to eat.

"Here, big boy. You stay in here and eat your peach. I'll be right in the next room."

He left Gabriel naked on the floor with his cup and his peach and returned to Cleo. She peered at him through slitted red eyes, but she didn't seem to recognize him. Her skin was yellow and hot, very hot, and dry. Phanor pulled the chemise off and sponged her clean. He'd have to get some water in her somehow. He held her up and tried pouring a cup of water in her mouth. Unaware as she was, she swallowed greedily. He must have fed her four or five cups before the sweat popped out on her fevered skin.

Phanor silently cursed the nanny. Likely she'd run off as soon as she saw Cleo had the Yellow Jack. How could she have abandoned Gabriel like that? *If I ever see her again . . .* he thought.

Gabriel toddled into the bedroom, peach juice running down his bare tummy. He steadied himself against Phanor's knee and gazed at Cleo. "Mama," he said, and lurched toward the bed.

Phanor lifted him to his shoulder. "See?" he said. "Maman is sleeping. Let's get you another peach. You're a hungry fellow, aren't you?"

Once he'd filled Gabriel's tummy, he took him outdoors to look for a pigeon feather near the neighbor's dovecote. Back inside he smeared some honey on Gabriel's fingers, as he'd seen his sister Lalie do with her baby, and handed him the feather.

He drew another bucket of water from the well and carried it back into the bedroom. Cleo had vomited again while he'd been outside. She hung half off the bed, her long hair falling into the bloody black pool on the floor. Phanor pulled her back onto the bed. When he saw the trickles of blood flowing from each eye and from her nose, he stepped back.

Cleo stared at him. At last, she said, "Phanor?"

He swallowed hard. The stench and the sight of the blood nearly undid him. "I'm here."

"Thank God," she said, and closed her eyes.

He'd have to get a doctor here to bleed her, or maybe to use the hot glass blistering cups. Some people swore that clysters pulled the poison right out of you. He cleaned up the mess and sponged Cleo down again.

"I'm going for the doctor, Cleo. I'm taking Gabriel with me. Hear me?" Cleo looked at him vacantly, her focus on some interior delirium. "I'll be back," he said.

Gabriel had grown fretful with the sticky feather. Phanor wiped the honey off his hands and tied a makeshift diaper on him. He hustled him out to the mare and held him tight as he wheeled the horse around.

He'd find a doctor and beg, bribe, or threaten to get him to Cleo's house. As he approached the foul hospital again, he hesitated. He didn't want Gabriel in that place. He cut down a side street. He'd take him to Josie. Cleo might still be afraid of her, but he wasn't. Josie—well, he wouldn't let her if she thought of keeping Gabriel. But Phanor thought he knew her better than that.

Gabriel clutched in one arm, Phanor pushed his horse through the muddy streets. The sun hammered the top of his head, and he wished for the hat he'd left on the floor at Cleo's house. Gabriel grew fretful and squirmed against his grip. Phanor pulled a handkerchief from his pocket to cover Gabriel's head, but Gabriel fussed with it until it was left behind in the muck.

Phanor knew exactly where Josie's two kitchens were. He'd scouted them out when he learned from Jean Paul she had set up business near the levee. Twice he'd walked by, just out of curiosity, he'd told himself. The first time, before the fever had come, he couldn't see whether Josie was at the

window of either kitchen since both of her stands had a
crowd of customers waiting to buy pies. The second time he
found her easily at the kitchen nearest the docks. People
stayed indoors as much as possible when the Yellow Jack
was in town, and only one man was at the window fishing for
coins in his pocket as Josie wrapped a pie in brown paper.

Phanor had watched her for a moment from beneath a
shady oak. The white cap on her head couldn't keep all her
hair tamed, and tendrils of it framed her face. She was
flushed from the heat, and she was much thinner than she
had been a year ago. But, he thought, she looked good. She
smiled at the man buying the pie, and laughed at something
he said. She looked very good.

Now he rode his horse up to the very door of the kitchen
near the docks. No one was on the street in this heat, and the
counter window and the door were open. Gabriel gripped
safely in his arm, Phanor slid off his horse and peered into
the dim interior. "Josie?" he called.

Josie stood up from bench at the work table. Her heart
swelled in gratitude to see him again. "Phanor!" She took in
the lovely boy in Phanor's arms, his light skin and black
eyes. "Gabriel?" she said.

"I need to get him out of this sun."

Josie made a space for Phanor on the bench. "You'll want
some water." Gabriel fought Phanor for control of the cup.
With the water splashed all down his bare chest, Gabriel
smiled in delight.

Josie could hardly take her eyes off him. She'd imagined
how big he must be as the months had gone on, and here he
was, a beautiful child who could hold his own cup.

"Cleo's got the fever," Phanor said.

Josie put a hand to her mouth. She already knew what the
Yellow Jack could do. Not long after Kathleen died, Molly
too had succumbed. Josie had seen the awful vomiting and

bleeding, the fever so hot it seemed to burn her hand when she tried to cool poor Molly.

"Josie," Phanor said quickly. "Not everyone dies of Yellow Jack. Cleo will get well, I'm sure of it." He watched her blink away the fear. "I need you to take Gabriel."

"But Phanor, Cleo won't want me to—"

"I'm asking you, not Cleo. She's hardly conscious, and I know you'll take care of him."

"I will, Phanor." She held her hand out to Gabriel, hoping he wouldn't shrink from her. He grabbed her finger and pulled it toward his mouth.

"You think he's hungry?" Phanor said.

"He's in the right place if he is," Josie said. She reached across the table for a small peach pie and handed it to him. He gnawed at the heavy crust and ignored the adults. When Phanor handed him to Josie, he accepted the transfer without taking his attention from the pie.

"I'm going after a doctor," Phanor said. "I'll be back in a few days, when Cleo's better."

"Where is she? I mean, where does she live?"

"On Rue Noisette, off the far end of Rue Dauphine. The green cottage with a persimmon tree out front." He hesitated. "But you don't need to come. I'll take care of her if you'll take care of Gabriel."

Phanor stepped into the glare of the street, and immediately regretted forgetting his hat again. "I'll see you soon. Don't worry," he said and mounted his horse.

He rode quickly through the quiet streets, the heated air still and stagnant. Smoke from small piles of burning bones, skins, horns, hooves—whatever people thought would drive off the infection—hovered just above his head.

At the hospital, Phanor found a shade tree for his mare and approached the open gates. He shuddered at the sight of so many bodies laid out in the courtyard waiting to be swad-

dled. The flies buzzed thick and black, and in the corner
Phanor caught the movement of rats. He averted his face and
crossed through the rows of corpses to the back gallery of
the hospital.

The immobility in the courtyard hadn't prepared him for
the noise and chaos inside the hospital. Men and women
filled every cot and even lay crowded on the bare boards.
Basins of blood and foul liquid sat here and there, alive with
flies. Phanor held a hand to his nose and waited for his eyes
to adjust to the gloom.

Three nurses moved slowly among the horde of fever vic-
tims, too fatigued and too hopeless to hurry. Across the
room, one of the nurses tried to restrain a man having a
seizure. In a cot near Phanor, a young woman in the grip of
delirium cried out and flailed her arms. Her eyes, yellow and
glistening, seemed to swell out of their sockets. Phanor
turned his head away.

He approached the nearest nurse, a white woman, who
was sponging a prostrate child with vinegar water. The
woman looked up at him with a face ravaged by sleepless
nights and too much death.

"I need a doctor," Phanor said.

The nurse stared at him. "You don't need a doctor."

"Yes. My friend has the fever. She needs a doctor."

"So he can drain a little blood from her arm? Use the
cups to make blisters on her back?"

"I don't know. But she's sick, she needs a doctor."

"Look, monsieur. Do what I'm doing for this poor child.
Keep her clean. Wipe her body to cool her, give her water to
drink, and pray."

Phanor looked around the large open room. There were
no doctors in the hospital. The only men on their feet were
the two who carried the dead to the courtyard. The three

women toiled alone for all these dozens and dozens of victims.

"Where are the doctors?" Phanor said.

"With their rich patients, of course. Who are no more likely to survive than this child here. I've seen your fine gentlemen bleeding their patients to a pale death. You don't need a doctor." She reached into her pocket and pulled out a small burlap bag tied with a string like the one she wore pinned to her dress. "Here," she said. The bag reeked of camphor, but Phanor accepted it. "For you, not for her. Wear it around your neck." She picked up a cup to offer her small patient a sip of water, dismissing Phanor.

Phanor returned to the open gallery and breathed in deeply. In the courtyard below, a tall, light-skinned colored man hollered, "And keep the damn cats out of here!" One of the orderlies Phanor had seen inside murmured something and backed away from the man's fury.

The angry gentleman wore the black frock coat and tall hat of a doctor. He was not a white man, but Phanor had heard there were colored doctors in town. He waited at the top of the gallery stairs for him.

"*S'il vous plait*," Phanor said. "Are you a doctor, monsieur?"

"*Oui.*"

"My friend is sick. Will you come with me, will you see her?"

"She has the yellow fever?"

"Yes. It's not far, only a few minutes from here. You have a carriage?"

"Monsieur," the doctor interrupted. He gestured inside. "You see all these people. I can only do so much, my friend. I'm needed here."

"But you could bleed her, or—"

The doctor shook his head. "I won't bleed another fever

patient. It does no good." He put a hand on Phanor's arm and spoke more kindly. "You might try placing a bowl of sliced onions near the bed. Keep her clean and give her plenty of water. Her life is in God's hands."

Chapter 39

New Orleans

Josie fashioned a fresh diaper for Gabriel with a clean dish towel. Sitting on the hard bench alongside her work table, she rocked him until he gave in and went to sleep. Long after she could have laid him down on a pallet of aprons, she held him close and admired the thick, dark eyelashes. His ears were just the shape of Bertrand's, she thought, but he had Cleo's upper lip. Love him as she might, he was not her child.

Whatever else God has planned for me on this earth, Josie thought, *he surely means for me to have a baby of my own.* She closed her eyes and said a quick prayer: "Mary, Mother of God, may it be so," she whispered.

At last she laid him down. She cleaned out the ashes in the grates, packed up the remaining pies, and shuttered the windows. With a bonnet on her head and an extra one on Gabriel, she locked up the kitchen, picked up her basket, and marched with Gabriel through the burning sun. In only a few minutes, a dark stain spread from where Gabriel slept and sweated against her, and though it was less than a half mile to the other kitchen where Louella worked alone, Josie felt faint by the time she reached it.

Louella had all the windows and the door open, keeping store for customers who had no appetite. When Josie entered, she found Louella napping in a cowhide chair next to the counter. At least a dozen unclaimed pies sat on the table, safe from flies under a linen cloth, and the smell of apples and cinnamon filled the little shack.

Josie lay Gabriel down and untied the oversized bonnet. She found a gauzy piece of cheesecloth to cover him and wiped his sweaty forehead with a damp cloth. He slept on.

Louella stirred behind her. "Law me, mam'zelle," she said, "what you got there?"

Josie pulled back the gauze a little and showed her. "It's Gabriel."

"De good God brought us lil' Gabriel? Where Cleo?"

Once Josie had told Louella all she could, she explained they would close the second kitchen for the rest of the summer. With the fever and so many ships quarantined in the river, business was too slow to burn two fires, heat two ovens.

"I'm going to Cleo's house, Louella," Josie said. "Phanor can't do it all alone."

"You go on den. Dem gran'chillen of mine half grown— I ready for a baby in dese arms. Me and Gabriel be fine."

Josie drank two cups of water before she left. She packed a small basket of fruit and a bottle of water, then dampened the neck and sleeves of her dress to cool her in the long walk to Rue Noisette.

By the time she found the house with the persimmon tree, Josie felt drained and light-headed. She'd drunk the bottle of water she carried half an hour earlier, and the sun dried the beads of sweat as fast as her body could produce them.

Phanor's horse switched his tail at the flies in the shade of an oak. He was here, then. Before going in, Josie pulled off her bonnet and searched in back of the house for the well. She drew a bucket up and wet her kerchief to wipe her face and the back of her neck. What relief. She opened her bodice and held her chin up to let the water drip from her throat down between her breasts. When she lowered her head, she saw Phanor watching her from the back doorway.

The unguarded lust in Phanor's face inflamed her instantly. Quickly he adjusted his features, and only sadness lingered in his eyes.

To cover her embarrassment, Josie picked her bonnet up from the grass, her own arousal as surprising to her as Phanor's. She turned her back to him to button her bodice and shake the wet fabric loose from her breasts.

At the door, she looked up at him. "Gabriel is with Louella," she said.

He nodded and moved aside for her to come in. The windows of Cleo's little house were open on every side for ventilation. The shutters kept out the direct sunbeams, and it was surprisingly cool inside. The main room boasted a lemon yellow settee and a matching chair. The mahogany table was scarred and scrubbed, though it had once been very fine. Josie followed Phanor into the nursery tinted with blueberry and buttermilk paint. Gabriel's crib, a carved oak bed draped with delicate netting, stood near a shuttered window. Toys, a peach pit among them, littered the floor.

"In here," Phanor said. "She's fairly quiet now."

Josie entered Cleo's bedroom. Having watched over Molly the last two days of her life, Josie knew what to expect, or thought she did. But this wasn't Molly, it was her own Cleo, and the dusky yellow of her skin shocked her. She put a hand to Cleo's forehead. It was hot, but there was no sheen of sweat on her skin.

"She needs water, I think," Josie said.

"I didn't know whether to wake her."

Josie considered for a moment. "I think we better."

Phanor sat on the bed and propped Cleo up while Josie held the cup to her mouth. She didn't really waken, but she swallowed, and Josie managed to get enough in her that she began to sweat a little.

Cleo groaned when Phanor laid her down again. Her head sank into the deep pillow, and she tossed back and forth.

"She's so hot," Josie said. She pulled Cleo's heavy black hair above her head and removed the feather pillow. She took up the cloth Phanor had left in a basin of vinegar water and began to cool her down.

Phanor leaned against the doorjamb watching her hands squeeze the water out of the cloth. As she wiped Cleo's arms, he said, "I didn't think you'd come."

Josie looked at him. "She's my sister."

After a moment, Josie asked him, "Do you think she forgives me?"

"Chamard comes here, Josie. Can you forgive her?"

Josie's hands stopped. "He comes here?"

"I think he loves her. And his child."

Josie waited for the pain to wash over her as it had so many times before, whenever she had allowed herself to think of Bertrand's teasing brown eyes full of light, his mouth on hers, or worst of all, of Bertrand in Cleo's bed. But this time, the pain seemed old, familiar, and muted. Life had moved on. She was not the Josie of two years ago. She was not even the same girl she had been after Gabriel's birth when she'd hurt so much she'd wrenched him from Cleo's arms. She felt shame, and regret lingered for that awful day, yes, but no more yearning for Bertrand.

So Cleo relives her mother's life, Josie reflected. *Like Bibi, she loves another woman's husband, a white man who can never be hers. Thank the good Lord I'm not playing my mother's part. Poor Abigail.*

Josie looked around the room, Cleo's own room. Three dresses on satin-wrapped hangers hung from pegs on the wall. One was red velvet, another blue silk, the third a bronze satin and lace. Fine dresses, costly and elegant.

Phanor followed her eyes. "She sings for a living," he said. "At Les Trois Frères, where I met you that Sunday afternoon last spring."

"So this is Cleo's house?"

Phanor nodded. "She makes her own money."

"Then she truly is free," Josie said.

Throughout that day and the next, Cleo sweated and moaned, tossed and flailed from her fever and aching bones. Josie and Phanor kept a cup of water at her lips whenever she seemed too hot to sweat. They cleaned her when she bled or vomited, and they wiped her skin with vinegar water. Phanor replaced the first onions in the bowl near the bed and burned the old ones, and he and Josie both prayed for her.

In the early morning of the third day, Josie left to help Louella start the baking. She was to return at midday to relieve Phanor and allow him to conduct his business in the afternoon. Still a block away from the kitchen, Josie heard Gabriel hollering. She broke into a trot and pushed open the kitchen door—Louella stood at the fireplace adjusting a roast on the spit. Gabriel sat on the floor, his dress tail stuck under the leg of the heavy worktable, his little face red and angry.

"Louella, how could you?" Josie rushed to lift the table leg off Gabriel's dress and grabbed him into her arms. "There, now, sweetheart, it's all right."

"Mam'zelle, you gon' spoil dat chile," Louella said. "He

gon' be underfoot, in de ashes, get hisself burned you don' put dat leg back on de dress."

Josie rocked him in her arms. "I'll keep him in my lap."

"You tink you can cut dem peaches and keep a chile's hands out of de way, you a better woman dan I am."

Josie pared and cut peaches, mixed in sugar and cinnamon, all the while taking care to keep the knife out of Gabriel's reach. In spite of her lack of sleep, her fear for Cleo, she took joy in the child. She fed him peaches, not minding at all that he smeared juice all over her dress. By the time the fruit was ready for the pie shells, Gabriel and Josie both had sticky arms and faces.

As they worked, Josie described Cleo's symptoms to Louella and what she and Phanor were doing for her.

"She ain't had no bleeding?"

Josie shook her head, worried again they'd had no doctor.

"Well, de Lord know you doing what all you can. Bleeding or no, it up to God."

Gabriel wanted to walk. Josie let him hold her two fingers and led him around the kitchen. He boldly let go of her hand and lit the room with his smile as he tottered from bench to chair and then back to Josie's arms.

"Dat's de thing," Louella said. "You get dat baby tired out 'fo you leave him wid me. I gone put him to sleep and finish up wid dese pies."

Josie kissed Gabriel good-bye and tied her bonnet on. For the twentieth time since summer began, she wished she'd brought a parasol with her to New Orleans. The sun sucked the life right out of her, and last night's rain only made the air thicker, not cooler. She resolved to try a shortcut to Cleo's house now she knew where it was.

The street she chose took her to the poor people's cemetery. No crypts here to keep the departed out of the muck and foul water. The dead delivered by the mule carts were merely swathed in old sheets. Only a few had been granted the favor of a wooden box for their remains, yet, distressingly, these coffins floated in their graves as water oozed up through the ground, the rains raising the water table even higher. The flies around the coffins and shrouded bodies buzzed loud enough to be heard across the road. Josie quickened her steps and put her kerchief to her nose, but she couldn't keep her eyes from the men tossing the bodies from the mule wagon into the pit they'd dug. With each thud, rats as big as possums scurried out of the way and then quickly returned to the feast.

A mound of stained bones flanked the mass grave, their burial space being usurped for the newly dead. In a solitary grave nearer the cemetery's wrought-iron fence, a man stood on a coffin and tried to rock it back and forth to settle it in the waterlogged pit. He gave up and punctured the lid with a pickaxe to let out the gases. Josie gagged from the stench and ran the rest of the way past the muddy graveyard.

By the time she reached Cleo's house, the smell and sight of death had chased all her courage away. Frantic to see if Cleo breathed, Josie burst through the door, startling Phanor into dropping the palmetto fan he was weaving.

"What's wrong?" he said.

Josie rushed into the bedroom to see Bertrand Chamard on his knees beside the bed, one arm flung over Cleo's waist, his head resting on the sheet next to her. Josie froze in the doorway. Phanor came up behind her and put a hand on her shoulder.

"She's dead," Josie said.

"No. She's the same. Come away," Phanor said.

He sat her on the yellow settee and held her hand. "Are you all right?"

"I just got scared," Josie said, and wiped the tears away. "How long has he been here?"

"A little while. He hasn't moved from her side since he came."

Chamard appeared at the door. His eyes were swollen and red and his skin was very pale. "When will the doctor be back?" he said.

"No doctor," Phanor said. "The man I talked to said to do what we're doing."

"Phanor says you have my son, Josephine," Chamard said. "Thank you." He picked up his hat. "I'm going for a doctor."

Josie took up the vigil at Cleo's bedside. When she placed a damp cloth on her forehead, Cleo opened her eyes. "Josie," she said, and closed them again.

Within the hour Chamard returned with a gentleman in a fine black coat and top hat. Circles under the doctor's eyes made him look tired, but his regal bearing promised medical wonders.

The doctor leaned over the bed and pulled Cleo's eyelid up. She fought him and cried out. Chamard held her hands. "Cleo, darling, lie still. He's a doctor."

The man felt her neck and her hot skin. With his foot, he shoved aside the bowl of onions on the floor. "What nonsense," he said gruffly. "Have you a basin?"

Josie fetched one from the cupboard in the other room. The doctor placed it under Cleo's arm, withdrew a lancet from his bag, and cleaned it on his pocket handkerchief. He tapped the blue vein in the elbow and cut through the soft skin until he had a steady trickle of blood. The three men and Josie stood mesmerized, all eyes on the stream pooling in the basin. When he'd drawn perhaps a pint, the doctor pressed his thumb over the wound to stop the bleeding. "A bandage, please," he said.

"That's all I'll do for now, Chamard. If she seems worse, come for me again, and I'll blister her." For the first time, he

looked at Josie. "Keep her cool, young lady." He nodded to
Phanor, picked up his hat, and left them.

Cleo moaned and tried to raise herself. Chamard sat on
the bed and supported her in his arms. He pulled the hair
aside and kissed the back of her neck. "My love," he murmured. Cleo leaned her head against his chest and closed her
eyes.

Chapter 40

In mid-October, a front moved through. People drew deep breaths of the cooling wind that dried up the puddles, hardened the mud, and blew the pesky mosquitoes out to sea. The odorous piles of burning hooves that countered the poisonous miasma fouled the air no more. Ladies ceased to wilt, and the planters from upriver began to drift back in to New Orleans.

The Yellow Jack had run its course, at least until the next fever season. Ships quarantined in the lower river were allowed to dock, and men bent their sweaty backs unloading silks and satins from China, fine wines and pianofortes from France. The smell of roasting coffee beans from the French Market wafted downriver to Josie's kitchens, where once again men stood in line in the early morning to buy their breakfasts.

Louella ran the original kitchen, and Josie ran the second one. They were training four girls to take over the pie shops and another who would help Louella in the new bakery. Josie hoped to deliver the first crème puffs to Les Trois Frères within the week, and with introductions from Phanor to the stewards at other clubs around the city, Josie expected a busy season.

When the second rush of hungry customers had come and gone after the lunch hour, Josie hung her apron on a hook and packed a basket of provisions.

"Maria," Josie told the new hired girl, "we need onions when you go to the market."

"*Sí*, senorita." Maria smiled and tapped her forehead. "I know what to do."

Leaving the kitchen in Maria's competent hands, Josie set off for Cleo's cottage.

Across town, Cleo sat propped up against a pile of pillows with a mirror in hand. "You are one ugly girl," she said aloud. She pulled down a lower lid; not a healthy red, not yet. She stuck her tongue out at the yellow image. *I don't know how Bertrand can stand to look at me,* she thought. She tossed the mirror on the bed and put her arms behind her head. *He does like to look at me though. Even in this old chemise, or better yet*—she smiled to herself—*without it. He must have dug a rut deep as his horse's hindquarters from here to Cherleu by now.*

She heard the back door open and Thérèze, the young woman Bertrand had insisted on hiring, say, "Dat one big basket, mam'zelle. Let me take dat fo' you." Cleo lay back and listened.

"Let's see that new tooth, Gabriel. Aren't you the big boy? Has he been fussing, Thérèze?"

Josie is herself now, Cleo thought. *Somehow, she's over it, Bertrand, everything. And with Phanor chasing after her, she's smiling again.*

"Yes'm," Thérèze said. "That big ole tooth in the back o'

his mouth been paining him. I keep rubbing a little turpentine on it, but he don't like it."

"And his maman?" Josie said.

"She been up most o' the mawnin,' but she gone back to bed now. I think she asleep."

"I'm awake," Cleo called. She propped herself on one elbow, and Josie appeared at the door with Gabriel on her hip.

"How are you feeling?"

"Pretty good, except I'm still a skinny yellow scarecrow," Cleo said.

"Thérèze will fatten you up."

"How long am I supposed to stay yellow? It seems like forever."

"How many days has it been?"

Cleo thought a moment. "Eighteen, I think."

Josie looked at her critically. "Well, it must be more than eighteen, then. But you look better, you really do. You're a pale yellow, now."

"Thank you very much."

Josie set Gabriel on his feet and he toddled off to find his ball. Cleo scooted over and offered a pillow for Josie to prop herself against the headboard.

"Sit down and tell me about the new kitchen," she said.

Josie brought her up-to-date. Business at the first two places had picked up and the money was coming in again. The new girls were working out well under Louella's supervision, and the fancy-goods kitchen should be ready by the end of the week.

"You and Phanor, entrepreneurs extraordinaire," Cleo said. "Both of you running your own businesses now."

"You remember the first time we saw Phanor?" Josie said. "He was barefoot, wearing a straw hat."

"I don't remember either one of us paying much mind to his feet, Josephine."

Josie laughed. "I guess not."

"Have you seen him today?"

"Not yet. Why?"

Cleo suppressed the urge to let Josie in on the secret. "No reason," she said.

For a moment they were quiet, and then Josie said, "Cleo?"

"Um?"

"Can you sit up?" She moved out of the way while Cleo swung her legs over the edge of the bed.

Josie pulled a folded sheet from her pocket and handed it to Cleo.

"What's this?" Cleo said.

"Read it."

Cleo opened the heavy velour paper. The official imprint of the state of Louisiana graced the top of the page. At the bottom was the signature of *Josephine Marie Louise Celine Tassin*. The text in the middle of this document testified that one Cleo Tassin, lately of Toulouse Plantation in the parish of St. James, and her son Gabriel, to be free persons of color.

"Oh, Josie," Cleo said, and pressed the paper to her heart. "Josie," was all Cleo could say. Her hand sought Josie's and gripped it tight.

Josie handed her handkerchief to Cleo. "Don't get the paper wet," she said.

Gabriel toddled back into the room and climbed into his maman's lap. Cleo whispered in his ear, "You're free, little man."

Josie stood up and wiped her own face. "I have to get back to Louella. Do you feel like eating? I brought a pork pie and some new apples."

"I better eat," Cleo said. She blew her nose and dried her eyes. "Nobody wants to watch a skinny girl sing in a saggy red dress."

Cleo handed Gabriel over and watched Josie swing him

onto her hip. Cleo's heart filled to bursting. She took a moment, and then she joined her family at the kitchen table.

After lunch, Josie set out across town to her new enterprise, La Boulangerie Toulouse. The two ovens had been reclayed, the floors and walls scrubbed, the windows reglazed. The new help, another Irish girl fresh off the boat, stood at the heavy worktable shredding coconut, and Louella sat in the light hemming kitchen towels made from flour sacks.

Josie tied an apron around her waist and took up her knife. As she picked an apple from the bowl on the table, she gestured toward a basket with a wine bottle sticking out from under the blue-checked cover. "What's this?" she said.

"Oh Lawdy," Louella said. She lumbered over to the basket. "You not spose t'see dat, Josie. Dat basket spose be a surprise." She took it off the table and set it in the corner. "Der," she said. "You jest forget you seen it, else I be in trouble."

Josie bent her head to paring apples, a smile on her lips. Through the afternoon, she acted as a second assistant to Louella as she perfected her recipes. When Louella slowed down long enough to cut a coconut cake, Josie came up behind her and wrapped her arms around her waist.

"Louella, I love you," she said.

"Shh, chile, I knows dat."

Josie straightened the lace collar on Louella's new dress. "Those shoes feel all right on your feet?"

"Dese de best shoes a cook ever had, and you knows it. You just fishing for compliments, and I gots work to do," Louella said. "Go on now, and let me get to it."

Josie hugged her and then let go. She glanced out the open door for the twentieth time. The day was cooling and the shadows were lengthening. He should be here soon.

Josie was wrapping a cake to put into the tin-lined safe overnight when Phanor darkened the door. At last.

Josie put a hand to her hair and hoped there were no flour smudges on her face. "Monsieur DeBlieux," she said in a syrupy sweet voice. "What a pleasant surprise," she said in a singsong simper she'd heard the belles of the ball use.

"Mademoiselle," Phanor said and bowed nearly to the floor. He swept a thick bouquet of goldenrods from behind his back. "For you."

"I declare, I do love goldenrods," she lilted and batted her lashes at Phanor.

"You get on out a here wid yo' nonsense," Louella said. "I take dose and put em in some water."

Phanor picked up his basket from behind the chair, cocked an elbow for Josie to take, and escorted her into the street.

"Are we having a picnic?" Josie asked.

"Of sorts."

Phanor took her through Le Vieux Carré to a quiet street shaded by mossy live oaks. He opened the gate at a blue house with galleries on three sides. A small oyster-shell path led to stairs on the side of the house, and without letting go of Josie's hand, he led her to the second story.

The sun lit the small apartment with golden autumn light. A fire was laid in the grate awaiting a match, and a blue and cream turkey carpet lay on the floor. Otherwise, no chairs, no drapes, no knickknacks—only Phanor's fiddle on the mantelpiece furnished the three rooms.

Phanor knelt to light the fire. Josie stood in the center of the parlor and breathed in the room's essence. She turned slowly to take in every window and sash, walked slowly into the other rooms. Phanor was waiting for her when she came back to the parlor.

Standing very close to Phanor, she said, "And this is all for you?"

He leaned his head down to kiss her gently on the lips. "Not necessarily."

Josie stepped in closer and wrapped her arms around his waist. "Meaning?"

"I might be persuaded to share it," he said.

She held her face up to be kissed, and Phanor pulled her in close. "What kind of persuasion would it take?" she said in his ear.

Phanor stepped back to produce a small velvet box from his pocket. "Only promise to wear this ring," he said. "Forever."

Josie admired the small perfect emerald for a moment, and then slipped it on her finger.

"I promise," she said.

Phanor put his hands on either side of her face and kissed her deeply. Josie's knees gave way, and he eased her down to the turkey rug.

"I know a priest in the next street," he said, leaning over her. "It would only take an hour."

Josie put her hands behind his neck and pulled him down to her. "I can't wait an hour."

Chapter 41

Toulouse, Springtime 1840

Josie gazed up at Phanor. His hair whipped back in the wind, and his eyes were so dark they seemed to swallow the sunlight. She wanted to kiss those lips, right there on the steamboat deck. "Are you as happy as I am, Phanor?" His smile told her all she needed to know.

Cleo's little Gabriel negotiated his way through the deck chairs, the rocking of the boat hardly slowing him down. Cleo followed with the leash in her hand. She'd declared she didn't care how awful it looked, she wasn't going to let her child fall overboard, and she'd attached a rope to Gabriel's waist.

Gabriel held out his arms to be picked up. When Josie lifted him, he tried to climb onto the railing, but Josie kept him on her hip. "I've got him tight, Cleo."

"Me too," Cleo said. She smiled and wrapped another loop around her wrist.

"How you feel about going back, Cleo?" Phanor asked. "You glad to go home?"

"I'll be glad to see Old Sam, Elbow John, and the rest of them. But Madame Emmeline—I don't know if she'll see me."

"But it was my fault you ran away," Josie reminded her.

"Madame may not see it that way."

"Does it mean so much to you?" Josie said. "Grand-mére letting you back in the house?"

Cleo's eyes teared, and Josie put a hand on her arm.

The heavy sweetness of magnolias wafted aboard from the plantation on the right bank. The front lawn stretched through the trees to a palatial white home with two-story pillars holding up the curved balcony. Josie recognized the Johnston place where she'd fallen in love with Bertrand Chamard, where she'd spent agonized weeks waiting to go home after the flood. A long time ago, she reflected.

Just upstream a new house was going up. The roof was already on, though the clapboards had yet to cover the skeleton of the cypress timbers. Albany Johnston's present to his wife, Josie was sure. She hoped he and her cousin Violette would be happy.

Josie had written to Grand-mére that they were coming, but she hadn't mentioned her marriage. Mr. Gale read the mail to Grand-mére, and as much as Josie appreciated the overseer, she didn't want him to deliver her good news—and she wanted to be sure Grand-mére understood that it was good news. Grand-mére had expected Josie to marry for money, for convenience, for the advantages someone like Albany Johnston could give her. But Josie had married the son of a poor Cajun.

Grand-mére could be a hard woman, and her wits were not what they were. Still, she had always liked Phanor, had seen his potential and his ambition. Maman certainly would never have accepted Phanor, but Josie hoped Grand-mére would be more forgiving.

The steamboat whistle blew as if the angels in heaven needed to hear it. Phanor cupped Gabriel's head against his chest and covered his ear. When the whistle had had its blow, Phanor told him, "Look." He pointed to the alley of oaks leading to the green and orange house. "We're here."

Elbow John and Thibault waved from the Toulouse dock, ready to help the crew with the gangplank and the luggage. "Look at that boy," Cleo exclaimed. "He must be two feet taller. Thibault!"

Cleo was first off the boat. She hurried across the boards between the boat and the dock, Gabriel in her arms, no thought of either of them falling in. She grabbed her brother with one arm and held him tight.

"Thibault, don't you let go yet, I'm not through hugging you."

Gabriel squirmed and pushed at Thibault when Cleo had the three of them crushed together, but once Thibault got loose from Cleo, he held his arms out for Gabriel and smiled. The radiance on his simple face won Gabriel over, and he lunged into his Oncle Thibault's arms.

Elbow John hung back. Cleo knew she didn't look like the girl he'd known. She wore a fine blue muslin dress embroidered in white floss, and her hair was wrapped in an elaborate blue *tignon*. She was a woman now, not a girl, but she still held Elbow John dear. She stood before him a moment and smiled into his weathered face. "It's me, John," she said.

"It sho is," he said and opened his arms to her.

While Phanor dealt with the luggage, Josie followed Cleo onto the dock. Thibault grinned when she stepped close to him. "You Josie," he said.

"That's right. Have you got a kiss for your sister?"

"I got lots of kisses. Dis here baby belongs to me now, don't he?"

Josie laughed. "You're going to have to share him, Thibault. Lots of us lay claim to this little boy."

Josie looked at Cleo. "You ready?"

Cleo nodded. She took Gabriel back from Thibault, and the two women walked up the alley to the big house. Grand-mére waited on the gallery in her rolling chair. When Josie approached the stairs, Grand-mére pushed Laurie away and tried to get up, but Josie hurried up the steps in time to stop her.

"I'm here, Grand-mére. Don't get up." She took her grandmother's trembling hands and let Grand-mére gaze at her.

"Ishu?" Grand-mére said.

"I de only one dat understand her," Laurie said. "She say, is dat you?"

"It's me, Grand-mére. And look who's with me."

Josie stood to the side and Cleo stepped in front of Grand-mére. The faded eyes peered intently at Gabriel. He laid his head against his maman's breast and peeked at the old woman with the deep-set eyes.

"S'mile?" Grand-mére reached for Gabriel. "S my 'mile!" She held her hands out. "My 'mile!"

"She say he her Emile," Laurie translated.

"I know," Josie said.

Cleo's face clouded up. She knelt down next to Grand-mére's chair. "Gabriel," she said, "say 'How do you do?'" He murmured the words and allowed his great-grandmother to stroke his black hair.

"S'mile," she said again.

"Grand-mére," Josie said, "You haven't said hello to Cleo."

Grand-mére stared at Cleo until at last the light of recognition shone in her eyes. She held out a hand to stroke Cleo's face. She touched her hair as if to bless her, and Cleo let her tears fall onto her grandmother's lap.

Phanor joined them on the gallery. While Cleo moved away to compose herself, he smiled at Grand-mére and bent over her hand. "Madame Emmeline," he said. "Good day to you."

Grand-mére seemed confused. "'sis?"

"It's Phanor DeBlieux, Grand-mére."

She stared at Phanor a good while, and then smiled at him with her half-frozen face. "'Day," she said very clearly.

"I have something to tell you, Grand-mére." Josie held her hand out to Phanor, who took hers in his. "Phanor and I are married, Grand-mére. I am Madame Phanor DeBlieux."

They waited while Grand-mére worked it out. At last she nodded emphatically. "'id good," she said.

Josie and Phanor lay in bed that night, listening to the house settle and the crickets rub their legs together.

"I like this bed," Phanor said. He idly pulled a curl of Josie's hair through his fingers.

"Better than ours?"

"In this bed, a man can stretch his legs out."

"So that's what you're thinking about. Stretching your legs?"

"What are you thinking about?"

"Whether our first son should be Phanor Emile Antoine or Phanor Antoine Emile. What do you think?"

"I think we need to get to work making that baby before we name him."

Josie pushed the covers back. "That's what I was thinking."